D0758037

The Arena Man

The Arena Man

Steve Englehart

A TOM DOHERTY ASSOCIATES BOOK / NEW YORK

This is a work of fiction. All of the characters, organizations, and events
portrayed in this novel are either products of the author's imagination
or are used fictitiously.

THE ARENA MAN

Edited by James Frenkel

A Tor Book
Published by Tom Doherty Associates, LLC
175 Fifth Avenue
New York, NY 10010

www.tor-forge.com

Tor® is a registered trademark of Tom Doherty Associates, LLC.

Library of Congress Cataloging-in-Publication Data

Englehart, Steve.
    The arena man / Steve Englehart.—1st ed.
        p. cm.
    "A Tom Doherty Associates book."
    ISBN 978-0-7653-2500-6 (hardcover)
    ISBN 978-1-4299-4620-9 (e-book)
    1. Immortality—Fiction.   2. Magic—Fiction.   3. Fantasy fiction.
4. Suspense fiction.   I. Title.
    PS3555.N4257A89 2013
    813'.54—dc23

                                                    2012037368

First Edition: February 2013

Printed in the United States of America

0   9   8   7   6   5   4   3   2   1

And Now for
My Brother
Thomas Ayres Englehart

That's not the way the world really works anymore. We're an empire now, and when we act, we create our own reality. And while you're studying that reality—judiciously, as you will—we'll act again, creating other new realities, which you can study too, and that's how things will sort out. We're history's actors . . . and you, all of you, will be left to just study what we do.

—said to be KARL ROVE, 2004

Greetings, my friend. We are all interested in the future, for that is where you and I are going to spend the rest of our lives.

—CRISWELL, *Plan 9 from Outer Space,* 1959

Author's Note

The Arena Man covers the lives of Max August, Pam Blackwell, and Vee from Sunday, March 20, 2011, through Friday, March 25, 2011, and Friday, April 1, 2011.

The Mayans, who worshipped Time Itself, devised a calendar made of two interlocking cycles. The first, consisting of numbers, goes around every 13 days, while the other, consisting of images, goes around every 20. So each day's name consists of a number and an image. Altogether, there are 13 × 20, or 260, distinct day names, and each has a meaning.

The Arena Man covers the lives of Max August, Pam Blackwell, and Vee during

12 Flint Knife	Fulfilling Magick
13 Milky Way	Managing Alchemy
1 Lord	Establishing All
2 Nipple	Encountering Reality
3 Wind	Advancing Possibilities
4 Night	Encompassing a Private World

and

11 Dog	Owning Embodiment

The Arena Man

12 Flint Knife (Fulfilling Magick)

Spring 2011 came to Libby, Montana, at 5:21 P.M. Mountain Day-light Time, with the pale sun framed by ominous, roiling clouds. As three black helicopters knifed over the hills above the Kootenai River, the slanting rays caught the blades with giddy intensity, but the black of the choppers was a dead black, with no reflection whatsoever. They looked like three holes in the sky as they dropped to hover two feet off the ground. Thirty men, dressed in similar nonreflective black, poured out and encircled the ranch house at the end of a long snowy road. Each one was carrying a Special Ops Combat Assault Rifle, Mk 17.

Jim Lasher was a Montana rancher. He swung his front door open but stayed partially out of sight, his hunting rifle at the ready. "Whatever you guys are doin', you're in the wrong place!" he shouted. "Get off my property!"

Thirty SCARs opened up on the house and killed Jim, his wife, his three children, and his invalid mother. It took no more than a minute.

Then the thirty men jogged with military precision back to the copters and clambered inside. The machines took off and swung south, over the central part of Libby, where they were seen for a fleeting moment.

At which point, in midair, the Black Helicopters vanished.

12 Flint Knife (Fulfilling Magick)

Spring 2011 came to Duluth, Minnesota, at 6:21 P.M. Central Daylight Time, exactly one hour before sunset. Peter Quince, the Wizardry link in the nine-member cabal called the Necklace, was in the cellar of the ancient house always occupied by the Necklace's magician, situated on the shores of Lake Superior. Spring marked the return of the Sun to the northern hemisphere, beginning a new round of life, but this far north, it was cold and gray, just above freezing, with a hard rain on the endless expanse of black water and forest. In the cellar, there was no light from the sun, and no life any sun would recognize.

The wizards had lived in the Issac Vernon Hill house with its wide lawn running down to the water and the Minnesota woodland out the back door since Fergus Skøord, the wizard of that time, had it built in 1898. But the wizards had lived in Duluth since Duluth was proclaimed to exist in 1854, so Skøord had the combined wisdom of his predecessors to draw on in designing a permanent residence for the Necklace's Wizard. There was a sanctum sanctorum in the cupola, a living room, bedroom, kitchen with a hidden chamber . . . and there was a dungeon. Officially a cellar.

It was wide and deep underground, painted a dreadful muddy blue, and today, with Peter Quince in residence, filled with comatose women. There were twenty-seven of them, laid out on parallel slabs of Oneota dolomite, a local stone much like marble, very solid, highly polished. The woman at the center was Rita Diamante, once the fearsome head of a Miami drug cartel, once a determined aspirant to the Necklace, once Peter Quince's lover—and now officially dead for nearly a year and a half. But Rita was not dead. Her color was pale and gray, marked with green and purple blotches, yet her chest was rising and falling with regularity. Like the others, all Latinas because Rita had been so. They were kept alive the way zombis are kept alive, but wizards had no need for lumbering bodies. They made up a sort of battery, their combined life essence funneling continually into Peter Quince.

On the slab to the left of Rita was the newest woman, Elena, fresh and brown and fighting her bonds. Standing over her was Quince, holding a knife. On the floor by his feet, so she wouldn't kick it away, was a kitchen clock with large numbers.

"Sixteen seconds," Quince said, looking at the floor.

"Fourteen seconds," Quince said, looking at Elena.

"This clock is precise, Master," Quince said, looking above his head.

"But Spring is an aspect of *this* world, Master. The ritual, with all respect—" Quince said, before suddenly dropping the knife to clutch at his chest, and fall forward, torso crashing onto Elena's stomach, driving the wind from her. Her struggles lessened as she fought to breathe.

Then all at once, he got control of himself, and pushed himself away from the dolomite. "Yes, Master," he mumbled hurriedly, head down. "I'm sorry. I'll do it now." He picked up the knife, threw back his head to roar in a strangled voice—**Now!**—and drove the knife through Elena's heart.

12 Flint Knife (Fulfilling Magick)

Spring 2011 came to Chicago, Illinois, at 6:21 P.M. Central Daylight Time, half an hour before sunset. Diana Herring, the Media link in the Necklace, was a gray figure in the light of the gray rain clouds clustered over Lake Michigan. She was calm and her eyes were clear—the Remeron had been carefully prescribed by a doctor whose son would have gone to prison for life if Di hadn't buried the evidence for just such an emergency as she'd found herself in after the summer of 2009. It was then that Max August, the "alchemist with a gun" determined to bring down the Necklace, had compromised her, forced her to become a double agent—and that was not the worst of it. He'd also told her that another member in the close-knit group of nine, the magickal link, Peter Quince, had been possessed by a demon.

So for a year and nine months, Di had helped to run the world, handling almost all the media, living always on the edge of the *now* that was cable news, knowing one of her allies was a creature from hell and the others would willingly kill her if they knew of her betrayal. It was no surprise that she'd found the best drugs to make her her best self, because there was not the slightest margin for error. All the terrifying what-ifs, all the threats to her very survival, they all stayed outside her daily zone. And Di, to her credit, could deliver breaking news in the midst of an air raid, with no second takes. Her training, her temperament, they were well suited for the life she had to live now.

Here she was, a year and a half later, standing in her high-rise on East Goethe and Lake Shore Drive. Here she was, trusted to run American media.

Max had promised that she would walk free when he took the Necklace down. Before the drugs, she'd had an ever-present lust to turn triple agent and feed him to her bosses, but Max could and would take her with him if he fell. He had the goods on her, and he'd demonstrated, more than once now, that he had power the Necklace couldn't counter. Assassinating him had been their top security priority since 2007, but they hadn't done it. So Max had the whip-hand in this story.

All she had to do to save herself was slip him advance information on Necklace moves. The two times he had interfered with those moves, he had been very good about leaving trails for them to find, showing he came at the threats from some different direction, a direction in no way connected to Di. But she hadn't given him everything. She couldn't, without revealing that the Necklace had a leak, and he was smart enough to know that. So she was the one who decided which things would hurt the Necklace, but not hurt them so often they'd start to wonder why.

In the gray light, she made her latest decision.

12 Flint Knife (Fulfilling Magick)

Spring 2011 came to Fort Wayne, Indiana, at 7:21 P.M. Eastern Daylight Time, a quarter of an hour before sunset. Ruth Glendenning, the Ops link in the Necklace, crouched over the master plan for the coming week, resting on her palms. It was going on T minus five days, and she had marked the remaining details on onionskin paper in the precise, almost architectural letters she had learned filling out forms in the District of Columbia police force. Eventually, she had risen to commander of the Special Ops Division there, the one that handled broken laws best left unseen. There was a lot of that in the District and she'd been very good at it—good enough to be tapped to leave the force and join the Necklace. In so doing, she became the only black on the council. She professed to be indifferent to such things and probably was. Her only criterion, for the agents she ran and for herself, was the ability to get the job done.

Ruth's normal bailiwick was Carlisle, Pennsylvania, but she and her men had relocated to Fort Wayne for this operation because it was tied so closely to the ordinance they'd be using. She'd done this a number of times before, so Franny Rupp had left a floor of her factory's newest brick building permanently at her disposal.

Now, as the clouds outside grumbled toward an approaching thunderstorm, Ruth added the onionskin to the low fire in her hearth. Within seconds, all written records of the plot were gone, and all that remained resided in her mind.

The objectives had come from Lawrence Breckenridge and Dick Hanrahan, the Gemstone and the Intel link in the Necklace, but the logistics were hers. There were two more flights in the run-up. Ordinarily, her men wouldn't need any extra drill, but with a wizard involved . . .

Ruth sucked air between her teeth: that was the part that always bothered her, and always would. She didn't understand what the wizard's doodad did. She had to build it into her calculations based on Quince's description—and he gave a good description of his toys, not a lot of gobbledygook—but until she heard back from the helicopters, she was flying as blind as they were. Nevertheless, at the end of the day, she alone in all the world got to plan ops with "elder doorways" in them. That's what had brought her to the Necklace.

Her radio squawked. "Mission accomplished."

SUNDAY, MARCH 20, 2011 • 7:21 P.M. EASTERN DAYLIGHT TIME

12 Flint Knife (Fulfilling Magick)

Spring 2011 came to Fort Wayne, Indiana, at 7:21 P.M. Eastern Daylight Time, a quarter of an hour before sunset. Franny Rupp, the Ordnance link in the Necklace, was watching Purdue vs. VCU on TBS-HD with pre-storm lightning flashing outside her office window. March Madness was in full swing, and Franny, like a lot of Hoosiers but also like a lot of people in general come March, was glued to the games and the point spreads. Her family had always been into basketball, their loyalty on the IU/Purdue split given to Purdue since it was northern Indiana like Fort Wayne. She'd followed the Boilermakers since she was four, but the love of her basketball life these days was the incredible Butler Bulldogs, who went to the finals last year and had won their first two games this year by a combined total of three points. They played again on Thursday, against Wisconsin. *And thank God it's Thursday,* she told herself, laughing at her own joke. Why not? She was on her second Bud since tip-off and she was feelin' fine, even if Purdue was getting its ass handed to it.

She had spent all day and half of last night making sure her birds were ready to fly through that "elder doorway" and fly back out again in one piece. Now she just had to wait to hear how they'd done, and so, Purdue. She liked doing things that any other inhabitant of Fort Wayne could be doing, because she was an *inhabitant* of Fort Wayne, not appointed to her city like the other eight links. And she was proud of it.

Franny's great-great-grandfather, Johannes Rupp, had been the Ordnance link in the cabal in 1854, when it decided to establish a geographical choke hold around the throat of the United States and call itself the Necklace. Johannes moved his Rupp Works from Detroit to Fort Wayne as part of the plan, and because the Necklace had never once had occasion to complain about his quality of workmanship, Johannes's son John Thomas had succeeded, and then J.T.'s son George, and George's son Randolph, and finally Randy's daughter Frances. No other link could claim any genealogy whatsoever, but Ordnance was always in the hands of the Rupps of Fort Wayne. Always had been, and always . . .

Cutting through the beer and b-ball, Franny remembered she was forty-four, with no heir in sight. Fortunately, her radio squawked and broke that up.

SUNDAY, MARCH 20, 2011 • 7:21 P.M. EASTERN DAYLIGHT TIME

12 Flint Knife (Fulfilling Magick)

Spring 2011 came to Wheeling, West Virginia, at 7:21 P.M. Eastern Daylight Time, just at sunset. Dick Hanrahan, the Intelligence link in the Necklace, reviewed the operation from his bunker deep inside his mansion. He had turned eighty-two in February, but he showed no signs of slackening the pace that had kept him the best-informed man in America since the Korean War. He had joined the Federal Response Council in 1953, straight off running COMINT, and moved up to the Necklace in 1968 when his predecessor, Nelson, had gone gaga—probably Alzheimer's, but Hanrahan's first act was to order second opinions and thoroughly investigate the original doctors. Turned out everything was above board, but it was pure Hanrahan: no stone unturned.

He shifted his butt in his padded chair, trying to find relief from his sciatica. He'd had his own doctors under surveillance for more than twenty years; he knew they were giving him every benefit they could. They were younger, but they were all growing older together so they knew what they would lose if they ever betrayed Hanrahan. His body was strong but it had its flaws now. His mind had none, as it summarized the first quarter of 2011, just ended, with solid satisfaction.

Nineteen years ago, in 1992, Renzo Breckenridge, the Gemstone of the Necklace, made like Kennedy saying America'd go to the moon. Renzo said that in twenty years, we'd hold all the cards, and he was right. A year and nine months from now, December 21, 2012, the day that all the nuts think the world will end . . . it will. For them.

This is mop-up time. The presidency belongs to us, all the Republicans and half the Democrats in Congress belong to us, the Supreme Court belongs to us, most of the governors belong to us, the media belongs to us. We're just tightening the screws. You gotta tip your hat to Renzo: he got it done.

No matter where a simple citizen turns, he finds us. Want to get what you vote for? Want to get paid? Want progress on anything that matters to you? Not unless we say so.

People feel it, but they're running out of places to go without it. Every bit of truth they personally know about ends up altered if it hits the media—made shallow and boring, or shallow and fearsome, and either way shallow, so none of it really matters. Soon they'll all be completely alone, and we'll have the corporation we've fought so long to attain.

Corporation America.

The old man with the young brain shifted his aching hip again, so he could lean back in his chair.

The only serious resistance left is Max August, and Pamela Blackwell. But they won't last.

You set the course and you brought the ship home, Renzo. Come the end of next year, the ship will dock, the mission accomplished.

But you won't be Gemstone then.

I will. Because you'll be dead. Like Kennedy.

SUNDAY, MARCH 20, 2011 · 7:21 P.M. EASTERN DAYLIGHT TIME

12 Flint Knife (Fulfilling Magick)

Spring 2011 came to New York, New York, at 7:21 P.M. Eastern Daylight Time, a quarter of an hour after sunset. Lawrence Breckenridge, the Gemstone in the Necklace, the boss of all bosses, was naked on the king-sized bed in his East Thirty-fifth Street brownstone, sliding his palm along the warm red back of his diabola. She was naked as well, and made of soft flesh, or something very like it. After many years, he could tell the difference, as subtle as her lover's scent. There was a velvety smoothness to it. He knew she wasn't human. He didn't care.

He had come up at the Politics link, recommended by his oldest friend, Dick Hanrahan. It was just under twenty years ago when Aleksandra appeared to him for the first time, and promised that they would rule the world in twenty years if he killed the existing Gemstone, who had not lived up to her expectations. He did, became Gemstone, and everything since then had unfolded as she'd seen it. He had contributed greatly, with his inner knowledge of politics and power, but she was the boss. He didn't care.

Anything he wanted he could have, but there was nothing he wanted more than Aleksandra. On a daily basis, he ran the world, and on many nights, he fucked the most beautiful woman imaginable. He grabbed her shoulder now and squeezed it as hard as he could, fingers pressing deep into perfect scarlet flesh, and she gurgled her delight.

He loved it all.

— 0 —

Spring 2011 came to New York, New York, on a wave of fresh power as the Sun's reign began. Aleksandra Korelatovna, diabola, was naked on the king-sized bed in Renzo's East Thirty-fifth Street brownstone, letting her lover overpower her and feeling the power of springtime surge through them both. In fact, she was neither naked nor there. Once upon a time she'd been human, but she'd fought her way to the top rank of humanity and then gone higher, to where humanity was just an illusion, a video game she could play quite well after living it for thirty-six years. Somewhere far away from Earth, she had created the perfect female form for the man who ran the Necklace.

She'd read about the Necklace in Academgorodok's long, cool libraries as early as 1959—but throughout her ascent, her people, the Russians, had seemed destined to rule the world. It was only after she'd become a diabola in 1988 that she saw the Russians crumbling and she turned her attention to the Necklace. She offered their Gemstone a private collaboration, just the two of them, to run the enterprise from a higher perspective, and they did well enough to push George Bush the First through. But in 1991, she could see Bill Clinton coming on and knew the cabal would have to work in new ways. Tom Jeckyl wasn't given to new ways. So she looked at his people, the eight others in the cabal, and chose Renzo. She could see the two of them having complete control of America in twenty years. He killed Tom for her, ran the world for her, and she gave him long life and unimaginable sex.

She felt the flow of the Solar System, the magnetosphere, the solar wind, and the interstitial gravity. She felt the Earth balance perfectly with the Sun at the moment of spring. She felt it all and focused it all through her power on Renzo.

She loved him in her way.

SUNDAY, MARCH 20, 2011 · 11:21 P.M. GREENWICH MEAN TIME

12 Flint Knife (Fulfilling Magick)

Spring came to London, England, at 11:21 P.M. Greenwich Mean Time, well into the cold, cloudy night. The nineteen-year-old girl now calling herself Vee knew nothing of the clandestine cabal called the Necklace, nor would she have been much interested if she had. Her focus for nearly two years had been the relationship between herself, a nineteen-year-old girl named Vee, and a leather-bound book.

Henry Cornelius Agrippa—His Fifth Book of Occult Philosophy

In 1519, the legendary Cornelius Agrippa had ensorcelled that magickal package and set it out for people like her to find—people who had been disciples of his, the book said. She could not have been the disciple of a sixteenth-century man—she was not from the sixteenth century; she knew that—but somehow, she knew she *had* been his disciple. Probably through other books, other packages left for the cognoscenti to find. And then she had somehow lost her way. She didn't know how. But Agrippa had written this book because he knew his disciples faced such dangers—though even he probably didn't think it would still be offering the way home in the twenty-first century.

She had been drawn to it and she had understood, deep in her soul, how to use it—as if he had taught her. She had read the book a dozen times now, cover to cover, but that was not how she used it. She talked to it, and it responded by opening an appropriate part of itself, revealing a passage highlighted in pale witchfire. It was a book—it could only reveal what Agrippa had thought important in 1519—but he had thought of many things by then. He was the premier wizard in an age of wizardry. His book had simple consciousness, like a computer running Magick as the OS.

Vee used English when she spoke to it, and the book appeared to her in English, though it must have been written in Latin. But Vee was far removed from 1519; Vee was all about 2011, because she was a fully functioning member of society, here and now. Until two years ago, she had been a schizophrenic named Eva Delia Kerr. She had lived drug-dozy days with two voices in her head. But whenever the drugs wore off, one of the voices told her she had to be more. The other voice told the first voice she had no idea what "more" was. The girl could not resolve them and so spent sixteen years in institutions.

But she ran away to London, and she came upon the book. She just liked it; she didn't know why. Then a demon tried to destroy her, but only succeeded in destroying her other identities, leaving just one at long last. That one called herself the Voice at first, then just Vee, though Vee loved to use her voice and did, singing in the clubs of Camden Town. Vee was *functional*. Eva Delia Kerr had completely ceased to exist.

Vee lived in a flat at 47 Hartland Road. It was not a large flat, but Hartland Road was the prettiest street in town, with every flat on its long, straight block painted a different pastel. There was something in Vee that loved those colors and she'd saved every pound she could until she could rent one of those flats. She'd moved in last November, to a flat with a canary yellow façade. Her neighbors sometimes laughed about Hartland Road looking like Carnaby Street, or San Francisco in the '70s, but that was just fine with Vee. She took that vibe and ran it through 2011 and turned it into something all her own. Something that got her onstage two nights a week at Eddie's Club, with a good chance for more. But two nights was fine just now, because the other nights, she was here, in her flat, learning from her book.

Two years in, Vee was *functional* in society and *functional* in wizardry. It wasn't as if she had to learn the magick from scratch; it was coming back to her, though from where she still didn't know. So tonight she stood naked in the center of her ten-foot-square living room, in the center of a series of concentric painted circles. This was the sixteenth-century way, with names of angels at the corners to fight off evil spirits while the magus and the universe found common ground. The book rested before her, on a table a foot bigger around than it was. There were candles in the half-foot above, below, to the right, and to the left of the book. She'd laid bouquets of gorse between the candles. As Spring came to London, she chanted, musically, her focus for tonight: "The lore of Spring!"

The book's pages flipped themselves with a quick intelligence, then settled slowly with the correct pages reached. Words on the upper half of the right-hand page were marked with a nonconsuming witchfire, so she read them.

The god of Spring is the young horned god—Pan, Dionysus, Proteus, Priapus, Pallas, the Green Man, Mars. He has so many forms because he is in all life, Male and Female. "Pan" is Greek for "All."

At Spring, the Sun is exalted in Aries the Ram, and Mars rules.

"I feel the Sun, and Mars," Vee responded, talking directly to the pages. "And I also feel Uranus, which happens to be conjunct the Sun this year. It makes everything extra crispy. But you, dear Cornelius, don't know about Uranus, since it wasn't found till you'd been dead two hundred years. There I'm on my own, following my own path." She pronounced it *Cor-nay-lee-oos*, the way he, as a German, would have pronounced it.

The pages flipped to a very familiar page. You are not me, nor should you be.

"Also this year, spring begins on a Sunday, the Day of the Sun."

Flip. The Day of the Sun is concerned with the communion with one's realm. It is good for leadership, vitality, creativity, and honors.

"This year it's in the Hour of the Moon, so that tempers it a bit."

Flip. *The Hour of the Moon is concerned with confidence and stimulation—the hallmarks of life. It is good for divination of cyclical events. It is good for the house and the home.*

Then the pages flipped again. *The god of Spring is in All. Soon enough it will divide, and this is a great mystery. The wise know of two secret sabbats at this time—the sabbat of women on March 25, which the Church calls Lady Day, and the sabbat of men on April 1, which the fools call April Fools' Day.*

"I certainly liked Lady Day last year—my first year. And I was a real April Fool."

Flip. *Thus ends the lesson.*

The book closed itself with a thump.

So Vee, left to her own devices, took her knowledge of Spring's power and her feel for it and made it more than the sum of its parts. In her small living room at 47 Hartland Road, in the center of the universe, Vee sang the power all night long, in a voice both strong and beautiful.

Vee was more than functional. Vee was *vital*.

SUNDAY, MARCH 20, 2011 · 11:21 P.M. GREENWICH MEAN TIME

12 Flint Knife (Fulfilling Magick)

Spring 2011 came to London, England, at 11:21 P.M. Greenwich Mean Time, well into the cold, cloudy night. Max August and Pam Blackwell, free alchemists opposed to everything the clandestine cabal called the Necklace stood for, were using Spring's power to seek Eva Delia Kerr. They were getting nowhere, as they had for the past two years, when the door to their hotel room flew open.

Two hooded figures stepped in decisively. As one, they threw back their cowls to reveal stunningly handsome beings, a man and a woman. He was majestic, well-proportioned, strong, with wavy black hair, piercing black eyes, and a commanding mouth. She was compact and voluptuous, curly black hair, piercing green eyes, bee-stung red lips.

Max locked on her. Her pink tongue peeked out, pointed; it flicked across her lips. He found himself watching her tongue intensely. Her eyes glowed emerald and he was transfixed, the light from them filling his eyes. In a smoldering voice, she said, "Maxxx." It was a triple-X voice. It was more than that. Max had to have her.

Pam could not believe how good the man's voice felt in her ear. His soft breath puffing her warm, soft ear. . . . She raised her head and kissed him hard!

Max's tongue speared the lips of the woman.

The man's hands stroked Pam's hair, her quirky blonde hair, over her ears, out along her shoulders, down her toned arms . . . over her breasts. She arched her back, offering herself.

Max had his hands up under the woman's hoodie, and he took it off her. Her body was naked beneath a soft red mid-mesh netting, more annoying than concealing, the kind you want to rip off with your teeth! Max did, in a frenzy.

· · · · ·

The man's lips were on Pam's nipple, playing it with the clear knowledge of what a woman feels. His right hand was sliding slowly down over her tummy . . . slowly . . . down . . . His left hand held her by the hair. Her head was back, lolling side to side.

"Get on your knees, Pam," the man commanded, and she happily slid down along his chest till she rested on the floor.

· · · · ·

Max remembered Pam.

But the succubus was cupping his crotch with her hand. He ground himself against her and ran his hand across her slim belly. His chin was buried in her hair of soft, shimmering, midnight curls. It was all he could do to look through the curls, at anything else. But he did, somehow, seeing the room, only to have his attention snap back to her. He could have let it all go then. But he forced his eyes to refocus again, moving past the soft black cloud, to the unbearable ugliness of the damned hotel room—to Pam.

· · · · ·

Pam was kneeling before the incredible man when suddenly he was gone.

She cried out in animal frustration. She opened her eyes frantically and saw Max, that fucking asshole, wrestling with him. He was hers, goddammit! The man's muscles flexed and strained in the lamplight, half hidden by Max's lumpy bulk and the shadow he threw. She looked desperately to see if she could turn up the lamp—and saw the woman.

"Don't look back!" Max yelled.

She began to look back. She wasn't into women. Then she realized for the first time that she was on her hands and knees.

Max yelled again, the strain of his battle evident in the sound. "Don't look back! She's your target! She has no effect on you!"

Pam came up off her knees in a stumbling hurry. It was true. The succubus—Pam knew it now—was naked and beautiful, and that didn't slow Pam's right uppercut to the belly one bit. The bitch's gorgeous hair flew as she fell on her rounded ass, but she was resilient. She threw herself at Pam's feet and bit her on the calf.

· · · · ·

Max kept his eyes always on the incubus. There was no question that the guy was a magnificent specimen, with all the muscles that entailed, but he didn't use those muscles in his line of work. His thing was sex and his combat was mostly attempted with his groin. Max knew exactly how to kill him. After two minutes of savage combat, Max did exactly that.

Max knelt beside the dead thing and did not look around, simply waiting, breathing hard. He heard the succubus make a soft mew of pain. The thought of it almost tore his heart out; almost literally yanked him around to look at her. But he did not look around, and then he heard Pam's shout of joy as a body fell hard to the carpeted floor.

"She's dead, Max."

"Make sure," was all he said, still not looking.

There was a muffled crack. "There's no pulse," said Dr. Pamela Blackwell, "and I snapped her little finger without getting a response. Is that good enough?"

"Yes," he said, and stood up at last.

Pam was crouched beside the dead female, her hair wild, her eyes bright, breathing hard. Max was marked with blood, eyes equally bright. The spell was broken and the things on the floor were just debris, and then Max and Pam were hugging and kissing and running their hands all over each other.

"It wasn't us!" Pam whispered. "We're not that!"

They stopped talking then. They had a lot of power to let loose.

MONDAY, MARCH 21, 2011 · 12:16 A.M. GREENWICH MEAN TIME

12 Flint Knife (Fulfilling Magick)

Some time later, Max and Pam lay utterly spent on the hotel carpet, and all was silence.

Then Max said, "Necklace assassins."

Pam nodded, then remembered he was looking at the ceiling same as her. "It took 'em long enough," she said offhandedly, though there was nothing offhanded about what they'd been through. "We first heard about this pair in Okayama."

"Shiraishi."

"Same difference." She took air in through her nose; let it out. "They had us completely, Max. They had *me*. I *never* would act like that. You *know* I wouldn't."

"I *do* know, honey," he answered her. "But they're everything humans find entrancing, everything humans want. And still, I wanted *more*. I wanted you. I looked for you, and stopped looking at the succubus, and saw that the incubus didn't mean a damn thing to me. All we had to do was switch partners."

"If they'd tackled us one-on-one . . ." Pam said slowly.

"We'd have figured something else out."

"I'm not so sure."

"We've beaten four teams now, all different," Max said. "A pair of mercs . . ."

"You and Coyote beat those guys," Pam said.

"True, but you and I took out the snipers in Hong Kong, the ex-KGB team in Kazakhstan, and these two. We've had our moments."

"Three and a half years of them for me," she said. "None for you."

"Oh no. I lived every minute of it, same as you."

Max was thirty-five years old, the same age as the moment he became Timeless in 1985. Pam was just thirty, with growing hopes of achieving the same state before she grew older than Max. Her mastery of alchemy was increasing by leaps and bounds; she'd been his disciple/girlfriend for all of those three and a half years, and his significant other since Midsummer '09, precisely half that time. The amount of commitment Max was willing to provide in the first half of their time together had been limited, because his first wife, Val, had been reincarnated somewhere on Earth, and he had sworn to find her. But in 2009 he had learned she'd become a girl named Eva Delia Kerr—and he had decided then and there that whatever might happen once she was found, he would stay with Pam. They had become a team, emotionally and magickally.

In 2009, he had thought that finding Val—Eva Delia—was a matter of hours, or at most days. But his agent in England, a woman called Hoodoo, reported that Eva Delia seemed to have vanished the moment she'd been discovered—and vanishing from practitioners of magick was a very unexpected thing. Max and Pam had flown to London and conducted a comprehensive alchemical search alongside Hoodoo, who could extend her consciousness into the Earth to know those who walked upon it. The three of them should have been able to find Eva Delia if she was anywhere in Britain. But there was no sign of their quarry at all.

"There's got to be competing magick involved," Max had told

Pam and Hoodoo over £35 Scotches at Boisdale, back in '09. "But I'll be damned if I know what it is." So some of Max's other friends, several of whom were new to Pam, came to London and devoted their energies to the search. But they all failed, and they all had their own business to get back to. As did Max and Pam, in their struggle with the Necklace. Now, the trail seemed irredeemably cold. It was only because Max and Pam had spent the past few weeks in Morocco that they decided to swing through London once more. Somehow, the incubus and succubus had found them here.

Max's iPhone gave a distinctive ring. Pam sat up as he raised himself with one arm and reached for the device with the other. Pam liked the way the light caught his mouth; it was the single most distinctive characteristic of his early life as a deejay. The one-armed push-up was the most distinctive of his ongoing life as a point man, forward-deployed in the war they were fighting. She really did like what she was seeing now better than what she'd seen of the incubus. But she hadn't been strong enough to break free on her own.

Max said, "Mrs. Peel, we're wanted."

She'd been with him long enough to know the reference. "Di sent you a message?"

"Coded in the ratings of WFLD radio. Something's going down in Fort Wayne."

"Fort Wayne?" she echoed. "Of all the places the Necklace has bases, that would be the last one I'd pick for something urgent."

"I hear that," he agreed, shifting around to sit with his back against the bed, already thumbing the apps on his phone. "But we're leaving London on the quickest flight out."

Day One

13 Milky Way (Managing Alchemy)

Max and Pam lifted off from Heathrow into scattered clouds, then a brilliant sky. British Airways flight 1542 was the day's first non-stop to Chicago, getting them in at 12:50 P.M. Central Time after a five-hour time change. As was their custom, they had the only two seats on the right in the last row of first class, they had new faces, and they had magickal shields around their conversation. Pam obviously wanted to talk, and as soon as they were airborne, she did.

"About last night . . ."

"Uh-huh."

"I believe doctrine states that power's just busting out all over at springtime." Pam's voice was carefully dispassionate. "And this year, the Sun's conjunct Uranus, to make it even more spectacular. It doesn't take an alchemist to see that power playing out last night."

"No," Max agreed, well aware that she was troubled by it. "But it takes at least an astrologer to know about it."

"D'you think Ken and Barbie timed their attack to take advantage?"

"Probably. I would have."

"Should we have been expecting them?"

"There was sexy stuff in the air last night, but that could have been us doing our ritual. An attack by incubus and succubus was certainly not probable."

"The whole male-female thing . . ." Pam mused. Her jaw clenched. "I remember when the Necklace made all their agent teams one man and one woman, because it made the teams more powerful."

"Yeah." He smiled at her in his breezy deejay way, refusing to join her mood. "Agrippa used to tell me the god of Spring is Pan, and Pan means 'All.' We all feel his power. And then soon enough, we settle in as one half of All, either male or female, and we go looking for our other half. That's nature, and that's gravity—the eternal coming together. We're all built for relationships. It's the nature of a dual world, and it's powerful."

Pam nodded, her lips tight.

"Beyond that, though," Max continued, "there are four seasons, and four days midway between the seasons, and out of that comes the eight sabbats of the world—Yule, Imbolc, Spring, Beltane, Midsummer, Lughnasadh, the Fall, and All Hallows' Eve. The wise begin their counting with Zero, and in this case that's Hallowe'en, the Dark Void. Then Yule is One, Imbolc Two, and Spring is Three, when the world, which has been kept under wraps all winter, becomes three-dimensional again. Then comes the hidden number pi, the number that never ends.

"Now, Archimedes worked out pi as approximately three and one-seventh, around 250 BC, but before him, people guesstimated at three and one-eighth, and they were the ones working out an understanding of the year. If Spring is Number Three, and there are forty days to the next sabbat on Beltane, one-eighth of forty is five. Five days from spring, March 25, is an ancient festival called Lady Day. It's when 'All' celebrates 'all the girls.'

"There are ninety-three days to the next season, at Midsummer. One-eighth of ninety-three is eleven and a chunk. Eleven and a chunk days from spring, April 1, is the equally ancient festival of April Fools' Day, which is when 'All' celebrates 'all the boys.' Alchemists, though on one team or the other, celebrate both."

"I know all this," Pam said sourly. "You're just trying to divert me with your dazzling repartée."

"No, I'm saying an alchemist celebrates both, because that's how our world is set up, because both count. Sex is a given, so don't beat yourself up over a fundamental part of human nature."

"It was so fundamental I couldn't do anything to stop it, Max. Unlike you."

"So you're human, and not as far along as you thought you were. Welcome to the club. But alchemy's a path, Pam, not a teleportation. You're getting there."

" 'Getting there.' '*Getting* there.' I want to *be* there already!"

"One step at a time, cowgirl."

13 Milky Way (Managing Alchemy)

Breckenridge ran on his treadmill, gloriously alive from his night with his diabola. The monitor in his private gym was secure on Channel Nine, the Necklace's intranet, so he conducted a lot of his consultations from there. Precisely at 6 A.M., as he did every day of the year, and had for nearly twenty years, he flipped a switch in a panel beside his hand and the image of Dick Hanrahan appeared before him.

"Good morning, Renzo," the old man said in his briefing voice. "Today is March 21, 2011, a Monday.

"The Brits took a shot at Qaddafi overnight, putting a missile in his compound, but he got away. Obama says he's not a target, and also says the U.S. expects to hand over military leadership to the allies within days.

"The Japanese say there's radiation in the food supplies around their four crippled nuclear plants, but eating it won't do anybody any harm."

"Can you believe we were going to detonate Yucca Mountain?" Breckenridge broke in. "This is much better, and it didn't cost a cent." He waved a hand. "Continue."

"AT&T plans to pay thirty-nine billion dollars for Deutsche Telekom's T-Mobile USA to create a new U.S. mobile market leader, and raise their prices ten bucks a month, so Carole is dealing with the antitrust boys."

"For a lot less than when antitrust had teeth, I'm sure," nodded Breckenridge. "That's just a business expense now. Tax deductible."

"You want the numbers?"

"No. Tell me about August."

"The succubus and incubus failed."

"Jesus. When we actually *do* bring that guy down, it'll be epic. What about the Black Helicopters?"

"Wiped out a family in Montana and were seen. I chose that guy who yelled at you in Kalispell, but it could have been anybody out there in the sticks."

"Now that's the way we like it," Breckenridge said, beginning to breathe just a little harder. "Friday night, they'll set off an uprising, and it doesn't matter how large, because it will legitimize the act of rebellion, and the fear behind the act. One of those rebels will kill somebody, like that lunatic in Arizona. Maybe more than one. But it won't have anything to do with us."

Breckenridge's shoulders were swinging back and forth. "One act of true violence and the pot begins to boil. The uprisers want it to boil, want it to boil over. Normal people want it to stop, and most don't care how that gets done. We can handle that for them. We can hold the lid on the boiling pot, as hard as we have to. And then comes Twenty-Twelve. Jackson Tower, in his time as the wizard, was too old-school to learn Mayan magick, but the Mayan End Times fit my plan so perfectly it's like it was preordained. December 21, 2012, will be the capstone of my twenty years as Gemstone."

Hanrahan blinked, once. "Unless August and Blackwell keep interfering—especially this Friday."

"You give these folks a lot of credit, Dick."

"You don't know magick any more than I do, Renzo. They've got real power."

"True," said Breckenridge, "I don't know magick. But I know human beings, and that's all Max and Pam are. No more, no less. They're not gods."

"Neither are we."

"Exactly. We're all humans here, and we have real power, too. The difference is, we're worldwide, and they're just the two of them."

"They have some friends. Maybe as many as a dozen."

"Humans, too."

"Let's hope so." Both men cracked a smile, but Hanrahan had another objection. "They've hit us three times so far."

"And we've succeeded forty-five other times," Breckenridge said.

"That's three in less than three and a half years. And each of those three was big. That's too much, Renzo."

"All right, Max and Pam have to die. The plucky rebel sweethearts have to die, and sooner rather than later. But I can't worry about, or bet all my chips, on any one operation, or any one source of opposition. I've got my eye on all of them. We may take some flak but we're getting this ship to Twenty-Twelve."

"Most of our other victories were in the back rooms of Washington, Renzo. Based on what he's shown us, August could have disrupted a lot of those. I think he hasn't because he hasn't wanted to. He holds his fire so he can focus on what, frankly, we're focused on. He wants to hit us where it hurts. And I believe that the threat assessment is very high on something this critical."

"Which is what I have you for, and what I have Ruth and Franny for."

"Thank you for including me with them," snapped the old man.

"Jesus, Dick, lighten up. It is what I have you for. The Intelligence link in the Necklace gives me what I need to know, and the Ops and Ordnance links give me control on the ground. I trust all of you to do your jobs, so I can run the ship. Until we kill Max and Pam, we will suffer a higher than normal failure rate, but that rate is six percent and I can *live* with that. One of our failures was Yucca, but the Japs just handed us what we wanted, so let's scratch that one off. *Two* failures. What's that, four percent now. Dick, if you saw the world the way I do, you'd see a far more complex, and ulti-mately forgiving, place."

"I see facts," said Hanrahan sourly. "I see August and Blackwell continuing to live, and my analysis says he'll be interested in Black Helicopters."

"He *would* be interested, but how's he going to know about them?" Breckenridge used the pad beside his hand again, to stop the treadmill and lope to a halt. "Let's just make certain we do every-thing we can on our end. Then it's in the hands of the gods."

"Yeah," said Hanrahan. "Finally Renzo: tomorrow is Stamp Act Day."

"I know. Huzzah! All hail the Loyale Nine, my friend!"

"All hail the Loyale Nine!"

MONDAY, MARCH 21, 2011 · 8:00 a.m. EASTERN DAYLIGHT TIME

13 Milky Way (Managing Alchemy)

Two hours later, Breckenridge stepped from his limo beneath Barker Chilton's spacious portico. It was a dismal, snowy day, but the portico's main purpose was to shield the arrival of visitors from non-Western satellite view. American and European satellites were recording a feed showing the Chilton estate with no visitors what-soever.

In fact, there had been thirty-three arrivals and departures this morning. Porter Allenby, the Values link, and Nat Whitten, the new Politics link, had massaged the gathering in preparation for Breckenridge; he was the centerpiece of the affair so his arrival was timed to be last.

"Larry!" It was Chilton, striding forward to greet him, hand out-stretched. For a nickname, Breckenridge preferred the "Renzo" his old friend Dick used; beyond that he preferred his given name. But this was trivial.

"Barker, how are you, old friend?"

"Excellent, Larry. Any problem on the flight?"

"No, I've had my pilot for a long time now. I hardly even notice flying." He turned toward the driver's window. "Roger."

The driver bobbed his head. The impression he gave was of so-lidity. Nothing would get past this man if it threatened the boss. Breckenridge said, "This is Roger, my pilot *and* driver."

"Your wingman," Chilton chuckled.

"Exactly."

"Nice to meet you, Roger."

"You, too, sir."

Breckenridge said, "One hour, Roger."

"Yes, sir." The limo moved smoothly to the parking area. Chil-ton led Breckenridge inside his mansion. There were thirty-three people there, almost all men. They broke into applause. Brecken-ridge flipped his palms up, humbly acknowledging it with a grin that said he wasn't humble at all. The applause went on for a while. He held up a palm and it died away.

"Ladies and gentlemen," he said, "I'm going to enjoy this day with you, and I'll tell you why. We are in the end days. The end of an era, ushered in by you. Soon those who share our beliefs will truly be the chosen ones, as the failures of the past, however noble, how-ever *sacred,* will matter no more. There will be a new day, with only promise ahead—and don't we all wish we could speed that day?"

Cries of assent were heard around the room.

"Well, we can't. But it's coming, coming because of you. Some say it's at the end of next year. Now, we're not Mayan—"

"Not hardly!"

"—but maybe they found the end of days on their own, to prove Christ's dominion over all the Earth, for surely he is Lord of all the heathens as well!"

"Yes!" "Yes!"

"Everything is speeding up, and it's spinning out of control. Everything's new and then everything's obsolete within months now. The tape, the CD, the DVD, the Blu-Ray. The film in the theater and the film on Blu-Ray with the two alternate endings. You can never get to the end of it, and so now people, somewhere deep in their souls, want to get to the end of it. In their heart of hearts, all of America is thinking, 'Can we just stop, please? Stop and let me finally find some work, let me enjoy my income, let me plan for the future, *let me relax*'—but I am certain that soon, maybe very soon, they will get their answer, and it will be 'No!' Our time on Earth is played out, and there is a new day coming!"

MONDAY, MARCH 21, 2011 · 8:00 A.M. EASTERN DAYLIGHT TIME

13 Milky Way (Managing Alchemy)

The Ohio River runs through the chaotic mountains of West Virginia—a river mighty enough to carve a valley over time, a long, narrow, north-south stretch of lowland passing eternally lowering ridges. Within that valley is the city of Wheeling, which has spread as wide as possible across the valley, to hold the twenty-eight thousand people who live there. But once you leave the city and head back up into the mountains, the population drops off drastically. An inhabitant of Wheeling like Dick Hanrahan could find complete privacy there.

It was getting to be warm, early on the first day of spring, but at this elevation the snow still clung to the ground and the trees. Hanrahan had left immediately after briefing Breckenridge and driven his personal Ford Expedition, a forgettable gray-silver, up Route 647 until he reached a gated turnoff on the left. It went without saying that he had hidden cameras watching the road for two miles in either direction, checking the gate and the narrow road leading up and away behind it, now covered in snow. But as soon as Hanrahan opened the gate with his remote and disappeared around the first curve, the road turned black and dry, thanks to the heating units running beneath it. Hanrahan continued another three miles upward to another gate, opened that one, and went to the ridge. where the road ended in a circle wide enough to turn around in. He left the Expedition and walked a quarter mile on a snowy path through the woods, giving his state-of-the-art electronic and mystical scanners time to decide that he belonged here, that they should not kill him. The walking made his back feel better, so he had no desire for death. His desire went another way.

He came to a small, windowless cabin and let himself in. No one had been here since his last visit, his sensors said. He checked his watch, then went to the bar and turned on the coffemaker. It was still two minutes to Charley.

. . . . .

In Duluth, Peter Quince sat cross-legged in the center of the circles ancient wizards had inscribed in the wooden floor of the sanctum sanctorum in the cupola of the house on Lake Superior.

At least, what was left of him did.

His body had become no more than clouds of mist, pulsing with rhythms only it could hear. Half of what he was, was here now, in Duluth. The other half, augmented by all the power from the women on the slabs, was a mist above a plane, the highest realm he could imagine. Two lights shone high above him, throwing vague shadows through him into the gaping, putrescent hole at the center of the plane. But four lines led from that center, in four directions, in four colors. The blue line led to the right, into a blue veil.

The half-Quince moved in that direction, passing through the veil, and entered the soul of Charley Posner, a loan officer at Chase in Dayton. Quince had the ability to enter a few select people, and Charley was the best fit of "distance" and "suitability" when it came time for Quince to choose someone to meet with Hanrahan in the cabin. Charley, who ordinarily lived alone in Dayton, lay unconscious twenty-three hours a day in West Virginia, but every morning at 8:15 he sat up as Peter Quince.

He did so now. "Good morning, Dick," said Charley with Quince's Western accent. "Enjoy your coffee. I've gotta go pee." He stood up and walked directly into the bathroom.

Quince was a wizard, and Hanrahan accepted his weirdness because he was good at wizardry. In the two years that he'd held the position, he had provided a steady stream of magickal devices to help the Necklace, including the bone that the Black Helicopter mission was built around. Moreover, he was the only one of them to have personally fought Max August and Pam Blackwell. His insights into their characters and methods had allowed the Necklace to keep August and Blackwell from forestalling the Wisconsin attack.

All of that was why the Necklace made allowances, but Hanrahan had one more reason: he and Quince were conspiring to kill Lawrence Breckenridge.

· · · · ·

Quince finished peeing. *Even with wizardry, coffee is coffee,* he thought. *None today.* But he lingered in the bathroom. He had no need to bow before Hanrahan, or any man, and he enjoyed these times when he could be the master and not the slave. *Let the old man wait, and wonder what I'm doing in here.*

But finally, he opened the bathroom door and Charley came forth, zipping his fly. "Where's Breckenridge this fine morning, Dick?" he asked his now longtime partner.

"Meeting with rich white evangelicals."

"As opposed to what?"

"All part of the buildup to Friday," said Hanrahan. "They'll give like crazy after Friday. He's very focused on Friday. Coffee?"

"No, thanks. So when I hit him Wednesday, he'll have to cram that crisis on top of Friday's mission—"

"—and Thursday morning, he'll be looking forward and backward, but not straight in front of him."

"That's the plan. And a good one it is," said Charley, "if you're right about him not suspecting you."

Hanrahan regarded him icily, but Quince/Charley didn't blink. "I've known him for forty-eight years," the old man said. "The only thing I don't know about Renzo Breckenridge is the cause of that strange noise I hear on my bugs—which I asked you about."

"I gave you my best answer on that, Dick," Charley responded impatiently. "It's a rejuvenation machine of some sort. Breckenridge's vitality is unnatural. Forget about it."

"I know for a fact that Ordnance didn't build him anything like that, and I find no record of any outside firm doing it, or of any wizard."

"But you wouldn't, would you? He's the Gemstone."

"And I'm Intelligence. So I would."

"Well, I found nothing on the wizard side, either. And after Thursday, it won't matter."

"I don't like loose ends," said Hanrahan.

"Then ask him, Thursday afternoon. You've got drugs."

"No, when I kill the snake, I kill the snake. And besides—I'll have a Necklace to run." The old man smiled his own reptilian smile. "Now, Peter, this will be the last time we'll be in contact before Thursday, unless something unforeseen comes up."

"We've foreseen everything."

"In all my years of espionage, I've never known that to be true. There's always something. And aren't you the one who says, 'There are no cut-and-dried answers in magick'?"

"Yes, but trust in yourself, and the world will be ours!"

"Are *you*," queried Hanrahan, "giving *me* a pep talk?"

"We're partners, aren't we?"

Idiot, thought the old man.

Fool, thought the wizard.

13 Milky Way (Managing Alchemy)

Peter Quince resolidified in Duluth. He opened his eyes. He was home.

Hanrahan doesn't suspect us.

"Then why haven't you engulfed him, Master?" Quince asked.

There's no magick in him—a major reason why he doesn't suspect. You are all I need here, my adorèd one.

He knew Belia'al was the Prince of Liars, but he'd come to enjoy the lies. "Thank you, Master."

I have had my way with great men since the days of the Patriarchs. I control one thousand humans, great and small. But never have I had my way with the world.

One thousand, Quince thought, preening. *And I'm his favorite.*

Control of your world is the ultimate response to the cruel and unjust fate that God imposed upon me. I have lusted after it forever. And now, finally, you and Hanrahan will seize control of the Necklace—then you will seize it from him. And I am you.

Quince's body shivered in anticipation.

God banished my brother Lucifer, creating me as an artifact of his arrival in the world of duality. Lucifer chose revenge through men's souls, but I chose men's minds. Belia'al laughed, deep in Quince's chest. **And I win!**

It was a conversation between two entities, but it all came from the one man in the room. Just a wizard being weird.

13 Milky Way (Managing Alchemy)

Breckenridge excused himself from the center table and gave a small wave of farewell to the crowd as he made his way to the exit. Porter Allenby and Nat Whitten got up as well and followed him. It was not done with pomp and circumstance, but it was noticed, and appreciated. Breckenridge, Allenby, they were the leaders, charting the course for the movement, and they had to do what they had to do. It would be worrisome if the leaders had nothing better to do than sit and make small talk. It was as if Lawrence Breckenridge was the president of the United States.

Outside, he and the two other Necklace members retired to the Gemstone's limousine, now rimed with a thin skin of snow. It was a mobile security spot, tricked out with every device the military-industrial complex had devised, augmented by the cabal's time-tested magickal shields. Peter Quince had offered to improve the shields, but Breckenridge knew from Aleksandra that they needed no improvement and had turned him down.

Roger sat in front, his back to the dense shield that slid up between him and the rear compartment of facing seats. Breckenridge took the seat facing forward; Allenby and Whitten sat side by side across from him and the latter closed the side door with a satisfying *chunk*.

Porter Allenby always dressed in a well-tailored suit—which is to say, one that didn't *quite* fit. It enforced his image as a man of down-home values from the heartland of America, which was exactly what he was. He stayed forever in tune with public sentiment, ready to ride it wherever he wanted to go. He was a minister, but seemed more like a professor, and the fact that he lived in a liberal state like Wisconsin showed he wasn't really a partisan. Thus, Diana Herring's media pushed him on the public as a serious person. He was the third guest at the party, the guy she put on as the center of balance between the right and the left. The fact that he was right wing, too, served to demonstrate that the center belonged there.

Little Nat Whitten had a face turned leathery early from all the close-and-personal battles he'd waged in the halls of the Texas statehouse. It was not a face designed for television like Allenby's; it thrived in the halls, filled with smoke and man-sweat, where it wheedled and roared and cajoled as needed to get a deal done, and preferably one they could sell come November. But last year he'd come to understand that deals didn't have to be sold any longer, they could just be announced, and he jumped at the chance to play for bigger stakes with the Necklace, replacing Michael Salinan. He was not surprised to learn that Salinan had been the previous Political link; if he'd known such a post existed, he'd have been in his top two to hold it. But Salinan had disappeared and the position was open.

Though he showed none of it, Breckenridge was weighing Nat's every moment, even now. Breckenridge had been the Politics link in his time, and he'd picked every one since, personally—including Michael Salinan. So he refused to give Whitten his complete trust at this early date; and Nat would have distrusted any man who did. They understood each other. "Give the contributions list to Carole," Breckenridge told Nat. "The money's not important. Tell me about commitment."

"Very high," Nat said, looking at the Gemstone with camaraderie. "We're goin' all-in for Wisconsin, Michigan, Ohio, New Jersey, Pennsylvania, Florida, Kansas, and Arizona. Everybody's pumped. There's strong pushback from the public, but those folks have no long-term strategy. If they stymie us here and there, we've still surrounded 'em, so the next time our ideas'll be well-known and long-held positions, not radical a-tall. I'd say our position is real strong."

"The governors and legislators may not be so sanguine about being cannon fodder," offered Allenby.

"They'll be taken care of if they're recalled. That's what think tanks are for."

"Ha! Then everybody'll be workin' for us—the governors as well as the slaves."

Breckenridge said, "Well, if any of the *governors* want to talk with me, set it up. We don't condone any backsliding."

"Sure. And then, come Friday, it's all forgotten. The Black Helicopters are the new Nine-Eleven."

Breckenridge looked at Allenby. "How's the mood?"

"Lots of unhappy people, fighting to hold on to their dreams. Not really ready to revolt, but the idea is out there. Problem is, revolt against what? Most think the rich are to blame, but how do you attack the rich? And the Tea Baggers think the liberals are to blame. So there's a lot of disjunction, a lot of unease, just below the surface. Ironically, the one thing holding it in check is the idea at the back of people's minds that the world ends next year, not this one."

"But after Friday?"

"Well, Black Helicopters have been a bête noir since the seventies. The original idea was that they belonged to the UN and would swoop down when America was converted to a one-world government. Unless they belonged to space aliens who were doing all the cattle mutilation. Their profile dipped somewhat when nothing further happened on those fronts, but they resurfaced in the nineties when Helen Chenoweth of Idaho charged they were being used to enforce the Endangered Species Act. 'We do have some proof,' she said, but somehow she didn't produce it, so they faded again in the public awareness. But they've stayed on the crazies' radar right along, and if that proof were finally to arrive, it *would* be another Nine-Eleven—*everybody* would *have* to jump on board."

"On a ride t' nowhere," said Nat.

"Not nowhere," said Porter. "A frightened mob goes wherever you point them."

"All we're doin' is givin' them something to rebel against, on the road to Twenty-Twelve. They'll take it from there."

"More falling in line. More allegiance," agreed Breckenridge. "One big happy plantation."

13 Milky Way (Managing Alchemy)

Eight hours and forty minutes after takeoff, Max and Pam touched down at O'Hare. They joined their fellow passengers on the long walk to passport control, and were waiting in line for customs when Max noticed a young woman two lines down. She had reached her customs kiosk and was having some trouble with the agent. He only had to extend his consciousness a little to hear their back-and-forth.

"You can't have my laptop or my cell phone," she was saying, trying to keep her voice under control.

"I'm sorry, miss, but it's the law," the agent said firmly.

"Nonsense!"

"Not nonsense. According to Homeland Security, you donated to Wikileaks."

"So?"

"So Wikileaks is under investigation, and since you support them, we can confiscate any evidence that may help pursue a case against them."

"My laptop? My cell phone? Wikileaks hasn't been charged with anything, and I don't work for them."

"You're holding up the line, miss. Please come with me to the interrogation room."

"I'm not going anywhere. This is bogus."

"It's the law. Now—"

Max had had enough. He ducked his head, concentrated for a moment.

The agent rubbed the back of his hand across his eyes. "Oh, go on through," he said, and stamped her passport.

The girl looked at him, but not too long. She grabbed her computer and phone and moved toward the exits as quickly as she could without attracting any more attention.

"These are not the droids you're looking for," Pam said at Max's side.

"Exactly," he said. "I just hope she's got sense enough to encrypt anything she wants to keep on a separate machine and leave it in America, because that'll happen every time she leaves the country and comes back."

"That *is* outrageous if she hasn't committed any crime."

"Well, a crime is whatever the government says it is, and the Necklace has been criminalizing whistle-blowers," he said. "I wish I could follow up with her . . . but we've got to get to Fort Wayne."

They came to their own line's kiosk. The agent looked them over, compared what he saw to the photos in their passports, and stamped them through. "Welcome home," he said.

MONDAY, MARCH 21, 2011 · 1:30 P.M. CENTRAL DAYLIGHT TIME

13 Milky Way (Managing Alchemy)

Max bought a copy of *Entertainment Weekly* to shoot up current American culture—evidently, Charlie Sheen, Charlie Sheen, and Charlie Sheen—on their way to rent an Altima from a no-name agency outside the airport. They set off toward the Indiana Toll Road over some of the worst pavement he'd seen in a while. He tried to find Jim Rome on the radio, but apparently Chicago still didn't carry him, so he settled on B96 and sat back to dance with his shoulders to Jessie J's "Price Tag." He was well and truly removed from his deejay days at KQBU, but a good pop song was eternal. *He can dance anywhere and any time,* thought Pam, with affection.

They'd last driven the toll road in September of '09. Diana had given Max the nine cities in the Necklace at Midsummer, and first they'd gone to London to help Hoodoo look for Eva Delia, but

when that had stalled after two months of no results, they'd flown
back to America for the scenic tour.

There were two reasons they'd begun with Peter Quince, Wizardry, in Duluth, instead of Carole van Dusen, Finance, in Boston.
First, they'd just beaten Quince and needed to know what he'd done
about that. Second, no member of the Necklace could be considered
"easy," but moving west to east put the heaviest hitters last, and it
was just as well to take it slow. They could *not* let anyone know that
they had this knowledge without bringing Di down.

So they took a room at the Holiday Inn in downtown Duluth
and went for a drive out London Road to see the wondrous houses
of East Duluth. In the early days the city on the great lake had rumbled with lumber, milling, shipping, and railroads. The tycoons of
the Gilded Age built homes to match their grandeur. Always solid,
with fine style, they ranged along the pristine eastern shore, where
the woods ran down to the water. They carved out lawns for private
views; some left the forest standing as it had since time primeval,
others cleared it out so drivers on London Road could see their
opulent houses. Peter Quince's place, known locally as the George
Kerrigan house, was one of those not visible. The obvious approach
was through the woods at the rear, but as soon as Max did his *wipe*,
where he "cleaned" reality by moving his hand from left to right,
he saw the haunting spirits there. So he and Pam went for brisk sail-
ing jaunts past the Wizardry house, up and back, where each time
both they and the boat seemed different.

Next, they drove down to La Crosse, Wisconsin, where Porter
Allenby, Values, held sway. There they took a tour of his mega-
church. Max found no spirits there; rather, there was the suppressed
tension, just below the surface, that roiled so many people. The
message was simple: "We deserve better." Subtext: "Because we're
the people who built this country." Subtext: "Because we were promised the American Dream." Subtext: "Somebody took that away
from us, and we don't know who that is, and it's *pissing us off*!"
Subtext: "So we hate everyone we don't know."

But the message was full of hope for a better tomorrow, and

Allenby delivered it with calm certainty. He was not a screamer, not an orator; he presented himself as simply a public speaker who happened to speak for God. Max and Pam—wearing name tags for "Eric" and "Mallory"—took in two of his services on many levels, feeling for the subtexts, experiencing the whole. The message was certain that it was true, and everything else a sad mistake. The message said "We will vanquish our enemies and claim the Dream!"

Next came Diana Herring, Media, in Chicago. If they didn't want to tip any of Di's compatriots, they certainly didn't want her to notice them, even though she'd naturally be on alert. Their theory was, there had been three months with no sign of them, so she'd have to be deciding that they'd been and gone. In any event, they took the tour at skyscraping Full Resource Channel three times.

For Pam, disguising herself with a twist of will was now very much second nature. She could see how you faced down a mass of new information, ground your way through it piece by piece, and finally came out the other side, where you understood the information, where it was something you could build on as you moved to the next course of work. Where you could see you had come a distance on the path to Timeless alchemy.

Which was why Max kept upping the ante, teaching her to "paint" her new identity with finer and finer brushstrokes. With his core knowledge of the 260 days in a Mayan cycle, and the 260 corresponding asteroids, he saw things with 260 facets—details you could easily overlook, but which worked around the edges of your attention, subtly confirming the reality of what you saw. By the time they left Chicago, she was almost as good as he was.

Next came Franny Rupp, Ordnance, in Fort Wayne.

13 Milky Way (Managing Alchemy)

Vee closed her canary yellow door and stepped out into Hartland Road. To her left, the road jogged across Clarence Way, and on the far side was St. Barnabas, an abandoned church. It was still hot out, and the early spring had put leaves on the old tree in front of it, which threw its own shadows on the narrow churchyard. People said the weather had changed, that spring didn't used to be like this. Vee wouldn't know.

She turned right and walked up Hartland Road, with its twin rows of color—a sight that always made her happy. Some of her neighbors were also out walking, and she greeted them as they passed. She liked most of them, but Vee in 2011 was interested in three things: herself, the book, and her music. She had gone so long without a self that she loved exploring all the things a Vee could be. It was one of the things that made her a rising star in the Camden scene, her ability to go deep inside that self when she sang. But the book was in there, too, and as she explored herself she explored the world of alchemy as well, and the two mingled. The Vee she was was a Vee she would not have been if she'd been allowed to live a normal life from birth. This Vee was a product of her distinct circumstances. She was literally born to alchemy. And so there she was, drawn inward toward a world larger than the one she walked on Hartland Road—and yet walking up Hartland Road to go perform in public.

That was the hard thing to explain: her real pleasure in singing for an audience. The book certainly didn't teach that, so it was all her, but she'd never wanted the spotlight when she was the girl who called herself Eva Delia Kerr. It was her real self, no longer held back by Eva Delia. It was Vee at her very core, the Vee she didn't know and so explored—and yet, she was immersed in alchemy at the same time.

Eva Delia could never have done that—held two sides together. But normal people could. All the neighbors could. Most of all, Vee could.

Sometimes that thought almost knocked her off her feet, it was still so new. Less than two years, after seventeen years of confusion and pain. No wonder she focused on herself.

And yet . . . she could not forget Eva Delia. That poor girl never asked to have another self thrust into her mind. She'd been the pawn of some evil force, who'd used her birth to hide Vee there. Vee was positive that it hadn't been Vee's own doing; she knew herself well enough to know she'd never do that to anyone, and the book spoke for a man who would never have taken a disciple who would. Vee was a victim, but so much more so was Eva Delia, doomed to a life of madness.

Vee was new to her life, but she had history, and she had curiosity. This is what she explored, and what she drew upon for her set.

She reached Chalk Farm Road and turned left, toward the High Street, but couldn't help noticing, in the market across the way, a wild variety of flowers. *Pan is the force that drives us all,* she told herself. *And this year he's extra explosive.*

Strolling into the heart of Camden Town, passing tinny CD players outside storefronts and stereos in flats above them and radios in passing cars and speakers in the pubs, she heard a continually shifting variety of music—all the sounds of 2011. Adele, "Rolling in the Deep." Bruno Mars, "Grenade." Keyshia Cole and Nicki Minaj, "I Ain't Thru." Cee-Lo, "Fuck You."

So very, very normal.

13 Milky Way (Managing Alchemy)

In New York City, Nat Whitten paid his cabbie and entered the Bismarck Hotel on East Twenty-ninth Street through fading rain. It was his longtime home away from home in New York—long enough for him to have bought the old building through a series of fronts. His room on the seventh and top floor was always available; more important, it was secured with state-of-the-art devices that were *not* provided by the Necklace. None of them were magickal devices or spells, but he had to know a good deal about security in his business and he was amply satisfied with his electronics, which had been engineered into the remodeling of the room. He had some things he had to keep private, even though he was one of the Nine. When he entered room 701, he could be certain that whatever he did there was private as hell.

He used his secure line to contact Gabriel Longchamps on his private laptop. The man's ruddy, horsy face appeared almost at once.

"Where are we, Gabe?" he asked him.

"I just got in," Gabe said. "The flight was ridiculous. It's too late to see anyone tonight, but I have an appointment with the commander in the morning. I'm sure there'll be red tape, but I'll be in touch as soon as I have a firm time."

"No one's lookin' at you funny?"

"Not at all. No one has ever known the bond between us, Nat. And if they heard a rumor, I doubt they'd believe it."

"Unfortunately, horse-face, I think so, too." They both laughed. "Keep at it and I'll talk at ya soon's you're ready."

1) Milky Way (Managing Alchemy)

"Listen, Senator, people are saying you're not pushing the debt hard enough.—Well, of course debt is irrelevant with this many people out of work, but that's the mission. If we don't sell the idea of a crisis there's no reason for people to accept losing wages and benefits, and nothing sells crisis like shutting the government down.—Yes, if we have to.—There'll be jobs *someday*. Once we're in charge and they're ready to take whatever they can get."

Another button on Breckenridge's secure phone lit orange.

"John, I've got another call. You've got your orders. Don't over-think it."

He punched the glowing button. "Congresswoman! How are you today?—Yes, of course we need that legislation. If they can organize, they can resist. Moreover, they'll think they have friends instead of competitors.—Don't worry about the money. The bank was indeed our primary operation, but we have more. By summertime, no one will remember if they go under.—Because no one will keep the story alive.—If it involves banks, no story will *remain* alive.— Right. Just do what we tell you and you'll get paid."

Breckenridge saw line nine light up with Diana's name. "Excuse me, I have another call.—Yes, I'll see you there."

He punched line nine.

"Good afternoon, Diana! We were just discussing the media. How are you today?"

"I'm great, Lawrence. How about you?"

"Fine."

"Good. I have a proposal for you."

"Shoot."

"I'd like to spend the next few days in Fort Wayne. The schedule doesn't require me to be in Chicago tomorrow or Wednesday, and

I'd like to watch Ruth and Franny in action, up close and personal. I'm always at the back end of events, but with a mission this elaborate and long term, the more I actually know, the better I can shape the storyline."

"And if you see Franny or Ruth screw up?"

"Well, I'd expect to see them *fix* the screwup, Lawrence. If they didn't, of course I'd tell you, but that seems unlikely. And naturally, *none* of it would go on air."

"You can imagine their reaction to your proposal, I'm sure."

"That's why I called you first, boss man."

"Diana, since Yucca Mountain, you've been an exemplary link. I've told you before how well you handled Wikileaks, and the wiretaps. But *my* worry is the possibility of your bringing unwanted attention to Fort Wayne."

"In all the time since August appeared, he's never broken any of our shields."

"That we know of."

"Well, Lawrence, by that standard, we could never be sure of anything."

"Welcome to my world."

"I hear you. But August is not a god."

"A point I myself made just this morning. But why should we tempt fate?"

"If I make a mistake because I'm uninformed, that would not benefit us. I'm trying to do my job the best I can, for everybody's benefit."

"All right. Make me proud tonight, and make certain you're back in plenty of time for Thursday night's work. I'll break it to Franny and Ruth."

13 Milky Way (Managing Alchemy)

Franny entered Ruth's office with a sour look on her broad face.

"What?" Ruth asked.

"Diana's coming to inspect us."

"Ah shit no!"

"Lawrence says she just wants to watch."

"Bullshit! We're at T minus four. I'll call him—"

"Won't do any good," Franny said. "He said he's decided and that's that."

"That bimbo has him wrapped around her little finger."

"I dunno about that, Ruth. I've never known Lawrence to be interested in any woman—"

"Trust me, Franny, powerful men always have a bimbo around somewhere."

"You think Diana? I don't. He was really pissed at her when Mike Salinan got put away. She had to walk on eggshells for a long time. I thought maybe she and *Mike* had a little something goin' on."

"And maybe Breckenridge was the man scorned."

"Umm. Maybe."

"In any event, she uses her sex appeal—"

"Her 'sincerity'—"

"Yeah. She bamboozles anything in pants. But not me," said Ruth.

"Or me," said Franny.

"But we're stuck with her anyway."

"Like a turd in a punchbowl."

Ruth held out a hand, waving the problem away. "Can you take the lead on this, Franny? You can work to a schedule; I've got to be plugged in all the time."

"I know it. I'll handle it." Franny sighed heavily. "And if she doesn't like it, she can go straight to hell."

13 Milky Way (Managing Alchemy)

Max and Pam pulled their rental car to a halt where the houses in Fort Wayne ran out. It was a year and a half since the last time they'd been here. The two blocks in front of them were open green grass on both sides, save for a Bud Light truck trailer parked on the left of the nearest block—then the street dead-ended at the Rupp Works. Behind a tall metal fence, a low, rather ominous citadel made of gray Indiana limestone faced the street. Six taller, longer, three-story buildings of brown Indiana brick lined up behind with all their windows blacked. Transparent walkways joined the top floors, adding a modern touch to Rupp's tradition of smart crafts-manship. Towering over it all was a high cylindrical chimney.

Railroad tracks ran past the compound, on its right, between the Rupp Works and what once had been the Dailey Company, according to the faded sign it bore. Now Dailey's was deserted, but in the fall of '09, Max had easily found the sensors there, in the most logical place to hide on this open ground. So he and Pam had picnicked in the park two blocks farther on and taken hikes back along the tracks, sightseeing. It had been a warm day in Indian summer.

Today was still in the high fifties, with warm days not too far away. The sky was gray with clouds, but light gray, not threatening to rain, and the sun, low but still behind the clouds, made a section of the gray almost translucent, making the ground seem dark. It wasn't the weather that made Pam shiver.

She looked at him intently. "Are you feeling what I'm feeling?"

His face was grim. "Like what I felt when we first arrived in Barbados, tracking Squire Omen."

"I couldn't feel it then," she said, "but I sure feel it now. It makes my stomach turn. Is that what we're here for?"

"No," Max said, opening the driver's door and getting out, his eyes locked on the Rupp Works. "It's not big enough. But it's the prelude to something." To any eyes but Pam's—had there been any—he was turning invisible. But there were no other eyes there, and she was becoming invisible as well. "Last time we got the hell away from it," she said, following him as he started off down the street at a brisk walk.

"This time I have to see what it is," he said—and abruptly broke into a run. Pam, startled, started instinctively after him, but *No*, he snapped telepathically. She stopped, and tried to see what he had seen. Now she did.

There was a man with a gun outside the factory's gates.

The gun was half hidden in the man's outer coat pocket, but Max and Pam were used to looking for danger. The man's hand was on the gun and his eyes were locked on the gate, which was now opening. He was to the right of it. A Hummer drove from the flat lot onto the flat street, not having to slow for the right turn. The man pulled his weapon, took aim with a professional stance, and began firing at the passing car. Windows spiderwebbed but did not break, before at least two people inside began return fire. The man on the street loosed two more shots, then turned and ran into Dailey's across the tracks. The Hummer hit the brakes hard and a man jumped out a side door to give chase, firing as he ran. Behind him, the body of another man flopped awkwardly out the door and landed on its head. The assailant ran into the building. The pursuer took a less obvious entrance. And Max, invisible, followed him.

In a long hall, Max saw the attacker ahead of him, passing shuttered office doors. The man ran through a doorway at the end of the hall and Max was right behind him, encountering pursuer and attacker on a vast open floor, two dark figures in late-afternoon gloom. Their shots echoed high and airy off the old brick. A bullet snapped past Max, who knew full well that invisibility didn't change the fact that he was physically here. But that was a game he'd been playing since 1972, a game he'd been loving. For all his magick, there was nothing like a fire fight. Though it changed things a little if they weren't firing at him.

The attacker suddenly turned and ducked and fired. He was clearly an experienced marksman but with that momentum it was still a lucky shot. It caught the pursuer in the chest, though he fired off another two shots before his knees went out from under him and he fell to the floor. The second shot went into the floor but the first one caught the crouching man and took him down as well.

Max ran to the pursuer; this man was dead. The attacker was lying twenty feet ahead, dying, spurting blood with less and less urgency. Behind Max came the sounds of other people entering the long hall, warily but steadily.

He dropped to his knees and yanked the pursuer's wallet and keys from his pockets. He searched quickly for anything else he might need but that was it, so he grabbed the gun as well and stood up again, shoving the booty into his own pockets, moving his feet comfortably apart. He put his hands out, palms out toward the pursuer's body, and made three distinct gestures, each hand a mirror image of the other, as his face hardened in concentration. Five seconds passed, while the sounds of the newcomers came closer—then Max gave a short, sharp shove in the air toward the body, and the body abruptly rolled over and disappeared as if falling into a hole. In fact it fell into the collective subconscious, the vast realm invisible to men but available to masters of magick.

Quickly, Max ran his hands downward in front of his face and chest, four times. When he was done he was indistinguishable from the man he'd hidden. He drew a finger along the left side of his neck and left a trail of blood. The newcomers would catch sight of him in ten seconds, so he pulled out the wallet and looked at the Pennsylvania driver's license. From that moment he was Dennis Aparicio.

Two men abruptly emerged from the hall, mirror images of pros, guns in front. After a moment to digest the scene, the one on the left asked, "You okay, Aparicio?" His voice, too, echoed.

Max had no idea what Aparicio sounded like, but that's why he had blood on his neck. He roughened his voice to say, "I'll live, but the bastard almost put one in my throat."

"He did put one in Lindemann, back at the Hummer."

"I was there, remember?"

The two newcomers approached the attacker from angles, still wary of him, but the closer they got, the more certain they were that there would be no more attacks today.

"Aw, Christ!" said the one on the right. "It's Cordover."

"Cordover?" Max echoed.

"You know. The guy they sent back to P-A for theft."

Max said, "Looks like it was a round trip."

"To a dead end." That was a new voice, but one Max recognized: Franny Rupp. She came striding into the room, weighing at least two hundred pounds, but it was mass, not flab. Max remembered Bertha Cool, a private eye Erle Stanley Gardner wrote about between Perry Masons, back when Max was a kid. Perry was now in the stage between forgotten and rediscovered; how many people would know about Bertha, who looked like she was made from a roll of barbed wire? That was what Franny looked like—just as she'd looked in '09, except for a very few more gray hairs.

"You okay, Aparicio?" she asked, making her way straight toward him.

"I'm fine," he croaked.

"You don't sound fine."

"My throat—"

She looked him over carefully, the way she'd inspect a new weld. "I see. You're a brave man, Aparicio."

"Just doin' my job."

"No. That was more. I appreciate it. Get that looked at, then come see me." She turned to the other two, and spoke to the man on the left, obviously the senior. "I didn't see you and Bragane movin' quite that fast, Royal."

"No, Chief." The man called Royal agreed readily, evincing no guilt. Bragane, on the other hand, narrowed his eyes; he was not a man to take a rebuke.

Max jumped in for his buddies. "I had an easier exit from the vehicle, Chief."

Franny snorted. "Job got done. That's all that matters here. Royal, you and Bragane get rid of the body. Come see me, Aparicio." She surveyed the body one more time, then turned on her wide feet and headed out, muttering, "March madness!"

Max looked across the room at Pam, who had watched all of this from the *astral*. Her real body was undoubtedly back in the car, slumped in the seat, but here, her *astral* thumb was decisively *up*.

MONDAY, MARCH 21, 2011 · 6:00 P.M. EASTERN DAYLIGHT TIME

13 Milky Way (Managing Alchemy)

Max's session with the doctor at the Rupp Works was simple enough. He hoped to get through it on deception alone, but when the man asked, "Where's your appendectomy scar?", Max magicked him. In the future, any exam would be pro forma and end with a clean bill of health. Max liked to avoid using magick when there was another way, because magick caused ripples that could lead back to him, but there was no other way so he rolled the dice.

Pam, still unseen by any but him, nodded in agreement.

MONDAY, MARCH 21, 2011 · 6:20 P.M. EASTERN DAYLIGHT TIME

13 Milky Way (Managing Alchemy)

Max rolled into Franny's office with the swagger befitting his rôle. The agents hadn't been there in September '09 so he hadn't studied them then, but they were everywhere now. They were highly trained, the élite of the élite, and therefore, all of a type. Max simply had to play the part, with no need for "Aparicio" to show any individuality. It made his deception easy, so he came to the office with his deejay's sense of a good show ahead, feeling pretty élite himself.

Franny was with Ruth Glendenning. Max had not seen the Ops link in person before, because her compound was the most heavily guarded of the nine, deep inside the forest of State Game Land Number 305 south of Carlisle, Pennsylvania. As he studied her now without seeming to, Ruth's face and body were both devoid of any excess fat—the genes of a supermodel grown middle-aged. And perhaps a supermodel would have the same eyes in an unguarded moment, but *Ruth's* eyes looked out upon the world at all times with no illusions whatsoever. In her skintight face they were chips of ice.

First Di and Mike at Wickr, and now two more links in the Necklace, Max thought. *Step by step, I'm closing in on them.*

"Sit if you want, Aparicio," Franny said in her rumbling contralto.

"I'm good, Chief," Aparicio said, still rough. "Medic just put some antibiotics on the throat. Doesn't even need stitches. It'll be tight for a few days but it won't slow me any."

Ruth, holding a piece of paper, looked him up and down, then came close to study the bandage. "He also says you shouldn't talk much for a while."

"I'm good," he said, not knowing what Ruth's men called her. Not "Chief," certainly.

"You look all right. I don't need speeches, but I do need bodies. Doc says you're still go for tonight."

He nodded.

"Now, do you know anything interesting about Cordover, and do you know anyone among the men who does?"

He shook his head.

"When I said I didn't need speeches, Aparicio," Ruth said sharply, "I still need the occasional 'No, ma'am.'"

Problem solved. "No, ma'am."

"He must have had some friends."

"If so," Max said, "I wasn't one of 'em. He kind of kept to himself."

"All right. I'll pursue that. Now, did Cordover say anything while you were chasing him?"

"No, ma'am. He wasn't much into conversation."

"How close to him were you when you shot him?"

"Twenty feet."

"Did he shoot you before or after that?"

"After, ma'am. He surprised me because I thought he was dead on his feet."

"And did you have any second thoughts about chasing down a man with a gun, who'd already shot the guy next to you?"

Max had wondered that himself, about the real Aparicio. "You know how it is, ma'am. I didn't want to be stuck in the vehicle, and once I jumped out, I just somehow didn't want to hide behind it, so I decided to take the fucker out. I think it spooked him a little. I mean, he was well trained, but he had to know he was on a suicide mission, and he probably was in no hurry to get to the end of it. So he ran, too, and probably figured to pick me off from Dailey's, but I knew both ways in. He picked one, I took the other." Max ended that speech with a rasping cough.

"Let the guy get some rest," said Franny.

"The machines are yours, the men are mine," Ruth answered, and it seemed to Max that it was a familiar statement between them. They'd be called upon to work together quite a bit, he imagined, and they were comfortable in their back-and-forth. "Aparicio: was there any sign that Cordover had help?"

"No, ma'am." Now that he'd spoken his piece, he figured he could dial it back from here on.

"So in your opinion, he was a lone gunman on a suicide mission."

"Yes, ma'am."

"I hate lone gunmen on suicide missions," Ruth said. "All right. Dismissed. But be back here at twenty-one hundred hours."

Aparicio nodded. "Ma'am," he croaked.

"Thanks again," Franny said.

"Chief."

13 Milky Way (Managing Alchemy)

With Aparicio taken care of, Franny and Ruth went back to their consultations.

"You think the attack has anything to do with the mission?" Franny asked.

"I'd say no," Ruth answered. "But I'll keep digging."

"I don't think so, either. We had Cordover for theft, which wasn't the act of an infiltrator."

"Still," Ruth said, "I'll raise the threat level. I can keep it low-key. Since your grandfather—"

"Great-great-grandfather."

"—surrounded the Rupp Works with empty fields that you own, it's unlikely that anyone saw or heard our little Wild West show."

"In a way," said Franny, "I'm glad we've got another flight tonight. If there's anything else that's hinky in this, that should show it."

"How are we supposed to know what's *hinky*," Ruth asked, "with the *bone* involved?"

"We're the Necklace," Franny said. "Take it as it comes."

Ruth cocked her head at her compatriot. "I don't see any need to alert Hanrahan at this point," she said pointedly.

"No," Franny agreed. "We don't want *another* of the Nine in our business."

Ruth nodded, and Franny turned to leave. Then she turned back. "You trained a good one in Aparicio, Ruth. I want you to know I appreciate it."

"They're all that good," Ruth said, uninterested in praise. "Or they'd better be."

"No," said Franny. "I think Aparicio's somethin' special."

13 Milky Way (Managing Alchemy)

Max rode with Royal and Bragane across town. He didn't want to say too much, and that worked out because Bragane monopolized the conversation.

"Here we are," he said, "driving our own cars to our own housing."

"Uh, yeah?" said Royal, rolling his eyes. Such a banal observation apparently had some previous context.

"If the U.N. had its way," said Bragane, "we'd all live downtown, in tenements, with no cars and spirally lightbulbs."

Max sat forward. Now he *really* wished he knew the context, so he'd react the way Aparicio would have. Fortunately, Royal took up the slack, saying with deceptive mildness, "You haven't mentioned the lightbulbs before."

"It's part of the U.N.'s Agenda 21," snapped Bragane. "We've talked about that."

"*You've* talked about it."

"They want to force all the countries in the world to go 'green'— preserve the ozone layer and manage forests and hug baby whales. The whole climate hoax. If we paid any attention to that shit, we wouldn't be able to drive, and we'd have to use their lightbulbs so they'd get rich."

"And we'd live downtown," agreed Royal solemnly.

"And we'd live downtown," agreed Bragane. "But the Senate's never ratified it, so America is still the land of the free."

"And we can drive across Fort Wayne," said Max.

"Yes, we can," Bragane said with great satisfaction. "You two can laugh, but if you think about it, there is nothing more American."

"You're an idiot," Royal told him, but Bragane was unfazed.

"Eternal vigilance is the price of liberty," he replied. "You'll get it, sooner or later. You both will."

Max decided that, of his two new acquaintances, he'd be getting along better with Royal.

They turned in to an apartment complex on Lake Street. It was a self-contained neighborhood, like the other subdivisions nearby, and Max had seen it on his previous reconnaissance. New renters in the other buildings were sometimes a little curious about all the buff young men who shared their complex, but those men were always nicely behaved, and everyone working for Rupp who'd lived there over the years had been the same, so the older renters calmed the newcomers' unease. In all respects, it was crushingly normal.

Mrs. Brenda Larrabee was having trouble getting her Kroger bags situated under both arms, and Royal sprang to her aid. "Hang on a minute, Bren," he called, and gathered the bags in his own arms. "Go on in," he called to Aparicio. But since Max didn't know where "in" was, he went over to join them. "I'll take one," he said, watching Royal and Bren to see if Aparicio knew her any better than as a neighbor. Neither one indicated as much, and Bragane simply leaned against the car to wait.

"Would you like a beer?" Bren asked, once the bags were on the counters and she'd begun to stow the cold stuff. "I've got some Diet Cokes, too."

"Thanks," Royal said, smiling, "but Dennis and I have to grab a quick bite and work out some boring engineering stuff tonight. We might have time tomorrow, though."

"Gee, I've got my book group tomorrow."

"Well, we'll figure something out. Take care, Bren. See ya."

The two men left, and walked across the parking lot, with Max letting Royal take the lead. "I hate lyin' to Bren," Royal said. "She's so easy."

Yeah, Max thought. *You and I are the ones with the similar interests.*

So he lied to his new best friend and said, "I'm taking a nap till we head back to the Works."

"No dinner?"

"I'm beat, Royal. I just *look* like Superman."

1] Milky Way (Managing Alchemy)

Max lay on Aparicio's bed, ostensively asleep, with Pam's voice clear in his mind.

This totally sucks! she said. *What am I supposed to do here?*

No girls allowed, he replied, the sensation of his internal grin as much in evidence as the words to her. *You're damn good at disguise but an ongoing gig as a macho man might be a little much.*

So what am I supposed to do?

Find a safe motel room and work on your alchemy. What's today?

Yeah, yeah.

What is it?

Managing Alchemy.

Exactly. So take the time and do the work—and maybe get out and enjoy the spring in the fields of Indiana, too.

You're loving this, aren't you?

What?

You know what. Being a soldier again.

Maybe . . .

1] Milky Way (Managing Alchemy)

Pam was a sucker for fast food that was available only in America. She hit Arby's and practically inhaled the Angus Three Cheese &

Bacon. Then she drove the rental car over toward the river and checked in to the Carole Lombard House, a B and B that was the star's birthplace. She liked a bit of glamour and had wanted to stay there the last time, but it was on the other side of town from the Rupp Works. This time, though, she was free to choose it *because* they hadn't stayed there, and she was supposed to stay out of the picture. In any event, one side of Fort Wayne to the other was not a terribly long commute.

The house was unimpressive on the outside, but inside, the décor was all about 1940s movie glamour. Her room was stylish, warm, and comfortable; just the place to leave her physical body while she exercised the *astral*. This afternoon had been the first time she'd been airborne in a good two weeks, and if she was on her own, that's what she would work on. Managing her Alchemy.

She lay down on the blue-green coverlet, rested her head against the reading pillows. She laid her hands at her side, utterly relaxing. Her first few years in the *astral,* her physical form, once she left it, was completely inert, save for vital life signs. But she'd come home to bumps and bruises too often, so she'd taught herself to leave enough consciousness to protect the physical form, let it roll over if necessary, curl up—but most especially, call her back if that wasn't enough. Leaving it completely vulnerable was an acceptable trade-off for a novice, but not for a *flier* with her experience.

So she lay on the bed and watched herself rise straight out of herself. The risen self was the *astral,* and *she* could roll over in place, in midair, and look back down at herself, and see herself looking up, to see herself above. But oddly enough, she was not schizophrenic. The gaze of the physical was almost fixed; it was the gaze of the *astral* that showed intelligence.

That gaze swept to the wall of the Carole Lombard House and then through the wall, into the Indiana night. She loved Midwestern skies. So huge!

13 Milky Way (Managing Alchemy)

"Aparicio. You awake?"

Max opened his eyes. He'd left the door unlocked so Royal could be his wake-up call, and now the man himself was standing there, dressed in night-camo fatigues. "Do I look like I'm awake?" Max asked, pretending irritation.

"You surprised me today. Surprised a lot of us."

"Like how?"

"You're the one that always says 'Look before you leap.'"

"Listen, Royal," Aparicio said, "when the mission goes down I'm all about the mission, and I'd say it went down when people started shootin' at us."

"I'd say so, too, but—well, anyways, good job today."

"Thanks. But you were right behind me," Aparicio said, sitting up.

"So we're both a couple of adrenaline junkies. And Brag; he was there, too. The rest of those slackers bought popcorn and watched."

"Not the chief, though. She was right behind you."

"Yeah. I was real skeptical when they sent us here," Royal said. "Glendenning's one thing, she's as tough as any man I ever met, but Rupp surprised me."

"You're just surprised by everything, aren't you? A real babe in the woods."

Royal punched his shoulder, hard, but not too hard for a man like Aparicio. "Better get goin'," Royal said. "She'll eat us alive if we're late."

Max swung his feet to the floor, and looked around the room. It was a civilian room but it felt like a barracks. And Pam was absolutely right: he'd missed the feeling.

Pfft! he could hear her say.

13 Milky Way (Managing Alchemy)

Max and Royal made the assembly with three minutes to spare. The tall brick buildings at the rear of the Rupp Works ran the length of the site along the outside boundaries, but in the middle they left a large open space that was invisible to outsiders. Satellites that could see it were fed a false image by NSA.

In the open space now were thirty men and three black helicopters. The moment he spied them, Max, in his own black fatigues, saw the outlines of the mission. He knew the legends of the Black Helicopters and the Men in Black who traveled in them. But he also knew that with the Necklace, it couldn't be quite that simple.

The choppers were modified MH-53Js. Military MH-53Js had been retired in September of '08, in favor of the V-22 Osprey. The Osprey was a cutting-edge turboprop, and as such it could do things the 53Js couldn't do—but it wasn't a helicopter. The 53Js were designed for low-level, long-range, undetected penetration into enemy areas under virtually any conditions, and could carry up to thirty-eight men. But one Black Helicopter wasn't threatening enough, so there were three.

The other men had done this before; there was no need for orders when 2100 hours arrived. Max stuck with Royal as their team of ten clambered into the right-most copter. The engines, idling to this point, began to rev, and all at once the first bird left the ground. Max was in the second, as it rose into the Hoosier sky. The team leader, whom Bragane called Major Duden, lifted what looked like a human finger bone high above his head, and—

. . . . .

they were flying through bright white liquid, passing birds of red and orange talking busily among themselves, heeling over till they were ninety degrees to the choppers, the tops of their fuzzy little

heads pointed toward Max, their wings wide and wonderful. Birds
and men soared into something like a spectrum strips of color
hanging like curtains, but each curtain hanging a further ninety
degrees so the choppers turned round and round, a dizzying whirl
into—

. . . . .

the black night sky over snow-covered fields, the sound of the ro-
tors echoing from the hard ground twenty feet below. It was hillier
than Indiana, much colder, *and Max knew why!*

They had just passed through a dimensional doorway, into the
subconscious and back out again. It was called an "elder doorway"
and was opened by a "bone key," made from the three small bones
of a finger, kept straight by a steel rod running through their cen-
ters. There were two such finger keys, and together they made
something called the Crossbones Key, but even one of them alone
was a powerful talisman. Now the Necklace had it—thanks, of
course, to Peter Quince. And now the choppers were somewhere in
the Midwest, but not Indiana. Black Helicopters, appearing from
nowhere . . .

Max craned for a look out the open side door. They were approaching a farm, following the furrows of desolate fields. A low
ranch was bracketed by a barn and a shed, set back half a mile from
the two-lane county road, a whole mile from the next habitation.
The moon had not yet risen so the only light came from the house
itself.

The choppers came to a halt a hundred yards from the light and
settled to earth. A horse whinnied in confusion. The men began to
leap from the choppers, Max right with them. Major Duden, a
lean man with a clipped moustache, raised his hand, pumped it
once, and the men ran to form a perimeter around the house. Max
had no trouble keeping up; the good thing about operating inside a
highly disciplined group was everyone else giving him clues as to
what to do. But one of those clues was, the men were about to
commit murder. This was not an exercise or a warning; Max knew
exactly what was in the air.

Once upon a time, in a land far, far away, Max August had participated in the wanton slaughter of a Vietnamese village. It had made perfect sense at the time to a group of angry young men, most of them high, who had just seen their own people butchered— but had stopped making sense when the first villager died. By then, of course, it was too late, and Max was no innocent bystander. It had happened in every war, on every side—it was what war did to you—but it was still something that sat at the back of Max's soul, always ready to remind him that he was nothing like a god. *It's kill or be killed, not kill or kumbaya. But that was war. This isn't.*

Positioned near the front left corner of the farmhouse, Max projected his consciousness inside. There were five people in there, watching television, playing games, doing homework—a father, mother, three kids. There was nowhere for them to go. So Max concentrated, his face masked by the night, and put the youngest child to sleep, before rendering him invisible. Even as he held his rifle at the ready, he moved on to the next oldest child.

The major pumped his fist twice. Max hid the oldest child. Four men advanced toward the front door, and four men moved toward the back. Max got the wife.

And then suddenly, the man whose house it was threw his front door wide and stood there pugnaciously, a shotgun in his hands. He was middle-aged, his face pale from winter months indoors and the threat before him, but he was steady and determined. "Get off my land!" he bellowed. Max thrust desperately at him, rendering him halfway invisible before the four men facing the front door cut loose. Their bullets stitched him in four streams and Max felt the life in the man flare and die. The alchemist quit trying to save him and let him fall, fully visible. In the adrenaline-fueled darkness, none of the attackers seemed to have noticed anything amiss.

Then those men and four at the back door raced into the house, looking to murder everyone else. Max went back to protecting the family. "Stay ready!" the major shouted to the troops on Max's side and those on the other side. "They may come out the windows."

But no one came out, except for the mercs who'd gone in. "There's nobody else here," their leader reported from the front doorway.

"Are you sure?" the major demanded.

"Sure I'm sure."

"They could have a hidey-hole."

"Believe me, Major, we know where to look, and we looked. Anything beyond that has got to be too good for a farmer"—he gave the sprawled body at his feet a kick—"unless he's more than that."

"No, that's exactly what he is. The family must be at the movies or something. Shit. All right. Panthers, retreat!"

The men began to jog purposefully back to the choppers. As they scrambled inside, the lights of a vehicle snapped on at the farm-house a mile away, and an old truck began to rumble down the farm road toward the county road. It wasn't a problem; the copters would be long gone before the farmer closed the distance to find out what had happened to his neighbor.

But strangely, the order to depart didn't come. The men in the copters sat and watched as the lights grew steadily closer. Those lights reached the turn-off to the farmhouse and swung wide into it, throwing a plume of dust to one side. They speared the farm-house, and then turned to the side, pinning the three copters.

"Now!" the major barked into his com link, and the copters rose as one. A man jumped out of his Ford pickup—Max could see it clearly now—and stood helpless, his hands at his sides, watching them go. That man could see them just as clearly.

The aircraft rose some fifty feet in the night sky, then banked toward the lights of the town in the distance. Three miles to their right, Max could see a small airport, with a single small plane com-ing in for a landing. The copters swept over the eastern edge of the town, a perfect grid of pale gray streets and normalcy, then crossed the east-west ribbon of highway. At this low height, all three were clearly visible, clearly audible, and it was clear people on the ground were registering them. There was no reason for them to be alarmed, since they didn't yet know about the murder, but they did see the Black Helicopters. In the southeast, the Scorpio moon was just rising, and the copters wheeled toward the moon—

· · · · ·

—and went back to Wonderland.

TUESDAY, MARCH 22, 2011 · 1:45 A.M. GREENWICH MEAN TIME

13 Milky Way (Managing Alchemy)

Vee sang, in the darkness of the cavern that was Eddie's Club in Camden Town. Eddie's was up the brick courtyard from Camden High Street, past the market, a famous venue—because it booked talent. Amy Winehouse had sung here, before the rehab. So had the Beatles, after they became the Beatles (but, to be fair, just before they made their first trip to America). They didn't come back as a group, but in 1978, John Lennon came solo. John Lennon meant something to Vee; she didn't know what, but she felt a connection, as if she'd known him personally. All Cornelius could tell her was "Everything you are is part of something larger." Sure, but what?

Vee sang in the darkness of the cavern. The lights were low and there was a mellow crowd, people scattered throughout the room even though it was a quarter to two on a Tuesday morning. Eddie's booked talent, and Vee had been here to kick off the week for close to four months. The word had spread throughout the city, and people who didn't worry about getting up when the alarm went off started riding out to Camden Town for her.

Her sound was big and dark and sensual, with a tang of fresh discoveries, like someone learning the joys of life for the first time—the voice of a slumming angel. She *felt* every sound she sang, deep in her soul, so her audience felt it, too. She connected with them, and they with her. That's how stars were born.

· · · · ·

When the set was finished, she accepted congratulations, thanks, veiled and not-so-veiled pickup lines with a thoughtful smile. It said she appreciated the compliments, but couldn't quite make herself believe she deserved them. She knew she was good, knew the effect of her voice, but like an angel, she kept her distance. More than one potential manager had marked it down as a particularly savvy stage persona. Then they talked with her and saw it was really her, like her strange mid-Atlantic accent, not quite British, not quite American.

Tonight the potential manager said his name was Matthew Raftery. "Not as on point as 'Vee,'" he said, "but we don't choose our names. We choose our future."

"We do?" Vee asked, not bothering to hide her skepticism.

"We choose what we want our future to be, then we work our arses off to get there," Matthew answered. "It's the people who don't choose who get whatever future happens by. I choose to make you a star, and both of us very rich, but you more so. I'd like you to choose me for your manager."

Vee sighed. "Sorry, Matthew, but I really don't want to be managed."

"I have a very light touch."

"I can tell."

"And I can tell this is fun for you, here at Eddie's, two nights a week. And it's a great step—but to what? There's too much involved for you to handle it all on your own. Let me do it while you just sing, just for three months. Then you decide what happens after that."

"No."

"Don't you want to be famous, Vee?"

"No, not really. I'm quite happy in my solitude. Stardom's fun but it's not all it's cracked up to be."

"How would you know?"

"I guess that's just how I feel."

Christopher Durban downed the last of his drink with a frown. He had wanted to approach her tonight, but the beefcake was ruining the moment, so he took what he could as he watched them from the corners of his eyes.

His colorless eyes in his bone-thin face.

13 Milky Way (Managing Alchemy)

Diana sat in the producer's chair at FRC, in Chicago, overseeing the feed of the sixty-second piece that would run during the ten o'clock news on every one of her stations in the Central, Mountain, Pacific, Alaska, and Hawaii time zones. The twenty-four-hour cable channels would get it, too. Everyone would find it again on their morning news.

It was a perfect piece, exactly what she wanted, with grainy cell-phone video of the helicopters, clear enough to show their existence, not clear enough to be certain of what they were. It had only taken one pass to process the raw video, bought by the local station from Mrs. Rosalind Gartenhier of the small gray town, to the required ambiguity. If Mrs. Gartenhier noticed a difference, she'd be told it was the natural distortion of television.

As the twenty second footage played twice, interviews with her and others established the absence of any definite opinion. Some guy named Murphy had said flat out that they were the Black Helicopters he'd been expecting; he was bracketed by someone claiming they were UFOs and someone else admitting he hadn't seen them himself but he'd heard they were military. So if you were also expecting Black Helicopters, you would find a clue there, and if you weren't, you would go along with the reporter's tone of detached amusement. If you were expecting Black Helicopters, you would see that tone as proof of the media conspiracy.

Stage Two of the Fort Wayne Project had gone off without a hitch, both there and here, Di thought. Now for my *private* show!

1) Milky Way (Managing Alchemy)

Vee arrived home in Hartland Road in a strange mood. After a performance, she usually rode the adrenaline high for another few hours and threw herself into her alchemy, but tonight she felt tired, out of sorts. *But that's what real life is like, right? Every day's different. I can let the book slide tonight; it's two thirty in the morning.*

Now if only the book would cooperate.

But as she passed the living room, she made the mistake of looking inside, and she saw the book flip open. She grimaced, irresolute . . . then went inside.

You are compromised, read the witchlit text.

"What?"

You are compromised.

"What do you mean, 'compromised'?" Vee demanded, knowing it couldn't elaborate. And when it didn't: "Okay, okay, okay!" She was in no mood for this, but she had to take it seriously. It was one thing to be tired, another to slack when there was work to be done. She balanced her weight easily on slightly spread legs, and raised her hands, the fingers making strange forms.

Sixteenth-century magick was always very careful to ground itself in sanctity, or at least the prevailing ethos of the day. Vee began to chant the spell the book had taught her, in the sixteenth-century style. "Every thing has something that it fears and dreads, that is an enemy and destructive to it." She paused, as if assessing her surroundings; then: "I call upon thee, in the name of thee, who art greater than all, the creator of all, the self-begotten who seest all but art not seen. Reveal unto me, if it be thy will, the hidden one who marketh himself mine enemy."

Her eyes were focused on the bamboo shade that stood just outside the outer circle, before the front window looking out on Hartland Road, and all the world outside her circle. She focused on the shade and saw the world outside. She let the magick flow through her, feeling its power, and on the screen she began to see . . . a face. Soon enough she recognized it: a guy sitting at table six in Eddie's. A bone-thin face. He had hardly seemed to pay attention to her. But now she knew he was a threat. No, not a threat—evidently, he had already done some damage.

The strange fatigue.

"What did he do to me?" she asked, in sudden fear for her newly won life. But the book answered, *You must learn it*, which was its standard line for such situations. As with the planet Uranus, she could get nothing else from Cornelius Agrippa.

"All right," she said. And then, looking into the night at that phantom face: *Drop by again tomorrow, skull-boy. Because if you don't, I'll come looking for you.*

MONDAY, MARCH 21, 2011 · 11:33 P.M. EASTERN DAYLIGHT TIME

13 Milky Way (Managing Alchemy)

The choppers appeared above the Rupp Works, settling toward the ground. Ruth and Franny were waiting for them.

The men slipped from the choppers a little more gingerly than they'd gone into them, either here or at the farmhouse. Two trips through the other world had taken a toll.

As Ruth came forward, they formed three groups of ten before her. "All right, men," she told them. "Well done. From what we're seeing here, the mission went like clockwork, and I'm very proud of your professionalism. That's twice the Black Helicopters have been spotted—twice they've brought death. Or so random hicks say. The actual story on TV is pretty vague, but it seems to be continuing. The more it plays out, the more it will be treated as the crazed imaginings of the lunatic fringe—which will simply confirm the uneasiness that fringe creates among normal citizens.

"So now we hold our fire. Tomorrow and Wednesday, the Black Helicopters will not be seen, and everyone out there will relax, figure it was a false alarm. Then on Thursday night, you will stage another raid, and again be seen. By Friday, the debate over a government conspiracy will be everywhere. Believers will feel they let down their guard too soon, and be determined to remain on high alert. Nonbelievers will fear the believers, and especially fear that they might turn out to be right. Then, on Friday night, you will stage an event that will outdo Nine-Eleven, for believers and nonbelievers alike.

"The final target remains need-to-know until you're in the air on Friday, but be aware that your actions on that flight will change the course of American history forever. In the meantime, you're on limited duty. Get your medical evals and then you're dismissed."

As the men began to move toward the infirmary, Royal said to Max and Bragane, "Let's go get hammered after, guys. We don't have to be sober for seventy-two hours."

"I *was* hammered," Max said. "Those dissolving colors, or whatever they were . . ."

"You mean the scenic route? I thought you were over that."

"There's 'over' and then there's 'over,'" Max said. "Sorry, man, but I'm done for the night. Gimme a rain check."

"You're not getting PTS, are you? All these naps?"

"Fuck, no. No trauma, no stress. But my throat's not happy. I'm gonna crash right after I'm done here."

"P-M-S," said Bragane dismissively.

"All right," said Royal. "But tomorrow, Brag and I are going to Show Stoppers around seven."

"I'm there. Absolutely. Can you catch a ride with somebody else tonight?"

"Sure."

"See ya in the mornin', then."

So once the doc had checked him through, Max strode straight toward their car and drove it into the quiet Hoosier night. Half a dozen other cars were headed for the same general area; all of them driving across Fort Wayne. Max was easily able to zone out and send his thoughts to Pam.

She answered almost at once. *What'd I miss?* she demanded.

And a great good evening to you, too, Doctor Blackwell.

Nuts. What'd I miss?

So he told her. Her emotion at the death of the householder was clear, as was her emotion at the survival of the family. And then he got to "the scenic route."

You'll remember, he thought, *on Omen Key, I put some sarin gas into the collective subconscious. Today I put Aparicio there. It's all the same deal—the unknown other side to this reality.*

You can stash things there AND fly through it?

It's the other half of reality. It has many uses.

But even though we can't see it from here, you saw it from the copter?

Just me, I think. The others couldn't grasp it; my new friend Royal was only talking about colors. But that, he said, *is not why I called you.*

Why, then?

I know how to close that doorway.

Cool! Pam said, but added, *Is that wise? We don't want to alert them.*

That's okay. It'll take a while to get the other key, because it's in Rome.

How're you going to get out of the army for that Her voice stopped.

Max said, *Right. You're going to do it.*

Me?

You.

On my own?

On your own.

Wow, she said. *Wow.*

I'm not worried about it. Are you?

Not even in the slightest, Pam said, with her crooked smile. *It's just, y'know . . . my first time.*

Hoodoo's deep underground in Cardiff, on our behalf. Everybody else's got something going on. Asking any of them to stop and run my errand—no. So it's a good one to start on.

Sure. Absolutely, Max, she said, her pleasure radiant. So—what am I getting?

A key made of finger bones. There are two of them; the Necklace has the middle finger, and the forefinger's in Rome. They used to belong to Louis the Pious, king of the Franks, son of Charlemagne, but they were repurposed from his corpse on Midsummer Night in the year 840. He was the first European to make witchcraft punishable by death, and the witches took offense. In the 1500s, the two keys came into the possession of Cardinal Janus.

Agrippa's archenemy, back in the day, right? Pam asked. And Janus was the Roman god of doorways. . . .

Give the little lady a hundred dollars. The good cardinal was no god, but he was heavy into sorcery, a traveler between worlds, and he took the name from his use of the bones. He's the one who combined them into the Crossbones Key. But he never became Timeless like Agrippa, and when he died, the keys got separated. The forefinger key has been exhibited at his old castle on the outskirts of Rome since 1953.

Just sitting there?

Just sitting there. After Janus died, no one but Agrippa knew what it was and no one but me knows now.

Why didn't Agrippa corral it? Why didn't you, for that matter?

I'm always on the move, and so was he. We both figured it would be there if we ever needed it, which it is.

But how do you know it still works, after twelve centuries?

Magick bones don't run out of gas. I told you about my own talisman, the lion carving. It was eight hundred years old and as powerful as the day it was created.

So this is just . . . shoplift the gift shop. She sounded disappointed. Won't there be spells around it?

Just an old Behenian chant.

I can handle that.

I keep hearing a "but," he said.

Max, I couldn't beat the incubus. I know I can't beat everyone I might run into out there. . . .

Neither can I, honey. But I know what I need to know to win, because nothing's cut-and-dried in magick. The next time you meet an incubus, you'll know how to win. And you'll be more experienced, starting now. He took a breath. *That said—*

Explore and verify.

Right. Do what I've taught you, keep your senses open, and you'll be able to CALL *me whenever you need to. Get the bone and come right back, because I ride the choppers again Thursday night. Okay?*

Okay!

So here's what you need to know . . .

Day Two

1 Lord (Establishing All)

At 6 A.M., the image of Dick Hanrahan appeared on Lawrence Breckenridge's viewscreen, and the Gemstone's appeared on Hanrahan's.

"Today is March 22, 2011, a Tuesday," the old man said crisply.

"Libya unfolds on schedule. A jet went down last night but the men have been recovered. The story is 'equipment failure.' There's some rumbling over Obama's use of force without Congressional authorization. Senator Webb told reporters, quote, 'We have been on autopilot for almost ten years now in terms of presidential authorization in conducting these type of military operations absent the meaningful participation of the Congress. . . . This isn't the way that our system is supposed to work.' Unquote. But there's no sign anyone's listening.

"The regimes in Yemen, Bahrain, and Saudi Arabia are handling repression just like Qaddafi, but there's no sign anyone's looking. There is zero chance of war with any of them."

"Make very certain."

"Of course. Now in Japan, after Fukushima hit its highest

radiation levels yet yesterday, it's back to normal today. It's not clear why, and it's clear that the process of stabilizing the reactors is far from over.

"On a brighter note, the earthquake and tsunami left a vault wide open at the Shinkin Bank in Kesennuma and somebody walked off with half a million dollars. Not us, sadly, but I have teams on the thief's trail. We'll get it.

"There's no further word on August and Blackwell. By the time MI-5 got to the hotel, the pigeons had flown and of course there's no way to peg them in the thousands leaving Britain every day. Each of our teams in London is trying to track them in their own way, but so far without success."

"So Max and Pam are invisible again."

"For the moment."

"They *are* good, aren't they?" Breckenridge mused. "If I didn't know they don't have a mystical backer . . ."

"How do you know that, Renzo?"

"Have you ever found any evidence of it?" Breckenridge snapped. "Has Quince?"

"No."

"Well, I have faith in you."

"Good. Just as Avery had faith on Stamp Act Day."

"Oh yeah. All hail the Loyale Nine!" said Breckenridge.

"All hail the Loyale Nine!"

"Huzzah!"

FRIDAY, MARCH 22, 1765 · 1:15 P.M. LOCAL TIME

8 Monkey (Connecting with Divergence)

In a close, windowless chamber, hidden behind a merchant's shelves on Front Street in the City of Philadelphia, Pennsylvania colony, eight men were seated, all smoking Virginia tobacco. Most of them had glasses filled with hard apple cider, the American alcoholic beverage; they'd have spit on whisky. They were uncertain how long they'd have to fit in this room just big enough for nine men—until the ninth burst into the room, fists clenched, eyes alight.

"They have done it, gentlemen!"

John Avery, closest to the fire, replied in an amazingly level voice, considering what this meant to the men in the room of nine: "You're certain, Joseph?"

"As certain as a wizard can be."

"And what might that mean?" thundered Thomas Chase. "You're asking us to bet our fortunes and perhaps e'en our lives on wizardry."

"No," Avery said, "as your leader, *I'm* asking. And I believe in Joseph's powers."

"Then perhaps someone else should be leading the Free Radical Commune," muttered Henry Bass.

Stephen Cleverly leaned inward. "The Commune has always included a wizard. Wizards have powers; they are real."

"Which is precisely the problem," responded Bass. "They are real men, and real men are fallible. We have no way to verify his assertion."

"Yet men today stand at the summit of all that has gone before," Cleverly answered. "We look back on the grinding darkness of the past and know that we have reached the age of reason. Men today can *think,* and judge Joseph's accomplishments."

"Furthermore," offered Benjamin Edes, "our final ascent to the peaks was driven by the Commune. It is due to our predecessors that we are the men we are, and they believed in wizardry. Therefore I, for one, will also believe our friend Joseph and vote to accept that the Stamp Act was passed."

"But this is the age of reason!" said Bass.

"Reason must include all facts," said Avery.

"Tell us *how* you know this, Joseph," requested Cleverly, "how you have certain knowledge of an event taking place in a country an ocean away, as soon as it transpires."

Joseph Field did not immediately reply. In his earlier days he had been a ship's captain. His private interest had always been in

the occult, but he was indeed a ship's captain for twenty-three years
and though now retired, he was no shrinking violet. "The captain of
a ship is navigating in featureless waters," he said slowly, "using his
mind and the tools men before him have left, from maps to knowledge of the stars. It is usually assumed that the captain knows his
business." He snorted. "I know because there is a practice known to
the wise as *the call*. It has always existed in wizardry, in one form or
another, by one name or another, but it has vastly improved since
we learned the secrets of the Caribbean. When Rupert, in London,
knows a thing, he *calls* to me."

"Across the Atlantic Ocean?" Chase demanded.

"Across the Pacific as well, if needs be. It travels the *ether*, not
the globe. It is as if I am speaking with him as I'm speaking with
you."

"How are his wife and mistress, then?"

Field frowned; his patience was at an end.

George Trott said, "So they passed the Stamp Act. They are truly
damned fools."

"And we have gotten exactly what we need," said Thomas Crafts.

"We can begin organizing at once, in district groups," said Avery, "but of course we must needs delay until the news arrives in
non-wizardly fashion before we *commence* the agitation."

"We will become known, then. We must have a public identity."

"The Freedom Rebellion Committee," suggested Cleverly.

"Much too verbose for the masses," said Trott. "I suggest 'the
Loyale Nine.'"

"I like that. But we don't want to limit our numbers," said Avery.

"No, of course not."

"What about 'the Sons of Liberty'?" said Field.

"I like that. For that's precisely who we are. The sons of those
who've fought for liberty since they arrived on these shores—those
who will see true liberty in these colonies with our own eyes."

"Liberty for ourselves!" said Edes.

"Free Radicals!" said Avery.

"All hail the Sons of Liberty!"

"Huzzah!"

"All hail the Loyale Nine!"

TUESDAY, MARCH 22, 2011 · 7:09 A.M. CENTRAL DAYLIGHT TIME

1 Lord (Establishing All)

Quince arose from his meditations, took a moment to get his legs steadied beneath him. He pulled a small box of hand-rolled cigarettes and a Bic lighter from a pocket in his robes, and lit up. He had never smoked before he met Belia'al; now he enjoyed the corruption of his lungs. He walked downstairs, two flights, to look upon his women.

He liked to look upon his women. They were completely in his control, the way he was in Belia'al's, and he enjoyed his own dominance. But he also enjoyed his submission. If any of the Latinas had any consciousness, they would probably not enjoy being anyone's slave, but they had no consciousness. To Belia'al, looking out through Quince's eyes, they were all the same, bags of flesh with tiny flames inside, flames he could draw forth and link to his colossal power. It was the same with Quince, except for Rita.

Señorita Diamante had meant something to him, before Belia'al. In the first flush of his servitude, it had not been hard to turn her into the first battery, but still she meant something more to him than the twenty-six others. *She* was going to be his partner in the beginning, a gang leader to deal with the outside world while he dealt with the inside and they wormed their way up in the Necklace. But he got a better offer—one that made him the bitch in the relationship, but the most powerful bitch on the planet, and part of the most powerful bastard. Hanrahan was going to be very surprised on Thursday afternoon, when Belia'al snatched his newly won power away.

Quince stared long and hard at Rita. A year and a half of immobility had wasted her form, but as part of a larger battery, she, like all the others, was continually renewed. Her body was thin but not deathly so; it was her color that was startling. Mottlings of green and purple, as if she'd been in a prize fight, as if she'd been thrown from a speeding motorcycle. As if she'd been used without regard by a demon.

Quince was a bitch but Rita was a loser. That was really why he came down here: to remind himself of that. Whatever he was now, he was better than her!

TUESDAY, MARCH 22, 2011 • 8:31 A.M. CENTRAL DAYLIGHT TIME

1 Lord (Establishing All)

Flying from Chicago to Rome offered Pam a multitude of possibilities. The earliest any flight could get her there was 6:50 A.M. tomorrow, but the departures that would make that happen left as early as 7:00 A.M. today and as late as 1 P.M.; it was simply a question of how long you wanted to wait for the connection at Newark. And there was another choice: a nonstop flight leaving at 4:45 P.M. and getting in just an hour and twenty minutes after the Newark flight. But she was too anxious to get going to sit around until the late afternoon, so she went with the earlier options and chose Continental 6748 at eleven, still giving her leeway if the flight was delayed.

And it looked like it might just be. There were thunderstorms battering the Windy City when Pam pulled into the rental lot at O'Hare, but thunderstorms were part of O'Hare's charm and she wasn't really worried. She had given herself two and a half hours before the flight, determined to do this as efficiently as Max. She completed the return process with the same credit card Max had used the day before; yes, she was surprised to be returning the car so soon, after its weeklong reservation; yes, she understood there would be some extra charges with regard to that. She paid the bill cheerfully. The credit card would indeed transfer money to the rental company the way a credit card should, but any attempt to investigate the personal data attached to the card would lead the investigator far astray. She couldn't be traced through the card.

She took the shuttle to the terminal and stood in line for her ticket and passport inspection. Both were in a different false name. It was, Max said, harder to get false identity papers ever since 9/11, but simple money would do the trick, as it always has done, and alchemy made it even easier. She and Max both had all the paperwork they needed to move swiftly and invisibly around the globe. Still, this was the first time she'd done this without following his lead and her antennæ were alert for any problem.

The overhead TVs in the terminal were showing Full Resource Content, the FRC's news channel. She saw several laptops streaming Full Resource Commerce, the money channel, or Full Resource Competition, the sports channel. The overheads carried a lighter-moment story at the end of the hour, about reports of Black Helicopters in Oklahoma. This after similarly spotty reports from Montana the night before. "It's an oldy but a goody when it comes to government repression," said the stunning blonde with the drop-dead smile and commanding eyes, "but it looks like it's making a comeback. Now this—"

Pam walked to the security line. She kicked off her shoes and put her bag in a bin. When her turn came she asked politely for the pat-down. The pilots association had advised its members to stay well away from the radiation, and who was she to argue with the pros? Plus, although the TSA swore the naked pictures the radiation provided were only for professional purposes, the machines were connected to the Internet and random nudes had shown up there. Finally, neither she nor Max wanted any pictures of themselves that they could avoid.

So she let the TSA lady recite a lengthy spiel covering everything she was going to touch, probably designed less to warn the passenger than to drag the process out, and then do her thing, as advertised. Air travel: *so* glamorous.

Pam had just the one carry-on. In coach, that might have raised an eyebrow, but she was in first class, in the seat by the window against the rear bulkhead, and those who sat up there were less likely to be on a long vacation than a short business trip. Sitting on the aisle would allow any passerby who wished her harm to slip a knife or a needle into her neck with minimal effort. By sitting in the window seat, she would have to fight her way out if attacked, but by the same token, any attacker would have to come at her across the intervening seat. And that seat had been purchased over the Net by yet another nonexistent person, so it remained empty. To this point, it had always been Max next to her, but this was her new world order.

TUESDAY, MARCH 22, 2011 · 10:40 A.M. EASTERN DAYLIGHT TIME

1 Lord (Establishing All)

Nat was feeling good about his prospects. Yesterday Tim Pawlenty announced he was running for president, today Ron Paul said he might do the same. Donald Trump and Newt Gingrich and Sarah Palin and even Michele Bachmann were in the green room, and there were half a dozen more out there, and by the time the Republicans narrowed it down to just one nominee, there'd be several left around to split the vote and send Obama back for a second term. Politics was politics, but stability was always the goal. Better the devil you knew. . . .

He walked down the carpeted hall to the first unused ballroom and carefully surveyed its interior, then went on to the second. He went inside and crossed back to the wall between the first and second rooms. If he was at the windows, mikes could pick up his words from outside. If he was close to the hall, local mikes could do it. The same would be true if someone had entered the first room after he scouted it, but he had to make his best play, and he'd be quick.

Longchamps's face appeared, from the other side of the world. "News?" Nat asked.

"I have permission for eight A.M. tomorrow morning. That's eleven thirty your time, tonight."

"I'll be ready, Gabe. See ya both then."

They signed off. Ten seconds tops.

TUESDAY, MARCH 22, 2011 · 10:45 A.M. EASTERN DAYLIGHT TIME

1 Lord (Establishing All)

Max, as Dennis Aparicio, parked his car in the lot at the Rupp Works and began to take a walk around. A thunderstorm was moving in from the west; it would already be in Chicago. But thunderstorms were part of O'Hare's charm; they could deal with it.

Nobody questioned his right to wander, and so for the first time, he got a good look at the interior of the complex. Surprisingly, despite the industrial nature of the buildings, the overall layout reminded him strongly of a headquarters complex at his old army bases. There was the gray citadel, which at least had the air of the big white structures favored by generals, but the long brown brick buildings were the very model of barracks, simple, utilitarian, and no more. A broad brick patio led from the rear entrance to the citadel across a small lawn to a faded asphalt street running back through the center of the complex. On either side, wherever a cross street didn't cut through, there was more good Hoosier grass, providing a sense of home at the minimum possible cost.

Of course, he thought, *since it's not a base, it is home—but it doesn't feel like it. It feels like Saigon in 1973.*

Being an Alchemist, he of course considered that feeling.

Once I became Timeless, I stepped off the people mover, which freed me up for anything I wanted to pursue—but before then, what I did used up discrete sections of a finite life, and getting sent to 'Nam was the

*first such section. I had no control over it, but I played the cards I was
dealt the best I could, and I won some and lost some. It was my educa-
tion in life, and no matter how far away from those days I get, they're
always where I started this little game.*

And the other half of his brain, that kept the internal conversation going, asked, *What about when Uncle Ed gave me his lion totem?
That would really be the start, because that's where the magick came
in.* But the first half responded, *I didn't understand that until years
afterward. 'Nam was square one for me.*

"Hey, Aparicio!"

He turned to his left and saw Franny Rupp on her knees, using
a wrench on the underbelly of a Black Helicopter. He strolled her
way, so into the military mind that he wanted to salute and say,
"Yes, ma'am!" But he was an Alchemist, so he said:

"How's it goin', Chief?"

"'Sawright," Franny answered. For a second, he felt another hit
from his past: Señor Wences on *The Ed Sullivan Show,* a ventriloquist
with a talking box who spoke that way. Franny, older than his
thirty-five years, had nonetheless been born later. She wouldn't
know Señor Wences. No one else here would know Señor Wences.

"Need any help?" he asked.

She looked up at him, neck-length hair sliding near the closest
eye. "You a mechanic, Dennis?"

"I know my way around a little, Chief."

"Well, none of my machines gets touched by guys who know 'a
little,' get me?"

"Yes I do, Chief."

"Fine. Now that we've got that settled, how are you this fine
mornin'?"

He shrugged. "I'm good."

"You packed a lot into yesterday, and I can see from my birds
that the trip through weird space ain't a walk in the park."

"I'm used to it now," Aparicio said. "Unlike machines, people
adapt. At least if they're working here."

"Adaptation is unpredictable. My machines can be brought back to spec after every mission."

He laughed. "There's no arguing with you, Chief. But I mean it: I'm fine."

"Glad to hear it." But she had something else on her mind, and hesitated on the verge of revealing it. She seemed to be casting around for a way to begin. Finally, as he started to move away and leave her to her work, she asked, "Dennis, you ever hear of gallium?"

"No," he said, though he knew full well it was an element. Number thirty-one.

"It's an element," she said. "Number thirty-one. Discovered in 1831. It's real important in LED displays for TVs and computer monitors. But since we're building lots o' those now, where we didn't used to, they figure we'll run out in 2017. One of our elements, gone extinct."

"Can't they recycle it?"

"Not easily. Not fast enough to matter. Hafnium's another—we put it in computer chips. That'll be gone by 2017, too. And indium, by 2020. But the real killer is zinc, by 2037."

"Zinc?" Aparicio spoke the word, but it was Max who was interested. There was always something new. "Zinc's in everything, isn't it?"

"Almost. You mix it with copper to make brass."

"I didn't know elements went extinct."

"Only people who work with metals know right now, but you can bet it'll be a big deal when the TVs stop coming."

"Wait," Aparicio said. "I thought I read somewhere—China has—"

"They've got rare earth metals, which we need, too, but those are different. We can do a deal with China. We can't do a deal with people and their cell phones. And so, one day I'm gonna need to fix a computer in one of my machines and I'm not gonna have what I need."

"You'll figure something," he told her, and added, ironically, "You'll *adapt*."

"I'll have to. But forever after I'll be working with fewer tools—fewer and fewer, over time. Things that used to work will have to be reinvented, or just forgotten about."

"Wow."

"Only one way to stop it, and that's to control everything from the top down. That's job one around here." She nodded up at him and turned her attention back to her chopper, but not without a little smile. "Nice talkin' with ya. Really. A pleasure."

Walking away, he asked himself, *Was that her flirtin' with me?* And the other side of his mind had no answer he wanted to hear.

TUESDAY, MARCH 22, 2011 · 2:55 P.M. GREENWICH MEAN TIME

1 Lord (Establishing All)

It was quite warm for March, and humid, as Vee rode the tube down to Tottenham Court Road and walked to the Atlantis Bookstore on Museum Street. She came down here reasonably often, caught in the flood where every book leads to new questions and new books, and today she had "fatigue" on her radar.

The area south of the British Museum was very near her old neighborhood in Soho, and that proximity, even after this time, made her, if not nervous, at least watchful. She had turned her back on Soho and had never once revisited those streets where she'd wandered schizophrenic. She never would. She hated every minute of every year she'd been forced to share her brain with Eva Delia Kerr.

But the Atlantis had a very eclectic selection—or maybe it was "eccentric." Either way, it was housed along the walls of one single room. And because there was no space to spread out, the room could get crowded with clientele as well. She liked all of that. People on her wavelength, either mystically or musically, were her kind of people. She knew full well that was selfish. She was entitled.

Girl cannot live by book alone, she often thought; even when the book was by Cornelius Agrippa.

But today there was a dark rumbling when she came through the door, and she quickly found out why. Last night, it seemed, a *bear* had attacked a young woman in the park by Addle Hill Road.

"A bear?" Vee echoed skeptically. She had to admit, she was skeptical about a lot of what she heard, even from fellow mystics.

"The CCTV on Knightrider Street got pictures," a ruddy young man with half a dozen rings in his right ear said. She'd spoken with him once or twice and he seemed grounded enough; his name was Roger, or Russell.

"A bear. In the center of London," Vee said with emphasis.

"Evidently, there were claw marks . . . and teeth marks."

"Well, damn, then. But surely they've captured it by now."

"Nope. It's a mystery."

"It has to have come from a traveling circus," offered another familiar voice. Vee turned and looked upon Matthew Raftery.

"Stalking me?" she greeted him.

"Perhaps the other way 'round," Matthew said, unfazed. "I come here all the time."

"*You* come here," Vee said skeptically.

"Ask Gwinevere," he said, flipping a hand toward the head clerk, who sat behind her low desk at the back of the room. Gwinevere nodded peacefully.

"He does," Roger/Russell concurred.

"Oh," said Vee, and turned to R/R. "Well, so do I, yes?"

"Yes."

Matthew said, "Good. Then no one's stalking anyone."

"That doesn't quite follow," Vee said to him. "It's still quite a coincidence."

Matthew held up his palms. "Relax, Vee. A coincidence is what it is—unless it's fate. Come have a coffee and I'll explain."

"This I'd like to hear," she said.

They went across the street to Giovanni's. He got an Americano; she got a mocha; and they sat outside. Matthew chose a table where their backs were against a wall, looking out at the sidewalk. "What a pleasure it is, seeing people dressed for warmth already," Matthew said, and Vee readily agreed.

"Listen," he said, after savoring his strong black brew, "have you ever heard of Mr. Cornelius?"

She laughed a little. "*Mister* Cornelius," she said. "No."

"Well, he was an unofficial consultant to rock stars in the sixties and the early seventies. He worked behind the scenes with Otis Redding, the Who, and the Carpenters. And certainly others we don't know about. Finally, in seventy-six he took on Valerie Drake."

Vee nodded. Names from the distant past, which was definitely, for her, a foreign country. "And so?"

"The services he offered were very special. Basically, he offered this," Matthew said, and swept a hand at the bookstore across the street.

"You're being very cryptic," Vee said.

He laughed. "Sorry. He offered a mystic overview—astrology mostly, but also Qabalah, Tarot. Some people said full-fledged wizardry. Before Valerie, he let traditional managers handle the bookings and billings—the stuff we talked about last night—"

"The stuff *you* talked about."

"Right. And with Valerie he did it all. My point is, he became a legend and his results speak for themselves, and he did it by knowing the occult. I'm learning the occult."

"You're doing what?"

"Learning. I don't know it all yet, but I'm doing pretty well with it, and with my business. I won't lie; I don't have anyone bigger than you, and you're not so big yet. But I honestly believe you will be, and I honestly believe I can help you take full advantage of that."

"But I don't want to take advantage."

"So you've said. But how about if I do your chart and let you see what you think?"

"I can do my own astrology."

"Then you'll be even better at evaluating me."

She sighed. "I don't want to be managed, Matthew. I just don't."

"No obligation. Just give me date, time, and place."

In an instant, she ran the tab on this situation. It wasn't *his* face that had appeared to her last night. His face was not actually all that bad to look at. What *would* another person say about her chart, whether he was any good or not? She'd never consulted another person. "All right," she agreed. "Thirty-one October 1991—eleven forty-five P.M.—Cardiff." She knew it to the exact latitude and longitude, but she didn't want to seem that hardcore.

"I'll come by the club tonight. . . ."

"No. I don't want this hanging between us in the room. Come see me tomorrow, after the show, at my flat. I'm at Forty-seven Hartland Road, by the overpass at the end. It's yellow."

"All right, Halloween baby," Matthew said. "I'll see if I can amaze you."

You can try, she thought. *But MY Cornelius Agrippa puts YOUR "Mr. Cornelius" in the shade, Matthew Raftery!*

TUESDAY, MARCH 22, 2011 · 4:05 P.M. GREENWICH MEAN TIME

1 Lord (Establishing All)

Vee decided to walk back to Camden Town. It was a hike but not an unpleasant one in the strange London heat, especially after being shut up indoors for months.

The book had taught her the basics of astrology—the planets, the signs, the houses. Because Agrippa had laid it down in 1519, his system was the classical one, with just seven planets, and two of those planets were the sun and the moon because that's what they called them for simplicity's sake. Because there were and still are twelve signs and twelve houses, the sun and the moon each ruled one, and the remaining five planets ruled two houses each. Saturn ruled both Capricorn and Aquarius. Jupiter ruled Sagittarius and Pisces, and so on. For each planet, a positive and a negative version. But not for the Sun and the Moon.

It was obviously an incomplete system. When Uranus appeared in 1781, it had to be integrated into it—as Vee had learned from modern books—and it was. Astrologers, and astronomers in that time, watched Uranus make contacts in the sky, and watched to see what then happened on Earth. It was found to be a revolutionary at heart; the correlations between events with Uranus and events on Earth were clearly telling a story of change, the shock of the new. That's what astrologers had always found in Aquarius, so they gave it the rulership there.

That's how all astrology was done, from its very beginnings two thousand years before the birth of Christ. People saw what happened in the sky and saw what happened in the street, and saw relationships. Some people believed there was something to that, and some people didn't. It went on like that until about the time of Uranus, when the astronomers decided their way was the only way. But some people still looked at both the street and the sky.

Astrology, Qabalah, and Geomancy were the cornerstones of Agrippa's wizardry, and they were the cornerstones of Vee's studies. Each system possessed an internal logic—a set of relationships. This made them solid structures to work with, and to test. Astrology said events in the sky corresponded to events on Earth. So did they or didn't they? That was the test.

Vee saw the correspondences right away, and that, for her, was the confirmatory moment. For her, it was never a question of *learning* astrology, but *remembering* it—including the new parts since 1519. Same with Qabalah, divination by numbers, and Geomancy, divination by the earth. She had no idea *who* she was when she was a disciple, but she knew she *was* a disciple. And so she sharpened and shined up somebody's memories, to the point where she didn't need a Matthew Raftery to tell her what was in her chart.

But that's what she had agreed to.

Why?

1 Lord (Establishing All)

Diana came through the terminal at Fort Wayne International. The overhead TVs in the terminal were showing Full Resource Content just like O'Hare, and the segment was last night's weather where the so-called Black Helicopters were seen, allegedly. It had been a clear night but very cold, which sometimes led to mirages. As far as Di knew, that was utter bullshit, and she was proud of her audacity in creating such a ridiculous theory that so many would believe.

Outside security, she was met by a neat young man in casual clothes and driven to the Rupp Works in a sedan with darkened windows—particularly dark since the threatened thunderstorm had arrived with her. As they cleared the gate, the driver called ahead on his radio, then pulled directly into a garage whose door was rolling up for them. The door closed behind them, and Franny entered through a back door as Di got out.

"Diana," said Franny, smiling as if her face hurt, holding out her hand.

Di affected not to notice any reserve on her hostess's part, taking Franny's hand with sincere enthusiasm. "So this is where the magic happens!" she exclaimed. But she registered the bland response on Franny's face and immediately dialed it down. "It's good of you to take me in on such short notice, Franny. I can learn a lot from what you're doing this week."

"Always a pleasure to see you," said Franny, not very convincingly.

The driver popped the rear hatch, hoisted Di's carry-on, and took it away. "I've set you up in a private suite, here in the Works," Franny told her. "No sense putting you in a hotel downtown." The women went into the building and up the stairs to Ruth's office.

Ruth was entirely civil to her visitor; she grew up in a bureau-cracy. "Nice to see you, Diana," she said, extending her hand with more vigor than Franny had shown.

Di shook it. "And you, Ruth. This is exciting."

"I'm sure you'll understand if I don't have lunch with the two of you," Ruth said, shifting a stack of paper on her desk from right to left. "Pretty busy after last night's raid, calibrating the next one. We're at T minus three. But there won't be much for you to see until then, anyway."

"That's all right," said Di, smiling reassuringly. "I'm here for the whole picture. I want to get to know Franny's machines, and your men, and how all of it fits into the normalcy of the heartland, before all hell breaks loose."

Ruth could read criminals, and that's how she rated Diana—which was all right in its way, because she wanted all of the Nine in the Necklace to be serious criminals. Diana, for her part, knew Ruth could read her. They all could, which was all right in its way, because she wanted all of the Nine to be serious criminals—and she wanted them to think they had her number so they wouldn't probe any deeper.

She looked back at Franny, who had stopped just inside Ruth's door. "Great video of the copters in the night, by the way. How are they doing, going in and out of whatever the hell they're going in and out of?"

For the first time, they'd reached a subject that interested Franny. "The second time through the doorway caused some anomalies. They don't touch anything solid in there, but the air or whatever it is around them carries the weirdness. The metal grows little extras. We shave them off and do thorough X-ray analysis. No internal changes so far."

"What about the people?" Di asked Ruth.

"No effects that we can see. We give 'em a physical after each run. Again, no internal changes—and in their case, no extras. I'll be keeping a long-term watch on them to see if anything develops, but they haven't been compromised so far."

"Good. But if anything *does* go sideways, I give you my word right now, it never happened. I have no ulterior motive, believe me or don't."

"I don't," said Ruth. "But then, I don't believe that of anybody."

"Very wise. Well, check me out all you want. My time here's not just to look at you." Di couldn't avoid stating the obvious, but with her cheerful smile she could avoid making it ominous. "So let's get to the elephant in the room, Ruth: it seems to me the X factor in any operation is Max August mixing in. Black helicopters are just the thing to catch his eye, especially since we crammed it down America's throat last night. When you're crafting a mission like this, how do you prepare for him?"

"I have two answers. One, there's no reason to think he knows we're in Fort Wayne. We've got our own wizardry, thanks to Quince, so the copters appear and disappear far away from here. Two, thanks to Quince, we've got the state-of-the-art defenses against August if he *should* find us. I'm not saying we're impregnable—I would never be that foolish—but we're ready, and on alert. He won't catch us by surprise the way he did the first two times, and the main reason is Blackwell. Her progress from Suriname to Wickr was quick; Quince said they made a great team two years ago, so I assume she's well down that alchemy road by now. But she's not as good as he is, so her being with him makes them more detectable overall."

"Sounds reasonable."

"But you don't buy it."

"Well, he's got skills that none of us has, except for Quince. It's hard to fight someone like that."

"I've never been in a war yet that was a slam-dunk. That doesn't mean we don't go to war."

"I'm just saying, wouldn't it be good to have Quince on hand here for the duration? He's our expert."

"He's on call. If August shows, he'll get involved; he doesn't have to be in Fort Wayne for that, since they'd duke it out on an astral plane or whatever, anyway. And he's caught up in some project of his own."

"Should we allow that, with this mission on tap?"

"Wizards are wizards. You knew Tower."

"Not well."

"Nobody knew him well. That's my point. But we're lucky to have guys like that, and we all have our areas of expertise. That's why we have a group of nine."

"All right," Di agreed. "Well, like I said, you know what you're doing. Now, according to my schedule, you two are lying low for a while. That being the case, I'd like to talk to the men, see what it's like from their perspective."

"Let's have lunch first," Franny said. "Then we'll do that."

"Yum."

As Di turned to go, Ruth caught Franny's eye—and rolled hers.

TUESDAY, MARCH 22, 2011 · 2:33 p.m. EASTERN DAYLIGHT TIME

1 Lord (Establishing All)

Diana and Franny entered the break room on the far side of the Rupp Works, where the men were playing World of Warcraft and gin rummy. The first man to spot them gave a peremptory "Ten-shun!" and the men snapped to as a unit.

Franny said, "This woman is going to ask you some questions. You can speak freely to her."

Diana approached the nearest merc. "Thank you, Chief. How're you doin', trooper?" she asked.

"Outstanding, ma'am."

"That's not speaking freely . . ." She looked for his name tag and saw that he wasn't wearing any. None of the men was. "What's your name, trooper?"

The man looked at Franny, who nodded. "Avilés, ma'am," he said.

"The chief said talk to me, Avilés." Her words were straightforward but her smile was warm and inoffensive. "I have to know the whole story of your adventures so I can spin the story we want. Now, how're you doin' after passing through the 'elder doorway'?"

"You mean the Stargate, ma'am?"

"Is that what you call it?"

"Yes, ma'am." He smiled. "Gate, door—it's somethin' special."

"No physical symptoms?"

"No, ma'am. We were trained for it."

"But a normal person would have problems?"

"Probably. You know the term 'gut-wrenching'? Well, it's like that."

"And everybody came through all right?"

"One hundred percent, ma'am."

She turned to the rest of the room.

"Anybody have any problems?"

They chorused back, "No, ma'am."

And as if it was simply the next logical question, she asked, "Anybody do anything special?"

"How do you mean, ma'am?"

"I'm sure you all did well, but is there any particular hero I should talk to?"

"On the mission, ma'am?"

"Yes," she replied . . . but her reporter's nose for news sensed something hidden there, and so she added, "Or maybe in the run-up to the mission?"

Royal answered that one. "Aparicio, ma'am."

"Aparicio," Diana murmured, looking around the room. "Which one is he?"

"Right here," Royal answered, jerking a thumb toward Max.

She went over to Max, her high heels clicking on the wooden floor. He watched her approach with bland regard. "How're you doing, Aparicio? What's your first name?"

"Dennis, ma'am."

"Drop the ma'am. You can all drop the ma'am. I'm not your commander, and I don't stand on ceremony. I'm Di, Dennis."

"Okay. Di."

"So what did you do yesterday? What time was it?"

"Five o'clock."

"Umm. At the end of a long day. So what did you do?"

"We had a little dustup with a former member of the team. It was nothing."

She smiled reprovingly at him, turned to Royal. "What did he do?"

Royal smiled back easily. "Guy took some shots. Aparicio chased him down and took care of him."

"That right, Dennis?"

"More or less," he said.

"I want to get your whole life story, Dennis."

Watching all this, Franny thought, *Star fucker,* and left her to her little amusements.

TUESDAY, MARCH 22, 2011 · 3:00 P.M. EASTERN DAYLIGHT TIME

1 Lord (Establishing All)

By three, Franny was back in her office, where she turned the television to Newschannel 15 and left it on while waiting for Butler University news. Soon enough she had live video of the kids getting on their bus down in Indianapolis for the thirteen-hour drive to New Orleans. They'd stop for some food in southern Kentucky and get a good night's sleep, arriving ready to go tomorrow morning. They'd be playing at 10 P.M. on Thursday, late but not too late—and probably just right for her plans.

1 Lord (Establishing All)

The flight to Rome left Newark pretty much on time at 5:31. Pam held the same seat and this time she had a seatmate, an attractive young man. They talked for the first half hour, with Pam simultaneously enjoying the conversation and matching her skills against Max's. He could tell you all about himself, or whoever he was pretending to be, and never leave a single checkable fact. She was just as good now; she never forgot her current name or bio, no matter how elaborate a tale she spun. Most of it was based on something real.

When it became obvious to the guy that it would only go so far, they let it come to a companionable halt. He ordered a Manhattan and asked what she wanted.

"I'm good," she said. "I'm real good. Thanks for the chat."

He nodded, pleased, and with a second nod, turned his attention to *The Economist* he pulled from his seatback pocket. Pam took Ian Rankin's latest paperback from her purse and sat back in her first-class seat, getting comfortable. With the book open before her, she could let her mind wander.

It was three and a half years since she'd met Max August. That first Hallowe'en night she'd been dying, in great pain, and he'd taken that away exactly as if by magick. She'd told him she couldn't trust him, and he'd said to simply trust her eyes. Then her eyes had been opened.

In this world we see around us, filled with petty grievances and shiny toys, there were just a few people, on the edges, who understood the ancient power of magick. They worked it, from the edges, where they were unlikely to be seen and even less likely to be credited. That was how it had to be, *because* magick was uncredited as yet, *because* magick worked behind the scenes, on the matrix of life. Max believed that magick was humanity's birthright, and in the fullness of time, it would be just another iPad, another fun and flashy tool. He thought about the fullness of time because he was going to be there to see it, if he kept his wits about him. He had achieved Timelessness, which meant he would live forever unless he was killed.

Naturally, he chose a life with a good chance of his being killed. That was him. But it was also her, as she found out in the days after Hallowe'en, the years after Hallowe'en. The two of them just fit. She shared his passion for righting wrongs, for making a better world, and she shared his exploring mind. Learning what remained a secret over centuries was both thrilling and deeply satisfying. This was what we were all supposed to be, and now she was. The two of them had a bond, a *flow*, between them.

His first wife—only wife, so far—had been Valerie Drake, the pop singer. Val had been murdered along with their mentor, Cornelius Agrippa, but the Timeless wizard had taught her the secret of living beyond the death of the body. He'd been too fundamentally damaged by Aleksandra Korelatovna, their dedicated foe, to do it himself, but Val had only been hanged. She came to Max every Hallowe'en from 1985 to 1990, while Aleksandra was rising on the planes to leave her own humanity behind. On Hallowe'en 1991, Aleksandra imprisoned Val's soul in the body of a newborn babe: Eva Delia Kerr. Max lost track of her, and swore to find her again. He spent the next sixteen years on that quest.

Then came Pam.

Now the quest continued, but there was no question of his becoming Val's husband again once they found her. He and Pam had committed to each other, and if Pam could master the art of Timelessness, they would be together for centuries. That was her goal, and nothing less.

Through Max, she knew that the universe was a unity and a duality at the same time. It had been hard for her to grasp at first, because she wasn't used to something that was two things at once. Until finally she stepped back and saw, say, "humanity" as a unity, but "male and female" as a duality, and both of them the same thing. As Max said, each of us was one-half of a whole. But each of us could put his mind to that and learn what the missing half held, so as to find the unity within the duality. Then you transcended the duality to work with the unified power, which was magick.

With the power she did have, she had learned to shape gravity, the most mysterious of all the primal forces—at least to science. Gravity held things together, drawing everything toward everything. The most basic fact of life in a duality was that everything related to everything else. Nothing on Earth existed alone. There was one thing and another thing—the duality—and there was the gravity, the relationship, the power between them. She was probably more than halfway home now—sort of a teenager—good enough to handle her own affairs in the other world.

But even without Max beside her, she could feel him in the power between them. They were a hell of a magickal couple. So yes, she needed to get her own feet under her, but that was just so she could be a better other half. Duality equals unity.

TUESDAY, MARCH 22, 2011 · 7:10 P.M. EASTERN DAYLIGHT TIME

I Lord (Establishing All)

Max drove the streets of downtown Fort Wayne. They were mostly empty now, two hours after the end of the workday and in the midst of the thunderstorm; it was second nature for him to avoid running into anyone still in search of food, while sending his consciousness into the *astral*.

Hey, Pam.

Hey yourself, she responded.

How's it goin'?

Goin' great! Much better than yesterday. How're you?

Great as well. Me 'n' the boys are goin' to a strip club tonight.

Lucky you.

It's a dirty job but somebody's gotta do it.

I'm in a first-class seat about to eat a first-class meal, with a handsome and charming neighbor.

I thought pets rode in the hold.

Ha ha.

Max?

Yes, dear love.

That's nice, she murmured. *Am I your dear love?*

Uh-huh.

That's nice. I miss you.

Same here.

Then get out of that strip club before I get back on Thursday.

Seems unlikely.

Try.

Duty may call.

Booty may call.

See you Thursday.

TUESDAY, MARCH 22, 2011 · 7:54 P.M. EASTERN DAYLIGHT TIME

1 Lord (Establishing All)

Once upon a time, Indiana and the entire Midwest were laid out on a grid: neat squares of green land and forest. Of course, the squares were on a map until the new owner took possession and began his new life in the new world. Sometimes the owner could only afford a half square, or even a quarter, but it was a place to start. America was limitless, with always something new over the western horizon. If Indiana didn't work out he and his wife and family could move to Illinois, or maybe Missouri.

But for most people, Indiana worked out fine, and people made good on their dreams. The men farmed the green land and the women saw to their growing families, and money and children

meant adding another square, or moving to the plot down beside
Eagle Creek. Little by little they put down roots and filled in the
territory and made it the nineteenth state. The "Hoosier" state, for
reasons no one, including Hoosiers, understood.

Farmers on the frontier needed government. In another distinctly
Hoosier moment, they created Indianapolis right in the geographic
center of the state. Then they put a circle at the geographic center
of the city and Miss Indiana at the center of that. Hoosiers have a
sense of design. Or of magick.

Other cities grew naturally, including Fort Wayne, because the
Maumee River came within ten miles of the Wabash and the Wabash ran into the Ohio. The Maumee was fed from Lake Erie and
the Ohio ran into the Mississippi, so this piece of green land and
forest was the shortest route inland from the eastern waters. The
Miami peoples' name for it was Kekionga, and the French built
Fort St. Philippe des Miamis for the fur trade, and the British faced
Pontiac's rebellion and lost, which might have caused them to re-
think the strength of the spirit in this land by whatever name, but
didn't. The Miami ruled Kekionga again for thirty years, until
George Washington ordered Mad Anthony Wayne to secure it for
the United States, and he did, so it became Fort Wayne.

The significance of the two worlds coming together here was
not lost on Max. It was the very definition of Earth magick, the
spirit in this particular land. But Indiana was settled by industrious
people who had no time for magick so it all just became a special
sort of background. "I dream about the moonlight on the Wabash."
That didn't show up on a grid. Or the design sense of Indiana's
James Whitcomb Riley, the National Poet:

> *An' the Gobble-uns 'at gits you*
> *Ef you*
> *Don't*
> *Watch*
> *Out!*

And so Indiana grew as part of America, and tonight Fort Wayne was suffering the general lack of jobs like any other American town. The new worlds were long gone, but the Hoosiers were cheerful enough. Everybody was running lean, but everybody *everywhere* was running lean, so why bitch about it? It's just the way life was. People still went out to dinner, bought their kids presents. And some guys hit the titty bar on a Tuesday night.

TUESDAY, MARCH 22, 2011 · 8:03 p.m. EASTERN DAYLIGHT TIME

1 Lord (Establishing All)

Show Stoppers occupied a quarter square a block away from the railroad tracks, which cut the grid at an angle parallel to the Maumee. Most of the square was a cracked parking lot, with the back third reserved for the one-story boxy red rectangle. Half a dozen cars were parked facing it, bathed in the glow of the gaudy yellow neon

Show Stoppers

running all across the front.

The neighborhood had the air of not-so-gentle neglect, with small white houses and untended lawns on straight north-south or east-west streets. Show Stoppers turned its back on the neighbors, looking across its parking lot and east-west at barren sycamores fringing the train tracks. Once again, this was not unique to Fort Wayne. He'd seen a place like this in every military town.

Aparicio pulled in on the far left. He ducked his head, came up out of the car, and sprinted through the yellow rain toward Royal and Bragane, who were waiting for him in the doorway, drinks in hand. He nodded at them and they all went inside.

Royal and Bragane had picked a small table at the end of the runway. One girl, no more than eighteen, was twining herself around the pole at the center of the stage, while another strutted out along the runway toward them. Aparicio looked her up and down, and then looked straight into her eyes. At first she didn't register it, any more than she registered most of what was going on around her near-naked body, but then she caught his glance and their eyes locked. He was looking at her not as a titty babe, but as another human being, and despite herself she smiled back at him. Then she gave him an extra look at how she was earning her living, and he nodded back with simple pleasure.

"I think she likes you, man," Royal said, flipping a hand at the girl.

"They all do," Aparicio answered easily.

"And how are we any different from this babe?" Royal asked. "Hookers by another name."

"Amen."

"Damn right amen. We're the elite of the elite, but even we do exactly what we're told," Royal said.

"Who tells Ruth and Franny what to do, d'ya think?" Aparicio asked.

"Does it matter? There's always a chain of command."

"Sure. But any idea *why* we're doin' what we're doin'?"

"You ask a lot of questions, Aparicio. Don't worry: we'll find out a year from now, when some final domino comes tumbling down."

"I don't get you."

"Whoever's runnin' the show, they're the smartest sonsabitches I've ever seen. They always send us out to do something, that causes something else, that causes something else, and two or three more steps down the line it knocks over somebody's domino, and he never saw it coming."

"Or saw it and couldn't do anything but watch."

"Yeah, that, too."

"So where does freakin' out paranoids with Black Helicopters get you?"

"Presidential elections next year."

"Yeah, but Tea Baggers don't have a lot of numbers."

"Well, but that's just what I'm talking about. You rile up the Tea Baggers, the TV and newspapers make a big deal out of it, pretty soon everybody's heard about it, or heard about what the TV told 'em."

"That's pretty sharp analysis for a merc, Royal."

"It's only happened about five million times."

"And it doesn't bother you?"

"Dude, it's the winning side."

Bragane said sullenly, "It's also the right side. And it's not 'Tea Baggers.' It's 'the Tea Party.'"

Royal gave him a pitying look. "You guys chose the name—" he began, but Bragane shook his head side to side.

"I'm not in the Tea Party! Fuck those lunatics! I'm a sovereign citizen!"

"Okay, okay," Royal agreed.

"What we're doing here is not just a job, Royal. We're in the final battle for our very souls."

"Who wants another beer?" Aparicio asked, but Bragane waved him back into his chair.

"You need to know this, Aparicio. In 1861, the American government set up by the founding fathers was replaced by a new government system based on admiralty law, the law of the sea and international commerce—the 'union.' This was no longer the Confederacy that the founders envisioned; once the war against the Union failed, America was gone. Those of us who know the true history of America are free of the Union—sovereign citizens. But under the laws of international commerce, we're slaves, because the Union still lives on our backs.

"In 1933, the Jew Roosevelt changed the money, so that it was no longer backed by gold, as it always had been, but by the 'full faith and credit' of the Union government. This means the government has pledged *us*, its slaves, as collateral, by selling our earning capabilities to foreign investors. *We* have to make good on the Union's promises in order to keep the Union afloat, because if we don't make them money, there won't be any.

"When a baby is born in the Union, a birth certificate is issued, and the parents *have to* set up the kid's Social Security number. The Union then uses that certificate to set up a secret Treasury account in the baby's name. Based on current annual earnings over forty-five working years, men are worth two million dollars and women one million six. So every newborn's rights are split between those held by the flesh-and-blood baby and those assigned to its corporate shell account.

"You can tell the difference by whether your name's in capital letters or not. Your name's Dennis Aparicio, right?"

"Right," Aparicio said, fascinated.

"But on your birth certificate, that's in all caps." He held his hands two feet apart, gesturing the size. "DENNIS APARICIO. That's your certificate self, and it shows up on all official documents: driver's license, marriage license, car registration, criminal court records, cable TV bill, correspondence from the IRS. That's why your real self, your sovereign self, not only *can* but *should* ignore all that. Except, you can't, because it's everywhere."

"So sovereign citizens need to band together. That's what the Free Range Corps is all about, for me, and it should be that for you. This isn't just some job. We're fighting for the Constitution!"

"Now you've lost me," said Royal. "I thought we were against the government."

"We are. But not the Constitution, and especially the tenth amendment: 'The powers not delegated to the United States by the Constitution, nor prohibited by it to the States, are reserved to the States respectively, or to the people.'"

"Tenthers," Aparicio said, understanding.

"Yeah," said Bragane. "There's nothin' in the Constitution about Medicaid, Medicare, the VA, or the G.I. Bill. Nothin' about the War on Drugs or federal surveillance, or . . ."

Royal jumped in. "But how do we know that's the Union?"

"What are you talking about? Of course it's the Union."

"*We* use that surveillance. We use a lot of 'the Union's' resources.

Who's to say this isn't a double bluff, with the Union itself sending us out there?"

"What *the hell* are you talking about?"

"Think about it. You say the Union's all-powerful."

"*Almost* all-powerful."

"Okay. But here we are, flying around their air space, and no one bothers us."

"Because we go through some phantom tunnel where they can't get us. We've got magick. That proves we're not them."

"But how do you know they haven't got magick? Aren't you guys still upset by the Masonic symbols on the money and the buildings in Washington?"

"That's a different thing altogether. That was the original Confederacy, and yeah, I'd wish they hadn't done that, but they're gone."

"Are they? Maybe they just staged the Civil War to make it look that way."

"You mean, the Union is the real America after all?"

"Doesn't that sound like something our side would do? A massive head fake?"

Bragane stood up abruptly, his face ashen. "It does, goddammit. I'm gonna hit the can."

Royal watched him go with sincere admiration. "Bring us some Buds on the way back!" he called. Then he turned back to Aparicio. "There's your real March Madness."

"So you don't believe we're his bad guys in disguise?"

"Hell, for all I know we *might* be! But I don't care. He was right about the only thing that matters: we're the winners. There's lots of weird shit going down right now, and I don't have any delusions that I can put a stop to it. So as a 'sovereign citizen,' in charge of my own life, I figure I'll live a much better life if I'm on their side."

"So it's all about you?"

"Of course it's all about me. At the end of the day, I don't care about anybody but myself."

"Good to know."

"That's why I didn't lead the charge for Cordover," Royal said, "and if *you* did that out of loyalty to anything but your own benefit, you're an idiot. We're winners, getting paid, and that's all there is to it."

The girl on the runway danced on.

1 Lord (Establishing All)

Vee's show that night was a departure from her usual sets. There were no ballads, no tales of love and weakness. Tonight Vee was tough and strong. It was high energy stuff for two hours past midnight. "Thank you," she said at the end. "It was something I had to do," and most of them, somewhere on her wavelength, understood. But only she knew how she'd kicked it up a notch when the skull-faced man walked in around onc.

She was waiting like a tigress to follow him when he left. But to her surprise, he came up to her among the other groupies as she was packing up. There was something about his face that was different from what she'd thought she'd seen the night before—more filled out. His deep black eyes were sunk back in his flesh as if he were an animal in a cave. They were hard to read.

"I just wanted to say, I really like your work," he said.

"Thanks," she said, thankful for her well-known diffidence before compliments. It explained her lack of warmth.

"My name's Christopher—Christopher Durban," he said. "Would you like to relax with a coffee?" His green eyes sparkled in the low light.

"Thanks, but I'm a bit nackered," she said, still smiling.

His face showed concern. "You should take care of yourself, Vee. You're important." Adding, "To us."

"I'll be fine. Appreciate your concern, Christopher."

He nodded, turned, and walked toward the door. Vee watched him go, and all at once felt a wave of lethargy flow through her, a great weariness, and she saw Christopher's retreating back swell, the muscles in his shoulders growing, putting strains in his shirt that hadn't been there before. He went out the door, a slab of meat, and Vee thought her legs might give way. The bastard had beaten her to the punch!

"I really like your singing," a tall, thin woman with cropped hair said, and Vee could scarcely nod as she stepped off the platform, steadied herself, and went out the door herself.

WEDNESDAY, MARCH 23, 2011 · 2:07 A.M. GREENWICH MEAN TIME

1 Lord (Establishing All)

Vee stepped into the courtyard silently, wishing she could make herself invisible. That would have been a nice power to have. But she was confident in the skills she did have. It was clear and cold, sound very crisp. To her right she could hear the soft footfalls of Christopher Durban, echoing off the old brick walls on either side. During the day, the stalls along one side of the passageway were flush with cheap clothing for sale, providing a distinct softening effect on sound, but at two in the morning the stalls were shut and the sounds were clear—if one made sounds, which Vee had no intention of doing. She set out toward Camden High Street in pursuit of her quarry.

Durban turned right and headed toward the tube station. He crossed the nearly deserted street and went inside. Vee never for a moment thought of letting him go, but she would have to play it smart. She knew the schedule for trains at this hour; there would not be another for six minutes. So she waited one, then went in. She took the escalator downward. She didn't see Durban below her on the stairs, so he was either in the passage leading to the platform or on the platform itself. If it was the latter, she could wait in the passage herself, out of sight.

He was not in the passage. A moment of adrenaline rush followed, as she wondered if he was hiding somewhere to come up behind *her*. But when she came to the entry to the platform, she stayed in the passage and cautiously looked to her left. There he was, his back toward her.

In a few minutes, the train roared in and came to a halt. Durban entered, and as he did so, his face turned toward the interior of the car, Vee ran out of the passage and into the car behind his. The doors closed and the train started south.

They rode to Tottenham Court Road, then negotiated the transfer to the Central Line.

WEDNESDAY, MARCH 23, 2011 · 2:54 A.M. GREENWICH MEAN TIME

1 Lord (Establishing All)

Vee waited in the shadows of St. Paul's until Durban crossed Cheapside and began walking briskly up St. Martin's Le Grand. She followed, staying well back, though down here near the Thames, the fog was filtering along the streets. He took an abrupt left into Postman's Park. She ran to make up the distance between them, but when she reached the park, she saw no sign of him.

Cautiously, she entered the dark green enclave. The fog hung around the trunks of the trees, with the bare branches clustering above like lightning turned to stone. This was not a bad part of town, but any woman alone would feel the peril of her situation. It came to her that if they had gone south from St. Paul's, they'd soon have been in the park beside Addle Hill, where the bear had attacked. But Durban was no bear.

Problem was, Durban was *nowhere*. She ran from tree to tree, hugging the shadows close. Still nothing. If she'd lost him, she'd have no other chance at him until he came to see her perform, next Monday—if he did.

She came out of the park into a narrow mews. At the far end was an open pub, half-seen through the fog. The mews was plastered with posters featuring a ram's head, surrounding a single one for *Swan Lake*. The mews was littered with rubbish cans, all limned by dim light from the pub.

Animals crept from behind the cans.

Vee thought the first one a cat, but it was just too big. A fox? The next one had to be a cat—but it was too powerful. And then came two dogs—she hoped.

They stood in the alleyway, limned by dim light from the pub, watching her. Then their heads went low, their haunches high. The dogs began to growl like something beyond dogs.

Vee stared back at them, her attention centered among them, waiting for movement. The very first thing the book had taught her was defense spells, because the entire basis for the book was helping a wizard who had lost his way. It did no good to teach the Hours of the Day if the disciple was already dead. So Vee was not afraid of Durban's little tricks.

She raised her left hand in a certain manner, and the right as its mirror image—remembering the instructions, trying to carry them out correctly—speaking the words:

"I conjure and confirm the angelic forces, sanctified and potent, which encloak a true wizard on her way!"

At once, an egg-shaped glow surrounded her, from eighteen inches above her head to eighteen inches below her feet, into the pavement. All four of the wild animals immediately leapt at her. But each smacked up against her protective sphere, and the sphere let her kick outward, so she booted them head over heels. The first one was definitely a fox, and the duo must be wolves. The cat-thing she had no idea.

The animals rolled from her kicks, the fox a great distance. But then they got up again and came loping back, seemingly unfazed. Their attack was less coordinated, her defense even more effective; again and again she repelled them. But much too soon she began to feel the effects of her lethargy. Her counterstrikes grew marginally slower, behind the curve, and the beasts kept coming and coming. She held them off another minute—two—three!—

But in the end, the fox finally sank its teeth in her leg. She tried to stomp it with her other foot and not lose track of its allies, but she couldn't. Something latched on to her calf. A wolf bit her clavicle and knocked her down. The sphere faded and the animals swarmed.

Then stepped away.

Vee lay, weak and bleeding, watching them. She wanted to get up but her body would not obey. Then from behind them, growing larger over them, throwing a shadow before him even larger in the fog, came Christopher Durban. He stood among them and looked down at her, a tight little smile on his tight little face.

"I felt your power and knew I had to have it, Vee. You are something strange and mysterious. But now I find rare strength of spirit as well, and intelligence. So you can certainly understand the situation you find yourself in. I want you alive to feed upon. If you'll allow it, you'll remain free. If you don't, I'll chain you in a room. Either way, I am your master now. Choose wisely, then, as you recuperate."

He moved his head and the animals walked away. He followed.

Vee bled.

TUESDAY, MARCH 22, 2011 · 11:30 P.M. EASTERN DAYLIGHT TIME

1 Lord (Establishing All)

Nat had returned to his hotel room on Twenty-ninth just after eleven. He'd been doing dinner and drinks with Donald Trump, and it had been a nice test of his skill to get home on time. Because what he was doing now was the real deal for him, the key to the unknowns that still existed for him in the Necklace. This would tell him where he stood.

He woke his laptop from its sleep and waited to be connected.

2 Nipple (Encountering Reality)

Gabriel Longchamps looked at the mustard-beige building ahead of him. It was standard Soviet army architecture, now painted to look like a San Diego mall. But then, everything here was beige, the snowcapped mountains, the wide flat plain, the camo'd guards. It even had San Diego's sunny weather.

"Gabriel Longchamps," he told the guard at the steel-reinforced desk inside the narrow entryway.

"Yes, Mr. Ambassador," said the guard. "We were expecting you."

"You don't make it easy to get inside," Longchamps offered.

"No, sir. We do not," said the guard, neither friendly nor unfriendly. "Please come this way."

He led Longchamps to a doorway at the back of the room. It, too, was reinforced. The guard moved to speak into a tube that protruded from the wall, set at an angle so he could keep his eyes on his visitor while speaking, and keep his words unheard. With a heavy thunk, the door unlocked and swung slowly open. An armed guard stood inside.

"Thanks," Longchamps told the first one, and walked inside. A second guard pressed the button that closed the steel door behind him, while the first one watched him, his weapon at the ready. Across the small room was a simple cage, seven feet high and four feet wide, made of steel bars. The top and all sides except the one with the door inside were flanked by rolls of razor wire, so even though the bars allowed a prisoner to reach out of the cage, no one would.

Longchamps himself was standing inside a full-body scanner, and he was given no opportunity to ask for a pat-down instead. The guard with the electronics studied the image for twenty seconds, then nodded. "All right."

The first guard now led Longchamps past the cage—"for prisoners being processed," he said. Inside security, he could afford to unbend a little more than the man outside. Inside security, he dealt with human beings. "You'll be the first visitor he's had in twelve months," he said as the two of them entered a corridor. This was not painted beige, or painted much at all. It clearly showed its origins as an aircraft machine shop in the '80s, as was no doubt intended. This was a gulag, and the despair here choked the air. Longchamps was wondering who that last visitor might have been. "Did you know the prisoner, before?" the guard asked him.

"Not personally, no."

"Good."

"Why 'good'?"

"He's not the same." The guard stopped outside a steel door numbered 27, with a small panel at eye height. He slid the panel open and looked inside. Longchamps could see some form of Plexiglas filling the opening. The room was air-tight, so the occupant would breathe whatever his captors chose to give him. As with the razor wire, the prisoner had to understand that there was no longer any way to connect with the outside, and he was completely in their power.

Satisfied with what he saw, the guard opened the door. Longchamps suddenly found he did not want to go in. But he had promised Nat, and they had known each other since he was twelve. He thanked the guard and went inside, and the door chunked solidly shut behind him.

The cell he was now in was six feet wide and ten feet long. There was a bed, a drinking fountain, a toilet, and a man; nothing else. The man was huddled against the toilet, his arms around it, looking up at Longchamps as if trying to figure out what he was looking at. His head was covered in a soft fuzz, a version of the standard military cut, so very different from the bald head that was once known to millions.

Longchamps took a long breath, then, keeping his back to the door in case the guard was watching still, slid his secure cell phone from his breast pocket, flipped it open, and slid it onto the pocket so the camera faced what he was facing. He thumbed the connection.

TUESDAY, MARCH 22, 2011 · 11:46 P.M. EASTERN DAYLIGHT TIME

1 Lord (Establishing All)

Nat studied the man on his screen the way he'd study a steer. There was no sign of spirit—no sign of the man who had dazzled everyone in his time.

His predecessor, Michael Salinan.

WEDNESDAY, MARCH 23, 2011 · 8:16 A.M. AFGHANISTAN TIME

2 Nipple (Encountering Reality)

Longchamps looked at the man against the toilet, and honestly didn't know if he should come any closer, so he stood where he was with his back to the peephole in the door. "How are you, Michael?"

Salinan turned his head away. "You're not real," he said sadly, in a soft, curiously deep whisper.

"I'm real," Longchamps said.

"No," said Salinan. Suddenly he began banging his head against the toilet.

Longchamps moved forward, alarmed, and touched Salinan's shoulder. "I'm real." But the prisoner flung himself away from his touch and scuttled to the side of the bed. Longchamps said again, "I'm real."

Salinan looked at him.

"What have they done to you, Michael?"

Salinan looked away. Then, keeping his eyes averted, he whispered, "Won't ever talk to me, when I'm awake. But when I go to sleep, oh yes, then they wake me every fifteen minutes, ask if I'm okay. They wake me up for good at five in the morning, and make me stay awake till eight at night. If I fall asleep they wake me up, make me stand up. Sometimes I fall down. It hurts."

"Do you ever get out of your cell?"

"Two hours. TV for one hour. *I Dream of Jeannie*. Walk round and round in an empty room for one hour. Can't stop. Can't sleep. Then here. They won't let me walk here, won't let me do anything other than sit; they stop me if I try. All I want to do is talk with someone. I need to talk with someone. Someone real."

"I'm real." Longchamps felt completely helpless before this helpless man.

Salinan abruptly lifted his head, and fixed his visitor with a thousand-yard stare. "Stay with me please!"

Longchamps spread his hands. "I can't do that."

"No. Course not," said Salinan, not in anger but in confirmation. "Why would anyone . . . ?" He scuttled back to the toilet, hugged it. "He's not real," he told it.

"Oh my God," said Longchamps. "Nat, can I go?"

But his words were garbled as his cell connection began to break up.

WEDNESDAY, MARCH 23, 2011 · 12:17 A.M. EASTERN DAYLIGHT TIME

I Lord (Establishing All)

Nat leaned forward, double-clicked the screen. The image of the cell was pixelating.

Dick Hanrahan's face appeared. "Good morning, Nat," the old man said.

Nat recoiled as if facing a snake.

"I'm calling to inform you," he continued urbanely, "that your attempt to sneak this past the Necklace was doomed from the start. You're new, so you need to understand that the Necklace knows *everything*. And we hold your fate in our hands at *all times*—just as we hold Salinan's. You can *never* try anything like this again. Do you understand me, Nat?"

"Sure, Mr. Hanrahan," he said, proud of the unwavering strength in his voice.

"Because if you *do* try it, you will be killed with no pushback whatsoever. Do you understand me, Nat?"

"I do, goddammit!"

"Good. I've scheduled a meeting for you with Mr. Breckenridge, ten o'clock tomorrow morning at his house. Good-bye."

"Wait!" Nat all but shouted. "What about Gabe?"

"We'll let him leave—since you were wise enough not to tell him about us."

"He didn't need to know."

"That's right. This is on you, Nat."

His screen went blank—and stayed blank.

WEDNESDAY, MARCH 23, 2011 · 12:30 a.m. EASTERN DAYLIGHT TIME

1 Lord (Establishing All)

Max was wide awake and determined not to be the first one to leave tonight, after ducking out twice yesterday. He matched Royal and Bragane drink for drink, burning the alcohol within himself to lessen its effects, telling wild, extravagant stories from his past with his usual skill at both storytelling and misdirection. He used times and places that made sense for times and places that didn't, transporting jungles to deserts and Saigon to Baghdad.

For his pains, he got to hear how Obama was a Muslim.

"He's not," Aparicio said, "but what if he was?"

"They're trying to destroy America."

"*All* of them? Believe me, Brag, if one point six billion people were working together, we'd hear about it."

"Some of them, then. And he's one. He's sure not an American."

"Because?" Royal asked.

"He was born in Kenya. The Hawaiian 'birth certificate' is a fake."

Royal was about to follow up but this time Aparicio leapt in. "And you know this how?"

"Jesus Christ!" Bragane barked. "It's all over the Internet."

"People can put anything on the Internet."

"So many people, working together?" Bragane responded triumphantly. "Didn't you just say that's impossible?"

"No, I said we'd hear about it," Aparicio said. "And there are more people saying the certificate is real."

"Sure. People who work for the government."

"You mean, like the people who store all the birth certificates."

"What else are they gonna say?"

"So the only way you'd believe it's real is if you saw it for yourself?"

"Hell, no!" Bragane exploded. "You just said, they generate those things by the thousands. They can put anything they want on it."

"So there's no way you'd ever believe it?" Aparicio asked.

"I know what I know."

"So little baby Obama was pledged to the futures traders of Kenya? His birth certificate secret account funnels cash to Kenya?"

"They don't have a system like ours. He needs to make his own money. That's why he's president."

"But it's not like you can just go out and become president. He had to pass through a lot of levels to get there. And he's half black. It seems like an extreme long shot for a Kenyan kid to bank on becoming the American president, don't you think?"

Royal piled on. "Here's the thing, Brag. There's definitely a lot that's shady going on—no question about it. And you look at history and that's always been true. There's a government you can see and there's behind the scenes. So we're left to take the facts we get and make some sense out of them. We can do that different ways by deciding which facts mean more than which other facts. We slant the picture, based on what we know we know. But then what we need to do is check that picture against new developments and see if it holds up. If it does, cool. If it doesn't, then we need to learn what's wrong and fix it. And yet you can't learn anything."

"That's where you're wrong. I listen to the news all the time."

"Whose news?"

"Fuck you," said Bragane. But though he could get steamed, he never got really mad. He knew in his heart of hearts that he was right.

"I think everybody's news says Obama's the second coming of Bush when it comes to government control," said Aparicio.

"Exactly. Thank you. Health care—"

"I was thinking of the ability to kill citizens or hold them forever without trial. That's all supposed to be illegal but it's expanded under Obama. Did you know everything that got Nixon impeached is now officially legal? Nobody cares because it's only Obama. But he's locked it in for any president down the line. You think that's a good thing?"

"So long as he doesn't do it to me," said Bragane.

"But if he does it to the bad guys?"

"Absolutely. You can't cut terrorists any breaks."

Royal pounced. "So why would he do that if he's trying to destroy the country?"

Aparicio said, "I think you need to raise your sights a little, Brag. Because the Folks Reachin' for Control don't want you to."

He watched both Bragane and Royal for any reaction to his slight emphasis on "FRC." There was none.

"You're sayin' what I know about the world is bullshit?" Bragane said. "That's nuts, Aparicio. You're a retard. C'mon, let's go home."

1 Lord (Establishing All)

Royal and Bragane backed their car away from Show Stoppers and rumbled away into the rain. Max stood by his car and watched them go. Then he said in a conversational tone, "What are you doing in there, lady?"

Diana Herring sat up from the shadows of the backseat. "Waiting for you," she said through the closed windows, her face now illumined in the yellow glow, but distorted by the rain.

"It's flattering," Aparicio said, "but why don't you show me your hands?"

She did. They were empty and yellow; he thought of *The Simpsons*. "Why don't *you* come inside?" she asked mockingly.

He unlocked the driver's door, then opened the rear door and slid in next to her. She moved back into the shadows, as far away as she could get, leaving space between them, saying softly, "The last time we sat this close, I tried to poke your eyes out, and the last thing I want is a misunderstanding."

Aparicio's face caught the light fully. He turned more toward her, his right hand casually rising to rest on the rear panel, his fingers making a subtle sign. He leaned toward her, one part of him surveying her with professional skill and the other part with all appropriate appreciation. "Whatever you say, baby. How much?" he asked.

"Don't give me that. I know who you are."

"Yeah? Who am I?"

"Max August. I got you here, Max, so I came here knowing you'd be one of the people I'd meet here. I know you can disguise yourself, and once I heard what went on here yesterday, I knew who you'd want to be: the one guy on the troopers' level who hobnobs with the Necklace bitches. Gives you access to everything."

"I thought you were supposed to be *my* fantasy . . . ," he began, then lashed out with his left hand before she could react. He struck her forearm at the nerve plexus above the wrist, stunning it, then reached past it and snatched the subcompact Glock 26 hidden between the seat and the door.

She regarded the gun in his hand with satisfaction. "Like I said: Hi, Max."

"What do you want, Di?" he asked her.

"I just wanted to see you, Max. Even though the face is phony. I just wanted to see your eyes."

"Why?"

"Because the eyes show the soul, isn't that what they say? Because whatever I saw in them at Wickr, it convinced me to throw in with you. Since then I've trusted that, but I wanted to see it again under less stressful circumstances."

"Then sit up where I can see you, too. We won't be seen from outside."

She didn't quibble. He remembered *that* from their first meeting. She was trained on live TV so she made her decisions on the fly, and she believed he could keep them private. So then he studied her face, looking for signs of over-strain, knowing she could fake sincerity, seeing nothing. He was trained in the jungles of 'Nam and he, too, made quick decisions.

"You look good," he said.

"You don't. I liked Greg's face better."

"I take what I can get."

"I suppose." She shrugged philosophically. "You like my analysis of your situation?"

"It seems to be correct."

"Yes. You did catch me at a bad time at Wickr, Max. I generally have a little more on offer. You should keep that in mind."

"I understood your distraction then. I understand you now."

"Do you?"

"Look," he said, "we can play that game all night. Let's take it as read, we're both mean mama-jammas. Now, did you want something besides my eyes?"

"What's the Necklace's plan here, Max? All I know is, it's Black Helicopters on Thursday and Friday night. They don't fill me in, because it's better when I'm as surprised as the viewers. In the moment, y'know. We relate better."

"I don't know any more than that. But I have a question for you, Di."

"Shoot."

"Last time we talked—"

"You had a proverbial gun to my head."

"Still do," he said flatly. "And you said the Necklace located to the nine cities at the time of the Civil War. I can guess, but why don't you tell me what the Civil War has to do with it?"

"This conspiracy goes back a long way, Max," she answered. "Centuries, at least. Its true origins are still not clear to me. But when it came to America, just before the Revolutionary War, it settled in South Carolina, so when the Civil War came, it had Southern sympathies. That's why it chose those nine cities to put a choke hold around the throat of the North, in 1854. Duluth was little more than a mining town then, but it was in the right place for their symbol."

"Then they were working in the North, for the South."

"No. They were always working for themselves alone. They just happened to be in the South."

"And this whole 'destroy the government' movement?"

"*Gone with the Wind.* There's a lot of romance tied up with destroying the *Yankee* government, and it's never gone away. It's a symbol."

"You're using all sorts of symbols now."

"Any symbol that works. Set your enemies to fighting each other, so they don't fight you. You know, Max, we're really doing everything right here, except for killing you. I really do think you'll prevent us from doing that, *and* prevent us from taking complete control, if you keep at it. But wouldn't it be fantastic if you joined in and took our ride all the way to the top?"

"No."

"No? That's all you have to say?"

"It's just that simple, Di. Or I am." He stared at her in the half-light. "We are one hell of a team."

"A match made in hell."

He nodded. "But I, at least, didn't help make it hell."

"I didn't join until October of oh-five. I had nothing to do with Nine-Eleven."

"The wars are still goin' on, though. Five of them."

"And I'm right where you want me to be, in a ringside seat for all of it."

"With an obstructed view, apparently."

"I got you here. Now you can take care of it."

"I appreciate your confidence."

"No. I appreciate *your* confidence. That's why I'm doing this." She opened her door. "Now would you mind walking me to my car across the street, in whatever manner Dennis Aparicio would, so long as it hides my face? I can't be seen here."

"My pleasure, Di. But we don't need misdirection; I can make us invisible."

"Now *that's* what I want from Peter Quince. Useful magick. Everything I get from him I figure's possessed. This is far more pleasant, Max."

"Membership has its privileges," he said.

Day Three

2 Nipple (Encountering Reality)

The sun, rising brightly over London in a clear blue sky, shone through a window and woke Vee. She was in an ambulance, racing, a paramedic hovering above her.

He saw her eyes open. "You'll be fine," he told her, first thing. "You've had a number of animal bites, but they're not very deep."

"Lucky me," she said.

He laughed, encouraging her spirit. "The bite marks look like wolves, and a fox. How did it happen?"

"You've got me," she said. "I was just walking through a mews and there they were."

"Was there a bear?"

"A bear? Like that poor girl on Addle Hill? No. Nothing that big, thank God. Now, how soon till I'm up and around?"

"Two days. You need bed rest."

I can give it two hours max, thought Vee—then repeated it. *Max.* It was a funny word, but for some reason, it made her feel better.

2 Nipple (Encountering Reality)

Having left Newark on time, Continental 40 battled headwinds across the Atlantic and arrived in Rome's Fiumicino Airport forty minutes late. Pam debarked as part of the throng—even this early, the place was packed—and went with it along the hallways and stairways leading to passport control. She was directed to one of the lines and waited her turn to present her papers. After a few questions, she was passed.

She made her way out to the taxi area. The day was chilly but clear; she pulled her jacket around her. The spotter motioned her to the next available car, but she abruptly waved him off, apparently having to take a phone call. She watched three more cabs be taken, then allowed herself to be given the fourth. It was highly unlikely that the cab could have been waiting for her.

She paid forty euros for her trip to the Hotel Sant' Anselmo, departed with a large but not memorable tip, and scanned the street behind her, noting the colors of all the cars and taxis in view. Then she walked inside the hotel, but crossed the lobby to a rear door and went onto the Via di San Domenico. There she flagged the first cab she saw that didn't resemble any of the ones she'd seen before and went to the Cavalieri Hilton in the Via Alberto Cadlolo. It was big and it was beautiful, but its main attraction was, it was big; there was no trouble getting a room at this hour of the morning without a reservation.

Upstairs, she hung out the "Non Disturbare" sign, locked the door, and made sure the windows were tight shut. Then she lay back on the queen-sized bed, centered herself, and shifted her *astral* form out of her physical form, entering the blue and silver *astral* world. It looked like our world but as if through a glass, with every point of interest having its own gravitational hot spot—blue glass, silver light. She simply had to stand in it to feel it in all directions, probing for any threat.

Finding none, she left one body on the queen-sized bed and went out for a walk, to experience Rome in the *astral*.

2 Nipple (Encountering Reality)

Vee came through the door of her flat and straight to the book. "Vampire spell," she said succinctly.

The book's pages flipped, and highlighted:

Now O thou vampire, since thou art pernicious and blood-red, in the name and by the power and dignity of the Omnipresent and Immortal Lord God of Hosts Jehovah Tetragrammaton, the only creator of Heaven and Earth and all that is therein, who is the marvellous Disposer of all things both visible and invisible, I do dispose of thee and thine evil to the depths of the Bottomless Abyss, there to remain until the Day of Judgment and beyond.

"I like it. What else?"

To destroy a vampire, cut its head from its body, fill its mouth with garlic, and drive a stake through its heart. You may also burn it with holy water.

"What else?"

Protection from a vampire. A crucifix, made of silver in the Hour of the Moon. Garlic. The wild rose. The mountain ash.

"The crucifix and the garlic, I can handle. Now, what about a spell against a master of wild animals?"

The book simply sat there for a moment—then flipped.

Two enemies. Utilize the power of Mercury.

"No, it's the same guy."

Two enemies. Utilize the power of Mercury.

Once again, Vee was reminded that for all its wonders, the book could only do what it could do. "Okay, say I used Mercury."

The best time to confront an enemy is when his particular strength is given to all. He will have no advantage then.

Flip.

The Hours of Mercury on Wednesday are the eighth of the Day, and the third and the tenth of the Night.

"All right. Sun comes up just before six and goes down just after. Divide both Day and Night by twelve, the eighth Hour is . . . one this afternoon, to two. Third Hour of the Night is maybe eight o'clock, and the tenth is three A.M. My Hours of Power."

A wizard cannot estimate. A wizard must utilize right measure.

"Right. You're right." She bobbed her head. "But I'm not going after him this morning. I'll probably take the evening Hour. I'll work that out and then figure exact times." She looked on the book, her oldest friend. "He wants to milk me like a cow, Cornelius. That's the last thing I'll ever stand for."

You are my disciple, the book told her.

But she was very tired.

WEDNESDAY, MARCH 23, 2011 · 6:00 A.M. EASTERN DAYLIGHT TIME
....
2 Nipple (Encountering Reality)

"Today is March 23, 2011, a Wednesday," the old man said.

"Turkey has done a complete one-eighty on the Libya mission. At first they were against getting NATO involved because, as NATO members, they didn't want to be part of an attack on Muslims. But then the French said the French should lead the NATO mission, which the French foreign minster called a 'crusade,' and now the Turks are all-in to keep the French from getting control."

"I look forward to the day when we have those people under *our* control."

"As do I. Now, the Senate leader in Wisconsin says if they had to vote a second time on stripping union rights, they'd lose, so they're going to defend the first vote in court rather than revote. It's not only realpolitik, it defuses the situation for at least two months."

"People will continue to organize."

"Yes, but as always, against what? They have no one to fight with until we bring it to a head again.

"Elsewhere in the world, Japan says the radiation wasn't as completely contained as they said at first."

"I'm shocked," said Breckenridge drily, "shocked."

"This one might shock you for real. Elizabeth Taylor died."

"Really? I liked her."

"As did I. And finally, Renzo, I had to take action against Nat. He was trying to get an interview with Mike in Bagram. I told him to come see you at ten."

"Fine. I'll have to move up my call then. But it's become predictable, hasn't it, Dick? Anyone we bring on board is so used to being their own boss . . ."

"One of the wisest policies you ever set in place was monitoring everyone the first year, Renzo. They have to learn who they're dealing with."

WEDNESDAY, MARCH 23, 2011 · 6:23 A.M. EASTERN DAYLIGHT TIME

2 Nipple (Encountering Reality)

Dick Hanrahan sat back in his intelligence bunker, a secure area inside a secure area inside the Intelligence link's mansion in Wheeling, West Virginia. He had access to the secrets of the world in here, and no one had ever intruded upon it without his gimlet-eyed presence. Not even Renzo.

It was almost sixty years since the Necklace had recruited him, he thought with some astonishment. Sixty years! How was that even possible? He had been running COMINT in Korea, and thought he was hot stuff. He didn't have to overthink it when the Foreign Response Council invited him to become a member. He didn't fully understand who they were so of course he stuck his nose under their tent. A spy's nature. But it was they who were studying him.

It was fifteen years before the Intelligence link opened up and they took him into the Nine. And forty-three years since then.

But in between, he studied with Professor Strauss at Chicago, and he met Lawrence Breckenridge. Renzo and he got to be friends arguing over coffee, upstairs in the Classics Building, surrounded by the glaring plaster busts overlooking the Midway. He liked Renzo pretty much from the start. The guy had no potential as a spy; he preferred manipulation to knowledge, so he let others handle the details. But the manipulation was first class. He understood Strauss's philosophy of the élite almost as well as Dick did. So when the Political link opened up in '76, Dick recommended him. Renzo didn't take to it at first—in '80, he was giving serious thought to jumping to Reagan's inner circle—but Dick kept him on board.

And then, the old man went on, *in '92, Tom Jeckyl died, and the remaining eight chose Renzo to take his place, instead of me—and Renzo began to use me, rather than work with me. For nearly twenty years, I've been his dog's-body, reporting to him every morning of the year at 6 A.M.*

Tomorrow, this dog has his day.

WEDNESDAY, MARCH 23, 2011 · 9:17 A.M. EASTERN DAYLIGHT TIME

2 Nipple (Encountering Reality)

Aparicio and Royal were playing pickup basketball on a side street inside the Rupp Works when Major Duden found them. "Aparicio. Chief wants to see you."

"Yes, sir," Max said, but made the man wait while he put a final dunk through the hoop. Then he turned and followed.

Franny's office was spacious, but every inch of it was filled with stuff. The side walls had no windows, or if they did, they were hidden by the cabinets. Those cabinets ran all the way to the ceiling, and rolling ladders, as in old-fashioned libraries, were in place before them. Nevertheless, there were stacks of papers all over the floor. Beside the entryway door was a box, four feet long, one foot high, with three computers atop it. The box was facing a mattress tucked into the corner; a command center if awakened in the night. The main computers were on her desk, on the far side of the room, and behind the desk, filling the wall, was a video screen. At the moment it showed a satellite view of Oklahoma, overlaid with radiant lines. Max made a guess: voice and e-mail mentions of Black Helicopters, courtesy of the NSA. Franny herself looked up from her desk, smiling. It was, surprisingly to Max, a somewhat appealing smile. She was thick but she had good bones. He simply had never seen her smile before.

"Aparicio, Chief," Duden said.

"Thank you, Major," she said, and the man left the room.

"Dennis," Franny said, standing up, "that was damn fine work yesterday. Made me proud."

"Thank you, Chief."

"Charging into an unknown venue after a guy who's already shot at least one man. That's a lot of balls."

"More like stupidity, Chief."

She came around the desk, crossed to him, watching him. Her nails were short but she made them felt as she ran her fingers across his chest. She flicked her head at the mattress. "Let's check your balls."

He stood where he was. "I'm sorry, Chief. I can't do that."

"It's not a request, Aparicio." The smile went away. "I can use a man like you, tough, and smart . . ."

"I understand that, Chief. Completely. But I made a promise . . . to a lady . . ."

"Is she here?" She looked right, left, back at him. "No, she's not."

"She's here in spirit, Chief."

"Save that crap for Oprah, Aparicio; it doesn't impress me. Move." Gone was all appeal.

"I mean no disrespect—," he began.

"Last chance!"

"Believe me, Chief, if I *could* comply, I *would* comply. There's nothing I'd like better."

"I will make your life a living hell if you turn me down, mister. I want this, and that's that."

He could stun her, take the last three minutes from her memory with a little work, but this deep undercover, stuff like that had to be saved for life-and-death challenges. Royal and Duden both knew he was here, and wiping them, too, just made too many tracks. He'd already handled the doctor.

"Chief, I just can't—"

"You're pissin' me off now." She picked up her phone and punched up Ruth. "Ruth, I want your permission to discipline one of your men."

"Who, and why?"

"Aparicio. For complete disrespect."

"Aparicio saved your ass yesterday, Franny. He's one of my best men."

"I know that. Now, do I have your permission?"

Ruth knew Franny when Franny was in one of her moods. "If you're sure that's what you want," she said.

Franny hung the phone up, and told Aparicio, "I want every urinal in this compound spic-and-span. And since they're all in use, you'll have to clean them over and over, until you change your mind."

"Yes, Chief," he said. "Over and over."

"So you are a pussy, after all."

"Yes, Chief," he said.

"Get outta here, pussy. Come back when you're ready to be a man."

"Yes, Chief."

He'll come around, Franny thought. *I can see exactly how this'll play out.*

Z Nipple (Encountering Reality)

At precisely the top of the hour, Peter Quince, who had once stolen a nuclear bomb from the Fortress, stole three carved talismans.

– 0 –

Aleksandra was floating in the Abyss—when the knowledge of the theft washed through her.

Z Nipple (Encountering Reality)

Max was at the janitor's closet picking out his brushes when the knowledge of the theft hit him. It came from right beneath his feet.

Z Nipple (Encountering Reality)

Franny had just rolled beneath a chopper, working out her frustrations, when her hip alarm went off. It was the signal for the Fortress, right beneath her butt, and any disturbance down there triggered an instant alert.

She pushed off on the chopper's belly and rolled out from underneath on her sled. She was getting to her feet, surprisingly quickly for her girth, when the secure phone pulsed. That would be Hanrahan.

"I've got a signal for a Fortress breach," the old lizard said.

"No sign of any external force. It's probably magick," said Franny heavily.

"Quince's bogies were supposed to stop that."

"Yeah, well, there's nothing topside."

"If it's something stronger than Quince," said Hanrahan, "it's a Code Red—probably Max August."

"I'll let you know as soon as I find anything."

"Careful of any residual magick."

"Why, Uncle Dick, I didn't know you cared."

"I need you to report."

Franny punched END and called Ruth.

"We're goin' down," she told her, and started bustling toward the hidden entrance.

WEDNESDAY, MARCH 23, 2011 · 10:03 A.M. EASTERN DAYLIGHT TIME

2 Nipple (Encountering Reality)

"All right," Breckenridge said reasonably, "so they think you're a wuss, or even a sellout. That was going to happen sooner or later. You're in the catbird seat. Sure, we're talking with them all, but you're our guy. It's all under control.—Hey, I'm sorry, B., but I've got a meeting. Yeah, we'll talk tomorrow."

He punched his phone. "Send up Mr. Whitten."

But abruptly, Dick Hanrahan's face appeared on the screen. "Belay that, Renzo," the old man said. "Something's been stolen from the Fortress. It looks like a Code Red—most likely Max August."

"What was stolen?"

"Rupp and Glendenning are on their way down there now."

"Why do you think it's Max?"

"Had to be someone with better magick than Quince."

"Quince's magick is pretty good."

"Maybe. You know I'm not sold on the guy, Renzo. Who are you to judge a wizard, anyway?"

"I'm the link that holds us all together. I have to be able to judge us all, even if I'm no wizard. I'm not a mechanic, but I can judge Franny. I'm not a crotchety old bastard, but—"

"Yeah, well, I don't know *anything* about magick, but I judge this: when we put the bomb from Yucca Mountain in the Fortress, August stole it back for a few moments, before the defenses Jackson Tower left us snatched it away from him. After that, Quince beefed up the defenses—but now someone on August's level has struck again. That doesn't give me confidence in Quince; I just don't think he's that good."

"Well, I think you and the wizard can never be bosom buddies, but let's wait and see what Franny reports. We don't even know what's been stolen." Breckenridge scowled down at his screen. "I think you've got Max on the brain."

Hanrahan grimaced sourly toward his screen, thinking *Just so long as you don't have Quince on yours.*

WEDNESDAY, MARCH 23, 2011 · 9:03 A.M. CENTRAL DAYLIGHT TIME

2 Nipple (Encountering Reality)

The last few vapors of his mist were dissipating around Peter Quince. He stood once again in his sanctum, solidly upon the floor, awkwardly but securely holding three bulky talismans in his arms.

Each talisman was about a foot and a half long, carved from sturdy wood, and heavy. There was an Angel, a thin human form with strong wings, but abstract, as if caught in the moment of revelation; the moment before and the moment after, it would just be a cloud. It was made of West African limba, inset with holly and quartz.

There was an Eagle of koa wood, whose wings were raised,

poised, about to drive downward. Its face was all fierce beauty, with flashing aquamarine eyes, and its claws were primed to strike.

Finally, there was an Ox, a rugged beast of red oak and black diamond. His head was lowered, his horns out front, maybe preparing a charge, maybe chewing his cud. Yet there was no denying his innate power.

Quince laid the three on the floor, and despite their size he was gentle. These talismans had been created at a conclave of wizards in Fez, in the year 1200. Along with the Book of Tarot, they were symbols of the sum of the wizards' knowledge, designed to last while wizards themselves lived and died. Somewhere along the way, the Necklace had acquired the three carvings, but now they belonged to Belia'al.

Excellent work, my adorèd one.

"Thank you for allowing me to take the lead, Master."

This is your realm, both of reality and unreality. The distinctions you make are foreign to me, so best if you make them.

"But you were with me every minute. I rely on you."

I shall protect you if you need it. You are one of mine. But you are the master of your magick and should not need me.

"I always need you, Master."

I dare say. And the alarms you gave them will have alerted them by now?

"It happened the moment I took them."

In a perfect world, I'd have preferred to keep this our secret, because these carvings are of great power. But this world is nowise perfect, and our control of the Necklace overrides that preference.

"We'll have the talismans in the end."

If Richard Hanrahan does his job.

"I have no doubts on that score. Do you?"

I have no doubts about what I control. Once again, it seemed wiser not to consume the old man, but now the human element comes into play.

"He'll be fine. The alarms have gone off, Breckenridge is focused on the theft and the coup on Friday, Hanrahan will be seeing him often in these next hours. The Gemstone will be completely blindsided tomorrow morning."

Then Hanrahan will be blindsided tomorrow evening, and we shall rule the world!

WEDNESDAY, MARCH 23, 2011 · 10:11 A.M. EASTERN DAYLIGHT TIME

2 Nipple (Encountering Reality)

Max held a ratty scrub brush in one hand and watched Franny and Ruth in the courtyard, through a window. His gaze was level and focused, his body unmoving. The two women entered the fourth brick building across the way, a building just like all the others, but Max knew it was nothing like the others.

He took his brush and walked out of his building toward the fourth building across the way. *The toilets over there look disgusting,* he thought. *Got to go in.* But when he reached the door they'd used, he found it locked. Under these circumstances, he moved his hand in a defined sweep and rendered himself invisible, gave it thirty seconds to see if there was any reaction—then set to work on the lock with his decades of skill.

WEDNESDAY, MARCH 23, 2011 · 10:16 A.M. EASTERN DAYLIGHT TIME

2 Nipple (Encountering Reality)

Franny made certain the inner door to the crypt was locked tight behind them, then she and Ruth took the elevator down to the Fortress. Back in Johannes Rupp's day, this had been a miner's platform on ropes and pulleys, but then again, it hadn't gone so deep. Over the succeeding decades, each owner of the Rupp Works had modernized the setup, while extending the underground vault. Indiana limestone made good caves.

They reached bottom in less than a minute and a half. Ruth kept her pistol at the ready, though it seemed unlikely they'd meet a flesh-and-blood intruder down there. Franny's hip device led them directly to the disturbance, through the rows of platforms and shelves. Wherever possible, the treasures of the Fortress were on display; there was little value in having a treasure if it was shut up inside a box. The platform they came to showed an open space among the remaining artifacts. There were no marks in dust because there was no dust; the technology in Franny's Fortress kept the archives pristine. Franny bent and read the plaque below the spot.

> **Three Talismans, from a Set of Four**
> **Ox, Angel, Eagle**
> **Carved 1200**
> **by Octavius Morgenus, Fez, Morocco**
> **Obtained 1988**

Ruth said, "Talismans, huh? Like the elder doorway?"

"Not our department," answered Franny, punching a call to Dick Hanrahan.

But it is mine, thought Aleksandra, invisibly watching.

WEDNESDAY, MARCH 23, 2011 · 10:30 A.M. EASTERN DAYLIGHT TIME

2 Nipple (Encountering Reality)

The next moment, Aleksandra appeared to Lawrence Breckenridge— and only to Lawrence Breckenridge. He had to excuse himself from the president again, and this time he indicated that he might be a while.

I bring bad news, she told the Gemstone.

"Let's have it."

The thief was Peter Quince.

"You're certain?"

Of course. I know his energy after his months in the Necklace.

"Hanrahan said it was better magick than Quince's."

Quince has evidently been disguising his true power—and he undoubtedly thinks he still is. No one but I could sense his involvement.

"So he thinks he's gotten away with it."

There's more. He took three talismans which I gave to your predecessor, Tom Jeckyl, for safekeeping. They are extremely powerful.

"What are they?"

There were originally four talismans, objects of power in the four elements. The Lion, ruler of fire, fell to Max August, and he has it hidden somewhere, feeding him its power. I had the other three, the Angel, the Eagle, and the Ox—air, water, earth.

"What can Quince do with them?"

He can bend air, water, and earth to his will.

"Is he stronger than you?"

No. I captured the three when I was still human. And that is the beauty of this situation, Renzo: he doesn't know about me. He stole those talismans and figured, correctly, that Max would be blamed.

"Do I need you to kill him?"

Not necessarily. But killing him will be my pleasure—once I learn what he has in mind.

"You're leaving him alive—with the talismans?"

Since I went to Tom Jeckyl in 1988, the Necklace wizard has never turned against us. I've always considered it a possibility, since they combine a lust for power with powerful skills, but Quince is the first to attempt it. I want to see why.

"What if—?"

Silence, Renzo. This is my decision.

"But evidently, you don't want to hear another opinion."

Evidently. This sort of thing is above your station. The magick man is mine.

"Well, what about Max? This is the first I've heard of his having the Fire talisman."

And you see, it has made no difference to you. It's just a power source for him, like a battery. It's part of his power, and you know his power without needing to know how he came by it.

"But couldn't we have tried to steal his talisman?"

We could have, if we had known where it is. But he's hidden it well, probably in the subconscious.

"What does that mean?"

It means that the collective subconscious is a realm underlying this one—the realm of dream, of fantasy, but still "real." Each individual connects to it individually, so even though you all draw from the same source, each of you sees it differently. If there are seven billion of you on Earth now, it appears in seven billion ways. That's why even I can't find something Max has hidden.

"Well, there are techniques to affect the subconscious. Drugs. It's not impenetrable."

No. In fact, your Black Helicopter crews penetrate it every time they pass through the elder doorway. But each one sees it differently.

"So we can't get Max's Lion. And what if Quince hides the Angel, Eagle, and Ox in his little corner of the universe?"

He won't do that before he uses them, will he? And I am fully prepared for that. Remember, they used to be mine. You just treat him as if you know nothing.

"If I know nothing I'm still in the midst of a crisis, and we've got Friday coming up fast. Since it was Quince who gave us the elder doorway, he could be planning something involving that."

He probably is. But if you had continued to think Max was responsible, that wouldn't have changed how you proceeded. So proceed, and we shall see what we shall see.

2 Nipple (Encountering Reality)

Max opened the door to the building Franny and Ruth had entered, and no alarms went off. He had seen this same collection of electronic and magickal sensors at the Dailey Company on Monday and had taken the time to determine the best way of negating them. He was invisible, he was inside, and he was feeling pretty good about himself until he came to the elevator door. There he found magick he had not seen before and could not circumvent on the fly.

I can get through it, sure, but not without triggering it. This has gotta be the magick that alerted me in the first place. And alerted Franny. If I go, any farther, and this seal gets broken twice, she'll never rest until she finds out why, and there's no way the Friday mission goes off as scheduled. He considered it, backwards and forwards. Finally he backed away. *Not worth it.*

He'd have to find some other way.

2 Nipple (Encountering Reality)

Hanrahan called Breckenridge. "Franny reports three talismans missing: an Eagle, an Ox, and an Angel. I checked the records: we got them in 1988, and August has the other one so it must be he who took these."

"Until we know for certain," the Gemstone answered judiciously, "come to New York. If Max *is* involved, I want to be right on top of everything as we head for Friday night."

"Sure, Renzo. Good idea." *If you hadn't suggested it, I would have. But I knew you would.*

2 Nipple (Encountering Reality)

Max was lingering near the building, prepared to stumble upon Franny and Ruth's return and ask some casual questions about their hurry. But he needn't have bothered. When they reappeared, Franny called to him first.

"Aparicio. You're off my shit list, at least for now. We need all hands on deck."

"Yes, Chief," he replied, accepting this turn of events like any soldier. "What's up?"

"We're locking down this facility and setting up a perimeter sweep. Go put that damn brush away and fall in inside ten minutes."

"Yes, Chief. And thank you, Chief."

"Before this is over, you may wish you only had to deal with latrines."

He went to do as he was ordered, and the two women continued toward Franny's office. "What was that about?" Ruth asked.

"Nothin'," said Franny. "My business."

"He's *my* trooper," said Ruth.

"Forget it."

"We're at T minus Two, Franny. Your sex life is not the most important concern here."

"Maybe not, but you don't need him until the mission tomorrow."

"We don't know that, now."

"Then wait until we do."

Entering the office, they found Di waiting impatiently. "Well?" she demanded.

"Three talismans," Franny responded, drawing it out a little.

"Pretty powerful, Hanrahan says. They were put in the Fortress during my dad's time, so I'm not familiar with 'em."

"Max August," Ruth added.

"Max August," Di repeated with sincere interest. "How do you know?"

"It's either him or someone like him."

"Doesn't sound like his m.o.," said Di. "He always strikes when everything's in play, and that's not till Friday."

"Are you an expert?" Ruth demanded.

"No," Di admitted. "I'm just saying—"

"Well, don't. You tell stories about what we do, but we do it. I suppose this makes you even more inclined to stay."

"Of course."

"Well, it's probably horse out of the barn stuff, but we're going to orange alert. Oh, and Peter Quince is coming to investigate."

WEDNESDAY, MARCH 23, 2011 · 3:50 P.M. CENTRAL EUROPEAN TIME

Z Nipple (Encountering Reality)

Pam!

What is it, Max?

There's something going on here, involving the talismans from Fez.

Your Lion?

No, the other three.

Does it affect what I'm doing?

Probably not, but I don't know for sure yet. Stay alert, and I'll update you as we go. Where are you?

On my way to Castello Janus, to scout the lay of the land.

Okay. Love you.

Love you, too.

Pam let her end of the *call* drift away and turned her full attention to her driving. She wondered if driving while *calling* should be an offense, and decided it shouldn't because *calling* worked behind the scenes and had no effect on the scene itself. The scene itself included a winding road along the cliffs of a mountain and increasingly beautiful Italian scenery below, glowing in the first sunny day she'd seen for a while, and she was fully engaged with it.

Even so, she envisioned various scenarios with three talismans in them, having one effect or another. As far as she knew, the complete group of four represented the four cardinal elements, fire, air, earth, and water. With sufficient magick, you could channel those raw forces through them, for use in this world. It seemed highly unlikely that they were connected to old French bones. Their purposes were totally different. But she considered what she'd do if the talismans showed up, so she couldn't wish later that she had.

And still she drove the mountain road with just one hand on the wheel.

WEDNESDAY, MARCH 23, 2011 · 10:53 A.M. EASTERN DAYLIGHT TIME

2 Nipple (Encountering Reality)

Max came to attention alongside his twenty-nine mates in the central courtyard of the Rupp Works. Ruth and Franny stood across from them, with Di in the background. Ruth spoke plenty loud enough for all to hear.

"Effective immediately, this compound is under lockdown. All entrances and exits will be guarded, and the perimeter will be patrolled." She let a subtle murmur work its way through the group, so that when she continued she would not have to stop. "There is magick involved so make sure you've got your wristbands on. Now, I want volunteers for perimeter duty."

Before her, half a dozen arms shot up. Dennis Aparicio's arm was most decidedly not among them. "Perimeter duty" was another name for "point man," and he'd be damned if he volunteered for Max August's favorite sport. He was never that obvious.

But that decision was taken out of his hands. Franny pointed at him. "Aparicio. I told you you'd long for the latrines. You're goin' out. The rest of you will rotate, four hours on, eight hours off. But you, Aparicio: you'll do four on, four off, till I say different."

. . . . .

Di looked on with pleasant, unassuming interest and thought, *You fucking idiots! He likes being a point man. Don't you see it?* But she knew that they did not. And since she'd thrown in her lot with him, that was a comforting thought.

WEDNESDAY, MARCH 23, 2011 · 2:55 P.M. GREENWICH MEAN TIME

2 Nipple (Encountering Reality)

It took Vee until the middle of the afternoon to feel that she'd mastered Agrippa's vampire spell. Like a new song, she first had to learn the words, and only then let herself flow into the meanings and the rhythms. There was a special trick to his spells, which she had learned by osmosis or blind luck or careful instruction sometime in the past. She could read the spells the way she'd read anything, left to right across the page, but when she let herself inside the spells, they had internal rhythms that only then revealed themselves. It was as if she was reading the words from top to bottom, catching relationships extant only in the calligraphy, even if she was chanting the spells without looking at the words at all. So she worked any spell thoroughly, until she could find no more within it. And later on, she went back to find hooks she'd missed the first time. She always found something more.

But by three, she had wrung the new spell as dry as she'd be able to without a break, so she brewed herself a cup of tea and found some Danish cheese for a sandwich. She sat at her kitchen table and realized she was starving.

Just as she finished eating, her doorbell rang. She went to the door, again checking the various alarms. Satisfied, she crooked her fingers to make a certain sign and waved her hand at the circle on the floor. The circle and the altar within it vanished, replaced by the image of a chair draped in a sheet and a half-painted wall beside the bamboo screen. A lank strip of tape appeared to run from wall to wall, to indicate "no entry." She opened the door and there was Matthew Raftery.

"Is this a good time?" he asked, looking at her bandages.

The obvious answer was no. ". . . Sure," she said, stepping back to allow him entrance. He came inside, looking around with interest as she led him past the tape into the rear of the flat. It was only eight feet wide back there, with a kitchenette fitting into the remainder of the space. Her bedroom lay beyond that, but it was hidden by a second bamboo screen. "You'll have to sit at the table," she said, clearing away her own dishes. "Tea?"

"I'd love a cup," he said. As she filled the electric kettle, he went on: "We didn't set a time for today, but I thought mid-afternoon . . ."

"That's considerate, Matthew, but I've actually been up since dawn."

"That's what it looks like."

"Pardon?"

"I can see that you look nackered."

"Yeah. Well. Darjeeling?"

"Excellent." He let her get started, then asked casually, "What's with the bandages?"

"I fought a corgi and lost. Big whoop."

"I love your seventies slang, Vee. And your American accent. It gives you a clear identity—one of the things I'd like to build on—"

"No. No management, Matthew. You're here to amaze me."

"I said I'd see if I could. And my management's amazing—"

She held up her hand. "No. If that's what this is about, you might as well go."

He held up his own hands in surrender. "All right," he agreed, smiling. "Only my amazing astrology."

She poured him his tea and brought it to the table. He put it aside to cool, and took a folded sheet of paper from his inside pocket. He unfolded it and laid it between them, so both could see it easily.

"To start with, you have a very interesting chart, Miss Vee. All the planets are below the horizon, and they're clumped in three groups. It means that your main focus is yourself, and your origins. Probably a Welsh nationalist, yeah?"

Well, all anyone can do is extrapolate, she thought. "Not really," she said.

"No? Then it's your own origins. Some mystery with your family, perhaps." She said nothing. "Well, you've got a lot of power, right at the bottom, in Scorpio. Sun, Mars, Mercury, and Pluto, all in Scorpio, with Pluto precisely on the bottom cusp. You are a very deep person, Vee. Your life is much more profound, and dark, than you let outsiders see."

"That's what the critics say, anyway."

"No, it's true; I see it. But it's like the darkness of Eddie's Club—only bigger. Like the stage at the O2. And you're the star of it, for certain. The second clump is Leo rising and a Leo moon, with a Virgo Jupiter very nearby. Leo is ruled by the Sun, so you're a natural-born performer, love that spotlight, right there at the center of that darkness . . . except that the moon waxes and wanes, so your love of the spotlight does, too. Your commitment to your music fades sometimes, *even though* you love your music. It's that Mercury down at the bottom, ruling its own house: you're trying to do two things at once. I'd say you're living two lives but I don't think that's true. The Mercury is moving away from the clump. It's like you used to live another life but put a stop to it, so now you only think of yourself."

He's pretty good, she thought, but said, "Only of myself."

"I'm showing you I can read, and that I'll tell you the truth whether you like it or not."

"All right." She smiled.

"Now, your planets, I said, are in three clumps—but the strongest clump is the one at the bottom. It's a core, very deep and dark, and very, very strong.

"So then there's that third group. Uranus and Neptune conjunct in the fifth house, which is also ruled by the Sun. The Uranus-Neptune conjunction marries awareness and the beyond; it's why you can so completely inhabit your emotions when you sing.

"And then, finally, there's Saturn, the manager, close to the third clump. Saturn's just moved into Aquarius, so anyone who manages you has to be on the cutting edge.

"You're tough, Vee, and you could go all the way to the top. But you don't think about going to the top because all your power thus far has been in yourself, at the bottom. There have got to have been times when that was tough. But what I'm here to tell you is, there is a top. I know how to take you there, so it won't matter that you haven't really considered it. You've been content to sing or not sing, outside your two nights a week at Eddie's. If that's where you want to stay, send me packing again. But even though the rising and moon feed into your deep, dark self, they're still Leo, still bright—and Jupiter, success, is right close by, but in a different sign. You know success is close, but somehow it seems to be in a different postal code. And with no dreams of stardom, that seems like the way it should be. But it's right there. You could reach out and touch it, reach out and take it. If you had me to use insight like this, to get you there."

"Wow," she said, and meant it. "First, no. No managing. But that was good. I mean it. I know a little something about astrology and that was good. But still . . ."

"No manager. Well, you may change your mind." He was good at rolling with the punches. She had to say, she liked that about him.

"More tea?"

Z Nipple (Encountering Reality)

Pam pulled her rent-a-car to a halt in the wide parking lot below Castello Janus, facing outward in case she needed to make a quick getaway. She was atop a high and narrow hill, seventy-eight kilometers outside Rome. A few birds were singing in the Mediterranean warmth below.

Crossing the crushed rock, she paid her admission to the ancient structure. The girl in the booth seemed to be a bored teenager. There were only a handful of other visitors; it was too early for a massive tourist influx. Pam stood just inside the entryway and raised her left hand to the level of her eyes, then wiped it across the scene from left to right exactly as if she were cleaning a window. The tourists in the room were all revealed to have no hidden side.

But not the old woman with the high forehead by the glass case containing a bone the color of old ivory. She seemed to be the docent, but she was actually the guardian.

Pam made her way around the room, admiring, generally truthfully, the objets d'art there—and making sure the old woman did not approach her unawares. At one point, the old woman *did* approach her, to inquire if she had any questions. Pam did not read any menace in her, any more than a watchdog would menace someone it did not find a threat, and Pam discussed the bone with her.

"It is said that witches stole the bones of their enemy, the French king, and used this bone as a wand in their midnight rites. You may know that witchcraft originated in Italy, so over the centuries the bone made its way to Rome. In 1492, Cardinale Janus, a high member of the Vatican staff, established a collection of such things and built Castello Janus to house it. After the cardinale's murder in 1530, by Cornelius Agrippa, the collection became scattered. The bone is all that remains in our hands."

"Cardinale Janus," Pam said. "Where was he from? 'Janus' is certainly not an Italian name."

"Actually, that's a common misconception," the old woman said. "Janus was a Roman god, the god of doorways. He was said to have two faces, one facing inward, one facing out. The cardinale was born Giuseppe Nero—no relation to the infamous emperor, as far as can be determined—and he took the name when he was elevated."

"Isn't it odd to take the name of a Roman god when you serve the Catholic church?"

"The Catholic church is the church of Rome," the old woman said with a small smile. Pam noticed that no matter what expression crossed her face, the woman's forehead never wrinkled. *Botox?* thought Pam, wondering as she so often did now at the infinite variety of human vanity.

If the old woman had not been imbued with magickal power, Pam would have tried to magick the bone herself right then. But since that wasn't possible, she used the remainder of her time learning the layout of the room and the rooms around it. For when she came back at midnight, for the rite of theft.

— 0 —

Aleksandra had no need for flesh in the forest around the house of Peter Quince. Since snowflakes were blanketing the bare branches, she wouldn't have wanted it anyway. She came as a red glowing light, hovering among the ancient trees. From her vantage point as a diabola, she could soon see the other lights here—the forest ghosts. There were a lot of them for a space this size: three native men, a white man and a white woman, a black man. They came to her through the forest that burned with the phantom fires of long ago.

I am Aleksandra, she said, and offered herself for inspection. They could see her only as a ball of fire, but they could sense her intentions. And as was generally the case since she'd become a diabola, Alexandra had nothing to hide. Her intentions were extremely clear.

One of the natives nodded judiciously. "I am Yellow Beaver." He paused briefly, knowing this being before him would not need more than that to read him. "What has Peter Quince done?"

He stole three powerful talismans from me.

"I'm not a bit surprised," said the old white woman. "Goodwife Brandwynne—English witch, my lady."

"Emanuel Woodhouse," said the black man. "What sort of talismans?"

Carved wooden figures—an Angel, an Eagle, and an Ox.

"Three of the four animals in the revelations of Saint John!" said the white man excitedly. Then, with a clear note of pride: "Arthur Raymond Roudebach, spiritualist." Then: "Where is the Lion?"

Not part of this set.

The oldest of the natives spoke. His tones were birdlike cheeps and trills, from a time when birds were everywhere, but Alexandra heard his intent clearly.

No, my talismans are not the ones in his faith, but they have the same meanings.

"What do they mean to Quince?" asked Yellow Beaver.

Power.

The shaman squinted up his eyes. "He needs more power?"

Aleksandra felt the bafflement.

Tell me of the power he has already, then.

"He is possessed."

Aleksandra pulsed.

Possessed.

"Yes."

By what?

"Something not of this Earth," said Roudebach, his eyes alight. "That's clear to all of us, but Quince has never spoken a name. And I must add, dear lady, that if your animals match those in the gospel of Saint John, that proves the truth of my so-called 'faith.'"

Aleksandra pulsed. The trouble with ghosts was, they never moved on.

What do you mean, exactly? "Something not of this Earth"?

The ancient one chirrupped: (We all live in the forest because we are of the Earth. We know the Earth. This was different.)

But different how?

Goodwife Brandwynne said, "It was very pleased with itself."

Woodhouse said, "It was like a wave of power. Once, I nearly drowned in the Cloquet River. I was being carried and tumbled and pushed every which way. That was what I felt in him at the end."

When did this happen?

"Nearly two years ago."

"Quince was helpless against it," said the witch. "It terrified him. He wanted to fight it but couldn't even begin."

"It was a bad, bad thing," said Woodhouse.

But you told no one. . . .

Yellow Beaver said stoutly, "We go nowhere and speak with no one who does not come to us. Had you come sooner, you would have known sooner."

Agreed. But because you told no one, no one told me. She moved her focus to the third native man, who so far had said nothing. *What can you add to this?*

But the man simply looked at her. There was intelligence in his eyes but his face was implacable.

"Three Wing never speaks," said Yellow Beaver. "But he knows no more than we."

Give me your hand, Aleksandra said to him. He touched her with his mind again, then extended his hand and plunged it into the glowing red light.

In the future, if you learn something useful to me, you must reach out to me. I will be grateful.

The old man trilled: (I shall see that he does, goddess.)

2 Nipple (Encountering Reality)

Peter Quince's private jet touched down in Fort Wayne some time after noon. He was met by a different man from the one who'd met Di the day before, escorted along a different route to the Rupp Works. Basic security. Quince couldn't help but laugh inside. What good did this shit do against someone like him? And now he was going to investigate his own crime.

Heh heh heh.

At the Works, he met with Franny, Ruth, and Di. The first two accepted him as their compatriot, and they got along well enough. Sometimes Belia'al was put off by the Hoosier's limited tolerance for magick, but he found Ruth a congenial spirit. The one who confused him was Di. She definitely kept her distance. He knew he wasn't completely stable anymore, not the way most humans at least pretend to be, but the others accepted it. Di didn't. She kept an eye on him at all times. Because he wasn't completely stable, he could never tell if it was fear or fascination. Either way, he did not care, because she was not Latina.

Di, for her part, was as sincere as she knew how to be with him, but she could tell he knew she was pretending. Very few people could read the real her, but then, he wasn't "people" any longer.

Ruth caught the tension between them. Franny did not.

"I came as soon as Hanrahan contacted me," Quince told them, lighting a cigarette. "I had something very time-critical going on this morning, so I'll have to start over on that, but when you all need a magick man you really need him. Now, did anyone actually see Max August?"

"No," answered Ruth, and Franny added, "We don't know who it was."

"We can make a pretty shrewd guess," said Quince.

"So why do we even need you, if the answer is already known?" asked Di.

"Who knows? I may uncover evidence pointing elsewhere," said Quince with a supercilious smirk. "In any event, no mystical break-in can be deemed completely investigated until a mystical man has seen to it."

"Breckenridge authorizes your entry into the Fortress," Franny said, "so we might's well get on with it."

"You're welcome to join me, if you maintain strict silence and make no effort to impede my actions," Quince said. "Otherwise, I'd prefer to be alone."

Di was caught on the horns of a dilemma. She did not like to be near Quince, let alone by herself in a secure vault—but she wanted to see the vault. "I'll stay quiet," she said.

"Sorry, honey," Franny answered, not sorry at all. "The big man didn't authorize you."

WEDNESDAY, MARCH 23, 2011 · 12:57 P.M. EASTERN DAYLIGHT TIME

2 Nipple (Encountering Reality)

Max patrolled a quarter-mile stretch of dirt road along the river's edge north of the Rupp Works. Royal had the other three blocks up there, and other groups of two covered the east, west, and south. They were dressed as civilians, but packing beneath the coats. The railroad had cut the area in half a hundred fifty years ago, so that north of the Works was nothing but open fields and the Maumee River; Max could look back and see other men positioned in the windows of the brick buildings behind him. Above them all hung heavy clouds. It would probably snow again tonight.

When Max had first taken on the identity of Dennis Aparicio, he had intended nothing more than espionage. Then, when he'd rediscovered the rhythms of the army, he'd counted it as a bonus. Now he was walking the paths of Fort Wayne, Indiana—not the trails of Vu Quang, Vietnam, but back on point just the same. Life was funny that way.

If there was one thing he'd learned in his years A.N. (after 'Nam), it was that he liked the cowboy life. He'd meant to live a life of roaming since he'd first discovered it. It was why he went into radio: jocks always moved. But he'd been good at it and so he'd been asked to stay, and he played that game the same way he played the war: big. He shmoozed the suits and got to jock in a window in San Francisco. He had a life, a post-war life. A normal life. And then came Aleksandra—and Val and Corny. Then he found the dark war, and the normal life seemed unsatisfying, when he could again go big.

But here he was: the point man.

2 Nipple (Encountering Reality)

Franny descended into the Fortress with Quince, after making him extinguish his cigarette. A sealed vault needed no second-hand smoke. Once she had him settled, she planned to leave him to his own devices. But he grew progressively less settled as they went, grinning at first, then chuckling, finally letting out a loud bark of a laugh.

"What's so funny?" she asked.

"I've imagined this place so many times since I learned of it," he told her. "Now I see where I was right and where I was wrong." But in fact, he was chuckling over the view of it through eyes in a body. In the mist, everything had seemed so shiny; in reality, it was unutterably drab. In thrall to a demon, almost everything on Earth was drab to him.

2 Nipple (Encountering Reality)

Little more than an hour later, Quince ascended once more to the outside world and delivered his verdict: "Max August, without a doubt."

"How can you be so certain?" Di asked. "What did you find?"

"A series of small indications," the wizard replied, with just a hint of condescension. "I would try to explain them but people who aren't into magick have a hard time comprehending such explanations. I'll just say that the only one of the Code Reds the Necklace knows who could be responsible for them all was Max."

"Was Blackwell with him?" Ruth asked.

"No. Though she continues to progress, she's not good enough for something like that yet."

"You're sure?"

"I'm sure."

"Well, that's it, then. I'll call Hanrahan."

"And I'll return to Duluth."

Di was disgusted. But unlike Quince, she took her pleasure in *not* revealing her true feelings.

2 Nipple (Encountering Reality)

The intelligence bunker in the subbasement of Lawrence Breckenridge's townhouse was used once or twice a year, whenever Breckenridge and Hanrahan needed not just instant communication but also instant consultation on some pressing issue. Though he never said anything about it, Hanrahan didn't like it because it wasn't entirely under his control. The room was his, but everything around it was the Gemstone's. Today, however, that bug was finally a feature.

Once he'd been driven from LaGuardia, the old man ran a thorough check to make certain the bunker's security was unbroken, and then took the elevator up to Breckenridge's room on the second floor to make his first report. "Quince says it was definitely Max August."

Breckenridge, at his desk, looked up mildly. "I'd like to hear his reasoning, Dick."

"Why? You don't believe it?"

"Oh, I believe it. But of all the facets in the Necklace, wizardry is the one I understand least. So I'd like to have him explain his reasoning." He reached out and punched Quince's button on Channel Nine. Soon enough the wizard appeared on-screen, standing beside a limo at the Rupp Works. His face was flushed but he answered Breckenridge's questions readily enough.

"There are certain mystical energies which only high-level wizards can use. I found traces of them, which limits the possibilities to five people we know of. August is one of them—"

"What about Blackwell?"

"Blackwell?" Quince smiled very faintly. "No, sir, Blackwell is not at that level. But as I was going to say, having narrowed the suspects to five, I studied the, shall we say, *signature* of the usage. Of course, I confronted August, and Blackwell, two years ago, and his signature is very clear to me. Everything about the infiltration was consistent with that."

"That still—"

"Doesn't prove it, I know," said Quince. Standing behind Breckenridge, looking over his shoulder, Hanrahan winced. *Don't interrupt him, you idiot!* But Quince kept right on: "I asked myself if someone else could be *impersonating* him, and ran tests for the other suspects, seeing if I could find any trace of one in the mix. I couldn't, so that made it a virtual certainty. And then I reached out for the items that were stolen, and though I'm sorry to say that I couldn't find them, I found a space where their power and August's coincided. That, to me, is conclusive. Sir."

Breckenridge seemed to consider that monologue, but in truth, he was simply watching this man lie to his face. After a moment, he said, "Very impressive, Peter. Thank you."

"Any time, sir."

Breckenridge ended the call, and turned his chair to face Hanrahan. The old man asked, "Any doubts about him, Renzo?"

"No. He seems to have thought of everything."

WEDNESDAY, MARCH 23, 2011 · 2:45 p.m. EASTERN DAYLIGHT TIME

2 Nipple (Encountering Reality)

Peter Quince flew away from Fort Wayne.

"They're all completely fooled, Master!"

What about Lawrence Breckenridge?

"You doubt him?"

I doubt everyone. And there was something about his stillness, his watchfulness. . . .

"He plays the spider, at the center of the Necklace's web. That's all."

What about Diana Herring?

"She's always like that."

Exactly, Peter Quince.

"You miss my point, Master. She doesn't like me, but neither does she offer the slightest threat. She is meaningless to us."

Don't correct me. Belia'al tightened the bond between them until Quince felt that every blood vessel in his body would explode. His face grew red and strangled and the veins throughout his body sprang into sharp relief . . . before the demon relented.

"Sorry," Quince stammered, collapsing to the floor. "Sorry."

She could be valuable. Once I am the Gemstone, I shall assimilate her.

Quince felt a stab of jealousy, literally painful in his still-recovering body. "But why, Master? She's no more magickal than Hanrahan."

Her resistance to magick can be useful to me. Most humans I meet approach me, one way or the other. Most humans are sluts.

"Now you're playing with me."

And why not, pray?

Peter Quince had no answer for that.

So, while you wait for tomorrow's morning, I shall examine our three new toys.

"I'd like to be involved in that, Master. I stole them, after all— on my own."

No, Peter Quince. You must remain here in case they call you again. The talismans are mine.

WEDNESDAY, MARCH 23, 2011 · 8:40 P.M. GREENWICH MEAN TIME

2 Nipple (Encountering Reality)

London was almost halfway though the first Hour of Mercury. The actual time between sunset at 6:18 and sunrise at 5:55 was eleven hours and thirty-seven minutes; divide by twelve and each "Hour" was in fact fifty-eight minutes. So Vee's time ran from 8:14 to 9:12. She could have struck later, at the second Hour of Mercury between 2:58 and 3:56 A.M., but she wanted this over and done with. Plus, in five minutes the moon would move from Scorpio to Sagittarius, and that would lead from danger to success. The question was, for whom?

The sky was a city's night, a gray yellow, the streets dark beneath its streetlights. Vee waited in the shadows off St. Paul's tube station, her silver crucifix unfamiliar around her neck. Durban had ridden to this stop last night, and the bear had been nearby the night before. Durban probably lived in the area, when he wasn't up in Camden Town stealing her power. Well, tonight he couldn't steal it because she wasn't performing, so he would have to strike at someone else. And he probably wouldn't strike at anyone around here because police presence had been enhanced in the area after two nights of attacks. So he would take the tube to somewhere else. Vee knew she was piling assumption on top of assumption, but it was the strongest structure she could devise. If she was wrong she was wrong.

If the cops didn't roust her for hanging around the shadows of St. Paul's for the past three hours. There were a lot of "if's". . . .

But she was doing what she had to do. Working her way back from the hell she'd inhabited was Plan A, and Plan B, and Plan C. Somewhere around Plan D was singing for a living. Matthew'd been right: she liked singing for a living when she did it, but she couldn't commit to it full time any more than she could commit to hovering in midair. It was too bad for pop culture, but Vee had a previous commitment.

And here he came.

Christopher Durban, nicely filled out, came from Old Castle Street, turning east on the Whitechapel High Street. But instead of entering the tube station, he carried on up Whitechapel. Vee followed him, staying among the other pedestrians, never standing out. He'd somehow become aware of her the night before, but she hadn't used all her protective spells then. Now she was using both her spells and her common sense. It might not be enough—maybe as a vampire he had a special feel for her power—but in the end, she was going to take his *chi* tonight.

Just before the Burger King, he stopped abruptly and spun to look back. His wrist was raised just enough to bolster a claim of having forgotten something, but that wasn't what he was doing. He was scanning the street for a tail. But Vee never broke stride, never changed her relationship to the girl in front of her and the two boys behind, all of them continuing their own journeys without regard to the man up the street. His gaze moved across them smoothly, sweeping the entire area, searching and not finding. Vee was certain that he didn't spot her, and exultant that he couldn't sense her.

Christopher gave the slightest satisfied nod and resumed his course.

He turned into the park at Brick Lane, finding a semblance of solitude off the thoroughfare. Vee hung back until he was halfway across the green, then followed, moving marginally more slowly than he. It increased the distance between them—*see, I'm not interested in you, I'm on my own walk*—but when he exited the park, he would be on one of two streets. She wouldn't lose him.

He left and she put it in gear, sprinting easily to the exit. He was not in sight on Alder but that was fine; she ran to the corner and looked down Mulberry, and there he was. She crossed to the other side of Mulberry, then sauntered along behind. There were still people walking here; she and Christopher weren't alone.

Claws clattered on the sidewalk behind her!

She looked back, and saw the fox loping toward her. He *had* known she was here! Looking ahead once more, she saw that he had stopped on the deserted street, and one by one, in the circles of the streetlights, the other animals appeared, watching her. But that just brought everything to a head. She began to run again, diagonally across the street straight toward Christopher, and she began to shout:

"Now O thou vampire, since thou art pernicious and blood-red, in the name and by the power and dignity of the Omnipresent and Immortal Lord God of Hosts Jehovah Tetragrammaton, the only creator of Heaven and Earth and all that is therein, who is the marvellous Disposer of all things both visible and invisible, I do dispose of thee and thine evil to the depths of the Bottomless Abyss, there to remain until the Day of Judgment and beyond!"

Nothing happened!

Now she was close to him, and he was looking right at her. She stared him down and shouted:

"Now O thou vampire—"

"I don't know what you think you're playing at, Vee," Christopher said, "but this has to stop." He raised his left hand, palm pointed past her, and the frantic pursuit behind her came to a clattering halt. Vee looked; the animals were standing ten feet away, their eyes unblinking on her. Across the street, a young couple was gaping at them—then turning their faces, hurrying away. An old man up the street was staring at them, but with a smile, as if this was street theater for his diversion.

Christopher stepped toward her. "They don't need to witness your shame, Vee. You can't cloak yourself in anything that I won't know, because I know your very essence. You can't follow me, let alone ambush me. You can't run away from me because I will find you. The only reason you're still alive is because I want it so."

"A vampire," Vee said, keeping her gaze on his. Surely that was right.

"A *psychic* vampire. I don't drink blood, I drink power. And yours is a very special kind. There's a purity in you, as if all the years that grind us into who we are hadn't touched you. It's a very clean sort of energy, like ambrosia."

"I like it," Vee said.

"I'll bet you do. But we're straying from the point, and we can't stand here all night. One more situation like this and your free-range life will end. I can't have these continuing contretemps."

"I will not be managed!" Vee gritted.

"Yes, you will, Vee."

"I will not be managed!" Vee started toward him, she knew she could take him, but she heard the claws again.

He smiled. "My animals protect me."

She spun, pulling her pistol and putting a bullet through the closest wolf's head.

Polyurethane flew. The wolf seemed not to notice, its eyes still on her, unblinking.

"Not real?" she asked Christopher softly, her eyes on the wolf.

"No, they're real. Merely dead, and stuffed."

She turned. "You give them life? You take mine and feed it to them?"

"I am a conduit," Christopher said, laughing.

"Conduct this, then," Vee said, and fired point-blank at his chest.

Polyurethane flew.

"Oh my God," she said.

"We're all puppets, Vee. Just like you."

She emptied her pistol, and still the pack swept over her. Durban was on top.

— 0 —

Aleksandra hovered in the void, looking out across the universe. She was absolutely still, as she filled the starry black space around her with her thoughts.

Quince is possessed. But by whom?

His duties as the wizard link in the Necklace give him plenty of room to explore.

Was he possessed when Renzo recruited him? No. I looked at him then. So later, in his explorations. He went farther than he was prepared to go.

According to the spirit woods, it happened at the time he stole the bomb and fought Max. Max would have known if Quince were possessed then, but he would love nothing better than to leave Quince in the belly of the beast. Perhaps Quince's choice of theft as a device should have been a warning.

What do I know of that event? Only what Renzo told me. Quince took the bomb from Yucca Mountain and put it in the heart of Wickr, to draw Max. They fought and Quince lost, but survived. A credible debut for any wizard. But of course, all we know is what Quince told us. It fit the facts Hanrahan could corroborate, but the space between facts is infinite. I cannot quite credit even the most

*headstrong or vainglorious wizard—which Quince may well be—
with attacking Max as his first official act. M<small>AX</small> attacked <small>ME</small>, but
Quince is not Max.*

*What happened in the interim? Renzo and Hanrahan grilled him
on his ideas. One was to make his own power <small>STONE</small>.*

Aleksandra pulsed. Her scarlet light flared briefly, stray tendrils
of flame escaping into the starscape.

He made the <small>STONE</small> and went too far.

*The place to <small>WITNESS</small> the truth is his sanctum—but I can't go there
without alerting him, and his possessor.*

But I know where I <small>CAN</small> go.

WEDNESDAY, MARCH 23, 2011 · 2:23 p.m. PACIFIC DAYLIGHT TIME

Z Nipple (Encountering Reality)

Madeleine Riggs, the redheaded young hotshot, crunched upon the
empty plain before the chocolate-brown mountains. The snow was
heavy on the peaks and a chill wind blew hard down the hills,
strewing bits of dust in her eyes. That was the good part. The bad
part was the wearing of the flesh. The weight of it, the limitation.
The longer she was a diabola, the less she liked fitting back inside,
even if she could have sex with Renzo. Being a diabola was better
than sex.

But when she had to, she did. And she could dress the flesh
however she wanted, so Madeleine was wearing a red North Face
Flash jacket that flattered her hair and white Salomon Snowtrip
pants. She looked damned good, even if there was no one to see it.
If she had to be human, she might as well please herself.

It was hard to believe that three months from now, this sweeping emptiness would be a living, breathing city, with defined streets
and shapes against the sky and fifty thousand people, all wearing
flesh. There would be light and noise and fifty thousand adventures: Wickr. Then, as if by magick, it would be empty again.

Madeleine had never been to Wickr, so she didn't know the layout, but she knew magick and she felt it at the base of the mountains. She strode across a plain that had hardened after brief winter rains had turned the dust to mud, each step a satisfying *scrunch*, and the closer she got the stronger she felt what had once been here.

BELIA'AL!

2 Nipple (Encountering Reality)

Aleksandra appeared before Lawrence Breckenridge, her perfect figure draped in red.

Stop!

Breckenridge was running through his plans for the murder of Peter Quince. He stood up and came around his desk to her. "What is it, diabola?"

Quince is not acting alone. He is possessed by Belia'al.

"Who—"

Belia'al is a demon, one of the four crown princes of Hell, second only to Lucifer.

"You know this creature?"

I read of him and his brethren in the long cold nights of Academgorodok. We have never met, but now we shall.

"How powerful is he?"

Less powerful than I, but you know that can mean little in the moment.

"What!?"

Exactly. So what I need from you is everything related to Belia'al on this planet that the Necklace can find—every spell book, every talisman, and the moment-by-moment whereabouts of every acolyte he has. I need you to start now and I need you to keep it a secret from the other links, not just Quince.

"Do you suspect others—?"

No, but I haven't looked at them. I will do that and let you know when I am satisfied one way or the other.

"It'll be difficult. Dick will notice soon enough. Ruth may hear if I put her troops outside Fort Wayne to work. And if it involves magick, Quince may notice."

It's worse than that, Renzo. Each human who succumbs to Belia'al becomes PART *of the demon. Their individual existence bleeds into the dark mass which is his true form. So if your people alert any owner of one of these objects, Belia'al will know. The goal, then, is to retrieve the objects without letting the owners know. That can't go on forever, but I need as much knowledge of the demon as possible, before he learns of it.*

Breckenridge had never seen this in her before, this lack of omniscience.

"I will make it so, Aleksandra," he told her, reassuringly. "But are you saying . . . Belia'al doesn't know about *you* yet?"

Yes! No one but you knows of me, so there was no way for him to learn.

"Excellent! That's excellent! He'll get the surprise of his, whatever, when he makes his move." But then the ramifications began to become clearer to him. "What can a crown prince of Hell do with *your* three talismans when he makes that move?"

A lot. I create multitudes, but he is multitudes.

"And when will he attack you?"

That's one thing I hope to learn.

Breckenridge picked up the phone.

❀ ✦ ❀ ✦

Belia'al descended into the talismanic world.

It was not a place he knew well. Every one of his humans knew it to one extent or another, calling it the subconscious, but a demon has no subconscious. He could reach the humans, and through them Earth, and that's as far as he could go. However, talismans served as magickal conduits between Earth and the subconscious, and demons could utilize *them*.

It was pure logic, and pure logic was demon power. Demon realms ran by logical rules, which the demon decreed. Their rule was absolute because they made the rules. But on Earth, they had to overcome Earth rules. That was why they sought to inveigle humans to bring them to Earth: they liked to overcome. No, they liked to *crush*. Without Earth, there was no matter to *crush*.

Belia'al used the power of the three talismans his slave Quince stole for him, to lower himself into the subconscious. He had been here before, through other talismans, in the long years of his existence, but even so, were he given to fear, he would fear this. Logic was unraveling around him, as he watched. Yet he was king of the demons, and had long since made the rule that he feared nothing.

The strands stretched out around him, appearing like trees growing from above, like ribbons waving in a wind. He couldn't apply logic to them, but he could regain familiarity. The subconscious began making sense to him, as his logic crushed its infinite possibilities to something manageable.

In time, in space, he settled onto a wide field of tall grain, bounded on two sides by steep and rocky mountains, all beneath a hazy orange sun. But even as he felt his feet touch the ground, clouds scattered quickly over the sun and the world grew dark and cold. He smiled.

Peter Quince could have stolen anything from the Necklace. All the plan needed from the Fortress was the alarm. But these are talismans of the first rank, as am I.

He began to stride toward the point where the mountains met. The grain he trampled died at his touch, and the death spread outward, so that as he crossed the field he left a widening V of extinction behind him.

2 Nipple (Encountering Reality)

When Aparicio went back for his second walk on the north side, he was given a new partner and a soft mist of snow. Royal and the other men had two shifts off while he had one, so the partners cycled. Thus, it was Royal who brought him dinner from the Works' mess hall, out along the semi-frozen road.

"Hungry?" Royal asked, holding out a paper plate piled with pizza and potato chips. In his other hand he held a can of Mountain Dew.

"Thanks, man," Max said, taking the gifts. He held the plate to his face and took a bite of the pizza, then did the Dew. He said, "Good pizza. Still warm."

"I could be wrong," Royal said, "but I think Franny values food." He snorted, clouds of mist around his face. "This sucks, man, sticking you on double duty. Franny's got her head up her ass."

"I thought you liked her."

"I do, by and large. But she shouldn't be assigning *us*. That's Glendenning's job. You're a part of the unit and we need cohesion. We *don't* need a member sleep-deprived when we go into action. We've got a thing tomorrow night and then the big one on Friday, for Christ's sake."

"Any idea what that is yet?"

"Not a clue. Works for them, sucks for us."

"Well, don't sweat it. I'll be fine, man. She's just having her fun, and you can be pretty sure that she wants the op to go as smoothly as we do."

"You're awful damn zen about it."

"What am I gonna do about it?"

"I suppose. All right, man. Take 'er easy." Royal turned and walked away, his boots squeaking in the pristine snow. Max watched him go and took his time finishing his pizza and Dew. After the last swallow, he let out a long, loud belch, willing to bet there was no one around to hear him.

He let the snow-deadened silence fall back around him, and then resumed his patrol. Walking alongside the river, he centered himself and *called* Pam.

The connection was made more easily than a phone call. *All set?* he asked.

Her voice came back loud and clear. *I've got this, Max. Don't hover.*

Well, good luck, he said, using their mission catchphrase. *Go get 'em, cowgirl.*

Yee haw!

THURSDAY, MARCH 24, 2011 · 12:00 MIDNIGHT

CENTRAL EUROPEAN TIME

Z Nipple (Encountering Reality)

Pam stood on the side of the hill, one hundred feet below Castello Janus. The heat of the day had vanished on the wind. The Sagittarius moon, just past full, was rising fat in the southeast, close to the Milky Way. Somewhere the church bells tolled *mezzanotte.* Midnight.

She was dressed all in black, because she had to do this physically. She wanted nothing more than to enter the castle as an *astral.* But unless the bone's magick fell within her sphere of knowledge— which it didn't, or Max would have said—she wouldn't be able to carry it back out through the castle walls.

She would have to be physical and invisible, by shifting the gravity around her. That would cause a gravitational lens and bend light—basic alchemical practice, and after three-plus years, second nature. She had no trouble with invisibility as a tactic. She just wanted to *fly.*

So now she worked her way up the ancient path that traversed the hillside, worn by the feet of the locals since before Rome was a gleam in the eyes of Romulus and Remus. She'd grown up in New Mexico and walked the narrow track with accustomed ease. She could see herself, and thus her feet, so there was no chance of her stumbling. In fact, she was making certain that she didn't even dislodge a stone—she was that silent.

She crested the hilltop at the parking lot, and continued along the grassy border, avoiding the larger rocks, until she came to the service entrance. There had been no magickal alarms there in the afternoon, and none had been added. The physical alarm would have been sufficient against anyone with no magick. As it was, she passed her hand over the spot in the door jamb where the alarm was installed, using her control of electromagnetism—the flip side of gravity—to add a bridge to carry the current when the physical circuit was broken. Then she began to reach into the lock with gravity and push and pull the pins. Picking locks was an area where she lagged far behind Max, but she could handle common locks. It took her seven minutes, but in the end, everything fell into place. She pushed the door open, listened to the silence that followed, did a *wipe* to see the inner room was empty, and slipped into its darkness ahead. She felt a smile at the corners of her mouth, told it *knock it off, it's too early,* but then let it come. Why shouldn't she enjoy this? She was in charge tonight.

After the *wipe,* she could see the passageway out of the room. It had a concrete floor, the better to roll supplies along, but the walls and ceiling were made of ancient stone. Unaccustomed to the un-evenness of the masonry, she banged her left elbow when the tunnel turned, but it was a minor annoyance and made no real sound. There continued to be no other sound from anywhere ahead, no other sights when she cleaned her view.

She came to an old stairway—was there any other kind in this place?—leading up and to the left. That was the direction she needed to go, and she took it with quick strides, questing upward and outward with her senses. She was gaining confidence but she wasn't overconfident. She was in the moment. She came to a door at the top and stopped. She heard nothing. She cleaned her view and saw nothing about the door that threatened her. She tried the door. Locked. But much easier to pick. She came out in the hall behind the visitors' gallery.

No sound as she padded the length of the hall. There were no electronic alarms, no mystical alarms. She came to the larger room. She cleaned. There was no threat there. Her path to her prize was open.

She was halfway across the room when the old woman appeared from nowhere, grabbing at her throat!

Pam instinctively brought her arms up, smashing the old hands free. She had no idea where the woman had come from, or how—

The old woman's hands snapped back to Pam's throat, like a vise closing. Her face, just inches from Pam's, was hideous in clean sight, eyes wide, mouth wider, a full set of clenched teeth. Pam grabbed the bony wrists and tried to pull them away, but they were as taut and as strong as iron bars. There was one way out—go *astral*—but her physical body remained in the harridan's hands, face turning purple and red. Pam's brain was reeling but she took the gravity on the old woman's arms and drove them apart. The fingers took bits of flesh with them but Pam could breathe. She staggered backward, slamming against the display case, rattling the bone, but her goal now was to keep the woman at bay, holding back her arms. Her hands were a yard apart now, a great bird of prey screaming with hate.

MAX! Pam *called* frantically. *MAX!*

WEDNESDAY, MARCH 23, 2011 · 7:18 P.M. EASTERN DAYLIGHT TIME

2 Nipple (Encountering Reality)

Max stopped where he was. *Here, Pam!*

2 Nipple (Encountering Reality)

There's a guardian—I couldn't sense her!

Max replied, *O thou spirit, I do here license thee to depart unto thy proper place, without causing harm or danger unto man or beast. Depart, then, I say!*

"O thou spirit, I do here license thee to depart unto thy proper place, without causing harm or danger unto man or beast," Pam repeated. "Depart, then, I say!"

The harridan abruptly stepped back, her eyes still wide but her screams now heavy breathing. Pam carefully relaxed the pressure within herself that had driven the gravity, but stayed on full alert.

The old woman brought her hands to her face.

"You have vanquished me, girl," she whispered. "I must do as you command. But first . . ." She took hold of her hair and pulled it down toward her chin, and her entire face turned over, as if on an axle running behind her eyes. For one delirious moment Pam could see the black oval inside her skull, and then the face turned over completely and revealed a new face. A mad young man. "I am not I, and thou hast not vanquished *me!*"

Pam ran for the door.

Max shouted, *No, Pam! It's Castle Janus!*

But Pam went on through the door—and fell into another world.

2 Nipple (Encountering Reality)

PAM! Max shouted. And then again, *PAM!*

Blessedly, her voice replied, but her tone was vastly different, way out on the edge. *Max—like 'm drunk—*

Stay with me, Pam!

Big 'n' crazy . . .

You're in the subconscious, but we're linked. Just turn around and come back.

Dunno where . . .

Come toward my voice. Just follow my voice. Do you have the key?

Do.

Then follow me home.

Can't. Trees.

What trees? he demanded.

No answer.

Max snapped, *Pam!*

Nothing.

PAM!!

Nothing.

He made a quick gesture, becoming invisible even as he created the image of himself, walking his beat. He moved swiftly to put his back against the strongest tree, bracing his legs. His eyes grew fixed on a spot ahead of him in the night. The tree behind him, the spot ahead, he joined them over the top, forming the symbol of pi with him inside. Pi was a gate, where the two worlds met, and in his mind he rotated himself, rolling through the gate into the other world and expanded, expanded, expanded. . . .

But the subconscious was vast and untrackable. *Wizards hide things there because it's a wilderness. The only good way to find some-*

thing is to already know where it is, and I have no idea where Pam is. What did she mean by "trees"?

He rolled back through the gate, into this world. His own tree was hard against his back. *I need some way to home in on her,* he thought. *What about the other bone, here?* He sent his mind to it, but realized a quick negation. *Her bone's as lost to this world as she is.*

He pushed off from the tree. *Elementals. They come from the subconscious. I can ask them.* He sat down against the tree, feeling its rough bark slide by, and opened himself to the nature around him. Elementals were nature spirits, earth and water and air and fire—the forces of nature that came from the subconscious, visible sometimes if you knew how to see. He knew, and soon they came to him. Neither could speak to the other directly, but he could make his desires and intentions clear. *When you cross to the other side, look for this woman and tell me if you find her.* It was a forlorn hope—the odds were infinitesimal that their place was the same place Pam was. But a forlorn hope was still something; he couldn't ignore it.

Then he got up again and, having done everything he could, resumed his patrol. Rhythmic walking was a chant of the body, good for setting it on autopilot. It allowed him to center himself and begin building the power he'd need to enter the building with the magick in the Rupp Works. *I could let it slide before,* he thought, *but not anymore; it's too big and too close in time and space to have no connection to this. I need to know what was taken, and why the seals around it are so good.* So he walked the riverfront road, closing out the world, focusing everything on one spot inside himself: the image of his tousle-haired Pam Blackwell.

LIGHT

Pam was in a forest of trees, but the trees were growing at all angles, literally all angles, Escher trees from the ground upward and from the sky downward and from the hills sideways. She herself was lying across two trunks. The sky was above her, but there were holes beside her and she could see sky down there, too. The world was circular, spherical, like the inside of a huge ball—maybe. She couldn't be sure. It was only a guess.

She'd fallen through a doorway. She couldn't get back through the tangle of trees and couldn't touch the ground. It was like a nightmare, except that it felt utterly real, and she knew she wasn't dreaming.

Max said it was the subconscious. The *subconscious*!

Panic played around the edges of her mind, like heat lightning, but she beat that down, like forcing snakes back into a can. She'd been on the path of alchemy long enough to see other strange worlds. Strange worlds came with the territory. This was just another one—though she'd never been on her own in one before. She let air out through her nostrils, breathed in, taking it slow. She was alive. That was step one. The subconscious was a world; Max hid things here. The subconscious was strange, but real. That was step two. She was an alchemist. Step three.

Max! she *called,* and then to be sure yelled his name out loud. But there wasn't a lot of effort in it. She was still having trouble just saying words, even the one-syllable ones. There was no response.

She started to press her palms against the tree below her, to raise her torso, and found the Crossbones Key still in her right hand. *Take me back!* she told it, still *calling* but not realizing it.

Nothing happened. She tried it again, making sure her lips formed the words, deliberately. But still nothing.

It needs a spell, she reasoned. *I don't know what that spell is.* But very carefully, she extended her hand back down alongside her body and shoved the finger bone deep into the front pocket of her jeans, then tamped it down. *I'll find it,* she thought savagely. *Or I'll find SOMETHING here that will get me out! Goddammit! I'll fight this!*

She pushed off from the tree. There was no nausea. Nothing in her seemed to be broken or bent. She put her feet against the nearest branch—her rising back thunked against another. It hurt.

That was a good thing. That made sense. She was in her physical body, definitely alive.

But she had another body. How was that one?

She used the side tree for leverage as she lowered herself again, closed her eyes and loosed it. She left as much consciousness as she dared in her physical body, because there was no telling what dangers might be lurking nearby, but she had to put all the rest of it into the *astral*. She had to *fly* and get an overview of this world without getting hit by branches, if she were going to figure out where to go.

She shot high above herself, passing through the trees that grew down from the sky, only to find that the sky was just more open space beyond those trees, and it was buttressed by more trees. It was as if she was trapped in a sponge, where each open area was just a clearing in the endless, all-dimensional forest. But there was no sign of the doorway. *How far did I fall before I got caught in those trees?*

Farther than she wanted to be away from her physical form, she finally decided, and dove back "down" through the thicket to return. This time the trees seemed thinner, farther apart—definitely not so tangled. It could be that the more she saw of this world, the more it made sense to her—that she was learning how to process what she saw. Or it could be the logic of a dream.

With that thought, still high above her physical, she took the corner of her mind reserved for it and lifted her physical arm and whacked it against a branch. *Ow!!* It still hurt, and immediately. So even if the world was made of dream, *she* wasn't dreaming.

In her final descent, she spotted a pattern to the thinning trees, that opened up an obvious path among them. Exactly what she'd been looking for. She settled back into her physical—it hugged her as she did—and she locked the two forms back together.

The standard advice, if you were lost but people knew where you should be, was to stay where you were. That did not apply in this case. If she was in the subconscious and the link between her and Max was broken, he couldn't find her. She would have to find her own way home. And that meant using her physical arms on what sure seemed like physical branches, and climbing across to the path.

At first it seemed this would be unbearably strenuous, climbing over, under, around, and through, but that didn't turn out to be the case. The trees were still tangled, but there always seemed to be an opening, so that she could move from break to break with increasing ease. It was actually a lot like hiking through an undiscovered forest, if you didn't mind rotating ninety degrees now and again. Pam didn't mind, because paths existed for a reason: to go somewhere people want to go.

As she found her rhythm, she began to *call* to Max again. It couldn't hurt.

WEDNESDAY, MARCH 23, 2011 · 11:07 P.M. EASTERN DAYLIGHT TIME

2 Nipple (Encountering Reality)

Snow was falling steadily when Max was ready to enter the building.

It had taken all of the three remaining hours in his shift, and a little more, but the rhythmic walking over dirt, alone in the darkness, had worked exactly as he'd intended. Magick was always in him now, like a banked fire, but turning up the thermostat for something this momentous took work and time. Time was no problem for Max, but it was *the* problem for Pam. When Josefovich replaced him at eleven, he still had moments to go, so he barely nodded as he rhythmically stalked away. Josefovich didn't care; he was contemplating his own four hours out here, beside the dank river.

Max was so close he had no worries about hitting his target, and five minutes later he felt the golden glow of success. It always amazed him at times like this that no one could see him shining in the dark. They *could* see him if he let loose a blast of power, but not otherwise. He passed the few men on duty in the Rupp Works with

just a nod—a nod that wasn't easy for Max to pull off in his current state. When he reached the shadows of the barracks across
from the vault, he became completely invisible.

The key was simple enough in concept: match his own power to
the power around the elevator door. It couldn't detect him if it
couldn't tell him from itself. He'd felt it clearly enough this morning, in determining what it was, and he was an old hand at the
nuances of magick—still, matching one's own power to that of a
rival magician was hard, not so much on the mind as on the spirit.
He didn't do it for fun.

He walked invisibly across the compound and picked the lock
on the outside door with the skills he'd learned in Alabama, 1989.
He crossed invisibly to the elevator, a solid, dependable Otis freight
elevator, big enough to transport an elephant. He stood completely
still before it for six minutes, attuning himself ever more closely to
the actual, present magick guarding it.

When he was ready, he pressed his fingers into the horizontal
crack between the doors. He did not feel what he'd felt before: the
sudden rush of power.

He pried the doors apart to where he could step over the bottom
door and entered the box. He was certain that moving the elevator
would trigger a good old-fashioned electronic alarm, so he opened
the trapdoor in the ceiling and pulled himself up and out, onto the
roof. He walked to the edge of the car, surveyed the space between
the cage and the wall, and dropped into it.

His most-used power was invisibility, but his most useful was
probably his control over gravity. Everything was connected to
everything through gravity, and manipulating those connections
was *the* basic tool in his alchemical arsenal. It was good not to be
seen while doing something; better to get it done. So now he dropped
down the elevator shaft, a distance of over one hundred feet, judging by his ears—and as he neared the bottom he lessened his gravity to slow and then cushion his fall. Landing, he barely needed to
bend his knees.

He opened the lower elevator doors and stepped into what felt like a towering cavern, invisible in darkness. But Max had a glow no one else could see. He let it expand ten feet out, for his eyes only.

What he saw seemed natural, an opening into one of the many great caves beneath Hoosier soil, but the next moment his eye fell on the Lucas Jennis edition of *De Lapide Philisophico* on a stand just ahead, and he realized what this place was: a trophy room!

Quickly, he began to work his way up and down the aisles, marveling at what lay before him. He was there to discover what was missing, with a time limit, but he couldn't help himself. There were historical objects—a bright golden 1933 double eagle, never officially circulated, caught his eye. There were Benjamin Franklin's bifocals (*why?*). But then he spotted legendary items in mystical lore—legendary because no one had laid eyes on them in hundreds, sometimes thousands of years. Everything was neatly displayed and labeled.

There was a cryptic, dirty Haitian mojo bag, its malevolence simmering, said by its plaque to have been taken by the first buccaneers to take the island.

A tightly stopped jar, inside an airless crystal cube, of Giordano Bruno's aqua vitæ.

A pencil study for *Les Bergers d'Arcadie*.

The amulet of Agamemnon.

A Connemara horned man.

The phallus of Pope Joan.

And always the books! Johannes Bureus's first book on Runes.

Andreæ's *Chymische Hochzeit Christiani Rosencreutz. Anno 1459.*

The Sacred Book of Abraham the Jew, Prince, Priest, Levite, Astrologer and Philosopher to that Tribe of Jews who by the Wrath of God were Dispersed amongst the Gauls.

Then, at last, the empty space. His first thought was, *Of course! Aleksandra had the three talismans when I met her; she wanted my Lion to complete the set. So of course she'd have given them to the Necklace after she became a diabola. But what have THEY got to do with the Crossbones Key?* A smile spread slowly over his face. *Answer: ask the Lion.*

He would have loved to make a complete inventory of what was down here, but Pam came first and foremost. Still, he dropped Pope Joan's phallus into his pocket as he sprinted back toward the elevator shaft.

LIGHT

Pam found the going easier after a while. The breaks through the three-dimensional thicket grew closer together, and finally became a sort of corkscrew tunnel, which swung her up the right side, up the left side, and once in a complete revolution. Then the tunnel began to spend more time at one angle, the one beneath her feet. There were still holes, voids that ate away chunks of the greenery around her. But the tunnel moved on between them, and the longer she walked it, the fewer the holes she saw. The clustering trees at all angles began to be merely bent trees whose lower trunks were rooted firmly on the angle beneath Pam's feet. With only the barest of shifts, she was walking through a forest of normal trees, no different from anything she was familiar with, and she came out into sunshine on a path that crossed a field. Instead of trees ahead of her, there were stalks of wheat, golden, swaying with the breeze and her passage. Still dressed all in black, she stood out clearly.

It's like a painting, Pam thought. *Like it's not real.* Then she shook her head. *Well, duh!* And still: *But in its unreality . . . it looks real.*

She stopped for the first time since she'd begun climbing through the thicket. *MAX!* she *called,* and she kept *calling* for another five minutes, as the waves of wheat shimmered around her. She projected her consciousness farther and farther outward, probing for ways she hadn't yet found, trying, not desperately, but with determination, to contact him any way she could.

But still there was nothing.

The wheat moved like waves around her, the breeze was fresh with the scent of Spring, and the sky was sunny and blue.

Alice in Wonderland, she thought. *Or Alchemist in Wonderland.* For the first time, she laughed. She liked that she could laugh.

She was no Max August, but she'd studied his ways. She knew that the human mind existed to make sense of things, and the reason this world was becoming more comprehensible was, she was comprehending it. It had seemed completely illogical at first, so different from the world she usually inhabited. But she'd been here for a while now, and she was getting the hang of it.

This was the subconscious. It was where the doorway took you. It was where Max had put the real Aparicio's body, and his Lion talisman, and half a dozen other things. But the subconscious was like a huge ocean; you didn't wander into other people's subconscious without some serious magick. So finding the Lion was going to take some serious magick.

So she turned amidst the wheat and surveyed Wonderland. The trees were still in evidence in the forests beyond the wheat field. Shafts of sunlight cut through their leafy canopies; she could see birds flying, and hear their songs. Behind her, the way she'd come, a low-lying fog had permeated the woods. Ahead of her, the path parted the wheat and ran through a valley; through its far opening she could see the sparkle of a lake.

Only the one path, she thought, and considered that. *But paths only go where people want to go. Whatever this world on the other side of the doorway may be, the way to get closer to the way out of here is to follow this yellow grain road.*

She walked forward again. The breeze shifted and the birds left the forest to sail high overhead. The wheat had a wholesome smell and she was sorry to leave it behind, but the lake past the valley beckoned. She entered the valley, whose hillsides on both sides were strewn with a riot of wildflowers, amid grasses that were waves in the wind. The lake sparkled brighter than ever. Birds— bluebirds—were swirling above, and singing. *Seriously,* Pam thought. *I'm a goddamn Disney princess!*

Then she smelled Belia'al.

She came to an abrupt halt, frozen in mid-stride beneath suddenly congealing skies. She could not be mistaken. She'd faced him directly at Wickr. She'd smelled him.

He's here, too! she thought wildly, and something grabbed her foot!

She tried to jerk free and almost broke her ankle when her foot didn't move. Instead, she lost her balance and fell back onto her butt. Something close to panic burst in her but she didn't let it slow her readiness to strike back—and then she saw for the first time what it was that held her.

A gnome.

Pam blinked. She knew what gnomes were. They were another facet of the subconscious, and probably the first magickal things she'd ever beheld, on the very first night she'd met Max. They were one of the four species of elementals, four forces of nature. Earth, air, fire, and water, they were servants, primarily of nature itself, but also of any magician who could see them—if you knew how to see them. That usually meant looking from the corners of your eyes, but Pam was looking right at this one. And it was looking at her.

"Hello," it said, and Pam realized it was female. She looked like a Keebler elf—pointy hat, blocky shoes, an overly large head with features like mashed dough. She wore a medieval simple brown shift closed by bright, shiny buttons, with a green collar. No more than six inches high, she held Pam's foot to the ground inflexibly. She needed to be reminded who was boss here.

"Please let me go," Pam said, firmly but pleasantly.

The gnome shook her little head. "There's bad in the realm. If you leave the valley, he might see you."

"He's right out there?" Pam asked, looking along the valley at the sparkling lake.

"Well, he's not in here," replied the elemental simply. "So stay here."

Pam looked around, gauging her surroundings. If she had to escape up a hillside, she doubted she could outrun the demon. But she definitely couldn't if her foot was being held.

"I want to stand up," she said, a bit more firmly and less pleasantly. "Now."

The gnome shrugged, and stepped back. Pam started to get back to her feet, but thumped back on her butt when something rapped her on the top of her head. Looking up, she saw an air elemental, a sylph, much like the one she'd seen at Mama Locha's on Barbados. That one had been a woman, and this one was a man, but the look of a lean body in a sort of Roman tunic was the same, as were the fluttering wings.

"Why'd you hit me?" Pam demanded.

"Funt wants you to sit still," said the sylph with asperity.

"But I *don't*! What the hell kind of elementals are you?" Pam said, and got up with a sharp eye on the sylph. He buzzed backward, keeping his distance, glaring at her. She glared back. *I really am Alice,* she thought. *Good or bad, I'm comprehending this as a fairy tale—complete with fairies.*

"Your name's Funt?" Pam asked the gnome, now five feet below her.

"Yep."

Pam looked back at the sylph. "And you—I knew someone like you, in Barbados. Her name was Cocorik."

"*My* name is Cocorik."

"No."

"Yep," a third voice said. "All sylphs are Cocorik, just as all gnomes are Funt and all salamanders are Chiss." Pam looked to her left and saw a six-inch man dressed in a reddish-brown hoodie, and black leggings. With the black below and the bright color above, he looked like a candle, and his image was always shifting slightly. His eyes were small and vivid; his cheeks plump and ruddy; his sideburns the colors of fallen leaves.

So Pam looked out at the lake. "That's three out of four," she said. "Where's your naiad?" And in response, a small female figure materialized from the water. She had black, shiny-straight hair pouring down around her wide-cheeked face. Large pointed ears stuck up through her hair; big blue-black eyes bracketed the wide nose between them. She wore a blue robe tied around her ample hips with silver cord. Her feet, as she stepped on shore, were broad and flat.

"I'm Mymla," she said in a burbling voice.

"I'm Pam," Pam responded. "And I'm *very* pleased to meet you all."

THURSDAY, MARCH 24, 2011 · 1:00 A.M. EASTERN DAYLIGHT TIME
....

2 Nipple (Encountering Reality)

Max left the vault the way he'd gone in, undetectable and invisible. There was snow on the ground outside to catch his tracks, but it was slushy and he dragged over it with his gravity to obliterate his trail as he moved quickly along the side of the building. When he reached the darkest shadows, where no one would be likely to walk, he put his back to the wall and reached out for his Lion.

Kalbu Rabu was the leonine spirit that inhabited a lion carved from amber, with delicate pieces of inlaid woods creating a flowing, fiery mane. In Max's world it was a foot and a half long, with some heft to it; when he had dropped off the grid in 1985, he'd stashed it in the subconscious, knowing it would be safe there. The two of them had maintained a continuous connection since then, but Max seldom had to contact the talisman directly.

Times changed.

HAZE
....

He found the Lion in a leafy glen. The sun above burned through a haze of unusual clouds, turning the bright green foliage a dark emerald. Here Kalbu Rabu was three times Max's height, his head among the treetops, the master of all he surveyed.

"Hail, Great Lion of Fez," the alchemist called.

"Hail, Max," the Lion replied, gazing down beneficently upon the man who controlled him.

"I bring news," Max said. "Your three fellows have been stolen, by a magus unknown."

"We have all been stolen, time and again. It is the nature of a talisman," said Kalbu Rabu philosophically.

"Can you find them for me?"

"You know I cannot."

"Then what about a woman, Pamela Blackwell? She is an obvious anomaly in this realm."

"Impossible as well. Why do you ask these things?"

"Leaving no stone unturned."

"I cannot feel a human. But I *can* feel the ethereal, and I must tell you, Max, that I *have* felt Belia'al in this realm, most recently."

"Oh, shit," Max said. That was bad news in and of itself. *But if Belia'al's involved, it must have been Peter Quince who stole the talismans.* "Is there anything you can do?" It was meant to be a straightforward question, but with Pam still on his mind, it came out a little raggedly.

"I can add my strength to yours, Max," Kalbu Rabu said, perhaps a little pointedly.

"What's the connection between you and the Crossbones Key?"

"None."

Max grimaced in acknowledgment, and bowed briefly. "Farewell, Great Lion of Fez," he said, and departed the emerald glen.

The great Lion gazed at the spot Max August had inhabited and wished, not for the first time, that he was more than the essence of Fire—more than a talisman for others. Then he might venture forth into the larger realm and seek his fellows or the woman. But talismans were only tools.

He stood among the trees and let the sun warm the mane around his neck, and accepted that which he could not change.

2 Nipple (Encountering Reality)

Hanrahan came to Breckenridge's room for his final report of the day.

"The raids are going well, Renzo. They might go better if I knew why . . ."

"I doubt it, Dick. I have perfect faith in you."

"Well, they're going well. The trinkets are being couriered here as quickly as possible."

"Fine. What do you have on Max?"

"There's a worldwide alert out, and I dispatched another four teams, but so far, no one at any level has seen him."

"Keep at it."

"Of course. I hope to have something by your morning briefing."

"I look forward to it."

"Good night."

The old man walked away, thinking, *It's tempting to indulge in a final, meaningful chat with Renzo, but I'm not doing anything out of the ordinary. When I come back at six it will be a smooth matter-of-course— right up until it's not.* His face betrayed nothing, not even to the empty hall. *Five more hours!*

CLOUDS

"I want to get out of here," Pam told the elementals. "Can you help me?"

The four looked at each other in perplexity. Then Cocorik, hovering above the other three, said, "No."

"Why not?"

"We can touch your world. You can't."

"I bet I can," Pam said. "I don't smell Belia'al anymore. The bad thing. If he can leave, I can, too."

"No," said Funt, with real empathy for her predicament. "I'm sorry. Someone put you here."

"Well, I can put myself out," Pam responded. "I'm an alchemist, and I don't have to wait for somebody else to use me." She squatted down, closing the distance between her and the three on the ground. Cocorik buzzed downward to listen in. "Speaking of being used, what do you know about a Lion talisman? Its name is Kalbu Rabu, and my man put *that* here."

The three elementals on the ground looked at each other, and shrugged.

"But there must be elementals where it is," Pam went on, her bits of knowledge linking together. "If you're all the same . . . you know what they know, right?"

"No!" said Cocorik with some satisfaction. "We're all the same but we're all individuals—that's how our world works. And you should be glad of that, Pam, because that's why any elementals besides us don't know where *you* are." He shot a glance at the end of the valley, where Belia'al had been, just making sure.

Pam scowled, in thought. "Okay, that may be true—but I still have to find that Lion. Can you suggest a direction to start off in?"

"No," said Funt, more conciliatory than Cocorik had been.

"Well, I was planning to follow this path. Do you have any reason why I shouldn't?"

"We don't know," Funt said, even more sorrowfully.

"Please don't wander away," said Mymla.

"Aw, let her go if she wants to," said Cocorik.

"But what about the other three?" asked Chiss.

Pam looked at him sharply. "Other three *Lions?*"

"No, silly. The Eagle, the Angel, and the Ox."

Pam's mind spun. "Are *those three* here?"

"They were just put here."

"But you don't know where they are," Pam pointed out, "so what good does that do?"

"We *didn't* know," said Chiss. "Until the bad thing went there."

"You mean you *do* know?"

"Yes," said Funt.

"Then which way do I go?" Pam asked excitedly.

"She doesn't listen," said Cocorik, and to Pam: "You can't go."

"Grab her foot again, Funt," said Chiss.

Pam stepped warily back out of range.

Mymla said, "She might be able to do it. She *is* different."

"But it's never, ever been done," said Funt.

The four elementals huddled. Then they offered a compromise. "You can stay with us."

"No," Pam said, gently but firmly.

They conferred again.

"Well," said Mymla at last, "we'll go *with* you, then."

"I thought you'd never ask," Pam said with a smile.

THURSDAY, MARCH 24, 2011 · 5:00 A.M. GREENWICH MEAN TIME

2 Nipple (Encountering Reality)

Vee woke up in hospital. There were bandages along her arms and legs, bandages beneath the hospital gown, and an IV inserted into her left forearm. She seemed to be floating, so she knew they were giving her painkillers, so she knew she was in pain. She could hardly wrap her mind around it, she felt so drained. But she knew exactly what Durban was telling her: if she fought him again, he would finish her off.

With floating slowness, Vee pulled the IV from her arm. She had to get ready.

Day four
. . . .

Aleksandra floated in space. Looking for something. What could it be?

The Belia'al tschotskes were floating around her in the obsidian void, nearer than the spectral stars, picked out by her lurid red light and bobbing softly on the waves of space. There were wands, sigils, even fossilized shit, all of it suffused with a certain evil odor, the stench of Belia'al. It wasn't an odor a nose could determine; it was an odor in the matrix, a violently twisted cord in the evolution of humans. They were animals, genus *homo,* with more brains than any other animal on Earth. They were homo *sapiens.* But they weren't diabolas. And so they took strange, dark turns they weren't prepared to handle. They brought their demons to their lives with plans of mastering them and ended as slaves. Too late then. There was nothing for it but to call the slavery glorious and claim it as their idea in the first place.

Looking for something. What could it be?

Belia'al wanted power, of course. But primarily, access to Earth. Demons never walked the Earth on their own. They formed hideous tumors in the matrix, a mix of magick and logic, in the realm

just below Earth—phantasms to humans, and yet part of their be-
lief systems. Demons *could* exist, if . . . And so the homo sapiens
reached out like Michelangelo's Adam and made the phantasm
real. The demon got a vehicle on Earth, the dual world where both
logic and magick coexist.

The demon was all logic. It had no magick of its own. Rather, it
got magick from the Earth through its human host and leveraged
it. The human thought he was getting demon magick but it was
truly his own, offered back to him by his cunning visitor.

The diabola was all magick, in the realm just past Earth. She
controlled her access to her old world, but had to force herself into
form to interact. She knew logic because she once was human, but
she couldn't use it directly anymore.

Earth was the midpoint between diabolas and demons. Each of
them needed the denizens of Earth to seek power there.

THURSDAY, MARCH 24, 2011 · 6:45 A.M. GREENWICH MEAN TIME

3 Wind (Advancing Possibilities)

Vee came slowly through her front door, bent and weakened, very
sore. Still, she came through the door, and hobbled directly to the
book.

Which, for some reason, slammed shut.

"What?" she demanded sharply. "Don't screw with me! I'm not
in the mood!"

The book lay quietly. At another moment in her life, she might
have thought more about its strange behavior. She might have
thought that it knew something she wasn't ready to know. But she
was on a mission, and this was not that moment.

"Christopher Durban is not real," she told it raggedly. "Or
rather, the thing I know as Durban is not real. It's being run by a
psychic vampire, and I need to know where."

The book simply lay there.

"Psychic vampire."

The book simply lay there. *Christ!* she thought. *Is this another thing they didn't have in 1519?* "No psychic vampire?" she asked. "He doesn't steal blood, he steals life-force."

Finally, the pages flipped open. *An Incubus steals magick from the female.*

"Thanks," she snapped. "But no. Not an incubus. A spirit."

A disembodied spirit can live after death.

A shiver ran up Vee's spine, though that was where she wanted to go. "How do . . . I find such a spirit? I need to know where he is."

Geomancy is an Art of Divination, whereby the judgement may be rendered to every question of every thing whatsoever.

"All right," she said. Geomancy—divination by earth—could well give her her answer . . . if only she didn't want so very much to go fall across her bed and sleep the day away. But she fought that lassitude and attitude, hobbling like some ancient crone to get the box of good English dirt she kept at the back of the closet, just for this. She set it on the kitchen table, and dropped gratefully into a chair before it.

The book again closed itself.

Vee groaned. Cornelius didn't know psychic vampires so she was going to have to take the lead on this—ask his advice when possible, but filter it through her knowledge of present realities. She would have to wing it.

Swell.

So: geomancy. The first thing a practitioner needed to do was to ascertain what Hour of the Day it was. First Hour on Thursday was Jupiter, and she was in the first hour. Well, on the horoscope, Jupiter was opposite Mercury, and Mercury had not worked at all well last night, so Jupiter might be just what she needed. She knew what the book taught about the Hour of Jupiter. "Concerned with the living of life in full measure. It is good for expansion, and good fortune." On top of that, Thursday, today, was the Day of Jupiter. So she'd seek Jupiter. She focused her mind on the concept of pure expansion, spreading out across all of London, and when she was firmly in that space, she put her question in words: "Where is the real Christopher Durban?" Simultaneously, she began to poke holes in the dirt with her forefinger, without thinking, simply reacting to whatever she felt. When she felt she'd done enough, she quit.

She took a knife and divided the dirt into sixteen horizontal sections, as evenly spaced as possible. Then she counted the number of holes in each section, and wrote down if it was an even number or an odd number. In the end, she had sixteen answers that could be translated to one dot (odd number) or two dots (even). In order, then, she constructed four figures of four lines each. The rules of geomancy led her from those four initial figures to just one figure—the answer to her question.

```
        •  •
        •  •
        •  •
        •  •
```

Populus, she thought. A place where people congregated. *Well, aside from being unlikely, it could be a million places. Hyde Park, Parliament, Eddie's Club. What the hell?*

Geomancy offered a final transformation in the case of uncertain answers, and she performed it. The figure now looked like this:

```
           •
        •  •
        •  •
           •
```

Carcer. Same root as "incarcerate." The Hebrew sages called it "the house of the warden." *Okay, a place where people congregate, but maybe not by choice. Jail? No.* But another shiver ran up her spine. Her penultimate night before becoming Vee had been spent in jail. She could not really remember it, since it had been wiped away along with Eva Delia, but the idea of "jail" always upset her.

She needed to know more, but the rules of geomancy forbade asking another question right away. No problem. She could try Tarot.

Forcing herself back to her feet, so she could get her pack of cards, she'd completely forgotten the strange behavior of Agrippa's book.

THURSDAY, MARCH 24, 2011 · 3:00 A.M. EASTERN DAYLIGHT TIME

3 Wind (Advancing Possibilities)

Max began his third shift on patrol with nothing more than a cat nap, but he could live with that. He could even smile, since his cat nap had followed his cat-rap. Out along the river, he checked with the elementals, but they had nothing, so there was little he could do now except wait and stay alert. With the temperature dipping into the twenties, the snow had turned to ice pellets, so staying alert would not be hard.

Now he had to see what day this would bring when it dawned. Alchemically, it meant Advancing Possibilities. That was good. But to the Romans, March 24 was Dies Sanguinis, the Bloody Day—part of a five-day festival of Cybele.

Cybele was the "Great Mother of the Gods" throughout Asia Minor—worshipped in the form of a black meteorite. Her son/lover, Attis, was about to wed the king's daughter when Cybele struck him with lunacy. In his delirium he castrated himself—so on the Dies Sanguinis, aspiring priests castrated themselves in his honor. Each castrato ran bleeding through the streets carrying his severed organs until he threw them into some house. The householder then had to give him a set of women's clothing.

Good times.

He reached the end of the road and turned around.

So it's woman-power today—that's what that comes down to. And they have it tomorrow, for Lady Day. So that's all good for Pam.

But he couldn't ignore a nagging doubt about Dies Sanguinis. It was woman-power, but it was the power of woman's blood.

He was still fully aware of his surroundings, and at that point he felt a golden glow flow through him—the sure sign of danger for forty years. He understood instinctively where to look, and indeed, there was the shape of Diana Herring in the area of greatest shadow.

"Two meetings?" he said, neither friendly or unfriendly, moving closer. "You must really love me, Di."

"I'm afraid not," she said. "There are many ways I'd describe our relationship, but 'love' would not be among them. No. I just came to say good-bye."

"Back to the salt mines?"

"Exactly. You guys are gonna make the news again tonight."

"But the blow-off is tomorrow night. Do you know what that is yet?"

"No. They think I work well under pressure."

"They're probably right."

"They're right quite a lot," she said. "*You* were good at working live, when you were on the air. I got your old air checks."

"To try to get to know me."

"Exactly."

"And did you?"

"Well, 'Barnaby Wilde' was showbiz, but I'd say there was a recognizable person behind him. I could hear the toughness, and the flair. You came across as a very hip king."

"Right," he said dismissively.

"You don't have to agree. But you've talked to me three times now, so I'm getting better at calibrating the current guy. His range has extended, and he's playing for much bigger stakes, but you're still the king."

"If I was king, the first thing I'd do is free my subjects."

"Well, we'll just have to disagree on that point. But I think you'll agree that you're running out of time. The Necklace has just about won."

"I'm not so sure," Max said. "Your problem is, nobody really wants what you're selling, so you have to lie about it—and when they do find out, they boot you out."

"We're dealing with it."

"Meaning you agree with me."

"Meaning we deal with anything. That's what we do."

Max looked her over. "Well, I hope you listened to the newscasts from my tapes, too."

"Why's that?"

"Because back then, there were only a few lies in the news. Granted, they were big ones, like Iran-Contra, but we could all trust *most* of what we heard, because there were half a dozen organizations all *trying* to be trusted. If anyone pushed a lie, the others would out it. Now lies are everywhere and nobody outs anybody, so we don't trust *any* of it."

"Yes," she said, nodding. "History is written by the winners."

"Duh," he said sarcastically. "Winning."

She smiled. "Charlie Sheen is much more entertaining than wars and unions, don't you think? Much more *useful.* Back in your time, he'd have been a little treat at the end of the newscast, if that. Now he's the lead. I don't apologize, Max. If we used our time for actual news, you'd be a lot more united. This way everybody's on his own. And yes they don't trust us, but each one doesn't trust us for a different reason, and in the end, the only thing we can all agree on is Charlie Sheen. Oh, and—after tomorrow night—Black Helicopters." She gave him her hand. "It's been a pleasure, Max. If you can put a stop to us, I walk, so I wish you well. But if you can't, I imagine I'll do a series about you, a very dramatic series with good guys and bad guys, and I'm afraid I'll make you the very bad guy."

He laughed. "I wonder who *would* have played me in that."

"Maybe Charlie Sheen. I was thinking of doing it like *Phantom of the Opera*—the mystery man behind the mask, pulling the strings—the demon king—"

"Stop right there!" Royal's voice, sharp from deep shadows of the trees by the river. "Who the fuck is '*Max*'?"

Diana snapped her head around but before he finished speaking,

Max had launched himself! A bullet spat out of the night, a second later, but Royal hadn't been expecting such a honed reaction and shot just behind his moving target. Then he was flying backward and landing hard on his head.

Still, Royal was tough and savvy. He rolled sideways, down the bank, getting distance and time to get up lunging. He slammed Max's diaphragm with his head and Max doubled over. Royal chopped at his throat. Max turned his head and took the blow on corded neck, chopped his elbow hard on Royal's chest in return. But there was no end game in this configuration and Max pushed them apart.

"Who are you, man?" Royal gritted. "What are you doing with *her?*"

"He can't report this, Max!" Di hissed.

"I'm on it," Max said, and added, "Sorry, Royal."

"Fuck you!" snarled Royal, coming at him with a looping right hook—a setup for a short left, as Max well knew, so he avoided it easily. He already knew that Royal had top-flight commando training, and all the other tricks he could pick up along the way, a hard-core dude—but Max had been UFC since 1987.

He came forward, hands ready, then snapped a right leg kick. It jarred Royal's thigh and the man's face tightened, confirming his assumption that Aparicio was a hard-core dude. But in no way was he worried; he was never worried. That's when Max threw an inside leg kick and knocked him back to the ground, dropping on top of him. Royal kicked upward, his boot in Max's face. But Max grabbed his boot, threw it to one side, and drove his fist as hard as he could against Royal's forehead. There was no give since Royal's head was flat against the frozen mud, and with a lesser man that would have ended the fight right then.

Instead, Royal struck upward and caught Max leaning in. Max jumped back, regaining his balance, as Royal twisted convulsively to his feet, following his advantage, laying two rights on Max. They were weakened but he was recovering visibly. Max took a step back, extending his hands, palms out, as if warding off the next blow. Royal launched it at Max's sternum, but as it passed between those hands, Max clamped them together on Royal's wrist and twisted. Either the arm would break or Royal would go to his knees; the second happened. Max kicked him in the face, which was beginning to bleed profusely. Max kicked him again, but this time Royal returned the favor by grabbing Max's foot and slamming him to the ground. Max hooked his left foot around Royal's ankle and kicked the held leg in the kneecap. Royal staggered backward and Max got up, a little slowly—then sprang forward with a running knee. Royal twisted but it caught him in the side. Max got his legs down as he grabbed Royal's torso and threw him across his hip. Royal got his hands down to break his fall but Max dropped both knees onto his back and drove him to the dirt once more. When Royal started to push up, it gave Max the room to stick his right forearm across the man's throat, his left hand grabbing the right and pulling up tight. His arm bar began crushing Royal's throat and the man tightened his neck muscles, fighting to dislodge his attacker. But Max could not be dislodged now. Royal's head began to suffuse with blood, turning a dark angry red. The blood was dribbling off his rigid face. He fought as hard as he could, and harder when he realized he was losing, but in the end, Royal fell back to earth, and lay still while Max continued the pressure for another thirty seconds.

Then Max got even more slowly to his feet. "Sorry, Royal," he said again. "But you knew the risks better'n anybody."

Di was watching with avid eyes. "You kept your face together, through all of that," she said breathlessly. "Max, you might beat us yet! Holy Christ, if only I had a camera!" And she kissed his cheek with real fervor.

He took hold of her shoulders . . . and took a second to push her away. "If only you had a camera and it wouldn't put your neck in a noose as well. Get outta here, Di," he said sincerely.

"Till we meet again, Max," she responded, apparently sincerely.

Then without a backward glance, she slipped away among the same trees Royal had appeared from, while Max began dragging his best buddy's body to the river.

LIGHT

The clouds over the valley parted as Pam and her fantastic foursome left it for an open green meadow around the lake. A number of paths, including the one Pam had been on, ran down to its golden reed-rimmed shore, to connect with a path that appeared to encircle the blue water. As soon as they reached that path, Mymla dove into the water.

Funt was the slowest of the four, so she set their pace. She *trudged*—an exact term—but she was dogged about it, plowing steadily onward. Cocorik buzzed along at the height of Pam's head, though he had almost nothing to say to her. Mymla swam alongside the others, leaving waves in her wake. And Chiss kept well away from the shore. The elementals were obviously still not certain that the bad thing wouldn't reappear; they were all on alert. But Pam wasn't worried. Belia'al hadn't come for her, and hadn't been looking for her, so it was *almost* certain that he didn't know she was here. *"No cut-and-dried answers in magick,"* she thought. *You take your best shot. And this is mine. If I can find any one of the other talismans, I can get myself out of here, so that's what I've got to do.*

Pam was beginning to get used to acting like an alchemist. The longer they walked along the lake without branching onto one of the paths leading away, into a forest or a valley, the more she saw in that fact. *My path to the talismans begins with water, and I'm a water sign myself, Cancer the Crab, born 7/9/79.* Pam stopped thinking about the three talismans as a group, and focused in on the particular ruler of Water. . . .

"I want to go to the Eagle!"

The elementals looked at one another. There was never any telling what humans were thinking.

"Longer trip," said Funt, raising one hand in a sign of reasonableness. "The Ox is closer."

"No," Pam said, certain. "The Eagle."

"We'll have to go right past the Ox," said Chiss, hopping around in place.

"Eagle," said Pam.

Cocorik made a noise of disgust. "Why not go all the way to the Angel?"

And Pam's alchemist mind accepted the question. *Why NOT one of the others?* So she ran through the elements in turn, to see why not.

Mymla, swimming in water . . . that still feels right. I feel the flow through the water she feels.

Cocorik. No. We are definitely not on the same page. I know it's just high mental energy, but it comes across as buzz.

Chiss. Maybe. His fiery spirit was comforting. But when he goes, he goes all out, and that's a little scary, frankly. Anyway, Fire is Max's thing, with his Lion.

Funt. Sweet. I really like her. But she's too slow for me. I like being on the cutting edge. She nodded, looking inward. *Yeah, I want the Eagle.*

She stopped, knelt, and dipped her hand in the water. Mymla stopped as well, bobbing on the swell, and looked up at her with kindred pride. Pam looked back at the water, saw her own reflection, and realized with a rush of pleasure that it *was* her reflection. She so rarely went out in public looking like Pam Blackwell anymore—but here she was! In the water, she shimmered with the flow.

"We turn here then," said Funt, unexpectedly. Pam came back from her thoughts to find them at the far end of the lake, at a junction with a path running into a forest of very normal-looking trees. Funt, now ahead of her, never broke her relentless stride as she made a sharp right turn and headed upslope toward the green and blue woods. The others followed, including Pam, but her mind was racing. *The first asteroid Max ever taught me was Artemis, named for the virgin goddess of the Forest and the Hunt. That sounds about right, too. Except for the virgin part, but hey, nobody's perfect.*

She laughed as they entered the forest, and it seemed to her that the sound echoed off the shining leaves. *I'm really enjoying this,* she marveled. She laughed louder, and it echoed off the trees. *I'm ARTE-MIS in Wonderland!*

] Wind (Advancing Possibilities)

At precisely six A.M., Dick Hanrahan walked into Lawrence Brecken-ridge's exercise room and stood beside the treadmill as Breckenridge took his daily run to nowhere.

"Today is March 24, 2011, a Thursday," the old man said. "Lati-nos are now one-sixth of the American population."

"Republicans are going to have to pivot off hating them," grunted Breckenridge.

"Eventually."

"Ten, twelve years. There's another couple of elections in it. But I'll have Allenby monitor it. We want out just *before* it goes side-ways."

"Okay." The old man made a note on his pad. "NATO has taken control of Libya's no-fly zone. America's now officially just a mem-ber of the coalition, still saying we'll be out any time now."

"Good."

"Radioactivity has been found in Tokyo's tap water and fresh vegetables. The government— Hold still. There's something on your hip—" Hanrahan swept his hand forward, the most natural thing in the world. But before he could touch Breckenridge, something punched his neck with a sharp pain that faded almost immediately.

That wasn't right. He reached for the spot and felt the length of a tranq dart protruding from his neck. The old man stared at Breck-enridge, who was slowing his run—turned to see the ops team emerging from a wall panel—toppled.

Lawrence Breckenridge stepped off the treadmill and stooped

to look closely at the compressed air syringe filled with blue liquid taped to the old man's palm. His old friend's palm. *It's exactly what I used on Tom Jeckyl,* he thought. *Twenty years on, it's still state of the art.* "Take him to the Cooler, Willingham," he said, straightening, his voice frozen nitrogen. Then all at once he had to let it go, so he drew back and kicked the old man hard in the head, one short, sharp shock.

I did not want to believe it, Breckenridge thought. *But the Gemstone has no choice.*

THURSDAY, MARCH 24, 2011 · 6:10 A.M. EASTERN DAYLIGHT TIME

3 Wind (Advancing Possibilities)

Willingham and his female partner, Jacoby, dragged the old man back to the elevator, with their Gemstone following. The elevator had three buttons, for the second floor where Breckenridge had his home and office, first floor that was nothing but the mansion of a very wealthy man, and the basement where Hanrahan and the other seven had private rooms. Willingham pushed the 2 and the B simultaneously, then the 1, and they all rode down four floors, to the secret subbasement.

That was where the Cooler was, where East Coast captives too dangerous to be transported to Chicago were kept as long as needed. Once they were no longer needed they were dumped down a wide tube running straight through Manhattan granite to the city sewer system. The Cooler provided two cells, a secure table for drug injection, and hosable tile walls.

Hanrahan began to come around as Jacoby was tightening the straps on his left arm. Willingham had finished with the right. But the old man looked past him at Renzo.

Renzo looked back, but spoke to the ops team. "He won't talk under torture. He'd take great pride in dying without giving in. So go straight to the drugs. His age is a problem but I trust you two to keep him alive." The Gemstone came forward and looked down upon his Number Two. He spoke directly to him. "Keep him alive until *he spills everything!*"

"Just the two of us still, sir?" Jacoby asked.

"This remains top secret. No one is to know of this until we've emptied him completely."

"Yes, sir."

Renzo Breckenridge had nothing more to say to his old friend. It might have meant something to have a fervent farewell, but Breckenridge couldn't see it. Fuck his old friend for fucking with the Necklace! He left the room, and the door closed with an airtight *thunk* behind him.

Willingham and Jacoby turned toward their captive. It gave Willingham a thrill to talk from the heart to the man who had always held his fate in his hand, and he savored it. "Here's what's going to happen, *sir*—as you well know. You are going to go on a great trip, be the happiest you've ever been. But you know full well that the time will come when you can't hold things together any longer, and everything we want to know will come tumbling out. So you know that all the time you're loving life, you're coming closer to the moment when we kill your sorry ass!"

Hanrahan looked him straight in the eye and said, "Are you gonna talk it to death, sonny?"

Jacoby jabbed a needle into Hanrahan's left forearm and attached its tube to an IV drip. Hanrahan strained his arm but it was completely immobilized, laterally, vertically, horizontally.

Well, that was how he'd designed the straps. He knew he wouldn't escape. But the one thing he also knew was, when he'd designed the drug regimen, he'd taught himself all the ways there were to resist it, just in case. He'd been plotting with the wizards for a good long time; this day had always been a possibility.

The old man was as ready as he'd ever be, for madness.

] Wind (Advancing Possibilities)

Breckenridge took the elevator back to the second floor of his brownstone. If anyone used it to ascend after him, or anyone used the grand stairway from the ground floor, or the kitchen stairs in the back, he would know. And without his active approval, they would not arrive alive. So even with others in the house, he was completely secure as he called out for Aleksandra.

But she, evidently, was not picking up. It didn't surprise him. And so he turned to his normal routine for Thursday and called Berlin.

] Wind (Advancing Possibilities)

Max said hello to Bragane as he entered the apartment. "What are you doin' up?" he asked. "Your shift's not till eleven, right?"

"Yeah, but I can't sleep. Don't you feel it?"

"Feel what?"

"The bad vibes, goddammit!"

"Dude, it's fine to think you can tell the U.S. government to fuck off and not care what they'll think, but at least you've got a theory for that. I didn't know you were a fuckin' hippie, too."

Bragane's jaw was set. "I grew up in Orange County, man. When the Santa Anas blow, you feel it, a lot more than just dry wind. You feel it every year, you know what I'm talkin' about."

"Well, I don't, and dry wind is the last thing we've got out there in that deluge, so I'm gonna leave you to it and grab a quick nap before I join you on that shift."

"Where's Royal?"

"Fuck if I know. Probably had time to eat breakfast, lucky bastard. I don't, so I'll *see you later.*"

Max went into his bedroom and flopped onto the bed, not even bothering with removing his damp clothes. It was time for yet another step, and he did hope to squeeze in some time for that.

He lay on his back and drew his power into a sphere around himself. It was golden, sparkling—it was him. It served as his calling card if a calling card was called for. It was, now, as he expanded his golden power into the universe. He established a metaphysical internet, to commune with his closest allies, his *friends.* Somewhere distant, yet seeming somewhere near, were Coyote, Scorpio Rose, Hoodoo, Korasu, Fetch, Lorelei, Mama Locha, Amba, and Kwasiba.

For the first few moments they all just took everything in, no one speaking. Max saw that Coyote and Rosa were not together, but he would not ask what that meant. He saw that Mama Locha still seemed ageless, but Amba and Kwasiba, the two young alchemists from Suriname, had grown in both body and magick since their time with him in '07. They were no longer apprentices.

Finally, Coyote, the primal totem, said, *Max,* and they were ready to begin.

Max projected his urgency to them. *Most of you know my woman, Pam. She was pushed through an elder doorway, and I have no way to contact her. So I ask, if anyone has a way, please use it. Either bring her back or get me a sign for finding her.* His power clearly stated that that was not all. *You should also know that the three unsecured Fez talismans have been stolen. The Necklace had them but someone else has them now. I assume the two things are connected but I don't know how yet.*

Coyote said, *Shit! We don't want to lose Pammy!* A blast of intense emotion came with his words, which Max understood. She was one that got away from him, which Max frankly enjoyed. But Max also knew Coyote would do everything he could to help find her.

Korasu, a *kisai*, spoke with a voice like a cello, full of deep harmonics. He spoke, in fact, Japanese, but it was the nature of this environment that everyone understood him. *I am very sorry, Max. I am fully occupied.*

I understand, Max said, and Korasu withdrew. *Anyone else?* Max asked.

Scorpio Rose said, *I am in the middle of a delicate arrangement, but of course I shall search the ASTRAL for you, Max.* Her face, the eyes and cheekbones well shadowed, grew brighter in his mind. *You will remember,* she added, *this was not unforeseen.*

It was spoken with no malice, or anything else. Max would never want to be like Scorpio Rose, but he knew her as only another Timeless one could—knew the void in her being, and the centuries she had borne it. He understood her desire to have him with her instead of with Pam. But she could not be malicious, not to Pam or anyone else.

I remember, Rosa, he said, but he was speaking to the crowd. *You'll remember that I have complete faith in her.*

Hoodoo said, *I can put Cardiff on hold. I'll speak with the gnomes. But Pam is a tough cookie.*

Lorelei said, *She reminds this one of you, Hoodoo, when you were her age.* Then, to Max: *But Pam has more power now than Hoodoo did then, and she seeks Timelessness. She will never let go of life.*

Max said, *I agree.*

Then this one shall seek her through life.

Mama Locha said, *That girl was born to the vodou, boy. An' remembah how she took to elementals? She's like the rabbit in the briar patch—exactly where she want to be. She prob'ly got the elementals workin' for her over dere.*

Amba said, *Our people know ways to the shadow world that no one else does. We'll walk them now, Max, deep in our forests.* Kwasiba continued, *But please tell us, Max, what are the "unsecured talismans"?*

Max said, *I'm sorry, ladies. I forgot you don't know.*

Amba said, *Not a problem Max. We know we're new.*

Max said, *There were four talismans carved in Fez, Morocco, in the year 1200. They represented the four elements. I have the Lion, but the Angel, the Eagle, and the Ox are now in play.*

Kwasiba said, *So our enemies control Air, Water, and Earth?*

At that point, Fetch sent a thought. He used no words at all, because he was incapable of them, but his thought was just as clear as the Japanese had been. *They have the CAPABILITY. It still matters who they ARE.*

Max said, *They haven't been used yet.*

Fetch thought, *That is a good sign. Pam was not sent to the elementals by the talismans, and is not being kept there by them. The coincidence of talismans and elementals may be just that.*

"Aparicio."

Max said hurriedly, *Gotta go. Let's talk again in half a day.*

Coyote said, *We'll get right on it.*

"Aparicio."

Max opened his eyes. "What?" It was Bragane, who said, "We're wanted at the Works."

"Why?"

"Royal's gone AWOL."

LIGHT

Pam followed the path alongside a tumbling brook, all lush green with trailing moss, framed by purple ferns. She heard the singing of the water, the murmur of the forest, and though it was all a sort of symphony, she heard nothing out of tune.

She once again took stock of her situation: The difference between a dream and reality was the logical connectedness of reality. In a dream, events took place one after another, as they did in reality, but there was nothing holding the events together. You started out one place with one set of people, and ended up somewhere else, with someone else. But in reality, even though you might not be paying attention all the time, anything that happened was connected to what went before and what was coming after. So whatever else this might be, she knew it was not a dream.

This forest was truly very different from her initial transitional environment. The trees were undeniably trees, ancient and venerable ponderosa pines, and shafts of sunlight contrasted with deep-woods shade. It was peaceful here, and she couldn't help but take a longer look at Funt, the elemental of earth. This was the sort of world she helped tend, the world of vegetation, sprouting from the soil. Her stoic nature, her measured trudge, it was all of a piece with the steady growth she promoted. And yet, Max had told her of his visions of gnomes *within* the Earth, loosing an earthquake—the earthquake he and Val had forestalled on the night he thought he'd killed Aleksandra. *Gnomes are not all about peaceful forests,* Pam thought. *They do whatever the Earth needs done. Could Funt—could any of them—turn on me?* She regarded the gnome with a more critical eye, but decided no, she didn't believe that. *They serve their elemental forces and they serve magicians, and now that they've bonded with me, they'll stay true to the end. I can rely on these four.*

Only, she remembered Max's teaching:

"Four" is just a mask for pi. Therefore, one of these elements is a mask of the infinite. She studied them. *Not Earth. It's always around. Not Air or Water; they're always here, too. Fire's the one that comes and goes.*

She focused on Chiss, skipping along. *I can live on Earth, in Water, and in Air. I can't live in Fire. It's fundamentally different from the others.*

But at that point, her thoughts were interrupted by a distant growl of thunder. . . .

3 Wind (Advancing Possibilities)

In Duluth, Belia'al reappeared within Peter Quince. **What news from Hanrahan?** he demanded, startling his slave.

"Nothing yet, Master," Quince said, closing his grimoire. "How were the talismans?"

Most excellent. Why is there no news, Peter Quince?

"Well, I don't know. I've been wondering myself. He should have contacted me by now."

He was always the weak link.

"No. That old man is tough as nails, and twice as mean."

Then someone even meaner has him.

"Breckenridge. Maybe. But we don't actually know that that's the case. He could just be busy."

Call Breckenridge. See if he answers.

"Master," Quince said diffidently, bracing for the tightening around his heart that always accompanied too much disagreement. "Master, we can't do anything to intrude on Breckenridge's routine. If Hanrahan has been delayed, we don't want to rouse Breckenridge, and if Hanrahan has been caught, Breckenridge will be alert to anomalies."

I understand that, but I still want to know. So make it work, Peter Quince.

"Of course, Master. You know I will. But please give it more time."

You are afraid, Peter Quince.

"I just know this world, Master."

And I know you. But I shall grant you one hour.

"Thank you, Master," said Quince. "Thank you." But in his heart of hearts, he knew: *He's willing to sacrifice me. Once he hears that Hanrahan has succeeded, he won't need me, and then what?* Despite his servitude, Peter Quince was a powerful wizard, and it took a powerful wizard to keep the part of him that was open to his demon placid, while in his heart of hearts he raged. *Adorèd one, my red ass!*

3 Wind (Advancing Possibilities)

Half an hour later, Quince was becoming convinced that something *had* gone wrong. But now he had been given an hour, and he wanted to keep that gift. He descended into his cellar.

Before him lay the sleeping women, and most important, Rita Diamante. She was the heart of his living battery, the linchpin in the web of power flowing into him . . . but looking down at her just now, he saw the prime link to the time, not so long ago, when he had been his own man. When he had been her lover, and they had conspired to find a way to augment their power, filling their days and nights with sex magick. He was not supremely happy then because his desire to relate to women was always low, but he'd been the undisputed master of the arrangement, and Rita was vibrant, vital. She was powerful when she was whole, and she was all his because that was how they were going to rise up in the Necklace.

Now, she was unconscious, blotchy, on a slab. And because he put her there, he was a slave.

When the hour ended, Quince went up two flights to his sanctum sanctorum and locked the door behind him. The only other conscious inhabitant of the house was his master, who was right there in the sanctum with him, but Quince said nothing and Belia'al had nothing to say. Quince seated himself in the lotus position at the center of his circle and began to work his will upon his essence. In just a few moments, his special talent grew manifest, as his body began to fade, to become misty, and in a few moments more, there was nothing in the room but a mist with two floating eyes.

Peter Quince had gone away.

] Wind (Advancing Possibilities)

The mist that was Quince centered itself in the subbasement of Lawrence Breckenridge's home. Quince knew that if Hanrahan had failed, that was the most likely place for him now, but Quince was hoping as hard as he could that the old man would not be there.

He was.

Hanrahan was strapped to a metal table, with an IV in each arm. He was high as a kite, the frantic high of way too much cocaine, the high that threatened to tear itself loose from its moorings and spiral far away. Quince could see the old man fighting it, and doing a surprisingly good job of it, by God—

Of course, Peter Quince. He chose the drugs in the first place.

Umm. And he is tough as nails. But he's no magician; he's never worked his will this far from solid earth. I'll see to him.

Peter Quince transferred his consciousness to the center of Hanrahan's mind.

"Partner," he said to him.

"Nnngghh," responded Hanrahan. There was consciousness there but it was inarticulate, using everything it had left to keep its mouth closed. Despite himself, Quince was touched by the old man's dedication.

"Partner," he said again. "I can put you under, so you can relax."

Kill him! snarled the demon. **We no longer need him. He's nothing but a danger to us now!**

It's not a question of "need," Master, Quince responded resolutely.

With my spell, he can do nothing but sleep. And his mind is a treasure trove, which we can use once we rule.

The demon never admitted a change of direction. **On your head, then!** was all he said.

"*Freem*," clamored Hanrahan.

"I can't give you freedom," Quince told the old man. "Doing that would reveal pretty much everything you're trying to hide. But you won't suffer any longer, and it will give me time to figure out what to do next. Don't worry, partner; you've had the worst of it." He laid his spectral hand upon the old man's mind and Hanrahan drifted into untroubled sleep.

Jacoby said, "He's passed out, Jimmy."

Willingham assessed the old man. "How are his vitals?"

"Still stable. That is one tough fucker."

"The drugs will keep tearing at him, anyway. When he wakes up, he'll be much worse off. So let him sleep and suffer the consequences."

THURSDAY, MARCH 24, 2011 • 8:47 A.M. CENTRAL DAYLIGHT TIME

3 Wind (Advancing Possibilities)

Back in his sanctum sanctorum, the mist with eyes re-formed into Peter Quince.

"All right. So Breckenridge knows about the plot—but not about me, or I'd already be under attack."

And does that not suggest something to you?

"No. What?"

Who could have betrayed him? You and he were the only ones who knew.

"Maybe the old man fucked up."

Did you sense regret or guilt? I did not.

"You're right . . ."

Breckenridge has his own demon.

"What? That's—"

Certain. Some outside force gave him his information.

"But if that's true, why didn't it know about me?"

We didn't know about IT. None of us is omnipotent, Peter Quince.

"It would explain a few things."

Hold.

Quince felt his master's force expand into the world. The wizard sat quietly in his circle and waited. . . .

None of the 999 others who serve me know of Breckenridge's demon.

"Not surprising, if we didn't. But you had to—"

Play, again, the recordings of Breckenridge's mysterious noise! I shall hear it with new ears!

Quince waved a hand like a conductor and the sound began to play in his mind with full fidelity. He felt his master listening, and Quince held still, fearful of distracting him.

At last: Leave Hanrahan where he is, and how he is. I must ponder this.

"I'll help you, Master!"

The answer does not lie in your realm, adorèd one. Wait, and be ready.

Quince felt the demon withdraw from him again—and shivered. His master's praise words failed to thrill him. He was empty now. He needed a smoke, and another woman in the basement.

THURSDAY, MARCH 24, 2011 · 1:30 P.M. GREENWICH MEAN TIME

3 Wind (Advancing Possibilities)

By the time she finished lunch, Vee had asked her questions every way she knew, and had narrowed Christopher Durban's hideout down to a large stone building, one you had to look up to. That was still maddeningly ambiguous—it could have been half of London if you were standing on the banks of the Thames—but it was all she could get at this point, so she'd spent the past half hour, while mindlessly eating fish-and-chips, creating her own "psychic vampire" spell.

The book was not going to be able to help her with that, but she took the spells she'd learned over the past two years and worked with them, trying to catch their flavor while turning them in the direction she needed—and in her case, phrasing her spell with all the internal rhythm and melody of those that had withstood the test of time.

Suddenly, her doorbell rang. She didn't get many visitors so she had a pretty good idea of who it was, but getting to the door included standing up and seizing up. She hobbled to the door and she was right: Matthew. He was holding a motorcycle helmet, and the bike itself was parked behind him on the street. It was red; the day was gray.

He had some opening line in place, but when he saw her condition, that all went away. "What the hell?" he blurted.

"More animal trouble," she said, waving it off. "I've learned my lesson. It doesn't matter."

"The hell it doesn't, Vee. You look like crap."

"More absolute truth?"

"No! You look like *yesterday's* crap."

She laughed. "Come on in, Matthew."

He came, but he wasn't laughing. "Seriously, Vee, what the fuck?"

Her laughter died, too. "Sorry, Matthew. That's not your business. You're not—"

"Your manager. I know," he said. "Can I at least be your friend?"

"Of course." She raised her palms in semi-surrender. "I'm sorry. I'm really—haven't had a lot of actual friends, lately. It's my choice; I have a lot of shit to work through . . . as I suppose you can see. But I'm glad you came by. Come on." She led him to the kitchen, moving a little better now. They sat down across from each other, she almost straight.

Matt was serious. "I saw private demons in your chart, but I thought you worked it out through your music."

"We all have demons. I'm Welsh."

"No, seriously—"

"Let's not," she interrupted. "I'm not going there. You just have to accept the fact that I like to keep myself to myself, as they say."

"Except when you tangle with tigers," he said, and leaned forward across the table. "Vee, are you in some sort of fight club?"

"No."

"Because those are a lot of bandages, and some of them are bleeding through."

She looked and saw what he meant. Her top showed dark blood along her side. "I'll fix it," she said.

"*I'll* fix it," he said. Scraping his chair back, he said, "Your medicine chest in the loo?"

"Don't bother."

"Vee, whatever's going on, let me help where I can. You may not want a manager but you don't have to do it alone."

I do, Vee thought. But she reviewed everything she knew about Matthew Raftery, and finally she nodded. "Look on the shelf above the toilet."

He brought out her kit and she turned her chair so she faced him. He gently lifted the bloody cloth, and said, "Hold that." She held it, and he began to peel the bloody bandage. It came away to reveal a gap in her flesh that had been well sewn up, but was simply too large to hold together at this early stage.

"Not a tiger," Matthew said quietly. "Large dog?"

Vee was ready to lie to him. But instead, she found herself saying, "Maybe I'll tell you later." Followed by, "Elizabeth Taylor died, yeah?" *Oh God! So lame!*

He took it in stride. "Sad thing, that."

"I didn't really know much about her. Do you? Being in the business?"

Now he smiled. "The *show* business?"

"Yeah."

"Not really my end of things, but Liz Taylor was a Brit who was so gorgeous she got to be an American movie star, and by all accounts she loved that life. She had a meteoric career, and then she got tired of the actual acting, so she just went on as a star. I thought it was brilliant."

"You like stars."

"I do. You've got to have big whatevers, to be a star. You've got to not only believe in yourself but you've got to get an audience to agree with you, to the point where they tell their friends, and you end up entertaining millions."

"And you end up doing drugs to get out on stage every night."

"Some do. Some don't. It's easy or it's hard, depending on the person. And if it was *too* hard, and I was that person's manager, I'd put her before her stardom. But I don't think it'll be hard for you."

"How'd we get talking about me?"

"*I* think you can be a star, and that *is* my end of things, so excuse me if I try to get you to at least consider it. But I plan on staying your friend no matter how many times you say no, so go ahead and say no again if you want."

Instead, she said, "Why do you think it would be easy for me?"

"Just the way you are. You're a private person, and you've got your demons, but you're a natural on stage. You could work theaters, arenas, and still go home and be yourself afterward. You're no diva."

Vee said nothing for a long moment. She was looking inside herself the way she'd looked at him before. Only then did she ask, "Are you about finished there?"

"About."

"It does feel better. The blood on my side was clammy."

He kept his eyes level, kept his tone casual. "So, what bit you, Vee?"

"I can't tell you, Matthew. I just can't. But," she found herself saying, "would you mind just holding me for a while?"

"Mind? No, I wouldn't mind. What are friends for?" He shrugged. "It's not as if we have any *professional* boundaries to worry about." He finished the bandage he was working on and stood up. "You can drop your top now."

"I think I need to change it."

"Sure. Where shall we sit, then? Not in these chairs. The front room?"

"No chairs there. It will have to be the bedroom."

He cocked his head. "Really?"

She stood up, creaky again, laughing at herself, feeling good. "Really."

"Because," Matthew said, "holding you might not be all I'd do, so far as you could stand it."

"I can stand a lot," said Vee.

THURSDAY, MARCH 24, 2011 · 8:25 P.M. MYANMAR TIME

3 Wind (Advancing Possibilities)

Twenty-five minutes later, in a time zone six and one-half hours away, two earthquakes struck the country of Myanmar, also known as Burma, less than a minute apart. They both registered 7.0 on the Richter scale and killed over 150 people immediately, but the survivors could feel it: there would be more.

THURSDAY, MARCH 24, 2011 · 10:00 A.M. EASTERN DAYLIGHT TIME

3 Wind (Advancing Possibilities)

The rain fell like blood on the Dies Sanguinis. It was *thick* somehow, not really blood-thick, but not really fluid, either. It had *weight*, no doubt from the freezing weather, and the mercs felt it, pounding down upon them, rolling stolidly down their jackets. It had a *scent*.

"Darryl Royal is AWOL," Ruth roared through the rain, with Franny at her side. "He was last seen at oh-three-fifteen this morning, when he and Aparicio"—here, she gestured at Max—"began their stints along the river. Royal had the west side, Aparicio the east, and they both started from the center, but after the first walk up and back, where Royal arrived just as Aparicio was turning around, Aparicio didn't see him again. But I don't believe a man like Royal would go AWOL on his own. I have to conclude that it's related to the lockdown we've been under. I have to conclude, gentlemen, that we are under attack. As of now, you will patrol in pairs, and you will check in every fifteen minutes. Those patrolling at eleven will demonstrate their combat prowess to me personally, and their weapons prowess to Chief Rupp, before heading out. We are at T minus one and we will not be stopped now. Dismissed."

"You look like crap, man," Bragane said to Max.

"Not getting a lot of sleep," Aparicio admitted. "But what's this shit about Royal, huh?"

Bragane barely nodded, his mind obviously on other things. "C'mon, hang back here a minute."

"Glendenning wants us to show how we'd rip out a throat."

"Let the others go first. I gotta talk with you."

"Really?" said Aparicio reluctantly, remembering their other talks.

"Really," Bragane said. "I'm serious, man."

"All right then." They *were* on the same team, after all.

The two men drifted to the side of the building across from the citadel, where they could keep an eye on the others' progress into the screening area and still talk among themselves until it was their time.

"What's up?" Aparicio asked.

"I think they killed Royal, and they're planning to kill us, man," said Bragane, sotto voce.

"What?" Max was genuinely caught off guard.

"Look, we're pretending to be the Men in Black, riding on the Black Helicopters. Meanwhile, the real MiB's are out there, but we're not engaging with them. There's only one reason for that, and that's that we've cut a deal with them."

"Or they don't exist," Aparicio said.

"Right. You've seen what *we* can do and you don't think *they* gave it to us? 'Elder doorways'? We didn't invent that. So look—we *think* we're pretending to be MiB's, and we're gonna do something spectacular tomorrow night. What if the *spectacular* thing is a bunch of *dead* MiB's, meaning *us*? I think that's the deal they made. I think the MiB's are gonna be shown to be a gang of thugs, which is what we can easily be made out to be, and not aliens. It *proves* that it was all bullshit, see, and that's the end of the last real legend of aliens. We've forgotten about Roswell, and the Grays, and the abductions, and now we'll forget about the Black Helicopters. We'll forget about aliens altogether, *which is what they want.*"

"Dude, really, you saw *Battle: Los Angeles* too many times," Aparicio responded derisively.

"C'mon, man. Think about it. *Somebody* killed Royal, and they did it for a reason. How about, he knew the truth about who we work for?"

"We don't know that."

"You see him going AWOL?"

"No, I don't. But that doesn't mean aliens."

"*Somebody's* gonna foreclose on our birth certificate accounts."

"Wait. How'd we get back to that? Or is that what you meant by 'foreign investors.'"

"Yeah," Bragane said. "The Men in Black. And don't you think, if they ever plan to foreclose, *now* is the time to do it? It's all about foreclosing right now."

"Bragane—"

"This is the time, Aparicio. It's the End Times. But most people don't see it because of tricks and deceptions like they've got planned for us."

"Look, man," Aparicio said, "I don't know. And I'm beat to shit. But I promise you, I'll keep alert tonight and tomorrow, and I will have your back if anything happens. If it does, we can talk about this again."

Bragane nodded. "Yeah, okay. I don't usually say so much, but I'm telling you, man, it's the smart move for them. It's what I'd do."

) Wind (Advancing Possibilities)

Ruth and Franny were deep in conversation when Di entered Franny's office. Ruth gave her a calculating glance, assessing her place in the new game, and Franny simply tightened her lips. Di could hardly miss it, but she could, as always, pretend she did. "Just came to say good-bye," she said cheerfully. "I really hate to go, with everything that's happening here. This is the eye of the storm. But I've got to get back to Chicago and get my own people set."

"I hope you got what you wanted here," said Franny, pro forma.

"Absolutely," answered Di. "I saw everything there was to see, I think. And although I told both you and Breckenridge that I wouldn't report on anything I saw to the public, I'll report to *him* that you two are amazing. I wasn't expecting all this drama, but you two rode right through it without turning a hair."

"We're a machine," Ruth said; it couldn't hurt to keep the relationship working, now that the intrusion was ending. "Franny's got the real machines, but we all do our part. We're prepared for the expected and the unexpected, and if we lose, it will have to be something tremendously unexpected that causes it. Otherwise, we're bound to win. Why overthink it?"

"Absolutely," Di said. "Well, it's all going in the Necklace archives, for future generations, and I want you to know, it's all good. People down the line will know what you're doing here."

"All right, then," said Ruth, glancing down at the papers she held. "Safe journey home."

"Umm," Franny concurred.

"Knock 'em dead," said Di sincerely, and left.

3 Wind (Advancing Possibilities)

Peter Quince took I-535 across the bridge to Superior, Wisconsin, and cut over to Tower—a street that still amused him, considering the name of his predecessor as the Necklace wizard. This Tower led straight to the Superior Walmart, where he reconnoitered slowly until he found his ideal arrangement: cars and trucks forming an inverted U. They blocked the rest of the lot seeing what went on there, and offered the promise of a variety of customers. He pulled his van to a stop across from the mouth of the U and climbed into the back to look through the tinted windows. He lit a cigarette and settled down to wait.

Lucrecia Gálvez came trundling her shopping cart across the lot as quickly as she could. It was fourteen degrees out there, and the wind from the lake made it colder still. The sky was endless waves of gray clouds and she was just four months from El Salvador. She had a winter coat but it wasn't thick enough for this, and she had no gloves. There was no ring on her left hand that Quince could see.

She came to a beat-up green Toyota in the U and popped the trunk, starting to transfer her purchases from the cart. Peter Quince slid open the van's side door and stepped out in a cloud of smoke. "Hello," he said to Lucrecia. "Need any help there?"

"No, thank you," said Lucrecia, giving him a wary smile.

He came toward her, smiling, thinking *How in the hell can anyone survive as a woman? Smaller, weaker—and always at the mercy of people like me.*

Pam and her pals were deep in the heart of the forest. The trees here were tall and black, and the thunder she'd heard in the distance a while before had moved overhead. In a very few minutes it was going to rain, hard. The trees sighed and moaned, their swaying branches intertwining to form faces of alarm.

"Can't you do anything about this storm, Cocorik?" Pam asked.

"Not me," said the sylph. "It's coming from the outside."

"You sylphs aren't doing it?"

"Didn't I just say—?"

"Then who is? Belia'al?"

"I don't smell him," said Funt quickly, as if to convince herself.

"Me, either," Mymla concurred, just as quickly.

"Me, either," said Pam. "But there's something wrong, and it's too coincidental for him to have been here and *not* be connected somehow."

"Well," Cocorik said, "everything's connected in this world."

"How long till we get to the Eagle now?"

Before anyone could answer her, they distinctly heard a crunching of branches nearby. They all turned to look and beheld a short, muscular shape, stepping out from among the trees on dainty hooves. Pam stared at it. She *knew* it, at least from pictures. It was the goat-god, *Pan*! His red eyes were alight in the shadows, staring fixedly at Pam. A crest of hair began low above them and ran upward, widening like a long widow's peak, the lines of it sweeping up into his tightly curling horns.

"It must be Spring where you come from," breathed Chiss. "That's when *he* appears."

"It wasn't Spring before *she* got here," buzzed Cocorik.

Then the storm broke and the goat-god launched himself, pounding toward them on his short, powerful legs. The elementals scattered and Pam had just time enough to put up a shield before he leapt upon her and sent them both crashing to the ground, rolling. Pam gave a sharp burst of gravity control to lessen the impact but she wasn't very good at that yet and hit harder than she'd have liked. She threw another burst straight at him to get him off her, but it did even less. He started ripping at her clothes—there was no mistaking his intention. The image of herself on her knees in London roared through her and she punched him hard in the face. He looked surprised, and more so when she did it again. He laughed, a thick, goaty sound of enjoyment. She hit him again and felt a knuckle give, and she hit him again and was nowhere near done. London had done that to her.

His face showed stirrings of anger. His thick lips drew back, exposing strong white teeth. Pam readied herself for his next assault. "Come on, then," she said. But before the fight could continue, Chiss leapt past her into the bristly hair between the horns, seething with white-hot intensity. The goat-god slapped at him but missed as Chiss skipped to one ear, then the other, like a spark from a conflagration. Pan slammed himself in the ear, then tried to leap back, only to find his foot pinned to the ground by Funt. He fell on his butt like Pam had, and that gave Dr. Blackwell all the time she needed to muster her magick and slam it into him, with all the gravity she could. His immobilized leg snapped and he roared in rage and pain.

Pam scrambled back to her feet, and stood over her assailant, who now began to hug his broken leg, bleating. "Let him go, Funt," she said, breathing hard. Funt looked up at her, then complied.

Pan instantly used his short, powerful arms to pull himself away from them, sliding on his butt back into the forest with his bent leg dragging painfully behind. Cocorik flew after him, chattering nastily while staying just out of any possible counterattack. Pam turned to Chiss.

"That was brave of you," she said to him.

He puffed up a little, made a small hop. "I would lay down my life for you, Pam."

"Well, please don't," she said, smiling to take the sting from her words. "I appreciate the sentiment, but I don't want any of you to get hurt. I don't want any of you going away."

"And yet *you* brought the spring to us," said Cocorik. "It wasn't spring till you came."

"I get it," Pam said. "My bad. Animal urges. But you know what, guys?"

"No," said Mymla, "what?"

"*I'm* no animal!"

THURSDAY, MARCH 24, 2011 · 3:32 P.M. GREENWICH MEAN TIME

3 Wind (Advancing Possibilities)

Vee and Matthew were lying in her bed, her hand on his stomach and his on hers, watching the lowering sky outside. It looked hot and sweaty out there—and it had been hot and sweaty in here. But out there it looked uncomfortable.

Vee was very aware that her only other companion for the past two years was in the front room, not very many feet from this bed. It was strange to have another companion after all this time, but Cornelius had no body beyond the book, and acted like it. He was a mentor, maybe a father figure—while she was quite happy being a woman, and not a crazy girl any longer. Quite happy. Even if her first word was "Ouch."

"Too much?" Matthew asked.

"Yes. But in a good way."

"You said 'ouch.'"

"Same as 'wow.'"

I've never had this before, Vee marveled. *Except I knew all about it, from sometime in the past. The blessings of my very strange life.*

She brushed Matthew's chest, lightly, with her fingertips. "How much occultism do you actually know, Matthew?"

"A lot. Astrology, Qabalah . . ."

"Do you do anything with it? I mean, can you use it for power? Combat power?"

"Combat power? What are you on about now?"

"Just humor me."

"Well, no, I can't use it for combat power. It's knowledge, and I can use it for *show business* power, like when to sign a contract, or scope the trends before they happen. I know with some certainty what to look out for in the next ten years."

"Really? Like what?"

"I'll tell you sometime—but right now I want to know why you're looking for combat power."

"*I* have combat power," she said, keeping her gaze on the clouds. "But not enough. And I'm being stalked by a psychic vampire."

"I've been called worse."

"I mean it, Matt. And he controls stuffed animals, and stuffed people. That's how I got bitten. It was a stuffed wolf and a stuffed fox, both with the original teeth." She dragged one nail back and forth, staring at the ceiling, dreading what she had to ask. "Still want to be my manager?"

He turned on his side to look at her. "Absolutely. Especially when you call me 'Matt.' Tell me about the vampire, Vee," he said.

"*Psychic* vampire. There's a difference, as *this* taught me."

"Psychic vampire, then. What's the story and how can I help?"

"The story . . . ," she said. "Well, his name is Christopher Durban, a very gaunt man who spoke to me Monday night. He took some power that night, so Tuesday I went after him, and met his animals. Last night I met them again, and discovered that neither he nor they was really alive. Apparently, they run off the power he steals from me, and probably others."

"Okay, run that part about 'I went after him' by me again."

"I told you. I take care of myself."

"How's that working out for you?"

"Not so well. But I can't quit. Otherwise, he'll make me his slave, and everything I've become, and everything you think I will become—it all goes away. I go away."

He took her chin in his hand. "You're serious. Everything you're saying?"

"Yes."

"Jesus," he said, thinking hard. And then he shrugged. "Well, fortunately for you, Vee, I like that sort of thing, and I like you. And maybe I *can* help a little, at that."

"How? You're not that Mr. Cornelius you talked about."

"No. But he didn't have my contacts in London. Let's see what I can turn up on Christopher Durban, psychic vampire and taxidermist." He stretched an arm over the side of the bed, retrieved his pants from the floor, and slipped out his iPhone.

In the front room, the book flipped open and words lit up, but there was no one to read them.

THURSDAY, MARCH 24, 2011 · 11:09 A.M. CENTRAL DAYLIGHT TIME

3 Wind (Advancing Possibilities)

Debarking in Chicago, Di was met by her personal limo and taken directly to Full Resource Central. There was a bank of four fourteen-inch flat screens in her seating compartment and she studied them all as they made their way along 90. The Black Helicopters had retreated from the main news, but Joe Keeler on the business channel managed to toss in a joke about it, just making sure it stayed on the edge of people's minds, and Harry Levine on sports hit it, too.

The limo exited on Grand and after several blocks turned south toward the river. After just two days in Fort Wayne, the buildings looked huge, massive and cold against the gray skies. Spring might have sprung on the calendar but it was at least two weeks away in the windy city. They pulled into the FRC underground garage and she exited with a sincere smile for her driver, then caught her private elevator. The button for "61" began her ascent.

There were sixty-nine floors in this riverside building. The public elevators had access to the first fifty-nine. Floor sixty, like floor sixty-nine, was a buffer zone, packed with the Necklace's standard kill-zone technology, in case anyone felt like accessing the inaccessible floors. Only Di's private elevator and one available to her top staff could reach the Middle Sixties, as they were called.

She stepped out on sixty-one, her private floor, and waved to her private secretaries. She was back in business.

❋ ❋ ❋ ❋

The demon went down to hell.

It was a closed-in cavern in the stifling claustrophobic chaos beneath the reality of Earth, not at all what Peter Quince had thought he'd seen when he'd first encountered it. The thrones, the fire, there was none of that in Belia'al's vision. It was a stark world, stripped of all finery, all magick, just tumbled boulders lying where they'd fallen when he had fallen, precisely as logic would dictate. They had all fallen from a great height, so the great hole they occupied was empty and singing with stillness the way only the underground can be.

Belia'al, king of demons, settled upon a crag, sharp edged and nearly molten, where he squatted and pondered as if taking a dump.

Who is Breckenridge's demon?

There remained no doubt in his mind of its existence, but what didn't ring true was its nature. **I am the king of demons and I know nothing of it. Logically, then, it cannot *be* a demon.**

It must be a diabola.

Diabolas don't need human hosts because they *were* human. Diabolas are humans who grew into the universe but insisted on maintaining their personal identity instead of becoming one with all. Their sin is pride, like my brother Lucifer, but they're not fallen angels. They're risen humans.

And *I* am *king* of the *demons!*

As a diabola, Aleksandra felt the thrust of his knowledge through the universe.

3 Wind (Advancing Possibilities)

She appeared before Breckenridge. *We have a problem, Renzo.*

"Hanrahan is taken care of—"

That's the past. I'm talking about the future.

"What is it?"

Belia'al has discovered my existence.

Breckenridge cocked his head. "How is that possible?"

He came to understand that you had a benefactor. There are very few possibilities. Discovery was inevitable.

"He knows *you*, diabola?"

Not me personally. He knows I'm a diabola.

"But you knew about him. Couldn't you hide—?"

Which part of "inevitable" don't you understand?

"I don't understand *why* it was inevitable!"

Because you aren't at his level, let alone mine. There is no hiding when forces are ethereal, only ignorance, and ignorance can end.

"But you're still above him?"

Of course. But I was superior to Max August when HE beat me. Belia'al draws power from his slaves, both human and demon, and they are legion. There are no guarantees in magick, so you and I must do everything we can, beginning now.

"Does he know you know?"

No. He will prepare himself, just as I'll prepare myself, to strike with maximum power. We still have time to surprise him.

"What do you need me to do?"

I need you to understand how this war will be fought, Renzo. Ethereal forces can only interact at set intervals, on the breath of the universe.

"The breath—?"

Call it a breath or a tide, but it moves in, out, in, out, reversing itself every three hours, or eight times a day. The standard time count on Earth was unconsciously set to it, so it tracks Greenwich Mean Time: noon, 3 P.M., 6 P.M. . . . Here in New York, it's four hours earlier, so the next reversal comes at 2 P.M., then 5, 8, 11 . . .

Breckenridge stood up straighter. "Two P.M. is half an hour from now."

The demon won't be prepared that soon, and neither will I. But when we go to war, one of us will launch it on the breath, and you will know it. From that point on, look for a reversal every third hour. Eventually, there will come a time when the flow should be with one of us and that one will not be able to handle it. That one will lose.

"Him." Breckenridge had no doubt. "I know your scope, diabola. After nearly twenty years, I'd better."

Yes. I expect to win. But we shall see. In the meantime, even as the universe breathes in and out, everyone on Earth remains in continuous danger from the demon.

The Gemstone laughed shortly. "I'm at risk every day. Just ask Dick Hanrahan. You do what you need to do to destroy that fucker, and don't even think about me."

THURSDAY, MARCH 24, 2011 · 1:23 P.M. EASTERN DAYLIGHT TIME

3 Wind (Advancing Possibilities)

Max walked his beat, and felt the vibes.

Vast things were happening, all around him, and his primary concern was Pam. None of it was directed at him, as far as he could tell, but was any of it directed at her? How was she handling whatever was going on? He'd done everything he could think of to help her, and now all he could do was feel the power wash through him. It didn't feel good.

Bragane was walking the other end of the road, and no doubt his every sense was alert, in case the Men in Black who killed Royal came back. And that was the crazy thing: there were Men in Black. Max had met one by way of Coyote, in 1990. The part of Bragane's theories that was most true was the part traditionally regarded as beyond imagining. The newer parts were paranoid fantasies, and they were considered possible. Max knew better than to believe in "End Times," but these were certainly *crazy* times. And they were getting *crazier* by the hour.

He spotted Franny walking toward him, stoically picking her spots past the mud puddles.

He came to a respectful standstill, if not attention. "Chief."

"How're you doin', Aparicio?" Franny asked, looking him over.

"Outstanding, Chief."

"Right. You're droopin' right before my eyes."

"Better now than yesterday morning."

"Pardon me?"

"Just sayin'."

Franny's homely face snickered. "I still like your balls, Aparicio. There's nothing I'd like better, normally, than to give you a chance to stop pullin' double duty to come on back to my bunk. But these aren't normal circumstances, so I can't spare either one of us."

I'll try to bear up, Max thought, but said, "Yes, Chief."

"I'm wonderin', now that you've a chance to think, if you've had any further thoughts about Royal this morning, or any time leadin' up to his disappearance."

"No, Chief."

"Any ideas on his disappearance itself? Royal wasn't the kind of man to go down without a fight, and you were closest to him."

"I didn't see or hear anything."

"Any chance you were asleep? Most natural thing in the world, the hour before dawn . . . after all your other shifts."

"No, Chief."

"Because I've talked with the two men working the sides of the Works, and the men on this end of the compound, and there's some feeling that there was a shot out here."

"Some feeling, Chief?"

"Some disagreement as to whether there was a shot or not. But o' course, you were closest."

"I did not hear a shot, Chief."

"Let me be clear, Aparicio. I have no inclination to punish you further, if you're straight with me. Royal was one of us, and I *will* find out what happened to him."

"I did not hear a shot and I was not asleep and I want him back as much as you do."

"If you're lying to me I will fuck you up good," she said grimly.

"It's the truth, Chief."

"Shit!" With that expression of disgust, she turned on her heel and walked away. Her foot immediately sank to the ankle in muck, and she let out a curse Max would have been proud to own.

But he did not like the vibes.

3 Wind (Advancing Possibilities)

"You're not going to believe this—oh wait. Why wouldn't you?"

Matt had his pants on, his shirt on but unbuttoned, and his iPhone in his hand. Vee was stretching slowly, keeping herself as limber as she could, wearing a leotard for warmth. She asked, "More weirdness?"

"There are records for a Christopher Durban, taxidermist, of 7 Cragmoor Mews."

"Yes?"

"In 1882." In his mind: *ba-dump-bump!*

But Vee just grew contemplative. "Could he really have been living off other people for all these years?"

Matt grimaced. "See, that's what I meant. You don't even question it."

"Of course not. I've seen his dummies and you haven't."

"Well, maybe I'm about to get my chance. Because Christopher Durban's home and shop are maintained to this day by a trust."

"Now *that* confuses me," she said. "His home is still there, at 7 Cragmoor Mews?"

"Yes."

"Then why did he give me his name?"

"To bait the trap? Get you to go to his lair?"

"He hasn't needed traps so far."

"That's what I thought, too. So let's go have a look."

"Not 'we,' Matt," Vee said, smiling but firm. "It's very sweet of you, but this is beyond even a manager's pay grade. Durban is too dangerous."

"But he won't be there; isn't that your theory? Mine, too. So there's no danger at all. Let's go."

"You don't even have a gun," she said.

"According to you, guns don't work against Durban. But I have *this*." So saying, he pulled out his lighter and flicked it to flame. "Polyurethane melts. Plus, you'll need a lookout."

"Matt," she said, "it's dangerous and it's against the law."

"But *you're* doing it, yes?"

". . . Yes," she said reluctantly. "I need to know everything I can."

"And whatever you do from now on, I get a cut."

"All right, all right," she said, judging it okay after all, surrendering. "You have one advantage—"

"Thanks."

"I mean, he thinks *I'm* a delicacy."

"And I'm fish-and-chips."

"Pretty much. He's wants me, not you. And not me until I regain some strength. But don't ever think he won't take you if he's cornered."

"Even then, he won't kill me; he'll keep me alive, so we'll have the chance to come out on top in the end."

"What happened to telling the unvarnished truth?"

"It's right there. I cannot believe that the future I see for you is going to be snuffed out before it begins. The unvarnished truth is, even if he is over a century old, we'll beat this guy, because you're going to be a superstar in *our* century."

In the front room, the book flipped open, banging the altar. "What was that?" Matt asked.

"Something loose on the roof," Vee said. "I need to get it fixed."

"No, it wasn't from outside. Stay here."

"Matt—"

"I'll be right back." He began to move stealthily toward the front room, so she reached out and took his arm.

"Matt," she said. "I know what that noise is, and I'm not worried about it. Beyond that, I don't *need* a *protector*."

"You can still use my help."

"No, seriously. You know more than I do about careers. I know more than you about Christopher Durban. When it comes to this, I'm calling the shots. I'm sorry, but that's how it has to be."

A look passed over his face, not so much "no" as "I'm not saying yes and I'm not saying no." It wasn't masculine pride, it was manager pride, reserving the right to disagree with the artist. What he said out loud was, "I still want to take a look around. I could bear to see the full extent of this place." He cocked his head, mildly. "Unless that's a problem."

Watching him, Vee read it all and once again figured, *I can live with that.* "Go on, then," she said.

He parted the sheets hiding the front room, and came to a halt before the magickal space—the ancient, intricate circles on the floor, the altar in the center, the implements upon it, the leather-bound book, lying open.

"Okay . . . ," he said.

"I was going to tell you in stages," she said from behind him. "I read somewhere, that's how it should be done. But this damn flat's too small!"

"You could tell me now. . . ." He turned back to look at her, his face a study in wonderment.

"I've been into magick . . . all my life."

"So you *do* have power." He looked again at the circles by his feet. "I know this layout. *The Lesser Key of Solomon.*"

"Maybe. I got it from somewhere else."

He stayed outside her circle but regarded the open book in the center of it. "From this?" he asked.

"Uh-huh."

Leaning, peering. "Looks like Latin."

"Yeah." But she could see the English of it, and the witchfire playing on it.

Reality is dual, but reality is real, the book read. *Forget neither.*

DELUGE

Pam and her friends came out of the forest to find the sky a vast jumble of angry gray, pelting them with rain. It had fallen hard enough through the forest's canopy, and with no canopy it was a deluge. They stepped back into the tall trees' shelter for a moment, and watched the water swirl across the path.

"This is caused by whatever's going on in my world, yes?" Pam asked the others.

"Yes," said Mymla.

"But you're not involved in it? This rain?"

"No," the naiad responded. "Elementals carry the will of nature to your world, but here, nature needs no help."

"So it's pouring down rain because . . . ?"

"It feels like it."

Pam regarded the rain coming out of the sky. "Something is going very wrong out there," she said with a touch of awe, remembering Max's words, "There's something going on here." *I think you should have asked for more specifics,* she told herself. *This can't just be Black Helicopters. It's like . . . a war behind the sky.*

"Come on," she said. "The sooner we get to the Eagle, the sooner we can do something about this."

"That's right," said Chiss, brightening a little. But Pam looked down at him, and asked, "How can *you* go on if it's raining like this?"

"Funt protects me," said Chiss, and only because he did not know Pam well did he miss the sudden amusement in her eyes, which she quickly suppressed. *You were going to protect me, and now you need Funt to protect you. I'm sorry. It just sounds funny.* But all she said was, "How?"

"I enclose him," the gnome said.

"Like armor."

So Funt stepped up close behind Chiss and held her arms around him, apart, the way Max held his power. And that was not a bad comparison, since when Pam gave the word and they went forward into the downpour, the rain splashed hard against an invisible shield encompassing the salamander. Of course, Funt had to stay right behind Chiss. She didn't seem to mind.

They soldiered on.

THURSDAY, MARCH 24, 2011 · 1:23 P.M. EASTERN DAYLIGHT TIME

3 Wind (Advancing Possibilities)

Hanrahan felt the bad vibes. This deep in the drugs he had no more filters. But it only made him laugh the louder.

THURSDAY, MARCH 24, 2011 · 2:00 P.M. EASTERN DAYLIGHT TIME

3 Wind (Advancing Possibilities)

At 2 P.M., Lawrence Breckenridge stopped what he was doing and tried to feel the breath of the universe. He stood stock still and waited, calling upon whatever he'd assimilated from twenty years with Aleksandra . . . but he couldn't feel anything. Neither was he attacked, so he went back to his business. The breath of the universe was out of his control.

THURSDAY, MARCH 24, 2011 · 8:15 p.m. GREENWICH MEAN TIME

} Wind (Advancing Possibilities)

The Hour of Jupiter is concerned with the living of life in full measure. It is good for expansion, and good fortune.

Vee had carefully calculated the Hours of the Night, and this Night the Hour of Jupiter began at 8:15 exactly. She and Matt had left her flat a little before 7 beneath a warm red sunset, ridden the tube to Clapham Common, and ascended to a cooling night. They walked briskly to a turning off Elsley Road. Fifty yards in, another asphalt path crossed the first one, and in addition to the crossing's four directions, a fifth passageway, barely ten feet across, curved away to the left. That was Cragmoor Mews. At 8:15 they entered it.

The first house to the left in Cragmoor Mews was Number One, while the first house on the right was Number Thirteen. That could put Number Seven at the end, beyond the curve. Though Vee and Matt both were wearing running shoes and trying to be quiet, any noise at all, even the jingle of change in his pants, brought small echoes off the close-in two-story buildings. The pavement was cobblestones and no help to footing. To Matt, this was not so much 1882 as 1782—a little piece of London that had gotten lost in the shuffle. Or maybe—

He touched Vee's shoulder, leaned in toward her ear. "I wonder," he said in a low tone, "if the preservation of Durban's house includes the preservation of Durban's mews."

She nodded. The same idea had occurred to her.

They rounded the corner, beneath the only streetlight. Somewhere above them, a cat howled, and the echo raced around them like panicked mice. Was it a real cat?

Dead ahead now appeared Number Seven. It was an old building but in excellent condition, better than any of the other houses in the mews. Money was being spent to maintain it, keep it painted. The first incongruous thing they'd seen was attached to the front window: a sign from Baldwin Security.

"There's no place to hide on this street. We have to be on CCTV," Matt said.

"I'm not worried about that," replied Vee. "I've sussed why he wants me here."

"Why?"

"To show me his power. It's a mind game."

"Is it working?"

"Not on me. I've got a tough mind."

"And I've got about ten percent of *that*," he said lightly. But his expression was wary.

Vee walked straight to the front door and tried it. It was locked. Then she tried the window with the sign, and it slid upward smoothly. She looked back at Matt to say, "See?"

She went through the window.

Matt followed. The interior of the house was lit only with the pale yellow light of the distant streetlight. With eyes well adjusted to the night now, they could see that in some ways it resembled Vee's own flat: a rectangular space divided by usage. But whereas in her space, the front area was a mystical room, Durban's was his taxidermy shop. A deer's head leered beneath its antlers from the right-hand wall. A tiger skin lay on the floor, and next to it, the rib cage of some smaller animal. A ram's head with great curved horns lay upside down next to that. To the left, several more small animals—ferrets?—crouched atop a glass-doored storage case, looking down upon a cubic stone topped with a mound of hair. A series of ducks, arranged from small to large, hung on the wall beside them. A hawk soared motionless near the low ceiling, which was fixed with heavy hooks. Several ropes were tied up there, drooping in loops low enough to catch an unwary throat.

But there were no cobwebs. The trust kept it clean.

Which made the slim trail of dust leading from the front door to the darker back all the more obvious in the gloom.

"He wants to show me," Vee said, her voice low but startling in the silence. She made her way past the rib cage, keeping an eye on the flattened tiger. "Do not trust any animal," she said. "Do not trust any *thing*."

Beyond the work area was a simple kitchen, and beyond that was a low bed.

With a body-sized depression in the mattress.

Matt thought of Hitchcock's *Psycho*, but Vee had never seen it. She went to the bed and peered closely at the dust gathered in the depression, then pulled out her small flash and looked closer.

"I think the doll I shot came here afterward. There's little bits of polystyrene in this."

"But it didn't come to recuperate. It wasn't alive. So—just to show you."

"Part of it was recuperation. Not regaining its strength, but sewing itself back together." She played her flash over a heavy needle and thread lying on the floor beside her foot.

She went back out to the front room and began examining the storage case, still keeping a watchful eye on the ferrets above. Matt lifted the deer head away from the other wall to look behind it, and she turned to remind him again, and in that instant saw the light of intelligence she'd seen in Durban's eyes flash from the eyes of the ferrets and then the ducks, one after the other, and then the hawk and then the deer lolling on Matt's shoulder.

Then it was gone.

Just to show her.

3 Wind (Advancing Possibilities)

At 5 P.M., Lawrence Breckenridge gave one more shot to feeling the universe breathe, and still felt nothing, so he resolved to let it go.

3 Wind (Advancing Possibilities)

It seemed to Max that he'd just fallen into a deep sleep when he felt Bragane approaching his bed. He opened his eyes.

"Good," Bragane said. "You're awake."

"Maybe," said Aparicio sourly. "What?"

"They moved the mission forward. We gotta go in."

"Fuck me!"

"Yep. Chief wants to get back in time to watch Butler play Wisconsin. Wheels up at seven." He leaned forward, overhead, a vial in his hand. "Five-Hour Energy. You'll need it."

3 Wind (Advancing Possibilities)

"I'm goin' with 'em," Franny told Ruth.

"The hell you are!"

"I'm not satisfied with what I'm seeing in the choppers. I gotta go out there and watch 'em in action."

"You sound like Di," Ruth said. "Are you saying the choppers are unsafe?"

"Would I be on them if they were? No, but I need to see how they stand up to the, the weirdness, in the moment."

"Franny, it's essential that we stay here, to guide the whole thing. I've got an overview, and so do you."

"Well, I want the underview, then. I want to *see* my choppers stand up to whatever's on the other side of that damn door!"

"Look, let's get serious here. You're one of the Nine. Getting killed is not in your job description."

"My—"

"Hang on. Your job description consists entirely of being part of the Nine. We rely on you. And especially you, because you're a Rupp. Your people are always here. But we've lost Jackson Tower and Mike Salinan in a little over three years. It's gonna take time with Quince and Whitten. So we need you to stay alive."

"Naturally. And do you know why us Rupps are still here? Because we do our job. My people didn't become an institution by accident. They checked and made sure what they said worked, worked, as specified and maybe beyond. You all rely on *us* because *we* rely on us."

But Franny let her shoulders settle, and her face grow solemn. "Things feel weird, Ruth. Don't you feel it? I hope we're not the cause of that, but whether we are or not, I've gotta see firsthand what we're up against."

Ruth nodded, grudgingly. "Yeah, okay. I hear you."

"No," said Franny doggedly, "you don't. Not really. I grew up in the Necklace, so I've seen wizard work all my life. You've only seen it these past ten years. And I can tell you, it's changed a lot since the late eighties. Tom Jeckyl started doing a lot more crazy stuff, and it's pretty generally worked out, but it's not what it used to be, and I don't like what it is. So I'm goin' out to see what I need to see and that's that."

"All right," said Ruth. "All right. But I'm putting you on the middle chopper for maximum protection. Aparicio's on that one. Is there a problem?"

"No," said Franny, but then stopped to consider it before continuing. "No, he's been solid through everything. That'll be fine. Now if you'll excuse me, I got work to do before we fly."

3 Wind (Advancing Possibilities)

The three choppers lifted off precisely at seven. The middle bird carried Franny Rupp, and Aparicio and Bragane. The mercs were well aware of their high-ranking passenger, but Franny wanted no special treatment and said so, as she stood up once they were airborne and began her last-minute instructions.

"Tonight we have a different mission from what was planned," she told them. "We are still going to waste a family and be seen escaping, but this particular family was switched out this afternoon for a reason. Somewhere inside their house is a magickal wand, consecrated—if that's what I mean—to some demon called Belia'al."

Aparicio twitched his shoulders, but said nothing. His eyes blinked twice.

"This wand is made of green jade," Franny went on, "and HQ wants it bad. If you see anything else that says 'Belia'al,' or looks like it might say 'Belia'al,' take that, too. HQ will sort it out. Make a thorough search but make it quick. Tip-off's at ten."

A murmur of appreciation for her attitude rippled through the chopper, though Aparicio appeared to be focusing on the task directly ahead, sitting quietly now at the end of the row.

The Necklace is at war with Belia'al. That's what all this is about—one of those battles that rages behind the scenes, so normal people never know why things turn weird on Earth. But does the Necklace know Quince works for their enemy?

Blink.

Di does. But she can't tell them because she can't say how she knows. Therefore, the Necklace is fighting blind.

Blink.

I can't get involved.

His eyes closed.

In the cosmos of his mind, he saw the face of Coyote, and it was not happy. *I tried every trick I know, Max. You couldn't think of a thing I didn't. But I had no luck.* His face grew closer, speaking on a level only Max would understand—a private word in a public forum about his fellow gods. *I talked with my tribe, and there's NO ONE who could find her. Totems are closer to the elementals than you are, but our world and theirs are separate things.*

Lorelei said, *This one flows with the life-force in many forms. It enabled her to follow Pam's life-force, to the elder doorway, and then beyond.*

Max and Coyote both said, *Lorelei!*

But she overrode them. *This one made her way easily among the salamanders and gnomes, and pushed onward toward the naiads, but she had no luck with the sylphs. In the end she could go no farther, and she did not find Pam.*

Korasu said, *I spoke with the sylphs. They say the same.*

I thought you were busy, said Coyote.

I am. But I found a way, for Pam.

Thank you, said Max, sincerely. They could all tell from Korasu's energy what that diversion had cost him.

I spoke with the naiads, said Mama Locha. *It's the same everywhere. The naiads I reach cannot say what's happening in other parts.*

Fetch thought, *Have you considered that they could be lying?*

Due respect, said Max, *but you don't know elementals.*

Elementals are forces of nature, yes? But they take humanoid forms. They can act humanoid. Humans lie. Pause. *Due respect.*

Elementals don't lie, said Kwasiba.

They don't, agreed Amba.

But they only know what's right around them, said Mama Locha.

So we know very little, said Scorpio Rose at last. *But we know this: Pam lives easily on the ASTRAL. She is close to a fée there. Any elementals she met would sense a kindred spirit. They will be her friends. Add that to her spirit, and her teacher, and one would have to see her fortune as a good one.*

Thank you, Rosa, said Max. *You're absolutely right. But we still don't know what we need to know.*

No one contradicted him.

All right. Thank you all. Please contact me any time if you learn anything.

He came out of his brown study to learn that the choppers had passed into the other realm. He stared through the open hatch and watched the veils of color spiraling past in long, thin streams. He could understand how someone seeing them for the first time, in amongst them, could think of them as trees. For all the good that did him, or Pam.

FLOOD

Pam peered through the rain, her hand shielding her eyes, and saw a swollen, raging river running perpendicular to their path. Everything everywhere was dark blue except for the foaming white of rapids.

"Is there a better point to cross?" Pam asked.

"I thought you liked water," said Cocorik cattily.

"This is the best place," said Mymla. "The river is narrow here."

"Narrow? It's—I can't even see the other side in this rain."

"It's not hard when there's no rain. I carry Chiss and Funt."

Cocorik added, "I fly."

Pam ignored him. She asked Mymla, "But can you carry them now?"

"Umm . . . ," said Mymla.

"No!" said Chiss.

"No," said Funt.

Cocorik said tartly, "So that's that. This is as far as we go."

But Pam turned to him now. "I can carry them."

"You? You're better in water than a naiad?"

"In this case, sure. I'm bigger, and I've done a lot of work on my survival skills. I can swim with one arm and hold Chiss and Funt above the water."

"They'll be heavy," said Cocorik with ill-disguised irritation.

"I can switch arms," said Pam sweetly. "But if I'm concentrating on keeping them safe, I'll need *you* to scout our route, so we take the shortest angle."

Cocorik looked doubtful.

"And I'll need *you,* Mymla," Pam went on, "to scout the water itself so I don't bang into a submerged boulder."

"Of course, Pam," Mymla said. "That's . . ."

"Ingenious," Cocorik said grudgingly.

"Just holding up my end," Pam told them. "I know there's usually just the four of you, so it's got to be strange having a fifth participant, but you would have thought of putting me to work soon enough."

The foursome muttered dubiously.

"Now, we'd better get started before the current grows any stronger."

So they all went down to the riverbank, where Funt made certain she was covering Chiss the best she possibly could, while Pam and Mymla walked down into the water, feeling the pull of the current, making their last calculations. Again, Pam had a moment where she *knew* she resonated to water, and naiads, and Eagles.

"Ready?" she asked, and everyone, even Cocorik, responded in the affirmative. And so, Pam picked up Funt and Chiss—who were actually not all that heavy, being elementals. She waded forward until the water was rushing past her chest, then pushed off strongly.

– 0 –

Aleksandra had focused on Belia'al. Now it was time to focus on herself.

I was on a rooftop in Moscow, 1963. On the astral, but plenty real enough to slow dance. We had music "on bones" from the West—transferred from a record onto X-ray film so it could be smuggled in. On the roof among the bright lights, big city, laughing with other boys and girls who had no idea I was huddled in Siberia, they played "Heat Wave" by Martha and the Vandellas. It was great, but what was greater was, I'd heard the Beatles play live. Moscow wouldn't know about the Beatles for months, and I'd shagged John.

I was superior. There was no way around it: I was.

But I was human, too. I wanted to dance on a rooftop in Moscow, with kids my age. I wanted to enjoy my humanity, even though I didn't know I'd leave it behind in twenty-two years. I was human and I shook my body.

That's the ticket of admission to Earth: a body. If you want to go on that ride, you pick a body and you go live where things have weight. Where when you've moved them, you've accomplished something. When you have a body, it's all real.

But you're not the body.

When the body wants food, you get it. When the body wants to dance, you dance. And when the body dies, you die, unless you've left it behind beforehand.

I became a diabola when I was thirty-six. Just a year older than Max. I had not even come close to using up my body before I ascended. I became a star, one of billions in the night sky. I burn deep red power and I look down upon the Earth. But I'm different from most of the stars. I kept my identity.

There are few diabolas. It takes a clear mind and an iron will. Why not simply let go and enjoy the ride as a star? Because I am Aleksandra Korelatovna!

If you're nothing but a body, then you'll believe in demon fables. You'll give the demon everything he wants, and you'll still die in the end. I hated my body. I was always as much more than just a body as I could be.

First my body trapped me in the Samarkand. Then it brought me Wolf Messing and his outsized appetites. But I had the talent to leave my body and I pushed that for all it was worth. I know bodies. I *know what pleasure Quince gets from Belia'al. The pleasure of the teacher's pet. You've accomplished something, for your master.*

I am no one's pet. I am no one's body. I am Aleksandra Korelatovna, and I am a star! I accomplished THAT!

I'll DESTROY that damned demon!

THURSDAY, MARCH 24, 2011 · 7:14 P.M. EASTERN DAYLIGHT TIME

] Wind (Advancing Possibilities)

Boom! Out of the doorway came the Black Helicopters, thirty feet above the ground, closing hard on an isolated cabin. The sun was setting behind them, so they'd flown east, and possibly north, with all that snow he saw below. Maine? Not Canada. The Necklace was not about Canada.

The other two choppers took the rear corners of the house as Aparicio's bird come down dead front. Shots fired from the right rear. The people in the house were trying to escape that way, and failing. It gave Aparicio's team a chance to move in. Fire was heavy as they closed the gap at a dead run. The defenders had numbers. Max protected everyone he could, on both sides, but the other two teams were coming in, too. Too many people. Too much commotion. A woman opened fire from an upstairs window, catching our team off guard. But the men in back had numbers, too, and the woman went down. No way to save her with everyone watching.

Then Aparicio's team was inside! He tried to take point but Franny shoved past him, her face eager, eyes gleaming. *She loves it,* he realized. *This is the woman who saw something she wanted in me and went after it. One of the Nine, and not that beer-drinkin' b-ball fan.* She fired off six rounds, cut a young woman in half, and went looking for more.

He let her go—because he felt the wand, below him. He put a burst in the flooring, chips flying, trapdoor shattering. Everyone else had his own problems; no one was watching him. He kicked out what was left of the door and dropped to a hidden crypt. The wand was hidden by a painting of St. Michael. The stench of Belia'al was all over it, but he didn't have to use it the way the people here did. *Magick's magick and I can use it any way I want!*

I can call Pam!

DELUGE

Pam could just see the other shore of the river when—

Pam!

Max!

Whoah! she thought. *Thank you, Jesus!*

She laughed in her relief and swallowed half the river, leading to a spasm of coughing. Chiss and Funt swung back and forth a little above the water. But she got it back under control, with Max's voice pounding in her brain.

Pam?

I'm—I'm here, honey.

How're you doin'?

I'm fine, Max. Just swallowed a little—water. I wasn't expecting—

Water?

I'm swimming a river. At least, I see it as a river. It's all good.

Really?

You sound surprised, she thought.

I am surprised, a little. Last time we talked, you were overwhelmed, and I was expecting . . . problems. He laughed, and she felt, as well as heard, the pleasure. *But I should have known.*

I've got four elementals helping me, Max.

Elementals? That's great! We tried every way we could to use them and got nowhere.

We?

All our friends. Yours and mine, he thought.

Well, tell 'em I'll see 'em real soon. We're going to find the Eagle. I know I can use her.

The Eagle Quince stole?

I thought it was Belia'al. He was here, Max—just before me, thank God.

I know. Quince and his master are in it together. I think they're at war with Aleksandra.

What the hell is going on out there? she demanded.

Dunno yet. But if Belia'al and Quince control the talismans—

He won't control the Eagle if I have anything to say about it!

He said, *This is a big load off my mind, honey.*

She could feel the pull of the current lessening as she neared the shore. *I've got this, Max. You take care of things on that side, and we'll be back together before you know it. I love you, Max!*

And I love you!

See you soon! And indeed, Max was no longer in her mind. But his words of assurance were.

Pam touched land.

3 Wind (Advancing Possibilities)

She's fine! She'll be fine!

"Aparicio? You find something?" Franny. Peering through the hole up there. Had she seen anything?

He raised the wand. "Is this your doodad, Chief?"

"Looks like it from here," she grunted, and squatted to get balanced before dropping down heavily beside him. He handed it over and she regarded it with a critical eye, not seeing any of the magick. "I hate these things. You scout the rest of this level?" she asked.

"Not yet," he said, knowing there was no one there.

"Then get to it, Aparicio. Don't disappoint me again."

"Yes, Chief," he said, and moved on into the shadows, which is where he wanted to be, anyway.

3 Wind (Advancing Possibilities)

Di sat in her producer's chair and looked down upon the darkened studio, and the three people sitting in front of the screens and the keyboards and the banks of electronics that filled one wall of it. It was dark to make the images on the screens pop, and the controls were marked out with small colored lights, like stars in space. All of it fed through her. She had total control over the reality that the FRC portrayed on televisions all across the country, and beyond. Push that lever, punch up number seven, match-cut *now* . . . and create reality, just like God.

She liked being back in her heaven.

"Annnd . . . *now,*" she said. In Studio 3-H, Andrew Fleming looked into camera one, sincerely truculent, and said, "We interrupt this program to bring you the following bulletin:

"At approximately seven fifteen this evening, an attack was reported upon an isolated home in Carrabassett Valley, Maine, a town of five hundred, two hours northwest of Portland. First responders say all eight people, including three children, who lived in the home are dead."

("One," said Di. The grainy cell-phone video of the Black Helicopters from Monday filled the screen.)

"Witnesses reported seeing Black Helicopters flying away from the scene. This is the third report of Black Helicopters this week, others coming from Montana and Oklahoma. Officials so far have made no comment on these sightings.

"We now return you to *Patrick Murtaugh Time.*"

ꓒ Wind (Advancing Possibilities)

At 8 P.M., Lawrence Breckenridge watched the broadcast on WFNY. Deciding what was to happen, telling Diana or one of the others to make it happen, seeing it happen before his eyes: that was where his power lay. And though he couldn't feel the universe breathe, he could sense a shift in the viewing public. It was visceral, that sense of public mood. There was fear out there. He was never wrong.

He picked up his phone and called downstairs. Jacoby answered.

"How's Hanrahan?" the Gemstone demanded.

"Still holding out, sir."

"He's a tough old buzzard," said Breckenridge, giving the devil his due.

"Would you like to see him?"

"No. Just let me know when it's done."

ꓒ Wind (Advancing Possibilities)

Peter Quince grew tired of waiting for his master to return, tired of being separated from the prizes he had entered the Fortress to retrieve, tired of being taken for granted, and tired of smoking. He could not and he would not do anything to confound his master's plans, but his master had no plans as yet, apparently, and Quince deserved *some* time with his talismans.

He locked the door to his sanctum, entered his circle, and began his incantations in a low, belligerent tone.

] Wind (Advancing Possibilities)

Vee and Matt got back to Hartland Road after midnight, having searched Durban's house from top to bottom. She was sure the psychic vampire's trick meant he was giving her all the time she needed to get her strength back, and she was willing to bet on it by staying. She was right—there was no further sign of Durban—but neither did they find anything of use.

"And you're sure it wasn't a trick of the light?" Matt was asking as they came through the door.

"I'm sure. It was him."

"So that is where he lives when he's not all dressed up as a wolf."

"It was. But we won't find him there again."

"No. He'll have moved out for the duration. He could be anywhere now."

"And yet . . . ," Vee said, eyes alight.

"What?"

"Geomancy."

"Divination with earth," said Matt dubiously. "Pretty simple stuff."

"*Very* simple. Binary, in fact—like a computer. And like a computer, you can do some amazing things with yes-or-no answers."

"What do you have in mind?"

"Durban has no real body. You and I can find his house, or his doll, but we can't find him. But divination operates on a spirit level, so it can find his spirit."

"Still, geomancy . . ."

"I divide a map of London in two and ask if he's on the left side. I perform the divination rite. When I come to the final answer, an odd number of dots means yes and an even number means no. I wait ten minutes, then I divide the remaining space in two and do it all again. Little by little I box him in."

"All right. And I'll try horary astrology, also designed to answer questions—though that's not one of my specialities."

"Good. But you know what, Matt? Before you do that, I don't have much food in the house, and all of a sudden I'm starving. Would you run down to the curry house, just to the right on Chalk Farm, and get us some takeaway?"

"Sure. What do you want?"

"Anything that looks good."

"Okay. Be right back."

He went out the door. Vee prepared herself quickly, then crossed into her circle and went to her book.

"He did fine," she said.

The phantasy, or imaginative power, has a ruling power over the passions of the soul when they follow the sensual apprehension.

"Look, woman does not live by magick alone. I deserve some happiness."

Deserve.

"Well, want. No, *deserve*. I lost so many years of happiness."

It is also manifest that such passions, when they are most vehement, may cause death.

"I understand. I haven't lost my way. But first he underestimates me, and now you do."

You are not me. You are you.

"Yes I am, Cornelius!"

STORM

Once Pam and the fab four crossed the river, the rain began to slacken a little. At first it confused Pam, because Max didn't sound as if any break in the demon-diabola war was coming soon. Then she wondered if it was because of her—if her solution to the river had changed some fundamental order, adding unexpected power to this realm. She couldn't know for sure, and she couldn't ask the elementals, since she *was* something new in their experience. But she let the thought warm her a little.

The path now led them over a series of small gray-green hillocks, as the land became more open. At each rise, they could look out through the lesser rain and see what lay before them, and the fourth time, Pam saw for the first time the mountains in the distance.

A ridgeline came in from the left of them to intersect a ridgeline from the right, and thus, the world around them was narrowing into a corner. The tops of all the mountains rose half-visible as writhing clouds ripped and re-formed up there. It was impressive.

But not as impressive as the fifty-foot Ox below their mound, between them and the corner of the mountains.

He was standing easily chewing his cud. Rain was sweeping from the left and he was facing full right, his butt to the rain, his face protected, water rolling off his back. His tail swished from time to time. Pam and the gang instinctively slowed their pace as they approached him, circling toward his face but giving him a wide berth. Pam brought them to a halt when looking up at him at eleven o'clock, as he might lean down to take a bite. The Ox, however, looked them over with benign interest, saw nothing alarming, and returned to his ruminations.

"Earth," said Funt proudly.

Pam could *feel* it. The creature was alive, at least in this fairy tale, but it was the prime conduit for earth power, that tight, compact, centering feeling. Solidity. She *felt* it with every fiber of her being, earth power beyond any doubt—and still, it was not *her* element.

That said, he's a god in this world, Pam thought. *In the real world, he's an eighteen-inch carving.* Then, compiling, *Come to think of it, in this world he's also an eighteen-inch carving. That's what Peter Quince put here. But this is how I see it. Fifty feet tall, and alive, and radiating that incredible power.* She looked down at her right hand. *Imagine power like that at your command, at your fingertips.*

And the Eagle was just on the other side of the mountains.

"Come on, guys," she told the foursome, and set out once more on the path toward that other side. "Up and over."

] Wind (Advancing Possibilities)

On the chopper home, Aparicio joined in the general celebration of their mission, without reservation. Sooner or later they would go back through the elder doorway and that would be his time.

"We'll make tip-off with time to spare," said Franny, to well-satisfied laughter from the crew. And soon enough, they did go on through.

STORM

Max saw the subconscious, gray and raining. The colors from before were completely gone. The woman and the men around him saw their dreams, but Max saw the subconscious and knew that he was on the same side of the veil as Pam—but he had no idea where. Fuckin' subconscious! They would both be seeing storms, but they weren't the same storms.

Nevertheless, Max saw the subconscious, unencumbered. The woman, the men, the choppers all faded away. Max was still exactly where he was, but everything from the real world was gone. He existed in the gray and rain, soaring through the air.

At least it looked like air.

Quickly, efficiently, the details of the gray and rain took shape as he understood them. He felt his feet pressing down on soft ground in a forest of bamboo. The rain was muted by the trees but the light cast everything in shades of gray. Max moved along the path, softly up and softly down, among the clacking trees, alert.

The *astral* was harder for him than it was for Pam. He didn't have her innate feel for it because it was a power of the Water energy and he was primarily Fire. An alchemist should be the master of all four energies, and he worked, off and on, to strengthen his control, so he was okay. But he couldn't do what she did.

The way grew grayer as he went, the light giving way to night. If anything were waiting to attack him, this would be the place to do it. And they might think he'd be complacent, having passed this way three times before. The colors of the path varied with the mood, but the path was always the same, leading a serpentine trail to the darkness in the deep woods.

The great stick trees wove in the stormy wind, smacking each other. There was continuous soft noise, hits of danger from all sides, and now there was the storm. On a night like tonight, anything could be hiding there. No longer unexpectedly, Max dug that. Woody Allen, of all people, said it best: "Eighty percent of success is showing up." Max liked showing up.

Also no longer unexpectedly, he could follow that train of thought while keeping his attention on the darkness, probing, receiving—living inside the darkness. Max saw the subconscious, and heard and smelled and touched and tasted it, too. Tiny thrills of adrenaline reacted immediately to any perceived threat.

This was magick of a different sort. Long before he'd wandered into the world of wizards, he'd been a magick junkie. He'd gotten it in the jungles of Viet Nam, when others around him were getting it from poppies. His version was more practical. Then, after the war, he "put away childish things," and he did radio on the edge, in the window on the street. He wooed and won the rock goddess. Only then did he learn magick from Cornelius Agrippa, and become Timeless, and lose Val, and set out to right the world.

"Set out to right the world." Max knew it sounded corny. He was no god, and he was not perfect. He could do stupid things with the best of them, and he had to face that. To do alchemy, he had to see clearly. But because he saw clearly, he knew that making the world a better place wasn't stupid at all. It was, in fact, extremely practical. Max knew that he was going to be living in this world for a while. If he wasn't killed, he would be here a hundred years from now. Five hundred. A thousand, maybe. There was no way of telling—other than being better than the bad guys—but he was going to live in this world this year, and next year, and the year after that, and the bad guys were nailing things down. His battles with them hurt them every time, but they were deeply entrenched, so it would take years to pry their noose from around the throat of America.

No problem. Democracy was worth that. That's what he believed.

Max passed through the heart of darkness, and out of the bamboo altogether, onto the shore of a tremendous lake. The night sky was a deep, deep gray, thick with barely discernable clouds, but less OBSCURE than the forest. Rain continued to plummet from it onto an exposed Max, the sloping ground, the water that sparkled with gray reflections as far as the eye could see.

This was where he'd stopped himself, three times before.

This time, he would go on.

He walked down the slippery slope toward the lake, and when he reached the lapping shore, he went on. He walked out onto the lake water, rejecting emphatically any comparison with anyone else. He was Max August, a guy who learned a skill. He learned alchemy, which taught him that the subconscious was all in how you understood it. He knew he was seeing what he could understand, which was different from doing it on the actual Sea of Galilee.

But the magick was the same. And it wasn't discomfiting to think that he and Jesus, and Agrippa, and Isaac Newton, and Ben Franklin, shared this bit of arcane knowledge. He was just Max August, but he had a killer skill.

He walked carefully over the rolling waves. Now any remaining danger would come from below, from the water into which he could not see. The water that twinkled with reflections of the sky, on all sides . . . that he came to understand, the longer he looked at it, he could see down into . . . all the way . . .

. . . until it wasn't water any longer, but was in fact deep space.

The twinkles were still there, on all sides, but now he could see that they were stars. They were cloudy at first, but soon enough were clear, sharp against the deep black of infinity, burning with a spectrum of colors.

They moved in relation to him. Or rather, he was still moving. He was soaring through space, effortlessly. Following an orbit.

The space-baby from *2001* was in his mind now: the huge Kier Dullea face, staring with childlike interest at the universe. But Max's interest was in no way childlike, and he was no child. He was exactly what he had expected he would be when he walked for the first time into unknown space.

He was a comet.

It wasn't just appearance. For all intents and purposes, here in space, Max had a different form, under the control of that shaolin mind. That form was a frozen lump of ice, dust, and small rocks. He was there but he could not be easily detected. That was the plan.

He soared through the void, toward a particular star. It was a red star, a young star, not long removed, as these things go, from its birth in a cloud of infrared dust. Its color was still infrared, though the human mind in the comet could only sense it, like an aura. The comet came near this star, moving in entirely predictable orbit, and as it came near, it began to feel the star's heat, so that its frozen surface began to melt, leaving a tail of dust behind. This sort of thing happened all the time. There was no reason at all for the red star to notice it.

The red star of Aleksandra.

Once upon a time, Max had kept himself and his buddies alive through infiltration. From the moment he understood that Aleksandra had moved to a higher dimension, he had felt that he would someday infiltrate it just as he'd infiltrated the 'Nam. He had never told Pam because she was just not ready. This required years of his time, but she would have wanted to join in, because that was her way. She would have tried to make use of it when she fell into the subconscious.

Pam was not the kind of woman to fail, nor the kind of alchemist. If Max did absolutely nothing for her, she stood a good chance of surviving her ordeal. But "good" was nowhere near enough, and Max was not the kind to do nothing if there was anything he could do.

The comet traveled past the star. There was no way to delay it.

The heat and light from the star began to strike the comet within a fairly narrow viewing range, like the sweet spot in 3-D. Max began to see the star with more detail than a simple scarlet glow, and he felt what he knew was Aleksandra. As he did so, the star pulsed once, and its consciousness expanded for a moment, encompassing space all around, encompassing him. But the pulse passed on and faded. She was alert for Belia'al, not for anything human, and to her the comet was only a comet.

So near now, Max wanted to strike at her with thirty years of hatred, but he had to accept that he didn't have the power for that yet. Not here. Everything he'd accomplished so far was nothing compared to what would be required for attacking Aleksandra on her home turf. But he would get there. All it took was time.

The comet moved on, the 3-D window fading, and Max flew still and silent, marvelling at what he'd witnessed. He had known Aleksandra as a woman, and he had faced her as a star, but he had never seen her as she truly was, as a diabola, a newborn star completely alone in deep space. He couldn't even say he'd seen her now. He hadn't fully understood what he'd witnessed, so his mind's attempts to see her as some sort of human woman had been incomplete and unsatisfying. She was just power, the fathomless combustion of hydrogen—with a consciousness.

He was nowhere near ready to try to destroy her when she was in her element. He could fight her if she came back down to human level, but not here. Still, he could read her, and from that moment when her consciousness encompassed him, he now knew that she was gearing up to attack Belia'al. That level of warfare was out of his league as well, and really, which of those two would he want to win?

When the comet had orbited far enough to be of no concern whatsoever to Aleksandra, he looked and saw the shores of sub-consciousness again.

THURSDAY, MARCH 24, 2011 · 9:33 P.M. EASTERN DAYLIGHT TIME

3 Wind (Advancing Possibilities)

Dennis Aparicio leaned back, shifting his position. Franny Rupp said, "You are one cool customer."

"How so?" Aparicio asked.

"You come down off a fire fight like no one I've ever seen before. You just zone out."

"I put everything I've got into the battles I fight," he said truthfully. "Then I need to regroup."

"Well, I'm not complainin'. You got me the wand," Franny said. "Keep goin' if you need to. We'll be home in fifteen minutes. And forget about . . . you know. You're off my shit list for good, Aparicio."

"Thanks, Chief," said Aparicio. "Appreciate it."

STORM

Pam and the foursome came to the Ox's corner, where the intersecting mountain ranges formed a cleft ranging upward, with a stream thundering down it, swollen with rain from higher elevations. The path up the mountain followed the stream bed as best it could, but there were plenty of switchbacks, forced by multicolored boulders and other obstacles. It would be a climb.

Pam didn't even slow down, keeping to the now-familiar pace of Funt as the path turned up beside the stream. *Water,* she thought. *There is water in the Ox's quadrant, just as there's air and fire, I'm sure. But that stream bed is pretty shallow on a normal day. Just my luck to be here in the rainy season.*

They made their way through an opening where a large rock lay solidly against the hillside, leaving very little room for someone Pam's size. The foursome had to wait for her, and even so, she scraped the side of her face against an outcropping. The next time they encountered an obstacle, she had to hoist herself over it.

Around a turn the trail forked. The right-hand path led upward, steeply, through a tumble-stone cleft to the path visible half a mile higher, when the rain allowed. Water racing down the cleft took a lower cleft near the top and left this cleft simply wet. The left-hand path led through a redwood forest, doubtless taking a less strenuous route up the mountain, and offering shelter from the storm. Pam gauged the two, then added her alchemical spin to it: left is shadow, right is light. The paths mirrored the traditional associations. Right now she was in a hurry, so there was no question, and she began to climb.

Up she went, thankful that this way was open to the sky; there were no low bridges. The rocks were loose and sometimes went tumbling from under her hand, but she knew how to climb, with her balance always beneath her. Funt, keeping pace, seemed to be obliged to struggle, heaving herself upward on rocks quite large for her, but actually never even breathing heavily. Rocks were her world.

Chiss went up as a salamander-lizard, skittering over the rough surfaces, holding as tight as flame to a wick. Cocorik flew, and Mymla dissolved herself to become humidity in the air, which clung to Pam.

STORM

Peter Quince stood spread-legged on a flat, metallic plane that stretched away forever everywhere. At the very center, between his legs, was a black, rotting hole. He knew it was the center, at least for him, because four lines led from it, at right angles to each other, in four different colors.

He turned his head to the left and gazed above the black line. Out there were strange trees and stranger holes among the trees. He calmly held his gaze, and over the next few moments, the trees resolved themselves into vague shapes, and then into recognizable shapes, as he knew, from his experience, that they would.

Peter Quince stood spread-legged on a point where two mountain ranges crossed. They formed a crude X, dividing the world around into four quadrants. As he looked to his left now, he saw, through shifting clouds, the Ox standing solidly below, guarding his quadrant. He looked ahead and saw the Angel, turned to his right and saw the Eagle, and finally turned to the last quadrant, where the Lion should have been, but was not. He said softly, but meaningfully, "Someday."

He looked once more at the solid *there-ness* of the Ox . . . and saw movement halfway up the hillside.

Then the movement resolved itself into a recognizable shape.

What the hell!? That can't be! It would just be too perfect!
BLACKWELL!

STORM

In what seemed to be a very short time, Pam was climbing onto the path again, much higher than when she'd left it, at the point where the redwood forest opened back onto open space and the path began to pick its way along a ledge. She had to take a minute or two, with her hands on her thighs, to catch her breath. The elementals clustered around her, none the worse for wear, and waited. She knew they were waiting, so the very second she could go forward, she said, "Halfway there," and started off up the trail. They went around a bend.

There stood Peter Quince!

If he'd have struck right then, he'd have won. But he knew he outclassed her, even without his master, so he had to toy with her first. This woman. "I really should have known you and August would stage some counterattack. But even not knowing, I was led to you, Pam. The power I'm a part of now can never be denied!"

Cocorik asked, "Who's this man?"

Funt said, "I don't like his smell."

Quince said, "So glad you made friends, but they can't come between us." He raised his left hand, holding a ball of seething power.

Chiss leapt at him, blazing.

Quince knew this realm too well. "Stop!" he commanded, and the salamander had no choice but to obey. Quince looked once more to Pam and the others.

They were gone, back around the bend.

. . . . .

She knew she was in serious trouble. The last time she'd faced Quince, he'd been well out of her league. She'd been on the point of committing suicide in order to stop him from killing fifty thousand people because it was her only option. She hadn't wanted to commit suicide then and she didn't want to do it now, so she ran like a rabbit, back along the path toward the redwood trees, but she was asking herself the whole time: *How do I get around it?* She ran but she remained the huntress.

Behind her, she felt the world open like a wound as Quince's power exploded toward her, and she dove aside, rolling into the forest. The power blast hurt her, and being hurled against the trees hurt, too. She'd trained with magickal warfare's best, and she'd come this far through Wonderland, but in times of real danger, Max had always been there for her. Getting to her hands and knees, she saw very clearly that despite her identification with Artemis, he'd always been her fail-safe—that if all else failed, he could save them both—and now she didn't have that. *But isn't that true of Quince, too?* she thought, and the possibilities thrilled her. *He's given himself to the demon. He hasn't fought on his own for at least two years! And I don't smell Belia'al!*

Nevertheless, Quince's next blast burst the needles on the trees around Pam into orange flame. Pam leapt up and ran, ignoring the pain from her cuts and bruises. *And why not?* she asked herself. *That's just one body!* She looked around and saw a moss-covered hollow between the great old trees. She dove into it and got as comfortable as she could, before throwing herself violently into the *astral.*

. . . . .

Quince approached the forest with all his protections in place. The last time he'd faced Pam, she'd been a spunky newcomer. That was nearly two years ago, so she had to be better; the question was, how much better? With Max August as her teacher, the answer was, undoubtedly, a lot. She was not to be confused with the wizard of the Necklace, but there were no cut-and-dried answers in magick. She could get lucky.

He missed his master; there was no getting around it. With Belia'al on board, this would be like shooting fish in a barrel, and there was nothing wrong with that. He had to admit he'd grown used to easy victories—and grown softer as a slave. But being a slave was his greatest joy, so he was not going to lose his master's favor by fucking this up.

Blackwell didn't attack him as he reached the edges of the forest—didn't attack as he slipped inside. It was dark in here, with clouds of fog drifting through, but redwoods gave one another space and there was plenty of visibility.

Enough to see her body.

She was lying sprawled among the trees. For a moment he thought he'd already killed her, but then he remembered her at Wickr and her *astral* powers—remembered just in time, because now she came for him invisibly. Only a trained wizard could have reacted so fast. He dove aside, and still one hand touched him to send her magick through him. It froze his side for a moment, but only a moment; if that was the extent of her power, she'd be dead in thirty seconds. Her progress in the *astral* was something special. He had almost underestimated her again. But he had more power. He got down on the ground, lay back, and let his own *astral* form come free.

. . . . .

Pam saw it all, and now it was her turn to be surprised. Quince was such a stocky man, so *thick,* that she had no idea how good he was at this. She should have guessed it from his position in the Necklace, but she didn't, and he almost overwhelmed her with his initial rush. She *flew* among the lowering trees, with him *flying* hard on her trail. More than a mile into the forest, she managed to put an extra thirty feet between them—then came to a sudden and complete halt, the way *astral* forms with their lack of mass could, and spun to hurl her power at him. It caught him head-on and blinded him for a moment, a moment she used to rocket straight upward.

But now she learned what experience could do. Quince knew that even though an *astral* could go anywhere, through anything, the natural thing for a new *astral* to do was go where her physical form could not go—upward into the sky, not downward into the Earth. As he staggered in *flight,* half-stunned, he threw an *astral* barrier above her, and Pam slammed into it. She fell back, herself stunned, and the barrier began to enclose her. Desperately, she tried to clear her head, and dove for the shrinking opening. Her *astral* body was her normal size; she couldn't shrink it; the gap grew narrower.

Too narrow! She was trapped!

A sapphire blue bubble surrounded her, and though she attacked it with every means at her disposal, every trick Max had ever taught her about spell-breaking, she could not get free.

Quince buzzed in to get a closer look at her startled face. His own face was wreathed in a smile, further compressing his features toward the center of it. "Nice progress, Doctor," he told her sincerely. "But you never had a chance against *me*."

Then he died.

. . . . .

Quince's mystical bubble died with him, and Pam's *astral* form came free once more, even as all of his power blasted its way into her. *It's what happens when a wizard dies!* she knew, barely able to withstand the rush. *And there's no taint to it! Whatever he did with Belia'al, magick is magick for me!*

But she couldn't spare the time to admire it just then, as she cast her mind back to her physical form. She could see it as clearly as if it were right next to her—see what she'd hardly dared hope she could actually pull off.

Her physical form, left with enough of her consciousness to maintain itself, lay across Quince's physical form, and her hand held her knife, buried in the wizard's chest.

❋ ✦ ❋ ✦

Deep in the heart of his hell, Belia'al felt it hard!

This is it! he told himself. **Peter Quince was my strongest weapon. Not my only weapon—999 remain. But Peter Quince was the key to this war, and the diabola has taken first blood.**

He was growling, low in his throat. **I must even the field!**

FRIDAY, MARCH 25, 2011 · 12:03 A.M. EASTERN DAYLIGHT TIME

3 Wind (Advancing Possibilities)

Max felt it. He was drinking beer with the strike team in Show Stoppers, caught in the rush of Butler's dominance, and nearly did a spit-take.

Pam killed Quince! Holy Mother of God!

"YEA-YAH!!" he shouted, and blended right in at the raucous bar.

— 0 —

Aleksandra felt it in unsullied space.

And she felt—

THURSDAY, MARCH 24, 2011 · 11:03 P.M. CENTRAL DAYLIGHT TIME

] Wind (Advancing Possibilities)

Rita Diamante woke up from a twenty-month nightmare.

Rita Diamante, the Latina thought.

Mi nombre.

She was lying, naked, on a marble slab in a basement. It was all she knew in the moment of waking. Except for this:

¡Rita Diamante, pendejo!

¡¡FUCK YOU, QUINCE!!

¡¡¡¡¡AND FUCK YOU, BELIA'AL!!!!!

FRIDAY, MARCH 25, 2011 · 12:03 A.M. EASTERN DAYLIGHT TIME

] Wind (Advancing Possibilities)

Hanrahan woke from the drugs.

He shot to the surface of his consciousness like a shark lunging for a leg. The time between his wakefulness and his memory of his situation was short, and then he was lying on a table in the lab, strapped at chest, hand, and foot, but that didn't matter because he had his wits about him.

He had trained against those drugs, and he'd been winning the battle when that idiot Quince decided to help. Quince had put him under with magick, but Hanrahan had still been on his way to a victory and he must have achieved it while magicked and out of it.

But I'm not under a spell now. It's only the drugs, and I can handle the drugs. But why aren't I magicked? Did something happen to Quince?

He had to *know*. That more than anything was what drove him now.

LIGHTNING

The sky was ripped by brilliant fractures as Pam stood once more within her physical form, looking down at Quince's body. She had the crazy urge to rip her shirt open and throw her arms wide like Brandi Chastain—but she settled for shouting at him as he lay dead at her feet, "You didn't die because of *Max,* Quince! You died because of *me*! Pam Blackwell, goddammit! *ALCHEMIST*!"

"She's like the Eagle now," said Mymla softly.

Pam looked away from Quince, and standing ten feet away was the foursome. She'd completely forgotten them in the moment. "Hey, guys," she said to them, her voice ragged.

"We couldn't help you," grumbled Chiss.

"I know," Pam said. "You had to take *his* orders, too. It's all right."

"It's not!" said Chiss. "We should have been with you, Pam!"

"That's not our way," Funt told him.

"We certainly can't change it," added Cocorik.

"But—"

Pam overrode him, riding her wave of success. "I like you all just the way you are," she told them. Hell, she liked everything, now. Quince's death would have to affect Belia'al, and that would affect whatever Belia'al had going with Aleksandra. Pam hadn't even been in the same realm and she'd struck a strong blow for . . . well, Aleksandra could hardly be considered the good guy, but Belia'al was certainly a bad guy. Bottom line, it would throw whatever was happening elsewhere into a cocked hat, and considering how bleak the weather had been because of the status quo, a change had to be a good thing.

There are no cut-and-dried answers, her alchemist's mind reminded her. But she would ride this wave until it broke. "How far to the Eagle now?" she asked them.

"Not much farther to the top of the mountain," said Funt.

"Then we'll go downhill fast," said Mymla.

"Let's do that thing," said Pam, and took three strides along the trail before stopping once again. She turned around and went back to Quince's body, and began searching it.

"What are you doing, Pam?" asked Cocorik.

"I can carry things between the worlds, so what if he can, too?" Her hands stopped moving over the bloodstained robe and her right hand slipped into a hidden pocket. It came forth again carrying what looked to Mymla like a wand. Pam studied it for a moment, then stuck it in her own pocket, still thinking. Not even Cocorik would disrupt that thinking.

They all knew Pam had found more magick.

FRIDAY, MARCH 25, 2011 · 12:13 A.M. EASTERN DAYLIGHT TIME

3 Wind (Advancing Possibilities)

In nine hundred and ninety-nine places, all around the world, nine hundred and ninety-nine people felt their master Belia'al surge into them, insistent, unstoppable—and this was strange to them because none of them ever resisted him. In Antarctica, Bangkok, Cleveland, Delhi, and almost five hundred other places, those people stopped whatever they were doing unless that would cause them bodily harm, and those who delayed found a way to stop as soon as possible. Within minutes, all 999 were filled with the same unholy spirit, boiling like sulphur in their guts. Then as one, all across the globe, in the dead of night and the blaze of day, seemingly ordinary citizens, reporters and graphic designers and oil men and lawyers and geophysicists and starlets and taxi drivers and university professors and animators and moms and senators, all turned and faced Manhattan—999 faces all pointed toward a single spot on East Thirty-fifth Street.

Each of the 999 had some degree of magickal power. None was the equal of Peter Quince, but seventy-eight were somewhat close. The others ranged down the magickal scale to some whose only real connection to the demon was a shared desire for degradation. But each of these turned from his or her spot on the planet to stare in the direction of an unseen Lawrence Breckenridge in New York City.

In his sanctum, Breckenridge began to look a little pale, a little queasy. He felt pressure on his heart, not the playful biting pain of Aleksandra's caress, but a heaviness, a leadenness. He thought it might be a heart attack, except that she'd taken those off the menu . . . except that it did feel bad, and getting worse. He picked up the phone—

=shit=

As Peter Quince had fallen, now fell Lawrence Breckenridge, the Gemstone of the Necklace.

— 0 —

Aleksandra felt it. Felt her lover Renzo fall, and felt the rolling shock that Belia'al had such extensive power on Earth.

But her focus had to be on how best to withstand that power. To that end, she continued driving herself into a form of Madeleine Riggs in the basement of the old house in Duluth.

3 Wind (Advancing Possibilities)

Hanrahan began to cough—a deep, gasping cough. It was a wheeze, a choke. He could not get his breath, and his face began to turn blue beneath the harsh lights of the lab. He shuddered, his movements slackening. . . .

Willingham came and stared down at him, but not for long. The old man had to sit up. So he removed the chest band and the wrist bands, while keeping the ankle bands tight, and helped the erstwhile head of intelligence to get upright.

Hanrahan's gasping continued for a moment, his face growing bluer and bluer, now marked by red veins and capillaries—but then he began to get some air down, began to move away from the crisis.

The old man turned his gray face to look at his benefactor. The old man's eyes were drugged and crazed. "Ha nama ku walla doh!" said the old man, smiling brightly.

As his left hand grabbed the back of Willingham's neck and his right hand grabbed Willingham's Adam's apple and yanked it from his throat!

The guard convulsed in death while the old man pulled him down on the old man's legs, so the guard wouldn't fall to the floor, out of reach. Hanrahan was more than willing to let Willingham's life play out its final few seconds while he himself got his breath back. He had trained for that routine back in '52, in Korea. It had saved him then, too. But that was nearly sixty years ago! He felt every one of his eighty-two years . . .

Finally, Willingham lay still. Hanrahan bent forward from the waist and took the key that allowed the guard control over the proceedings. Hanrahan used it to unlock his ankles. Then he still kept the body on the table while he gingerly pulled his legs out from underneath. He left it there when he got down off the table.

3 Wind (Advancing Possibilities)

Maddy Riggs undid the straps that held Rita Diamante to her slab.

"Who the fuck . . . are you?" Diamante gasped, her spirit in no way impeded by her weakened body.

"A friend," said Maddy.

Rita's face grew crafty. "Where's my . . . friend Pete?"

"Pete is dead. Why else do you think you're having this conversation?"

Disappointment flickered through Rita. "Who killed him?"

"You mean who robbed you of your chance? Well, it wasn't me. But now listen, Quince was working for Belia'al—"

"Yeah."

"—and I need to know everything you know about him, because I'm going to fight him."

"You?"

In a heartbeat, Maddy Riggs was replaced by a glowing red sphere, hovering in midair.

"*¡Mierda!*" snapped Rita, recoiling, nearly rolling off the slab. "*¡Siempre la santería!*" She hated that shit, now more than ever. But if this *thing* could fight Belia'al, it *should* fight Belia'al, because Rita knew in her heart of hearts that she could never do it herself. And it had to be done.

"Okay," she said. She slowly but adamantly maneuvered her long-unused legs around, dropping them over the edge of the slab. She took a long look at what had happened to them, then lifted her head toward the red star, and the red star became the redheaded woman and helped her stand up. Finding her balance, holding on to both the slab and Maddy, Rita said "Okay" again, tightened her jaw and started to continue, but Maddy put her warm hand against her forehead.

"You don't have to talk. I'll take it directly." Maddy's blue-black eyes looked deep into Rita's black diamond eyes, and the information Aleksandra wanted flowed directly mind to mind, so that Aleksandra heard it without any emendation that Rita might ordinarily make before reporting to someone of such power.

He's the Prince of Lies, the king of demons. When I say it's all about him, I mean it's ALL ABOUT HIM. He lives in his own world where he makes all the rules. And rule number one is, he CRUSHES everything else. If he can fool you into thinking it won't happen to you sooner or later, he just enjoys it more.

Maddy replied, "I see that you know people, Rita Diamante."

"Men," said Rita indistinctly. "Just men." Then, spent, she collapsed into Maddy Riggs's arms.

FRIDAY, MARCH 25, 2011 · 1:09 A.M. EASTERN DAYLIGHT TIME

} Wind (Advancing Possibilities)

Hanrahan used Willingham's modified iPad to call Jacoby into the room. She opened the door and she wasn't unwary, but the old man simply lunged around the edge of the door and drove his knife into the heart before she could defend herself.

"Mama woh doh gah labba," Hanrahan said to himself. He was still within the influence of the drugs, but every minute off the table washed that influence a little farther away. The fight against them grew easier; he'd be back in this reality soon enough. But by then, he wanted to be strangling his old pal Renzo. Let's face it: after the Necklace marks you for dead, you're not going to escape for very long, so you might as well be all you can be in the meantime.

He disposed of the two bodies down the shaft, just as they'd planned for him. He locked the lab door behind him, carefully, and made his way unsteadily down the hall. He couldn't use the elevator because it would alert his quarry. Neither could he use the main stairs. But he had inserted a code in the back stairs that would allow him passage.

He avoided the guards because it was better than killing them and letting their absence spark an alert. He was sorry he'd had to kill the first two—although, they were Renzo's palace guard, so that was something. There was no guarantee that Renzo would be in his sanctum, or even in the building, but if he was, he might have no protection. Hanrahan didn't know anything that had happened since six this morning, so this could all be for nothing, but it was his only play.

He came to the top of the back stairs and looked along the hall leading to all the rooms. Renzo's door was just past midway. How many times had Hanrahan walked this hall, back and forth between the sanctum and the smaller meeting room? Thousands of times. But what he found inside the sanctum had never been more important.

The sanctum door opened. Gillebrand and Larkin came out. In the hallway there was nowhere for him to hide. Now he'd have to kill them, both, without the element of surprise.

"There you are, sir," said Larkin. "We've been looking everywhere for you." *Jeez, he looks old,* Larkin thought.

"Why were you looking?" said the old man, smiling, steadily closing the distance between them. "Didn't you know where I was?"

"No, sir," said Larkin. "And do *you* know, sir, that you're the new Gemstone?"

Day five

It was 2 A.M. Eastern Daylight Time when the universe breathed in and Aleksandra launched the god war.

She pumped her scarlet light, harder harder harder, wider wider wider, till she held it on the edge of a precipice, then collapsed it all at once to force a laserlike beam from her core that was recorded but ignored as an anomaly by astronomers at Cerro Tololo. This beam speared blank space at the speed of light and then beyond, into the Earth and through the veils until she blew through Belia'al's defenses to impale the demon in his lair.

In the center of the demon a proto-star began to burn, 4,000 degrees. Belia'al instantly burst into flames, foul-smelling, sooty flames that filled the vast caverns of his realm with choking smoke. His body began to boil and bubble, writhing with harsh farts of putrid gas.

He laughed.

Not enough, diabola! I'm far more dense than that!

Your density is dispersed with the loss of Quince!

No more than yours with the loss of Breckenridge.

Fool! I don't need him!

But in all else, he was right: she now knew that she didn't have the power to destroy him head-on. He knew it, too. So they would each take that knowledge and work from that, when the universe breathed out.

She left.

. . . . .

A 4.8 aftershock struck Myanmar, killing dozens more people still reeling from last night's quakes, and now the tremors were continuous.

FRIDAY, MARCH 25, 2011 · 2:00 A.M. EASTERN DAYLIGHT TIME

4 Night (Encompassing a Private World)

Max was exhausted, deep asleep, but when the god-war began in earnest, he awoke at once. Getting out of bed, he went to look out the window, knowing everything was happening in other dimensions, but wanting to see what *he* could see in his. He saw the clouds in their familiar heavy-laden gray blotting out the sky, and nothing more But—

"It's on," he told himself. The universe was in play between a diabola and a demon, Pam was on her way to the Eagle. But his job was to stop another 9/11 before the day was out, and that had to be his main concern. *Now all we can do in THIS world is hang on tight!*

FRIDAY, MARCH 25, 2011 · 6:00 A.M. GREENWICH MEAN TIME

4 Night (Encompassing a Private World)

Dawn was just breaking over London when Vee moved for the first time in half an hour, by leaping up from her seat. "Got him!" she shouted, and then reacted a little as the pain from her bites kicked in. Matt looked up excitedly from his charts. "Where?"

"You won't believe it! You really won't! That cunning old bas-tard! C'mon!"

She went out the front door and led him to the shadows under the overpass. In the chilly, pale air, with shafts of pale orange sun-light painting the sky, she turned him toward St. Barnabas at the end of the block.

He queried her silently, with his eyes, and she nodded with happy certainty. They went back inside.

"At the end of *this road?*" he continued.

"A good spot, don't you think?" She marked a figure on her left palm with her right forefinger. "First division I performed on his location—Populus, a place where people congregate. Then Carcer, incarcerated. He's in the church but in a crypt, or something like it." She put on her jacket. "Right down the street."

He took her arm. "Where are you going?"

"I'm going to finish this!"

"You're not ready yet," Matt said firmly. "You need to be at your best."

"No, I don't. I've thought about it and that just gives him more to feed off me. I need to be lean."

"Yes, *you do,* because you're not going to out-body-fat him. You're going to out-magick him, and for that, you need to be at your best."

"I can't just leave him right down the corner, ready to attack at any time!" Vee shouted.

"Yes, you can," Matt replied, very calm, "because you know he won't attack until tonight."

"But he didn't attack this *past* night," she said. "He's giving me time to fatten up!"

"Exactly. So do that!"

"Listen, Matt, this is why I didn't want a manager."

"I get that. And this is why you need one. I don't know the magick you know, but I know divas."

"Thanks!"

"Stars. Goddesses. Performers at their peak."

"You don't have any!"

"Yes, I do," he said. "I've got you."

"First, I'm not at a peak. Second, you don't have me."

"Vee, I know divas because I've studied divas. Some of them are nice, but all of them live at the peak of their star power. When they go out there, they're at their best. They don't half-arse it.

"And they get that way by working themselves up throughout the day, so they're *at* their peak come showtime. There's a science to that, and an art—you could call the whole thing 'magick'—and I know that very well. I can work you today, build you step by step toward the Hour of Jupiter tonight, so you're the best Vee you can be, not the skinniest. It's the best Vee that will destroy Chris Durban at last."

Vee said, "The Hour tonight is at twelve oh six A.M., and it's six in the morning now. That's eighteen hours!"

"Think of what you can *be* in eighteen hours, Vee."

She looked at him, her eyes hooded. She wasn't used to this at all—people telling her what to do—people who *could* tell her what to do. And she didn't like it. She'd stayed away from it right from the start, that day she'd found Cornelius and lost Eva Delia. If she made Matt a part of her life, it meant crossing a bridge she'd never even gone near. Or, she could stay where she was—a girl and her book. . . .

A girl who wanted to live more than another eighteen hours.

"All right, Matt," she said at last. "Make me a star."

WHITEOUT

....

Pam and the gang felt the changes for the third time. Pam felt them especially, filled as she was with new power. She knew without doubt that the changes weren't good, that whatever she'd done to Belia'al through his servant hadn't derailed the drama outside. But she was inside, with her own drama—now reaching a climax. Literally.

They were within two hundred yards of the mountain peak—the

mountains' peak. Toiling upward, they'd begun to see, in the brief moments when the clouds did not obscure everything, where the four mountain ranges came together to form their close-to-perfect X. The elementals weren't tired because they never were tired, and Pam wasn't tired because she was filled with new power. She was Pam, definitely, but a much grander Pam than before—very much like Max in his most magnificent moments. She was as close to the mastery of alchemy as she was to the top of the mountains. She was close to Timelessness. And just as surely as she knew she'd cross the mountains into another world, she knew she'd cross into eternity with Max, sooner rather than later.

She was going over the hump.

And then the chimæra appeared.

A chimæra was a combination of the four elements, and this thing had a lion's head with an ox's horns, wings like an angel, and claws like an eagle. There might have been a snake's tail thrown in, but that was hard to see past the flames writhing from the creature's mouth.

"Uh, guys . . . ?" Pam asked.

"It's horrible," breathed Funt.

"Hideous," said Cocorik.

"So you've never seen it before?" Pam pressed.

"No!" snapped Chiss.

Another artifact of whatever's going on outside, Pam thought. *The goat-god was tough but he was home-grown. This thing is unnatural, even for here—but it's in my way.*

Without pausing, she focused her newly won power to her center, reared back, and hurled it at the chimæra. It recoiled in pain and surprise, but was in no way overcome. Pam immediately expanded her power, forming a silver sphere around herself and her friends, who were clustered at her feet. Notwithstanding the bravery they'd all shown thus far, none of them knew how to fight something that lived outside their four-fold division of the elements. The chimæra belched its fire at them just as she completed her maneuver. The fire dented her sphere—that's how Max always phrased it—and she had to smooth it out again, make it structurally strong. The chimæra charged her but ran into the sphere's edge, breaking one of its horns, roaring in pain and rage. It stood with its snout against the sphere, huffing, the sphere glowing orange before Pam and the elementals, who looked up at her fearfully.

Then Pam expanded her sphere explosively, right in the chimæra's face, knocking it ass over teakettle. It rolled heavily back up the path and went off the right edge with a churning of legs, landing on its back. That kept it from flying, and they all heard it tumbling down the mountainside, scattering the boulders.

The fivesome ran onward, straight to the top, unwilling to wait a moment longer. As they crested the mountains, the clouds rolled back one final time, revealing the X in all directions, and a tiny broken chimæra halfway down the mountain's side, buried in rocky rubble.

FRIDAY, MARCH 25, 2011 · 2:00 A.M. EASTERN DAYLIGHT TIME

4 Night (Encompassing a Private World)

Hanrahan sat sprawled behind Breckenridge's desk—the Gemstone's desk—*his* desk. He, who had spent a lifetime processing information with unemotional efficiency, could still not wrap his brain around the turn events had taken. More than once, he looked hard within himself to see if he was still on the drugs. But he knew he was not.

He really was the Gemstone.

Renzo had had a heart attack. But before that, he had kept the news of Hanrahan's betrayal and capture a close secret, between himself and his elite team, and with all three of their deaths, there was no one left who knew the truth. So as the Necklace Number Two, Hanrahan was the successor. Unbelievable.

Less than an hour had passed since he'd assumed command. Not an undue amount of time to read the past twenty hours' reports from the rest of the Nine on Renzo's desk and process them, even without drugs passing out of his system. But as the drugs washed completely away, he savored the whole crazy situation. He'd schemed for so long, made perilous allies of three different wizards, looked Renzo straight in the eye every morning for decades—and even though the old bastard had somehow known, Hanrahan had come out on top. Now he'd gained the world, to run as he saw fit, just as he'd always wanted.

And the world never stopped spinning. The Black Helicopters still had to fly tonight. The five wars still had to be fought, and bin Laden still had to be finished off when the Gemstone decided it was most useful. Unions had to be busted, drilling in the Gulf had to be brought back on line, the Twenty-Twelve Project had to proceed, and nothing could be disrupted, by this or anything else.

He activated Channel Nine for a private call to Peter Quince. Peter Quince did not answer. But the wizard's status was a piece of information the old man needed without delay. That was a loose end that could so easily rise up and bite him in the ass. He used the phone on the desk to wake up his man in the Minnesota State Patrol and send him to Duluth to have a look-see. There was nothing else he needed to do before continuing to his next step.

So he straightened up in his chair, envisioning himself behind the desk in the pose assumed by all presidents when addressing the nation, and used Channel Nine for his conference call with the rest of *his* Necklace.

FRIDAY, MARCH 25, 2011 · 2:03 A.M. EASTERN DAYLIGHT TIME

Y Night (Encompassing a Private World)

"Today is March 25, 2011, a Friday," the old man said, "and I am extremely sorry to report that Lawrence Breckenridge suffered a fatal heart attack just past midnight, two hours ago. I am now in command."

Di, unflappable even rousted from her bed, possibly even at her best, said, "That's terrible news, Dick. My condolences on your loss; I know he was your friend. He was a friend to all of us." Hanrahan could not but remember himself and Renzo torturing her.

"Terrible news, yes," said Allenby. "But we couldn't be in better hands. You have my complete support, Dick. Anything you need . . ." Hanrahan remembered Allenby's campaign to have Jackson Tower removed, and Renzo's smackdown of it.

"Hear, hear!" said Franny. "We're with you, Dick." Hanrahan remembered everything about them all.

"Did Lawrence suffer?" asked Carole van Dusen.

"The doctors say no," answered Hanrahan. "It was very quick."

"Thank God for that," said Franny.

"Then you, as the Gemstone," said Ruth, "should know that we're still go for this evening. It's T minus zero and we're fully prepared."

"I'm not worried, Ruth," Hanrahan said. "I'm not worried about any of you—not even you, Nat." The others instantly wondered what he meant by that, but he would not enlighten them, and neither would Nat.

"Will ya be maintainin' Breckenridge's schedule?" the Politics link asked with a perfect poker face.

"Probably not today," Hanrahan said. "I'll review it and take care of what can't be postponed, but some things will have to be. As you can imagine, this comes as a shock and there's a lot to consider." Something about that made him sound old and infirm to his own ears, so he added, "It's still full speed ahead. Nothing has changed with any of our missions."

Carole van Dusen, as was her wont, moved to another point. "Where's Quince?" she asked.

"A very good question," said Hanrahan. "I'm checking on that as we speak."

"How big a problem is his absence?" Carole asked. "If Quince is unable to answer this call, he could be in trouble . . . or part of the problem."

"Believe me, Carole, that has not escaped me. I don't see Quince as a conspirator. He's weird, yes, but you know wizards. Until I get firsthand intel, it's best not to speculate, but I would certainly advise you all to maintain alert status until that intel is to hand."

"Well," said Carole, the next most senior member of the Nine, "this can't be easy, Dick, but you seem to have it well covered. Call on me for anything you may need in the hours and days ahead."

"I will," the old man said, "but what I need most from all of you is business as usual."

"You got it," said Allenby.

"Lawrence was a great man," said Franny.

"It's hard to imagine us without him," said Ruth. "But I'm sure we'll be fine under you, Dick."

"Absolutely," said Nat, though it was all he could do to look Hanrahan in the eye as he said it. What the hell was this going to mean to him, with no one above his nemesis?

"We'll talk again after the Black Helicopter run," said Hanrahan. "All hail the Necklace!"

"All hail the Necklace!" the others responded, and signed off.

FRIDAY, MARCH 25, 2011 · 2:30 A.M. EASTERN DAYLIGHT TIME

4 Night (Encompassing a Private World)

Ruth thought about going back to sleep but rejected the idea. She was up now, and despite her firm assurances to Hanrahan, she needed, if only for herself, to reconsider her plans to see if this change at the top affected anything.

Driven by the same impulse, Franny began rechecking every aspect of her birds.

4 Night (Encompassing a Private World)

It was beginning to snow, great fat flakes floating lazily past the window at the back of the private ambulance that carried a listless and emaciated Rita Diamante to St. Mary's Medical Center in Duluth. The hospital was quiet, though the emergency room had seen a few extra mental patients tonight—and now this. The sister of the woman in the ambulance had called and made all the arrangements.

"Fulana de Tal?" the admitting nurse asked the ambulance driver, and he nodded. "That's her."

The nurse moved closer and lowered her voice. "What kind of a name is that?"

"I dunno. Spanish, I guess."

"Never heard of 'Fulana.'" The nurse looked around, lowered her voice still further. "Not Muslim?"

"Don't think so. The woman who arranged transport had red hair. And you have to take her."

"I know, I know. I was just asking." Now the nurse told the residents to move the patient's gurney from the ambulance. As the woman came into view, the nurse was shocked at her gaunt appearance—the fighter's brother in *The Fighter* came to mind—but the nurse was a pro. "Don't worry, Miss de Tal," she said cheerfully. "You'll have the best of care from now on. We'll get you back on your feet before you know it."

Rita was a pro, too, and smiled wanly, especially since "Fulana de Tal" meant "Jane Doe." The scarlet star had a sense of humor. But a wan smile was all Rita could manage before slipping back into blessed sleep.

4 Night (Encompassing a Private World)

The Minnesota state cop reported back to Hanrahan. "I broke down an upstairs door in Peter Quince's house and saw the man lying dead. I'm certain it's he but I can't get at him. He's inside a circle, painted on the floor, and for whatever reason, I can't cross into it."

"Don't worry about it," said Hanrahan. "I have that under control. You say you're certain it's Quince, but how certain are you that he's dead?"

"As certain as I can be from ten feet away. I sat down outside the circle so my point of view would stay steady and watched his chest against points painted on the wall beyond the circle. I saw no movement in his chest, over the course of five minutes."

"All right. Get out of there and seal the building. We'll take it from here."

"There's one more thing, sir."

"What's that?"

"There are twenty-six naked women in the basement, all heavily sedated."

"Get them all out of there. Call Diedrich and Marino to help you, and make it fast."

4 Night (Encompassing a Private World)

Belia'al launched his counterattack on the outward breath of the universe.

He now understood the unitary nature of his opponent. There was just the one of her, one who had failed to destroy him, and he had all of his hosts—nine hundred and ninety-nine of them. Not one thousand, because the demon had to leave Quince's spot open until a suitable successor could be found. Nine hundred and ninety-nine, as Breckenridge had discovered, was plenty.

In all those places, all around the globe, he began to attack anyone nearby. His hosts weren't zombis because they were all controlled by one cold, alien brain, but they could have passed for them. They began to work their way toward the most populated part of town, whether it was noon or midnight for them, killing everyone they could. Some of them, a few, were themselves killed, but most were too ferocious to resist. Nine hundred and ninety-nine paths of destruction began to carve themselves onto the Earth. When those who could reach a city, did, they set about sowing widespread panic.

. . . . .

Japanese experts stared stunned at their latest test results: Iodine-131 in the environment was 1,850 times the acceptable dose. And as they stood staring at that number, shouts began out in the street.

FRIDAY, MARCH 25, 2011 · 5:10 A.M. EASTERN DAYLIGHT TIME

4 Night (Encompassing a Private World)

Reports began to come into Hanrahan's information center, now functioning from the Gemstone's office—reports of insurrections in all parts of the globe. Quickly, the old man began prioritizing the dangers to Necklace installations and personnel. Then he began issuing orders to his local commanders. Whether noon or midnight, they needed to assemble their men and protect their local assets. As more reports came in, he adjusted the orders as needed, running his world in real time.

He was loving every minute of it!

4 Night (Encompassing a Private World)

Di was awakened a little after five by her overnight editor. He filled her in and despite this being the second time she'd been rousted tonight, she was crisp and clear in shaping the report. She told him she'd be in in half an hour, called her driver, then stepped into the shower and shampooed her hair as she watched the results of her work on the flatscreen.

"This is a breaking news report from FRC. Good morning, America. Coordinated terrorist attacks were launched throughout the world in the past hour. Gangs of thugs are striking in many cities, and are being confronted by local police and military. The terrorists apparently hoped to overwhelm first responders through sheer number of simultaneous attacks, because their armament varied wildly, from fully armed assaults to simple muggings. Full Resource Central will keep you up to the minute as events unfold.

"Now back to *First Round Chat*."

This works to my advantage, she considered. *Something to ramp up the anxiety before the Helicopters hit San Antonio.* And, remembering telling Max that she had no idea where the grand finale was being staged, her laugh echoed in the shower stall.

4 Night (Encompassing a Private World)

Matt had access to a studio up the Abbey Road, and on their way there, they couldn't help but notice a fire and the sound of sirens in central London. Matt, however, was adamant: "It has nothing to do with you."

"It could be Durban."

"A guy made out of polyurethane doesn't start fires."

"Good point."

"We have our own business to worry about."

The studio, up a flight of narrow stairs, was a large black room, with variable lighting and one wall a window into the engineering booth. Mikes on stands were clustered in a corner, awaiting their call. Incense hung heavy in the quiet air.

"Who's recorded here?" were the first words out of Vee's mouth.

"Everybody," Matt said. "It's been here in one form or another since the fifties. They say Miles Davis and John Coltrane were here."

"What about Amy?"

"No. Not her vibe."

"No . . ." Vee was feeling for the vibe, and it did seem more like her own. "Did you have a choice?" she asked.

"Yeah, there are a couple of places I can usually use. But this felt right."

"I think you're right." *He knows what he knows.* "So what do we do, Matt?"

"You need to do some stretching and some boxing—"

"Boxing!"

"No contact, just moves. But you're going into a fight, right?"

"Not boxing, I don't think."

"Mind-set's the same. Reflexes are the same."

"You do this for all your divas?"

"No, Vee. Just for you."

"Yeah, well . . . Continue."

"Exercises pointed toward your fight tonight. At intervals," he told her. "Interspersed with time for singing, time for specially se-lected meals, time for studying your geomancy, time for medita-tion, time for rest. The intervals will cycle, building throughout the day, so you can walk out there tonight and *kill!* So to speak."

" 'Kill' works," Vee said, showing some cheer at last.

Pam and the elementals were all but running down the mountain. Their elation at passing the X in the peaks was still high, but the weather grew worse, not better, as they descended the precipitous path. The parting of the clouds which had so thrilled them turned out to be the result of rising winds—winds now threatening to sweep them right off the mountain. Funt again sheltered Chiss and held Cocorik's hand, and he held Mymla's, and Mymla held Pam's, as the little creatures anchored themselves to the big human. They weren't heavy so a good deal of the gale's power slid right off them. Not so Pam, who was buffeted continuously by it. She seriously considered finding shelter, but she still felt strong, and every step brought her closer to the Eagle. So they ran, hoping to get below the strength of the blow.

But as they turned a corner, they turned directly into the wind, and all at once Funt cried out. "Chiss!"

Pam looked and saw nothing in the gnome's embrace.

"Where is he?" she shouted above the shrieking blast.

"Gone!" bawled Funt.

"Oh my God!" said Pam. *It's my fault!*

"Don't worry, Pam!" shouted Mymla. "He'll come back sooner or later! Keep going!"

"Really?"

"It's his nature."

A new blast of wind rocked Pam, but she took it in stride, savoring yet another step on her path to cosmic knowledge.

4 Night (Encompassing a Private World)

Across the globe, agents of the FRC fought the 999 tooth and nail. The 999 were full of Belia'al, but the mercs, all trained by Ruth Glendenning and equipped with both magickal shields and SCARs, were close to impervious. Once they arrived on the scene and encountered a blood-smeared, snarling host, many found it like shooting fish in a barrel. But even a barrage of bullets could only rip and tear the enemy's body. Even a head shot wasn't enough. As long as there was any sort of body at all, it would crawl, still striving for more blood. It had to be completely dismembered or burned to a crisp.

From his spot at the center of the FRC web, Hanrahan could see a worldwide coordination among the attackers. As one of the rioters fell in la Place de la Concorde, another grew stronger in Darfur. It happened too many times to be coincidence. Some one thing was driving them all, he was sure. Quince could probably have given him intel that would help him shape his response, but Quince was dead in Duluth.

The first ones who could be incapacitated but not killed— something they resisted to the last gasp—were interrogated on the spot. The mercs went straight to torture, Jack Bauer methods that were entirely suspect as to their accuracy, but there was no time for more sophisticated work. A picture began to emerge, of people suffering the same delusion, that their "master" commanded them, but what good did that do? Unfortunately, the old man was at a loss to explain what he was seeing. He could only fight the symptoms, not the cause—but because he was Dick Hanrahan, and in the first flush of command, he fought them with skill and success, and even verve. Little by little, the mercs were turning the global tide.

. . . . .

On the Big Island of Hawaii, Kilauea began to spew lava, higher and more sulphurous than usual.

4 Night (Encompassing a Private World)

In San Antonio, Texas, Joe Diggs, a cameraman for the local FRC station, positioned his instrument at the corner of Market and Cherry outside the Alamodome. His assignment was to capture some street scenes, to show the morning show what the area looked like before the big crowds arrived. He'd be back at five for those crowds. Somebody upstairs thought the quick-cut transition would be interesting tonight, but Joe couldn't see it.

Still, the normalcy of Market Street was also a contrast to the reported riots elsewhere in the world. Joe would have preferred to be recording those. All he got was a hot and hazy street.

He realized someone was standing beside him, and took his face from the viewfinder. It was some young guy, who said diffidently, "Please. I don't want to interrupt you."

Joe paused to take a look around. There was still almost no one else around them. "What do you need?"

"Hi, sir. My name's Kevin. Kevin Stallworth. I'm looking for work, and I'm hoping you know of something at your station that wouldn't be public knowledge yet."

"Doing what?"

"Whatever you all need. I'm smart and I'm strong and I don't mind hard work."

"You don't have a broadcasting degree?"

"Degrees don't get you anywhere now, sir. I came down from Fort Worth because I couldn't get anywhere there. But I can do any job, whatever it is, and you never know when something will turn up." Kevin's jaw grew tight. "I've been looking for work for a while now. Please just give me a chance."

"I'm busy, kid, and I don't know anything. Take off," snapped Joe. The kid gave him a hard stare, more sorrowful than angry, and moved on down the street—probably to ask some other random stranger for help.

Generation Fucked, thought Joe. *Shit, kid, I'll give you MY crummy job.* But he didn't mean it.

4 Night (Encompassing a Private World)

For lunch, Vee had hearts of celery filled with organic almond butter—fiber, nutrients, protein, fat, all together—and Matt had a steak and cheese pie. As they ate, she had had a chance to consider what she'd be able to do at midnight, and she gave him the outline of her plan. At first he was stunned, then horrified, but in the end he saw that it was the best way, and soon he was adding practical details. After lunch, he sent a text message, gave Vee a written schedule for the afternoon, and went out to pursue his part.

· · · · ·

An hour later, he was standing, leaning back against a wall, across from a boot store. A guy around his age, wearing a backpack, came alongside, took off the pack, laid it against the wall, put his feet up against it, and leaned against the wall himself.

Both kept their eyes on the passing scene, as befitted a random event.

"Surprised to hear from you, Matt," Fagan said in a soft tone. "I thought you were managing unknown musicians."

"Still am," Matt answered. They could have been side by side at the urinals.

"Is this involved with the riots?" Fagan asked.

"I don't know anything about any riots."

"Quite the little war zone in Mayfair. And there's more like it all over the world. Anarchy in the U.K. and everywhere."

"Not interested."

"Must be one hell of a show *you're* planning, then," said Fagan.

"Let me worry about that."

"I'll let you worry if you've got pictures of the queen."

In response, Matt handed Fagan a small pouch. Fagan undid the drawstring and looked inside. "I won't be counting this here," he said.

"It's all there."

"So's this," Fagan said, and walked away. "Cheers." Matt stooped, picked up the backpack, and shrugged it on. Then he walked away.

. . . . .

Vee, untethered to a microphone, roamed the empty studio, going deep inside herself and finding every last nuance she could summon for the spell she would sing tonight. Her purpose tonight was to live, and live free, so she went back to her earliest memories of the life she was trying to save.

They were not good memories, and they were blurred by all the drugs, but they were hers. The voices, the voices in her head, arguing, competing, talking over each other, the poor frightened girl and the desperate Voice—yes, desperate, because the Voice knew this was wrong, that she shouldn't be here, and if she was, she couldn't fight it, because the girl . . . the girl *should* be here. It was her body and the Voice was an intruder, but the Voice was a wizard's disciple, and so neither one could silence the other and they ranted on and on. The Voice couldn't put any of that into words, not with the girl's words there, too. It was only when she became Vee that she could look back and know.

So the memories were painful and confusing and hard, but they were the only memories of the only life she knew. She wouldn't lose that life. She would *not*.

4 Night (Encompassing a Private World)

The 999 had been decimated, almost literally. There were fewer than 125 hosts left when the universe breathed out again and Belia'al began to augment them. Every place was like Shanghai, where Chen Qingshi staggered into Huaihai Road and began grabbing people in the Friday night throng with his bloody hands. He grabbed Maxine Weijiang, a petite student who screamed but wasn't strong enough to pull free, and the bystanders who weren't running for their lives smelled a sickly, sulphurous stench—and Maxine turned to grab anyone she could.

In many cases, bystanders were hard to come by due to the prolonged battles all over the world, so the hosts broke through windows or boarded a passing bus or train. They took anyone they could find, from grandmothers to children. If they could move, they could be made to move as Belia'al desired. And as their numbers swelled, they began to overrun the now exhausted FRC units with sheer berserker inevitability.

In New York, Hanrahan saw his numbers begin to fall, and he called out reinforcements from the military.

· · · · ·

Tropical Cyclone Bruce began to pick up steam on its way toward Fiji.

4 Night (Encompassing a Private World)

"Good day, America. This is the top of the hour, and this is the top of the news. The terrorist uprisings around the world have been mostly contained at this hour. Outbreaks continue in Bangladesh, Moscow, and other places, but there has been nothing in the United States for nearly two hours. We can thank our brave men and women in uniform, both state and federal, for that. We value their sacrifice on our behalf."

FRIDAY, MARCH 25, 2011 · 12:00 NOON CENTRAL DAYLIGHT TIME

4 Night (Encompassing a Private World)

At noon, Rita slipped from deep sleep into a coma. Her monitors alerted the intensive care staff at once and measures were taken within thirty seconds, but it appeared it was going to be touch and go for the next forty-eight hours.

FRIDAY, MARCH 25, 2011 · 2:00 P.M. EASTERN DAYLIGHT TIME

4 Night (Encompassing a Private World)

At 999 places across the globe, a Madeleine Riggs appeared.

There were again 999 hosts of Belia'al. Some of those 999 had become hosts just three hours before, but that didn't matter. Old or new, the bodies all held Belia'al. The demon looked from every eye.

He looked at Maddy Riggs, and was caught by surprise, nine hundred and ninety-nine times.

He had thought the diabola was a single entity, and she was, but long before she'd become a diabola, she'd created the illusion of multiple people where she was, and now, as a diabola, she could create more than the illusion. Each Maddy was made from her, and was solid enough for her well-remembered KGB combat skills to take an immediate toll on Belia'al's hosts.

Her consciousness flicked from form to form. She chopped the gun hand of a lottery winner in Düsseldorf, and kicked the legs from under a CFO in Brasilia, and dodged a bullet from a locksmith in Hong Kong, and turned the gun on an airline pilot in Nairobi, and took a bullet from a circus clown in Delhi, and dove into the gut of a county commissioner in Fort Wayne—

FRIDAY, MARCH 25, 2011 · 2:00 P.M. EASTERN DAYLIGHT TIME

4 Night (Encompassing a Private World)

"You see that?" Bragane demanded.

"More than you know," Aparicio said, staring at Madeleine Riggs.

It was twenty-two degrees and there was a thin film of ice over the mud path out by the river. The Madwoman who'd once seduced him was grappling with a fat man that Bragane recognized as an Allen County commissioner. The man seized the woman in a bear hug and dropped backward, hurling her over his head. She landed, hard, and slid five feet, but she was up in a flash.

"Which one do we shoot?" Bragane asked. "I hope not the redhead."

"Hold your fire unless attacked!" Aparicio barked urgently. "There's shit goin' on everywhere. This could be a diversion, hoping we're beat at the end of our shift." Another patrol had killed a crazed intruder two hours before on the south side. Everybody knew it was getting squirrelly out there.

Maddy ran forward, her feet not slipping now, her feet hardly touching the ground, moving more quickly than the commissioner expected. But a wave of rage seemed to explode in him and his own hand moved more quickly than it should have, grabbing her face and pushing her off course so she went to one side and he turned and clubbed the back of her neck on the follow-through. She stumbled, then rose completely from the ground and whirled in place and kicked the commissioner full in the face. The sound of his breaking nose was completely audible to the onlookers.

He went into a crouch and she came in for the kill, but at the last second he proved to be shamming as he uncoiled with a knife that went deep in her gullet.

"Shit!" snapped Bragane, raising his weapon.

"Wait!" snapped Aparicio in turn.

"Why?"

"Just wait!"

Madeleine Riggs went to her knees, bent just as the commissioner had bent, her red hair parting, exposing her neck. The commissioner went for it with his knife and Madeleine's right arm shot straight up at an impossible angle to grab his hand in mid-thrust. She twisted the wrist, snapping it, bringing him around by the arm still attached to it, and shoved the hand and knife into his left eye. It took him some time to know he was dead and fall to the ice, time Madeline used to straighten her arm and stand up and size up the men with guns and eyes locked on her. She evidently decided she had other places to be and so left the men to run toward the river. She was not quite out of sight through the trees before she vanished.

"I did not see that!" said Bragane.

"See what?" Aparicio agreed. And he thought, *Neither did she see me for who I am. Not even after I scouted her.* He smiled. *I like that.* But his next thought erased that. *If she's in the front lines, things must be going badly.*

He didn't even know that Breckenridge was gone.

SHELTER

Pam and the three remaining elementals finally got below the gale. As the mountain's slope began to flatten out, they took a corkscrew turn . . . and the winds stopped. Below them, at the end of the trail snaking downward, they had a clear view of the valley below. There was a small, colorful hamlet, set against the right angle where the mountains met, facing a wide green marsh leading out to blue ocean. It was a beautiful sight. But Pam brought them all to a skidding halt as soon as they saw it.

"Can we relight Chiss now?" she asked.

"*We* can't," said Mymla. "A human has to use fire."

"I can do that," said Pam.

"She means a human in the *human* world," drawled Cocorik.

"Maybe not," said Funt. "We never had a human here before."

"Well, how can you make fire anyway, Pam?" snapped Cocorik.

"The wand I took from Quince. It makes fire."

"It *does?*" said Funt. Pam had to use every ounce of her alchemy to not burst out laughing at the stunned looks on their faces.

"It *should,*" she said, suddenly realizing that it might not work in this world. She pulled it from her black jeans and thumbed the lever.

It lit.

"It does," she said. "So now we need tinder." She saw tall citrine grasses on the slope above them, dry from lack of rain. "Cocorik . . ."

"Of course," he said, equally dryly, already on his way up.

"I'll get sticks," said Funt, trundling off to do so.

"And I'll stay out of your way," said Mymla. "I'll go back to the turn and make a shield against the final winds."

"We won't need that," said Pam. "This wand is powerful, and you should be here when he comes back."

"All right," said Mymla, smiling. "If *you* say so, Pam."

Cocorik flew back down with every last bit of grass he could carry. He was sour but he was one of the four. *And this, of course, is why he doesn't like me,* Pam thought. *He can't boss the others while I'm here.* She shrugged. *I'm doing my best to leave, little guy.*

Funt came back with all the twigs she could carry, and watched along with the others as Pam built a small pile of twigs and grass in the shelter of a rock.

"Okay," she said, kneeling beside the pile. "You guys stand uphill there, just in case there's a breeze. And I'll just . . ." She thumbed the lighter, held its small flame to the kindling. The grass began to burn. . . .

Poof! Chiss appeared in the flame, looking unchanged from before. He stepped out of it, apparently unconcerned with it. "That was fast," he said, looking quizzically at his friends.

"*She* did it," said Cocorik, tossing his head in Pam's direction.

"She *did*!" agreed Mymla wholeheartedly.

"We just wanted you back, Chiss," Pam said, her face nearer to him than usual as she knelt above him. "But when you say 'That was fast'—I didn't expect *you* to appear as soon as I touched the grass."

"All flame is the same."

"But not the flame in my lighter," she said, giving up on calling it a wand.

"That flame doesn't belong here. It can't bring me here."

"But it lit the grass."

"Grass belongs here. That can bring me."

"Right," Pam said, filling in the blanks. "Because you're not the flame, you're the element of flame, in the elemental world."

Mymla spoke up. "Pam's an *alchemist*!"

"I wish I could hug you, Chiss!" Pam said.

"I understand. But it's not my nature," he said sadly. He straightened his shoulders and stepped out onto the trail. "I'm glad to be here, with you all again, but there's no more time to be wasted on me. We need to get you to the Eagle."

"Yes, that's right," said Cocorik. "The sooner the better."

"Well, welcome back anyway, Chiss," said Mymla. Something in her voice caught Pam's attention. Was there an unrequited love there—?

"Right," said Pam. "Time to go."

4 Night (Encompassing a Private World)

At six, Vee called a halt to her preparations. "I'll see you at Eddie's in an hour."

"Vee, I wish you'd stay with the program," Matt said. "There's more that we can do."

"I believe you. But although you've proved your skill at diva-making—I feel good, Matt; I really do—this particular diva has things she needs, just for herself, if she's going to be ready for her big show."

· · · · ·

Half an hour later, Vee returned alone to her flat, and went straight to her book.

"I'm sorry I haven't talked to you much lately," she said.

I am a book. You are alive, said the book.

"What do you think of Matt?"

Time will tell.

"Do you like him?"

Time will tell.

"Are you jealous?"

I am a book. You are alive.

"All right," said Vee, though she'd have wished for more. "I want you to know, I am fighting for my life at the next Hour of Jupiter."

The Hour of Jupiter is concerned with the living of life in full measure. It is good for expansion, and good fortune.

"I know. We're in the last Hour of Jupiter by daylight. The next one, in seven hours, is when it all goes down. Either I get free of Christopher Durban or I die."

Jupiter is a fire planet. Fire is life.

"Yes. I'm going to save my life. But, just in case . . ." Vee couldn't say the words, and then all at once they were spilling out. "I wanted to tell you how much you've meant to me, Cornelius. I was so lost, and now I'm found."

The book sat silently . . . then finally began to flip its pages, toward the end, *to* the end. It sat with all its pages turned to the left, and only the cover to the right. And then a seam began to open along that cover, marking out three sides, so that when the seam completely opened, it formed another "page" which the book then flipped to the left, revealing words she had never seen before.

You are my disciple. I trust in you.

Vee stared. She had read the book cover to cover, many times. "You never showed me that. . . ."

The seam closed. She ran her finger along the line it had been, put her nails where she'd seen it and tried to find a purchase. But there was none. The leather was whole.

The entire book glowed briefly with witchlight.

Vee sniffed, and her mouth softened. "Thank you, Cornelius. . . ." She wanted to continue, but she couldn't speak.

Pages began to flip, back to front, until they revealed the first lines of the Fifth Book of Occult Philosophy.

Magick always disappears. That is its nature; it is unseen. It is nonetheless real, a force always available to the wise. Magick must become so familiar that you see it when it is unseen. Only then can you become one with magick.

She nodded, said, "I love you, Cornelius."

And she went out the door.

4 Night (Encompassing a Private World)

When Vee came in the door at Eddie's, Matt was sitting at a table in the corner. The weirdness in the air cast a strange spell over the crowd, but that didn't matter: there *was* a crowd. As she settled into her seat, Matt waved at the waiter and he immediately brought her a pint. "This is *way* off the diva procedure," he said laughing, "but I'm guessing it's what you'd like."

"Very much so," Vee said, again marveling at how well he knew her already, and how well he rolled with her punches.

"So why are we here?" he asked.

"I had a chance to think today," she said after savoring her lager. "About Durban, but also me. A significant part of my life has taken place inside these walls, with these people. I have always held them at arm's length, with my 'mystique'—but I realized today, I can't perform if there's no one to perform for. I put my songs out there, and they like them so they support me, and I get to keep doing it. I used to think I was alone, but the truth is, I'm not alone and I never have been. So if I'm going to defend my life tonight, I want to rise to my peak where I've lived it."

"I'll watch your alcohol intake then, shall I?"

"You shall, but so shall I," she said, smiling. "When the Hour of Jupiter comes, I'll be right where I want to be. In the meantime, Matt—I want to dance!" And then she added, oddly, "As if I was in a window!"

Matt let it go. The truly magickal were just different.

4 Night (Encompassing a Private World)

Once again the universe breathed out and Belia'al took the offensive. His remaining hosts continued to resupply their ranks with the innocent, and any host, old or new, who found a way to hold a Maddy Riggs caused a great change in that body. Boils, arthritis, spasms, contractions, all of them and more wracked Maddys worldwide, driving them to their knees, where they died at Belia'al's many hands. They were only her illusions but Aleksandra felt every one of their agonies. . . .

They vanished. All of them, all around the globe. Aleksandra could create new Maddys as easily as Belia'al had created new hosts, but she had had enough.

. . . . .

Power engineers were working to restore power to fifteen districts of Russia's southern Krasnodar region, where 70,000 people were without power and in the dark after-winds up to seventy-five miles an hour severed power lines.

CALM

The hamlet in the valley by the intersecting mountains was a beautiful little fairy-tale village, with thatched roofs and gables and everything Walt Disney ever dreamed. But Pam couldn't get through it fast enough. She and the reconstituted foursome walked through it so quickly it irked some of the peaceful inhabitants. Who did they think they were?

But Pam's sole goal was the marsh beyond the hamlet, and the ocean out beyond that. The marsh was a vast plain, almost flat, covered in patches of green grass and blue water. *I can pick my way out to the edge,* thought Pam. The sky was blue, but a warm blue, like a living thing stretching from horizon to horizon. The clouds were gone, for the first time in what seemed like forever, and a good bright light shone over everything, even though there was no sun in the sky.

Pam started forward, onto the cushiony grass. This really was a charmed land. She looked down to say so to her companions, and they weren't there. She turned and saw them back where the marsh began.

"What's up?" she asked.

Mymla answered for the crew. "This is your space, Pam. You go the rest of the way alone."

"But why?" asked Pam. "You came with me to the Ox. The Eagle is *your* totem, Mymla."

"But she is *your* goal. She'll always be with us, and we with her, but you need her *today.*"

Cocorik cut in. "Watch. She won't leave us."

"Oh, guys," Pam said, going back across the hillocks to them and dropping to her knees. "We'll see each other again."

Funt was startled. "We will?"

"A good alchemist communes with the elementals. I can do it more than I have."

"But it won't be *us.*"

"Are you sure? Because I think the experience you four had with the strange human who fought her way to the Eagle is going to become part of elemental lore—something that *all* elementals will know. Something in the *essence* and not in the *individuals.* So even though it won't be you . . . it *will* be you."

"We'll know you?" Cocorik asked dubiously.

"I'll do everything I can to make sure you do."

"Then we'll do the same," said Mymla. "We'll tell everybody, and tell them to tell everybody."

"So don't worry," Pam said. "I'll see you again before you know it. But I do wish you would go with me now."

"You came in alone, you go out alone," said Mymla. "You're an *alchemist!*"

So Pam leaned down and embraced each of the three she could, and gave Chiss her most dazzling smile. They all cheered as she stood up again. And she walked away fast, so they wouldn't see her cry. *It's just because I'm in the water quadrant,* she told herself. *Artemis doesn't cry!*

FRIDAY, MARCH 25, 2011 • 4:00 P.M. CENTRAL DAYLIGHT TIME
....
4 Night (Encompassing a Private World)

"America, I want to talk with you a little bit about zombis. For, make no mistake about it, there are zombis in our streets and our fields right now. The *government* says they've contained them, but I have Mrs. Nancy Olsen of Piscataway, New Jersey, on my telephone. Nancy, tell my viewers what you're looking at."

"Zombis, Norman. My neighbor Mrs. Sanderson has been taken over. She's outside my house! I'm afraid she'll break my windows!"

"Have you seen her eat the living?"

"No, but she looks . . . hungry."

"Thank you, Nancy. Keep in touch with us throughout the day, if you can. And you know, America, eating the living is just the tip of the iceberg. This zombi rebellion ties in directly with the Black Helicopters which have terrorized Montana and Oklahoma and Maine this past week. Because, of course, if the government wanted to stop the zombis, they could. If the government wanted to stop the Black Helicopters, they could. They have the strongest, most powerful military in the world. They could stop them. But they don't. And that's why I know the Black Helicopters will be back, with something even more horrifying than this.

"At first, you know, I couldn't understand why the Black

Helicopters would attack in three such different places. But then I saw the *plan*. Look at this map. See, here's Montana. Then here's Oklahoma. And here's Maine. Now you draw a line from Montana to Oklahoma, then another from Oklahoma to Maine. You see it? You see that it forms an angle? And if you draw another line, parallel to the line from Maine to Oklahoma, starting in Montana, you go through Las Vegas—right?—and then Los Angeles. Now look at the symbol. It's like an 'S,' but not just any 'S.' That's the lightning-bolt 'S' of the *SS*. Could it be any clearer? You know, they like to say I'm crazy, but I'm telling you, the Black Helicopters are coming for California next. And so the zombis, as terrifying as they are—as terrifying as they're meant to be—are in the end just the shock waves in the assault of the United Nations, all across this great country of ours! The final assault of the one-world agenda that will end the world and bring about the Rapture! The Black Helicopters will destroy the sinkhole called Los Angeles and Jesus shall return to judge the world!"

FRIDAY, MARCH 25, 2011 · 5:05 P.M. EASTERN DAYLIGHT TIME

4 Night (Encompassing a Private World)

In Ruth's office, the two leaders spoke through Channel Nine with their new Gemstone. The old man looked more gaunt than usual, but his eyes were bright with Necklace pharmaceuticals. They knew the signs of uppers, and saw them; it never occurred to them what other drugs Hanrahan might have faced recently.

"Listen, ladies," the old man said, "this is the first mission on my watch. It remains the first mission in the Twenty-Twelve Project. Be sure it's a success."

"We're very confident," said Ruth, anxious to get the mission started.

"Still, you've flown without opposition thus far. In and out, of out-of-the-way places. Tonight you're on a much bigger stage, in a much more populated area. And I have no doubt that some pilots will be in the air tonight, hoping to catch a glimpse of the Black Helicopters."

"If they do, and we don't want to be seen just then, we'll take them down."

"Are you still determined to go along?" Hanrahan asked Franny.

"Yes, sir. I've got to know the stresses my machines will face."

"Don't bullshit me. You want to pull the trigger."

She smiled. "You know me, Uncle Dick."

"I do. If someone had to take over at a moment's notice, we're fortunate it was me, because I know just about everything."

"Meaning there's something you don't know?"

"I don't know what caused those riots last night and this morning. It's clearly something magickal but we can't contact Quince, so, you need to remain on high alert until the mission is absolutely complete."

Ruth nodded. "Mysterious terrorists, nosy pilots—it'll be a wonder if we don't just get stuck in rush hour."

They all laughed, while Franny added, "We'd better get started then."

"Godspeed," said Hanrahan, and clicked off. As he did so, he felt a creeping sensation, like a chill shadow. *Conscience?* he asked himself, and answered, *Hardly*. But he contacted his tech team and ordered all occult barriers double-checked.

4 Night (Encompassing a Private World)

When the men assembled for the final Black Helicopter mission, the sky was so low that Max felt he could reach up and touch it— that once they took off they'd pass not only through an elder doorway but also the sky itself, like Flammarion's famous picture of the alchemist crawling into the world beyond. But that was Pam's situation now; Max, who'd begun the week crawling into the latest balls-out scheme by the Necklace, had seen that become almost mundane compared to everything going on in the world beyond.

The men entered their ships and three helicopters rose directly into the elder doorway, opening for them above the Works. No one saw them go. But to the men's surprise, they passed back out again in just a few minutes, somewhere over a river.

"We're taking the scenic route tonight," Franny told the men on her chopper, and the men on the other choppers by radio. "We're over Missouri now, and we'll be flying visibly for most of the trip. We'll go back inside the doorway twice in order to maintain a schedule, and maybe some other times if people get too close. We don't intend to be caught. But we do intend to be seen as much as possible, so the conspiracy buffs can trace us back along a false path. We'll be in the air for three hours, forty-five minutes. The attack will take place precisely at nine our time—eight local time."

She paused, took a breath. "You'll have seen the rocket launchers we have on board tonight. That's because our goal is the Alamodome in San Antonio," she said, and looked around to see who got it. Only two didn't, and they declined in her estimation. Aparicio did, she saw. "At nine tonight—eight in Texas—Number One Kansas and Number Twelve Richmond will be in the final minutes of the Southwest Regional Semi-Finals. It'll be a shit game, but Friday night, Elite Eight, the game in Newark almost surely over—the TV audience will be there, watching as we obliterate the fifty thousand people in the dome." She put her hands together, flipped them apart: boom! "The folks who've been waiting for the Black Helicopters to do their thing will get the night they knew would come."

4 Night (Encompassing a Private World)

Twenty minutes later, the Black Helicopters passed one hundred feet from the top of the Saint Louis arch, and Max began planning what he'd do if Pam didn't bring him the key in time. It would not be pretty.

PEACE

Pam came to the end of the marsh, where the grass died out and only beautifully sparkling blue water remained. Standing there on the edge of this world, she thought she caught a glimpse of something flashing out over the ocean. The second time she saw it, she knew it for the light on the Eagle's wings as it circled above the ocean.

Now she would have to leave her physical form behind and proceed in the *astral*. To this point, she hadn't been able to become *astral* and see a comprehensible land at the same time, but that was *to this point*. Here, with all the land behind her and all the water ahead, the Eagle finally in view, she was sure that that had changed.

If she was going to be afraid, this was the time. And there *was* fear in her—but she was *not afraid*. She controlled her fear, because she knew what she was doing. It came to her very clearly then that she *did* know, that all of her work with Max had led her to this place where everything was magick, and her mind was far more exalted than afraid. No more than a handful of people in the world, in any world, could understand her now.

She lay down on the soft grass and looked up at the blue sky, and rose into that sky. She looked down at her body on the grass, and once more saw Pam Blackwell, the woman she always was before she met Max August. That tousled blond hair, that crooked smile. In some ways, even now, she missed the old Pam Blackwell. But her future far outweighed her past.

So she turned her eyes toward the Eagle and *flew* out over the sparkling waves. The land at the edges of her vision quickly slid away and there was nothing around her but ocean below and sky above, two shades of blue, as far as the eye could see. She was soaring in the middle of immensity.

FRIDAY, MARCH 25, 2011 · 11:50 P.M. GREENWICH MEAN TIME

4 Night (Encompassing a Private World)

The Hour of Jupiter would begin at 12:06, so Matt moved into position fifteen minutes in advance.

In all the time they'd spent in Cragmoor Mews the previous night, there had been no more sign of habitation in the other houses than in Number Seven. Tonight was exactly the same. Either the denizens here minded their own business, or they didn't exist. Either way, he was more concerned with passersby in the quadrant behind him than the curving lane in front. Just inside the mews, between the last streetlight outside and the first streetlight inside, he knelt and opened his new backpack. He took from it a U.S. Navy SMAW rocket launcher.

The launcher was a fiberglass-epoxy launch tube, 760 mm long. The tube was just over 83 mm across, to hold one of the two rockets he'd bought with it. There was a British-made spotting rifle to sight it.

Now it was all up to Vee.

4 Night (Encompassing a Private World)

It was the extension of Friday night in Camden Town, so even here, on a side street, there were people. Vee kept her wits about her as she walked briskly across the intersection, wearing her jacket over a black tee and jeans, her hair pulled tight. It wouldn't do to let her guard down now.

She moved into the shadows overhanging the stone walls and stopped, expanding her awareness. No one around slowed his pace. So she went on to the front doors of the church, blue like all the doors for some reason, and locked like all the doors. She smiled a little grimly as she placed her hands on the handles. Cornelius had taught her this one:

"I call upon thee, in the name of thee, who art greater than all, the creator of all, the self-begotten who seest all but art not seen. I call upon thee to open the way for me, that I may strike down evil in thy world."

The doors opened.

The flattery in the spell made it archaic. We see ourselves a little bigger now, and God doesn't need his ass kissed. But the spell was potent all the same, for things like doors. It did for her what it did for Cornelius in 1519. Magick from across the centuries was in her hands. She could feel the hidden forces align themselves in response, feel the world *shift*.

She pushed the doors wider with the low squeal of old and un-used metal. The interior was barely lit, by streetlight through old and dirty stained-glass windows. It was the nave, a high, vaulted room with pews, where people once knelt. She would never kneel.

She went inside.

There were echoes from the stone floor, the stone pillars. Some-where in here was Durban's crypt. She moved watchfully to the

right-side wall, before creeping down the aisle there, alert for al-
coves. There were three, but none had anything she wanted. When
she reached the steps to the altar, she was beginning to sense each
passing moment in her Hour of Jupiter. She ran quickly before the
altar to reach the other side, rather than retrace her steps, and as
she did so, she caught the faintest line of light in the altar floor.
She went up onto the platform—surely deconsecrated now—and
remembered the secret at the back of the book quite well as she
dug her nails into the seam and slowly got a purchase on a hidden
trapdoor.

She opened it. Below her were stairs, running down some fifteen feet to an open doorway. A single candle burned in a plate at
the bottom of the stairs, throwing a wavering circle. *It's a trap or it's
not,* thought Vee, *but there's no time to screw around. I have to meet
him to kill him, and there's no other way this ends. Not for me.* She took
a deep breath, let it out. She felt her right pocket. Then she started
down the stairs, as silently as a cat.

Halfway down, the door slammed shut above, and Durban
stepped through the doorway below like a wolf, or a lynx. "Trapped,"
he said, and his gaunt face was sad. "I'm truly sorry you chose this
path, Vee. We could have made such beautiful—"

She leapt at him, knowing it was just what he wanted, knowing
her strength was flowing into his. Even as they went down in a
heap he was yelling, "Yes!" and she could feel the first touch of her
fatigue. She stuck her right hand in her right pocket and thumbed
her phone.

SATURDAY, MARCH 26, 2011 · 12:16 A.M. GREENWICH MEAN TIME

4 Night (Encompassing a Private World)

Matt's phone began vibrating. He took one deep breath, let it out,
sighted the launcher, and pulled the trigger. A vast blast exploded
from both ends of the tube, lighting all of Cragmoor Mews for a

moment, showing the rocket arcing from his shoulder to blow the front of Durban's house to splinters.

As the flash faded, he was already sliding the other rocket into place.

4 Night (Encompassing a Private World)

Vee felt the blast through its effect on Durban. He spasmed under her hands, shouting sudden gibberish. His eyes went blank and she took her advantage.

"I call upon thee, in the name of thee, who art greater than all, the creator of all, the self-begotten who seest all but art not seen. I call upon thee that I may strike down evil in thy world!"

The doll went slack, all consciousness gone. She rolled away from it, but thumbed her phone once more, just for luck. Ten seconds later, Durban spasmed to fly two feet off the floor, and split along its right side, spilling stuffing. Vee watched its immobile form slowly sag for another sixty seconds . . . then reached for her phone a third time. *We did it, Matt. I'm free.*

Durban lurched up without warning and grabbed her throat. More stuffing flew; the hands and arms were flabby, slack, but the strength in them was undiminished.

"I call upon thee," she shouted, but the face before her, now falling in upon itself, still grinned like a palsy victim. "Not enough," it said hollowly. "You value your life, but I value mine more. I've kept it far longer." And Vee knew it was true. She threw a fist at his chest and the doll split open like a pillow—and the *astral* Durban still held her. She could see him, a pale, pale man, inside the empty body, still with that hideous grin. The magick she knew could not beat him. This was beyond everything the book taught her, beyond everything she somehow just knew—

—except for one thing.

She jammed her left hand into her left pocket. She came out with a small capsule and stuck it down her throat. His clutch made it hard to swallow but she could force it. She *would* force it no matter what. She *did* force it.

The cramps started almost at once.

This is my End Game, she thought with almost ludicrous calm. *Go!*

SERENITY

Pam was soaring over the wide, wide ocean, in a beautiful blue-green sky. She could feel the wind in her face, and wondered: *Why wind and not Cocorik?* Then her mind responded, *Because this is MY space, here very literally between me and my Eagle. Not even Mymla could be with me now.*

She looked out at the water, stretching away in all directions to the horizon. It brought back a memory, of flying with Max from Barbados to Suriname, in the bright sun over the Caribbean, still very early on. He was explaining the Mayan calendar, and she'd looked down at the ocean and thought, *Could there really be 260 things contributing to this view?*

Now she thought, *Easily.*

She looked up to the air. The Eagle was closer now. Circling lazily, the bird was beginning to come into range. Soon Pam could make out the sharp lines of her carving, the artistry that had gone into making an eighteen-inch talisman. But the Eagle before Pam was fifty feet long. Soon she could easily make out her expression, as her beady eyes remained fixed on Pam.

Pam came alongside the bird, flying twenty feet away from it. She had thought of making her greeting somewhat more flowery, but at the end of the day, this was a talisman. Its purpose was to be used by humans. It was one of the 260 things Pam had weighed. So as the two of them soared side by side, she looked straight across the distance at the watching Eagle and shouted, "O Great Eagle, I have come to free you. In return, I ask that you open yourself to me."

"I can't be freed," answered the Eagle, her voice harsh and loud from her massive throat, carrying clearly through the blue-green sky. "I serve another master."

"That can change," said Pam. "I live and work with the man who controls Kalbu Rabu. He told me how he freed the Lion. I know how to free you, and myself."

The Eagle studied her narrowly. "You chose not to work with the Ox."

"He's not my talisman."

"And you believe that I am?"

"I know that you are."

"Well, you're correct in that." The bird nodded once, briskly. "You are of the Water clan. What is your name, woman?"

"Pam Blackwell!"

"So what do you propose, Pam Blackwell?"

"I propose to enclose us both within my power, to block the connection to your current master. I propose to be the only power around you, and so become your mistress. You will then be able to do what I command, and you will send me, *astral* and physical forms both, back to my Earth. Is that acceptable to you?"

"It is *possible*," said the Eagle. "But I cannot *accept* it, for you are not my mistress."

"But if I just *do* it . . ."

"I am not responsible," said the Eagle, eyes glinting.

"Then I'll begin!" called Pam.

She closed her eyes, and continued to fly. It was an exhilarating feeling, flying blind, knowing there was nothing to run into, and so she centered herself. She opened her eyes again but now was looking out from her spirit, neither *astral* or physical. Her spirit was the heart of her, a silver sphere of power, sometimes inside her and sometimes out. Keeping her eyes on the Eagle, she pushed it out, expanding it. It began to resemble a silver soap bubble, wobbling and rippling with the strain and concentration, but holding together nonetheless until it was a huge sphere, large enough to enclose both Pam and the Eagle.

The sphere began to glow a soft blue-green. *I'm one with her!* Pam knew. She felt electricity, magnetism, and the flow within. She felt Water.

The Eagle abruptly nodded her great head.

Pam *flew* closer, still looking in the Eagle's eye. "I am free," said the Eagle. "I am yours, mistress."

"Then free *me*," said Pam.

"Go."

⟡ ⟡ ⟡ ⟡

It was 8 P.M. Eastern Standard Time—or Midnight Greenwich Mean. The universe breathed in and Belia'al knew he had exhausted the possibilities of Earth. It was time to give the diabola what she had given him and take the fight to her.

He centered himself in the 999, on Earth. He was the king of everything below him, and through the 999 he brought it all to the planetary plane. In 999 places, Belia'al stood upon our world and drew all the power from all the realms below, and in 999 places, Belia'al turned his gaze to the sky above. In the night over Lake Tanganyika, he saw a sparkling spectacle of multicolored pinpricks; in the daytime in Madrid, he saw none. But from his 999 places he saw it all.

One star among the billions up there was the one he wanted. One star was red, and young, and—there, near Sirius. It was notable as the only red one in the area, but there were a million other reds in the heavens. It was very hard to see from Earth, for someone without 999 pairs of eyes. Professor Luther Blážek's copy of The Tycho-2 Catalogue called it TYC6539-2404-1. But Blážek knew, because his master knew, the way ethereal beings do, that that small red star was the one that Belia'al sought.

And so, as the professor stood hunched in an alleyway in Vincennes, gore dripping from his beard, exhausted by a day of brutal warfare in the streets, exhilarated by the sky, he and the 998 others felt their master rise up on their shoulders and reach up toward the star and go there.

There is no direct connection between Earth and hell, but there is nothing *but* connection between Earth and sky. With his base of 999, Belia'al could go up to space just as he'd gone down to the subconscious, but without the hallucinations. Space was part of Earth's reality. The demon could rise up from the Earth until the Earth became a blue dot behind him, and then was lost in the glare of the sun, and he could keep on rising until the small red star near Sirius began to grow larger, and then filled his view, and he could still be in touch with the Earth. He could not be denied.

Now you learn, little diabola!

Learn to laugh at you, demon? mocked the star.

Belia'al threw the power of hell against her, and Aleksandra felt the fires within her flicker and fume. The plagues he visited upon her human forms found their counterparts in the burning hydrogen at her core, disrupting its very structure. But she rode them out, enduring what could only be called pain, if stars felt pain. Her color grew more crimson but she rode them out.

Belia'al drew upon specific hells and flooded her with power that had disgusted dinosaurs. But this was better for Aleksandra, because she felt no disgust at anything. In this form, as a diabola, she could not be overcome by sensations. Belia'al gathered the spoor of the demons he ruled and hurled it at her. Still she burned on, if anything growing more scarlet again. Belia'al . . .

. . . began to realize where he was. The star was before him, yes, he was connected to the 999, yes—but space was all around. Empty space, infinite space . . . the kind never found in an underground cavern . . .

You exist to crush, demon. But there is nothing to crush here, except me, and with each passing second, your ability to do so is being revealed as insufficient. Here there is the opposite of "crush." Here is expanse—and dissipation . . .

Belia'al the king of demons threw all the power at his command against her—and it was pathetic. Her fires barely surged at all now. She had encompassed his power, and was burning it! While he could see pale green effluvia drifting from his form, into the void.

Damn you, diabola! he screamed.

I'm beyond damnation, she answered. *But not beyond realizing that a creature of logic and form could not long exist here. And so I attacked you in your sphere to begin this war, and fought you across the Earth, until you could finally see that logic dictated you do to me what I had done to you—attack me where I live. But I can live below; you can't live above!*

On her final word, Belia'al collapsed, his presence in the midst of space falling backward, downward through the increasingly hallucinatory emptiness, leaving a smear of green fog behind, until finally, *finally!* he tumbled toward the bright light, then eventually the blue dot, and then the South Pacific where he struck like a meteor. But he had no physical form at that point and passed through the ocean with no tsunami, into the Earth below, into his personal hell, where he broke his cavern's ancient crags before he struck rock bottom and split it wide while boulders pounded down from the walls, burying him.

In the years to come, he would recover. He would not dissipate here. But for now . . .

The bad vibes ended.

FRIDAY, MARCH 25, 2011 · 7:15 P.M. CENTRAL DAYLIGHT TIME

4 Night (Encompassing a Private World)

Aparicio shuddered.

"What's wrong?" Bragane asked him.

"Nothing," Aparicio said. "Absolutely nothing." He grinned and punched Bragane's shoulder. "Not a goddamn thing, thank you very much!"

"You're nuts, Aparicio," Bragane said.

The Black Helicopters banked into a single file and trailed a two-mile convoy rolling straight down I-Three-Five.

4 Night (Encompassing a Private World)

"What did you do?" Durban demanded, his voice no more than the echoes in the stairwell.

"I've killed myself," Vee grated, the pain growing exponentially worse.

"Nonsense!" Durban snapped. "I know you! You're too full of life for that!"

"Too full of life . . . to give it away," she murmured, and felt the floor of her very being begin to dissolve. Durban held on to her ever more tightly, trying to force her to live, but there was no question now. She was expiring. The floor gave way. She felt the darkness rise around her as she fell, faster and faster. Durban was absorbing the last of her, striving for every crumb. At last he saw no more to be gained from her and decided to let go.

He couldn't.

The life he'd taken was the dying life, and death was in him as well. He panicked at the thought and tried to force his fingers from her phantom form, but he couldn't. She was swirling into oblivion, pulling him down and down, an anchor. Christopher Durban called upon everything he was, everything he had been for over a hundred years, a true son of Queen Victoria, survivor of the Blitz, to stay alive.

But he had gone too far.

His sight began to go . . . but he saw her looking at him.

"Die!" he mumbled. His hands grew weak.

Her response was lost.

He died.

Still they descended. Vee had to be sure this time. She had to pull his fingers from her throat and let him spiral away from her, into the invisible. Only then, when he was too far below to play any sort of trick, did she slow her own descent. She had little more than simple existence left—but she had that, because she knew how it was done.

She had done it before.

LIGHT

Pam flew toward the blue-green sky. The first time she'd seen it here, she had thought it was full of holes and trees, but she'd walked a path since then, and arrived at someplace else entirely. Still, she had never forgotten that there were other ways to see it, and now, as she rose like a blue-green star in the sky, she let the sky dissolve and saw the trees again. And the holes. Now they were blue-green.

Onward and upward Pam flew. She darted through the holes like an expert surfer, following the paths they made in all three dimensions. She knew the paths had to come together at the point where they entered the tunnel to the other world.

The Real World.

Home.

Now the path she was following was paralleling another, and then they came together. Here was another path coming in, and another. It was all coming together!

She emerged from a hole like any other, to find just one hole ahead. She *flew* into it and found herself in a long white tunnel, the hole to end all holes, running straight through the impenetrable trees. In all the chaos was a single strand of order that led out of the subconscious. Pam could barely see it, but she did see it and she *soared* through it as fast as she could go, her excitement escalating every second.

Ahead, she could see the elder doorway. It was closed to her, unless she had a key. She had the key. She sailed to it and into it—

> And then Pam's face appeared to Vee,
> and Val's appeared to Pam,
> and for one pure moment in time,
> each saw the other clearly!

SATURDAY, MARCH 26, 2011 · 12:50 A.M. GREENWICH MEAN TIME

4 Night (Encompassing a Private World)

And then Vee was flying upward, rising and advancing, leaving the darkness behind for the light, and she felt the pulse of life in her veins, with the faint scent of sweat and adrenaline, the tickling of the hair across her ears, the sounds of a living universe. She was overwhelmed by it, all but crushed by it, and exulting in every bit of it. She had no time to think about the blonde girl. Fighting the pull of death was something only a powerful wizard could do, or teach. It would be *so very easy* to just relax and fade away. But she had fought it before, and she could do it now.

That was what she knew about herself, when there was so much she did not know. She had ruined Eva Delia because that girl had died and Vee lived on, but Durban had never died. He couldn't go where she could. He couldn't come back.

Liquid on her tongue.

"Don't you die on me, Vee!"

Never!

And then Pam was flying upward, through the white tube, and she felt the feel of life in her veins, with the faint scent of sweat and adrenaline, the tickling of the hair above her ears, the sounds of a living universe. She was overwhelmed by it, all but crushed by it, and exulting in every bit of it. She had no time to think about Val. She was all about the ride!

But at long last, the white tube widened, and this time there were no holes and trees. There was a helicopter with Max in it!

Aparicio jolted upright.

"What the hell?" grumbled Bragane. "Are you losin' it, man?"

"Sorry," Aparicio said distractedly. "Guess I drifted off."

"Easy to do in this muck, but keep it together."

"Yeah," Aparicio said, lying back and closing his eyes. Rising in the *astral* in his funny, not-quite-easy way, and in the center of the Black Helicopter on its way to slaughter, he held Pam tight and she held him tighter and they kissed harder than the night they beat the London demons. . . .

4 Night (Encompassing a Private World)

And Pam, for the first time, thought, *Val!* Her eyes opened.

Max loosened his embrace, and she felt it and loosened hers. "Sorry, honey," he said, occupied with his own situation. "I'm running out of time here. Did you bring the key?"

"I did," she said, and held it out to him, triumphantly. *No time to talk!*

Max kissed her again, and when he took the key, he used two hands, leaving the empty one resting on hers for another moment.

The key itself, which had felt solid in Pam's *astral* world, felt just as solid in this one. He clutched it tightly and told Pam, "Get some popcorn. Here we go." He laughed, his warm Max laugh that saw the fun in everything. Turning away, he raised his empty hand to form the telephone sign against his ear. "We'll talk later. Call me."

So as Pam stood more or less on the floor of the helicopter (her feet stayed steady while the floor rolled a little), she watched Max go to work, and she thought, *I did it!*

"Now hold tight," Franny told her troopers. "We'll be passing through the doorway into our world, and stay out just long enough to be sure we're clearly seen. Then back inside, until we pop out just ten blocks from our target. We'll hit it hard and then we're gone. Any questions?"

"No, Chief!" thundered several of the mercs.

"Outstanding. Here we go."

Major Duden held up his Crossbones Key, and the doorway opened wide around them. They came out of the muck over rugged Texas land, gray-tan, cut with white-tan paths and black shadows. In the far distance, the city lights were just stronger than the crimson sunset skies. Hot air suffused the chopper.

Above them, a US Airways regional jet 900 was on landing approach, headed straight for them. There was a moment for the pilots to realize what they were seeing, what ground control had never warned them of. They flashed their lights and took evasive maneuvers.

The major nodded with complete satisfaction and held up his key to open the door.

Max held his own key by his side and turned the bone at right angles to the major's. *For America!* Max thought. *For America . . .*

The Black Helicopters flew full speed into a closed doorway.

There was no sound, with nothing material to hit. But the effect was the same as flying full tilt into a wall. The choppers crumpled and the men were thrown hard forward. Their seat belts kept them from injury there, but in the next instant, the crumpled copters were falling straight down. Some men grabbed ahold of their belts, praying they'd help, while others unsnapped them, fearing they'd share the chopper's fate when they crashed to earth. Max was one who unbuckled, but only to allow his control over gravity full sway. He curled into a ball and produced an invisible shield that would cushion his fall.

WHAM! The Black Helicopters, pride of the Rupp Works, dropped like dead ducks and crumpled yet again against the ground. Half a dozen men died, crushed in their seats; all the others suffered injuries and concussions, with one exception. Dennis Aparicio stood up and made his way to the lolling figure of the major. The other bone key lay beneath his dangling fingers. Max took it, and slid out the compacted doorway.

Pam floated and watched. The fire in Max was crystal clear to her eyes.

He looked upward to make sure the US Airways flight hadn't lost control, that it wasn't for some crazy reason barreling down on him, and found they had handled it fine. Only then did he gauge the country. They were on a ridgeline, very rocky, carpeted with scrubby grass and creosote bushes and twisted trees; open land outside San Antonio. Other planes on approach to the airport provided a distant buzz, and there was gunfire in the far distance; Lackland Air Force Base, if he had to guess. Rescue teams would be here soon enough, spurred by the airliner's report. Max began to jog along the ridge at a ground-devouring pace. He'd be well away from this wreckage before anyone arrived, and he'd be well removed from being Dennis Aparicio.

A shot snapped past his head.

He dove for cover, what there was of it in the high grass. As the night came down, there was enough; he crawled on his knees and elbows to his left, toward a pile of medium-sized rocks. Then he took a cautious look and saw Franny Rupp, covered in blood, one arm hanging limp, the other holding a sidearm, leveraging herself from the wreckage. The one arm was useless; it was only her bulldog determination that drove her. Then, behind her, came Bragane. He said something to Franny and she nodded decisively.

When Max had a choice, he chose not to kill, so he moved on.

This mission was over. He backed crab-wise away, using the rocks for the little shelter they provided, and dropped beyond Bragane's view by reaching the rocky hillside. It was getting very dark now, so there was no way to tell how hard it would be to go down that way, and the odds were that he'd set at least one set of rocks clattering in the process, but if he stayed on the ridgeline, the odds were worse. However, even as he decided that, another shot came his way. There was no way Bragane could see him—unless there were night-vision goggles on board the chopper.

Max slid down the side of the hill until he was certain his head was out of any view, then got his feet under him and started running. As luck would have it, there was a trail below him, and he dropped onto it. He took the downhill direction, just as another shot snapped past. This one was close; the goggles worked. Max gave fleeting thought to shooting it out but still saw no reason to take that route. The trail was better.

Bragane came over the top of the ridge at a spot forty yards away from the spot Max had chosen. The man was running so it must be where the trail began. He was firing as he came, with little hope of hitting a moving target but with more hope than if he didn't shoot. Worries about ammo didn't seem to be on his mind, so he must have stocked up when he was grabbing the goggles. Max put a gravity shield around himself and ran on.

He came to the bottom of the canyon, which was filled with trees because that's where the water was, when there was water. Max got in amongst them, definitely putting himself out of sight—there were no tree-vision goggles—and ran full tilt along the trail, his every sense alert for low branches or stray rocks. He saw several of each and dodged them, hardly slowing his speed. At last, the trail turned to the left, and as soon as it did, he took an abrupt left turn and pushed through the trees back to the hillside, which he went up as fast as he could. By being around the corner, he should still be invisible to Bragane, who would seek him in the valley while he was back up on the ridge.

He was breathing heavily, but still moving well, as he crested the rise. He kept low and found a vantage point where he could look down into the canyon. It was dark down there, but Max knew all about seeing in darkness. He would spot Bragane when the man came through those trees, a silhouette on the lighter trail, and Max would pick him off. Now he had no choice.

A shot kicked dirt before his eyes.

Now he was rolling back over the edge, but just out of sight. Then a low fast run across the rocks around the corner, earth breaking away beneath his feet, scrambling upward against the downward slide. He leapt for a big rock, got his hands on it, chinned himself, got his elbows over the top, pulled himself up onto it. There were trees and brush at this point. Max went up and in.

The trees were ten to fifteen feet tall, and their low, wide foliage rendered him all but invisible. It was *thick* in there. Max stood and listened for a full minute.

Bragane was also in these woods. A distance, but coming, slowly, alertly. He was no Royal but he was an elite merc. And unlike Royal, he had no questions when he went after Max. Bragane was coming to avenge his men and repay a betrayal, and those were motives that drove a man like Bragane hard. He knew Max would come up near the edge so he was moving along the edge, looking for sign of his quarry. But not right at the edge, where a sudden rush could send him flying out into space. Bragane was doing it by the book. There was almost no sound.

Use your shield! said Pam abruptly.

No, he said firmly.

Why not?

Because if you'd have invented Facebook, you'd have invented Facebook.

What?

I call myself an alchemist, and I prove it every day. It's easy to be an alchemist, now. But I also call myself a point man, and I need to prove that when I get the chance.

I get that, Max, she said. *I was channeling Artemis in the subconscious. But I used magick when I had to.*

That whole place was magick, he told her. *This is Texas. I don't need magick for this, and I don't want magick for this. If I let one side of me go, I stop being me. I like being me. Now, in the immortal words of Pam Blackwell—don't hover.*

Max began to move silently inland, away from the edge. The sign he'd already left was not worth going back to cover; his play was to get out of there and at some point disappear, stopping Bragane for a moment and then forever.

Ahead of him was a run up a gully, where thirsty tree roots sought rain runoff and thrust themselves across the slope, turning it into a series of stairsteps. The brush on both sides was thick from their water, and there was a turn to the right on the stairway that was partially obscured. He went up the gully, landing by landing, and when he got to the turning he took it. The pathway went six feet to the right, then turned back toward its original flow. Max looked behind and saw a spot on the far side of the original path, a place where a man could slide into hiding in the thick brush and have a clear view of his quarry's back while he navigated that six-foot jog. *A place, in fact, where other men have had the same idea.* It was the natural idea. But so was the idea he'd had when he'd come to the jog: while I'm looking right, I'm not looking left, so what am I exposing myself to?

Max made a snap decision, based on what he knew of Bragane. With his paranoia, the man would wonder long and hard about what he was exposing himself to before he went around that corner— and Bragane would notice that spot where a man could hide. Bragane would come around that corner trying to focus on two things at once. But Bragane would assume the worst: the hidden sniper. Bragane would be partial to the man who might be lying in wait. So Max stayed where he was, inside the jog, moving the full six feet from the corner, and turning back to face whatever came around it.

In the quiet, Max listened again. Bragane was coming at the same deliberate speed, moving forward somewhat, doing his own listening, then moving again. He could see the obscured turn even better than Max had, with the night goggles. He stopped as he neared it, twice, to study the view. There was silence. *He's spotted the ambush point.* More silence. *Scanning the point.* A slight shift in the silence. *He can't see me there, but he can't rule me out.*

Bragane swung around the corner, his back against it, a gun in each hand, his head steady as his body turned. But his eyes couldn't leave the ambush spot, and for a split second he didn't see Max standing six feet away from him. Then he did, and Max fired.

. . . . .

Max approached Bragane with respect, though he had no doubt the man was dead. Standing centered six feet away, knowing his target's moves, he put his shot right where he wanted it. And still, he double-checked. The art of survival.

Then he heaved a great, long sigh. He stretched his neck left and right, relieving the tension there. He centered himself again and held his hands as if he was holding an invisible beach ball, shook them once to get the power centered, and then he yanked his hands apart like any stage magician. From the open air before him fell the unchanged corpse of Dennis Aparicio, to sprawl across a creosote bush.

Geez, said Pam, who was still in the *astral* close by, *I'm glad I didn't run into HIM in there.*

Aparicio will be accounted for, he said. *Somebody might notice that he's wearing the same clothes as the day he became a hero, but he was probably planning his escape all along and had them on underneath his uni. With Peter Quince dead, there's no one to tell the Necklace how it could be otherwise.*

They'll get another wizard, Pam said.

In time. It took 'em almost a year to get Quince. Folks like us don't grow on trees. And when they DO get another wizard, he'll have to be special to catch up with US!

Even in her *astral* form, Pam would once have blushed at that, no matter how much she agreed with the sentiment. But not anymore. Pam Blackwell, alchemist, just accepted it, as demonstrated truth. *I'm going to be Timeless,* she said simply.

You are, honey, he said, equally certain. *You're comin' up on it fast. But it would probably be a good idea to get out of this war zone.*

Thank God they didn't blow up the arena in San Antonio, she responded.

There have been a lot of arenas these past few days, Max said.

He took the two bone keys from his pockets and locked them together at the large knuckle, so they formed a wide V. Then he took the V in his left hand, and held that hand across from the right as if holding a ball, and this time he forced them together. The Crossbones Key went into the subconscious.

Pam, you need to go get your physical form, and I need to get far away from here before dawn. Meet me at the airport at dawn. Then I want to hear every single thing about your time with the talismans.

So we're done here? she asked.

Yeah. Unless . . . He looked at her, through the veil. *Why?*

Because . . . She went for it: *I saw Val.*

What? In the subconscious?

BETWEEN *here and there. There was* ONE *moment, passing through the elder doorway, when her face appeared.*

You're sure?

She looked exactly the same, Pam said softly, *but really, at that moment, who else would it be?*

They locked eyes across the veil—the way a couple does in a room of strangers. *Was there anything else you could tell from her makeup, or her hairstyle?* he asked her. *Any sort of hint to where she is?*

No, Pam said. *I'm pretty sure it was her spirit. She looked like she did in the seventies—unchanged. The only thing I could tell for certain was—her chin rose—she was pretty.*

She was that, said Max clearly. *But that was then, and this is now. All we have to do is find her, and then we're on our way.* He reached out to her, through the veil, and turned his hand *astral* to take hers. *She survived death. She's fought long and hard to still be here, so she needs to know who she was, so she can decide what to do with her spirit.*

When she's making her decision, she'll be looking at us and seeing I've taken her place. You know that, right?

It's been twenty years, and I'm not only alive but Timeless, Max said. *Val understood sex and magick very well. Hell, she introduced me to it.*

Yeah, Pam said.

(And added in her heart of hearts, *I'm Mistress of the Eagle. I'm Artemis—an alchemist. And still, at the end of the day . . .*

(*I'm Pam.*)

4 Night (Encompassing a Private World)

Vee sat up. She was cold and quivering, she couldn't get warm, but she had enough fire to get herself up off the floor. The thermal blanket Matt had brought, per the plan, dropped into her lap, but he took it and wrapped it around her torso again.

She had gone into the realm of death, and she had come back out again. She had not died, as she knew she would not. There was something about death that she just *knew,* something she couldn't understand because she couldn't understand so much about herself, but she knew it. She could face black eternal emptiness and be a tourist.

She emitted a sort of strangled sound. It freaked Matt until he realized she was laughing.

"What's so funny?" he asked, encouraging this show of spirit.

"A tourist," she chortled, softly. Everything was sunny now, coming back from the infinite darkness. "Matt . . ."

"What?"

"I saw the woman who . . ."

"Who what?"

She clutched the blanket and pulled it tighter around herself. Her cheeks were beginning to show some color. "Who's in my dreams," she said. "At the moment I passed between death and life, I saw this woman, clearly. She's always laughed at me in my dreams. The same woman!" She looked up at him, her face pale and gaunt; with the blanket around her she looked like Death. "She's got to be important! Maybe she can even tell me who I am!"

"You're Vee," said Matt.

"That's my name. That's not me," she said. She pivoted toward Matt, scrunching her shoulders to hold the blanket while she hugged him tightly. "We have to find her, Matt. We have to search for that face!"

"We will," he told her, feeling her shivering lessening. Then she was laughing again. "What?"

"You teased me, that you could say 'Durban lived a hundred years ago,' and I wouldn't turn a hair. Don't you realize it sounds just as weird to me, to say 'Let's go search the world' and you say 'Okay'?"

"That's what a a manager does, Vee. I get you where you need to go. But I am thinking, searching the world for a specific woman will take some income."

"No problem," she responded, feeling very certain. "I'm going to make us rich!"

FRIDAY, MARCH 25, 2011 · 9:00 P.M. CENTRAL DAYLIGHT TIME

4 Night (Encompassing a Private World)

From her perch in the producer's chair, Di rallied the troops to contain the story. Fortunately, though she'd never breathed a word, she'd had her Plan B ready in case Max pulled it off. And maybe it was really Plan A. In any event, the San Antonio crew was scrambling to reach the crash site, but she couldn't wait for them to arrive, or, God forbid, one of her competitors' crews to arrive. There was no time to wait for facts; she had to get out in front of the story and make it her own. In the movie of her life, Di was always the star.

She personally wrote the copy and flipped the switch so Andrew

Fleming could intone "Good evening, America" from Studio 3-H to his nearly two million viewers. "This is the top of the hour, and this is the top of the news. A group of three military helicopters, on a training mission from Lackland Air Force Base outside San Antonio, Texas, has crashed in remote Texas Hill Country. The number of survivors is unknown at this hour. Early reports state that these copters were part of a country-wide sweep to search for the so-called 'Black Helicopters' that some people claim to have seen this past week. Ironically, the government says they had just determined that those sightings were of new-generation crop dusters, unknown to the observers.

"And just a few miles from the crash spot, in San Antonio's Alamodome, Number One Kansas beat Number Twelve Richmond seventy-seven to fifty-seven. . . ."

FRIDAY, MARCH 25, 2011 · 10:19 p.m. EASTERN DAYLIGHT TIME

4 Night (Encompassing a Private World)

Dick Hanrahan was running down. His sciatica was killing him, but the FRC mercs were finally wiping out the last of the rioters, just as the long, long day caught up to him. Most of those rioters had suffered heart attacks or something like, about an hour ago, making things easier. He had no idea what had been going on across the world today, what tied them all together—and therefore, he was determined to find out. He would not rest until he had an explanation. And now the Black Helicopters had gone down. That was the cherry on the sundae. But he'd warned Renzo, and they always had the next plan in place. *He,* Dick Hanrahan, always had the next plan in place. It had been a rough first day, but he had handled it all, fighting his way free of the drugs and then guiding the Necklace moment by moment, hour by hour. He stretched his shoulders and leaned back in his chair, ignoring the pain. "I *truly was* born for this!" he told himself, with true satisfaction.

"Unfortunately, Dick, so was I."

Hanrahan's brain processed the information instantly. His brain knew it was Renzo entering the room, holding a pistol. But for once in his life, he could not make himself believe it.

"I have a friend," Renzo was saying. "She figured your friend would try to kill me, so she created the illusion of my dead body. She does that sort of thing. So I've been watching you, invisibly, since you thought you became the Gemstone. You were actually good at this job, Dick. But I'm good at it, too—and I have a friend!"

"What the fuck, Renzo?" muttered Hanrahan at last. "I don't—"

"No," said the Gemstone. "You don't know *everything*, Dick."

He shot his oldest friend right through the heart, twice.

He had plans for the brain.

Day Twelve

11 Dog (Owning Embodiment)

Even in Denver, spring was beginning to make itself felt now. It was in the air from farther up the mountains. And if spring didn't make an older man's fancy turn to love, it did turn it to money. At the Vesta Dipping Grill, Renzo leaned across the table and said to Di, "I'd like you to take over the Intel link."

Di cocked her head the way she did. "You can't be serious!" she said sincerely, while her mind was screaming, *This would be TOO SWEET!*

Renzo said, "Dick Hanrahan filled that spot for forty-three years. I've been here just under twenty. He was my oldest friend. I've never had the need to look elsewhere. His coup attempt caught me completely by surprise. So as I look around now, of the people I know, you're the one with the widest network of sources and contacts."

"Except for you," she said, leaning into it. "Come on now, Lawrence. This is April Fools', right?"

"Not at all. The day is completely coincidental. Once I made my decision I came straight to you, even though you're in the midst of your conference."

"But surely you had *some* contingency plan in place. The man was *eighty-two*."

"I had three names. They were all said to be good—by Dick. I didn't get outside opinions, and his is now completely untrustworthy. I have to go with what I know, and I know you've gotten your act together since your little excursion to Wickr. You're a solid member of the team, and as I say, you've got the contacts—plus, you're *not* a part of the military. We like wars but those guys are beginning to like 'em a little too much. I want a more contemporary viewpoint with my reports."

And a grateful subordinate, she thought, and waited for his next line about celebrating this. But he seemed to be finished. Waiting. "Well," she said, "I'm very honored, both by the job and your vote of confidence, Lawrence. Needless to say, I accept." *Now he'll say it.*

But he said, "I'll need you to pull double duty until you pick your successor at Media. We're all short-handed—again—with the loss of Peter Quince. I have to find a replacement there, too, but there we have no one else familiar with magick."

She thought, *I might know someone . . .* and stopped that train dead in its tracks. Her promotion was more than enough. Sneaking Max into the Necklace would be certifiably insane!

So she simply said, "I accept, Lawrence."

"Call me Renzo," he said finally.

"Okay, Renzo," said she.

FRIDAY, APRIL 1, 2011 · 1:00 P.M. CENTRAL DAYLIGHT TIME

ll Dog (Owning Embodiment)

"Miss de Tal?"

"Yes?"

"You have a Mister Juan Mengano to see you."

"Thanks, Loretta. Send him in."

Rita collapsed back into the pillows, looking around her room. This was a high-class place. When she got out of here—in another month, the doctors said, but she would cut that down—when she got out, she was going to find out who her mysterious benefactor was. Even if it *was* santería. There'd been more than enough of that since she'd hooked up with the FRC. It was time she faced it head-on. *Long past time. ALMOST TWO YEARS PAST TIME FOR EVERY GOD-DAMN THING!* she raged inside her skull.

But now she lay, thirty pounds underweight, feeding tubes in her arms, a bag of wretched colors watching *Oprah* and *Ellen* until she leapt at the chance to do exercises, or she got her very first visitor.

Mérides came into her room. He looked tan and fit, well turned out—very much the acting head of Miami's largest drug cartel. He brought the Florida sun inside, when outside it was still snowing.

"*¡Hola, Rita sweeta!*" he said with his flashing smile.

"Hello, *Johnny*," she replied meaningfully, but with significantly less energy. He understood that she wanted to seem American up here in the frozen North.

"My God, you look like death, Fulana!" Johnny said, at her bedside. "We thought you *were* dead. What happened to you?"

She laughed. "Sit down. It's a long story."

He pulled up a metal chair, and sat forward. "You could have knocked me over with a feather when you called—"

Her left hand, palm up to provide the arm vein for the IV, opened wide to say *Eh.* "What else could you think? I dropped off the face of the Earth."

"Exactly. There I was, middle of the breakfast meet—you know—and I hear from a woman I thought was dead. It was some spooky stuff. But I came right up. Brought the private jet—I got a new one. We'll get you back down to Miami and get you some sun!"

"Problem is," said Rita, "you *didn't* come right up." Her right hand, under the covers, clenched hard. A searing pain rocketed through him, outward from his groin. He tried to throw himself off the chair. He couldn't control his muscles. But he got enough momentum to rock the chair and then tip the chair over and fall away from it, so he lay squirming in a fetal position on the green linoleum floor. She relaxed her hand.

"I've got family in Miami, *pendejo*! They were actually happy to hear from me. They were more than happy to keep a watch on you. You called in Lecuona before you left."

He tried to answer but it was just a croak.

"You kinda like being the boss, don't you, Mérides? Kinda settled in after two years."

"I—I don't . . ."

"Careful. I'm a little stronger than I look. I wired the chair to hurt you, but I've got a silenced pistol, too. I can play this any way you want."

Mérides gradually began to unclench his body. "What—do *you* want?" he gritted.

"Well, if I wanted you dead, you'd be dead, so I guess I want your undying loyalty again."

"You could never trust me now," he responded cynically.

"That's where you're wrong. I know you. You do like being the boss, so you can *be* the boss, just like now. I'll be working on something a little higher. Something that will show my appreciation to the FRC."

"Are you high?" he said, an edge in his voice but still on his side on the floor. "Those guys are players."

"I'm tight with Breckenridge. He's got his eye on me. He was checking my potential when I got this shit from their wizard. I'm gonna get a few breaks now, and I'm gonna work them, until I blow those bastards up and then pick up the pieces."

"You *are* high. Why don't I just kill you some other night and get on with my business?"

"Because you know me. You know I mean what I say. You'll finance it for me, and I'll give you everything."

"*You'll* rule the world?"

"*We'll* rule the world!" said Rita. "It's a big place."

Mérides sat up. He spread his hands. "Okay, *padrona*. It's a deal."

– 0 –

From the moment Aleksandra'd met Rita, she'd seen something of herself in this Cuban gang lord, hell, Cuban *spitfire*, and that deserved the most careful nurturing. She'd keep watching her for a while and see what developed. Renzo was okay on his own.

FRIDAY, APRIL 1, 2011 · 2:00 P.M. EASTERN DAYLIGHT TIME

11 Dog (Owning Embodiment)

Franny Rupp, her right arm in a sling, used her left hand to call Ruth Glendenning in Carlisle. It wasn't easy but she took it one step at a time.

"How's everything shakin' down?" she asked after their hellos.

"We lost ten men, including Aparicio and Bragane, and put the other nineteen in the hospital for up to eight weeks. Fortunately, you walked away with a broken arm and the next phase for Twenty-Twelve isn't till Norway, so I've got time to train the replacements."

"Norway just needs a bomb and some guns, so it's slow here, too. But Butler's in the semi-finals tomorrow night!"

"I've got twenty bucks on 'em, Franny. Meanwhile, with no Intel link, I asked Breckenridge who Aparicio was working for, and he couldn't say. I asked when he'd get an Intel link and he couldn't say."

"Thank you for not mentioning, um . . ."

Ruth said, "Nothing happened, right? So why should it concern anybody?"

"It concerns me. I should have known."

"Crap, Franny. *I'm* the one who should have known. You handle the machines, I handle the men. And he fooled me, so if you want to blame somebody, blame me."

"I'm not blamin' anybody. I just wish I'd been able to go after Aparicio myself, instead of Bragane."

"Let it go under the bridge, Franny. Aparicio did die, so we got some of our own back."

"Yeah. But the whole thing . . . ," said Franny resignedly. "Did you hear about the kilogram in France—the hunk of metal that's the official kilogram?"

"No, Franny, I can't say that I have."

"It doesn't weigh a kilogram anymore."

"April Fool."

"No, really. It's decay of some sort. Maybe of gravity. Whatever, the official kilogram can't be used as an accurate representation of the kilogram anymore." She went to wave her hands and rediscovered that the right one was in a sling. "It's like the whole world is really falling apart. Like 2012 really is gonna be the end."

"You're taking March Madness *way* too seriously," said Ruth. "You need to get laid."

"I tried, didn't I? Fuckin' Aparicio!"

FRIDAY, APRIL 1, 2011 · 7:00 P.M. BRITISH SUMMER TIME

Il Dog (Owning Embodiment)

Matt, jogging, sweating from the balmy heat, caught Vee just coming out of 47 Hartland Road. "Hey," he said excitedly, breathing deep. "Eddie's let you out of your deal. I had to slip him a little under the table, but you can take the two weeks in Manchester, starting tomorrow night! I texted Harleigh. We can leave first thing in the morning—or even tonight if you want."

"Is this April Fools', Matt?" she asked him.

"Not a bit of it."

She grinned. "Well, I can see which choice you want." She was back to her old self now, not just alive but alive the way she was before she ever set eyes on Christopher Durban. Vee was once again *vital*.

She was certainly vital to Matt. "The journey of a thousand miles begins with a single step, Vee. We're going on the road, headed for the peak and the blonde! Remember this moment, because one day you're going to say, this is where it all began!"

"You'd better come inside," Vee said, and took him by the hand.

"That's not an answer," he said, but he went with her. She led him into her shadowed house, into her circle, up to her altar in the center.

"Well?" he asked.

Looking down at the book on the altar, Vee said, "Cornelius, this is my friend Matt."

The book flipped itself open. A word lit up. *Welcome*. Pages flipped to another part of the book, where it also said *Welcome*. Pages flipped. *Welcome*.

Pages flipped. *Sworn by Cornelius Agrippa on this 31st day of December, anno domini 1519.*

Matt took a step back. He looked at the book. Looked at Vee. Kept looking at Vee. "All that we went through," he said narrowly, "the psychic vampire, the cheating of death—and *this* is what you decided to keep a secret? A book by the greatest medieval wizard? A book with a *mind*?"

"I didn't forget. But it wasn't my secret alone."

Matt looked at the book again, obliquely. "You mean," he asked, "you had to get *the book's* permission?"

"Yeah."

All of a sudden, his face split in a delighted grin. "And it *gave* it!" He turned to the book, but spoke to Vee: "Notice how I turn no hair at this news. I am unfazed."

Then, to the book: "Thank you, Cornelius," he said. "I wouldn't have thought I qualified."

Pages flipped. *A Magician is no other but a studious observer and expounder of divine things.*

"But you two are obviously much better magicians," Matt responded.

Magick is the connexion of natural agents and patients, answerable to each other, wrought by a wise man, to the bringing forth of such effects as are wonderful to those who know not their causes.

"Well," Matt told the book, "I swear to you, as I have to Vee, that I will do everything I can to get her where she needs to go."

Sworn by Cornelius Agrippa on this 31st day of December, anno domini 1519.

Thus ends the lesson.

"I'll just pack," Vee told Matt, rising on her toes to kiss him. But she didn't start to pack for an hour.

11 Dog (Owning Embodiment)

Max and Pam stood on the rocky hillside a hundred feet below Castello Janus. The Pisces moon had already gone down, leaving the evening to the deep indigo before full blackness, but it was still hot. The invisible planet Sedna was on the horizon, with Gemini sparkling high overhead. It was a magickal night.

They all were, now.

Pam looked down from the stars to the Crossbones Key in her hand, turning it back and forth, admiring its design. "Last time that *thing* in the gift shop sent me through the doorway," she said, "using her one bone. But this time I have *both* bones, and she has *none*. We'll see how *she* likes it over there. I can already guarantee that the elementals won't befriend her." Her face was growing gray in the night. "But if she hadn't sent me, Max—I wouldn't have seen Val, the way I did. Now I *feel* she's out there, the same way you do.

I have a connection with her now that I didn't have before. And I think that's a good thing."

"I can see the ending from here," Max said lightly. "The two of you will become BFF's and run off and leave *me* behind."

"Not likely, cowboy," Pam said. "I've invested too much time in you to start over now." She touched his arm in the dark. "Why didn't you sleep with Franny, Max?"

"You know why."

"I do. But I like to hear you tell me."

"I did not sleep with Franny because I promised you I'd avoid that sort of thing."

"If you could."

"If I could. And in this case, I could, so I did."

"Did it help that she's not pretty?"

"Actually, she can be. But that wasn't a factor."

"So you scrubbed the latrines and walked extra shifts just for me?"

"I'm guessing," Max said, "you like the whole male-female thing now."

"It *does* have its moments. Yes." Pam withdrew her hand and straightened her shoulders, looking up toward the castello, blotting out the stars. "So does alchemy. Let's go have one of those alchemical moments with the two-faced bitch. My treat."

"And then afterwards, one with just us."

"I'll be quick, then," she said.

LIGHT

At the top of the mountain, at the X where the four crests met, the fifty-foot Eagle, Angel, and Ox stood waiting. Today there were no clouds in the sky, no wind and no rain. From the X the threesome could see for miles, over the blue ocean, the green meadow, and the purple forests of trees. They could also look down on the fourth side, a vast verdant jungle, and the bronze path leading up from there. They were standing and watching as up the trail loped a fifty-foot Kalbu Rabu, the Great Lion.

He came to the top with a warm smile on his leonine visage. "Hail, my good friends," he said. "Hail!" The others moved forward in joyous reunion.

"Finally," said the Ox, standing steady to study him. "I'd forgotten what you looked like."

"Welcome home, Lion," said the Eagle, reaching out a wing to him. "He's just joking."

"This should have happened much sooner," said the Angel, ethereal but all too human. "*Your* wizard," nodding to Lion, "and *your* wizard," nodding to Eagle, "are connected."

"*My* wizard," said the Lion, "had no idea where you three were. It wasn't until *her* wizard found you and told him that the connection could be made."

"She took control of me, and then all three, so she could pluck us from the place where Belia'al put us and put us where *she* wanted," said the Eagle with the same pride in her eyes that had shone in Mymla's. "Alongside her man's Lion." Then her head turned sharply. Way, way out on the blue horizon, she'd seen something appear—something resembling an old woman. It fell into the sea.

"May we remain together for many years now," said the Lion.

"Under the control of *two* great wizards," added the Eagle.

"All's well that ends well," said the Ox, gazing around benignly.

"Except," said the Angel, "that the elementals are now much too full of themselves." And he kicked aside a nearby boulder, revealing Chiss and Funt and Mymla and Cocorik, laughing like little children. But Mymla clapped a hand over her mouth to get control, and when she had it she shouted toward the huge figures high above her, "She's an *alchemist*!"

11 Dog (Owning Embodiment)

Di reached across the table and took Renzo's dry hand. "This is exciting!"

"Between you and me, it's exciting," he said dourly, calling for the check with his free hand, but leaving his other where it was. "Out there"—he swept his arm at Denver—"it'll be just another wave on the sea of life, barely noticeable."

"You sound like a poet."

He chuckled. "Nobody calls me that, Di."

"I do, and I will," she said brightly. "When there's no one around, of course. Because you *are* a poet, Renzo. Your poetry, if I may say, takes place in reality."

"I try to make it smooth, yes. You never want attention—the exact opposite of your profession. But as to that, when it happens—"

"The Twenty-Twelve Project?" she asked, clarifying.

"Right. On Twelve, Twenty-One, Twenty-Twelve, you have to keep that wave as invisible as can be."

She smiled; a very nice smile. "Twelve, Twenty-One, Twenty-Twelve." She savored it. "That sounds really good, Renzo. I can use that. I'm tellin' you, a poet." She squeezed his hand. "So you can rest assured that on Twelve Twenty-One, and in fact from Hallowe'en right on through Christmas, we'll be focused on the Mayans and 'time' and all that spooky shit, not on you. On Twelve Twenty-One, we'll be reporting from Mayan pyramids and scanning the skies." She laughed, sincerely. "Black Helicopters are *nothin'* compared to the End of the World! People are going to *love* that!"

"So when we take full control, for the next five thousand years . . ."

"No one'll hear a word."

About the Author

Steve Englehart has had a long and prolific career writing for comic books, films, television, video games, and children's books. He is best known for his work with Marvel and DC Comics on such franchises as Batman, Captain America, and the Avengers, among many others. His original stories were the basis for the films *Batman* and *The Dark Knight.* His Night Man comic became the NightMan television series. *Countdown to Flight,* his Wright Brothers biography, was NASA's top selection for science in American schools. Previous Max August novels are *The Point Man, The Long Man,* and *The Plain Man.* Steve lives in Northern California with his wife, Terry.